LORI FOSTER

FAST BURN

HQN™

ISBN-13: 978-0-373-78998-6

Recycling programs
for this product may
not exist in your area.

Fast Burn

Copyright © 2018 by Lori Foster

Praise for *New York Times* bestselling author Lori Foster

"Teasing and humorous dialogue, sizzling sex scenes, tender moments, and overriding tension show Foster's skill as a balanced storyteller."
—Publishers Weekly on *Under Pressure*
(starred review)

"Best friends find hunky men and everlasting love in Foster's latest charmer.... Her no-fail formula is sure to please her fans."
—Publishers Weekly on *Don't Tempt Me*

"Foster brings her signature blend of heat and sweet to her addictive third Ultimate martial arts contemporary."
—Publishers Weekly on *Tough Love* (starred review)

"Emotionally spellbinding and wicked hot."
—New York Times bestselling author Lora Leigh
on *No Limits*

"Storytelling at its best! Lori Foster should be on everyone's auto-buy list."
—#1 New York Times bestselling author Sherrilyn Kenyon
on *No Limits*

"Foster's writing satisfies all appetites with plenty of searing sexual tension and page-turning action in this steamy, edgy, and surprisingly tender novel."
—Publishers Weekly on *Getting Rowdy*

"A sexy, believable roller coaster of action and romance."
—Kirkus Reviews on *Run the Risk*

"Steamy, edgy, and taut."
—Library Journal on *When You Dare*

Dear Reader,

I'm excited to introduce the fourth and final book in my Body Armor series, featuring hot alpha males whose überprotective instincts are put to good use in their roles as elite bodyguards.

Brand Berry is the only one of his closest friends who hasn't yet left MMA fighting behind to join the elite Body Armor personal security agency. Being a bodyguard definitely appeals to him—but so does the agency's gorgeous and fearless owner, Sahara Silver, and Brand isn't one to mix business with pleasure, so he's been resisting her efforts. Yet when Sahara's quest to find her missing brother puts her in a kidnapper's crosshairs, Brand doesn't think twice about appointing himself as her protector—even if working alongside her brings him to a closeness he *can't* resist.

I hope you enjoy reading Brand and Sahara's romance as much as I enjoyed writing it. Many of you have said you don't want to leave the series...but all good things must come to an end. I promise to do my best to make the next series just as much fun and every bit as sexy.

Have some thoughts on the books? You're always welcome to reach out to me. I'm active on most social media forums, including Facebook, Twitter, Pinterest and Goodreads, plus my email address is listed on my website at www.lorifoster.com.

Happy reading!

Lori Foster

FAST BURN

CHAPTER ONE

SAHARA SILVER SAT behind her enormous desk in her posh office on one of the upper floors of the elite Body Armor agency. Bright October sunshine splashed through tall windows. A large vase of fresh flowers, delivered that morning from a very content client, filled the air with sweetness.

For the most part, she was content.

She ran the most elite security agency in the area, probably in the whole country. To stand out from the crowd, she'd taken a different approach in selecting her bodyguards—sexy competence. To prove the old mantra that "sex sells," she'd acquired a trifecta of studly employees, ex-MMA fighters with ability, skill and yes, sexiness. Her agency was recently instrumental in solving a high-profile case, but she was no less satisfied with the outcome of other, more personal, cases.

Body Armor saw results. Clients could come to her with a wide array of needs and know they'd be in good hands.

Yes, her life would almost be perfect…if her brother weren't missing, presumed dead by everyone except her.

Once she found her brother—because in her heart she knew he was still alive—he'd reclaim control of the company he'd founded. He wouldn't be thrilled with the changes she'd implemented over the past year and a half, but always, from the time she was a know-it-all preteen, he'd encouraged her independence, her fearlessness and her confidence. Scott would understand why she'd had to put her stamp on the agency once she'd inherited it.

Not that it mattered. She'd turn it all over in a nanosecond to have him back. She'd live in a cardboard box on the street if she could just hug her brother one more time.

"Brand Berry is here to see you."

Surprised, Sahara glanced at Enoch, her right-hand man and very good friend. "Brand is here?" She immediately felt flustered. *Absurd*. "I wasn't expecting him. Did I miss a meeting?"

"No." Enoch lowered his voice in a conspiratorial way. "He said he only needed a minute of your time when you were free, and since you're free right now—"

"Yes, of course. Show him in." Even as she said it, a tiny unfamiliar thrill ran through her.

She'd made a point of surrounding herself with some of the finest male specimens on the planet—professional fighters that she'd turned into prime bodyguards, each of them in high demand. It was her vision for Body Armor, to get rid of the stuffy *Men in Black* clones and offer instead *real* men, with real muscles, certifiable machismo and lethal ability with or without a weapon.

No, she didn't fire the previously established bodyguards; that would have been disloyal to her brother, who'd hired them. She simply reassigned them to the more boring cases, and overall they were happy with that.

Anything to do with a celebrity, a dignitary or a politician her elite team now covered.

She desperately wanted to add Brand to that team.

Thinking she'd have a minute, she was just circling out from behind her desk when Brand stepped in around Enoch. Instead of waiting in the guest area, as a client would do, he must have been hovering right outside her door.

Her toes curled in her high heels.

Enoch was on the small side, five-two, slight of build, with average brown hair and eyes. It was his keen intelligence and attention to detail that made him so perfect at his job.

But his size didn't really matter when he stood next to a man who made most everyone seem small, her included. Brand was a big and badass professional MMA fighter with a solid steel frame of muscle all wrapped up in a cocky attitude.

Faded jeans molded to his thick thighs, going well with his running shoes and an ancient Aerosmith T-shirt that stretched over his chest and broad shoulders. Reflective sunglasses pushed to the top of his head made his golden-brown hair messy. Darker brown eyes held her captive as he murmured, "Sahara."

Leaning a hip against her desk, she drank in the rugged, virile sight of him. "Be still my heart."

Wary exasperation rooted him to the spot.

Yes, she always spoke her mind. Why not? She was the boss and her employees knew her interest in them wasn't personal. Of course, Brand wasn't yet an employee.

Putting her hands together, her fingers extended to frame him in a square, she remarked, "A photo of you looking just like that could launch my new line of advertisement."

He crossed his arms. "Advertisement for *what*?"

"Bodyguards with ability and sex appeal." He'd look great on a billboard, maybe with a gun in his hand. She could already see it. Maybe she should ask Enoch to keep a camera at his desk for occasions like this?

When Brand just stood there, his expression amused, she smiled. "Tell me you've come to give me good news." She'd been after him for a few months now to join the agency, constantly throwing out bait, trying to reel him in. He'd nibbled, but he wasn't caught. Not yet.

"I came to talk about that, yes."

Elation conflicted with disappointment. There were times when she hoped they could take a different path from employer and employee, one more personal, intimate.

Even…sexually satisfying.

But in the end, the business came first. Always.

She hadn't given up hope for her brother, and when he finally returned, he deserved to find the company thriving.

She'd put her heart and soul into making that happen. There was no time for anything else.

"Perfect." She tried to be excited, but it wasn't easy.

"Actually," Brand said, coming to stand very near her, "I've been offered another fight."

That gave her pause. She'd thought he was done with the Supreme Battle Challenge, better known as the SBC, for very difficult, personal reasons that he'd shared with her, but not many other people. "I thought you needed to be around more for your mom."

"My mother," he corrected, "not my mom."

For Brand, there was a huge difference between the two. Sahara knew because he'd explained it to her. "Right, sorry." Still, the woman had suffered cardiac arrest and, due to complications, had almost died. Personal conflicts aside, Brand had overseen her care. "But don't you need to—"

"I decided an influx of cash would be better."

So he could pay for what was needed, instead of getting so closely involved? That, too, made sense given their backgrounds. "I see."

"The SBC would reward me for taking the fight with a nice bonus."

"Oh?" If that's all it took, she could offer some signing bonuses of her own. "So how long do I have to wait for you to finish up—"

"It would be my last fight, *but*," he said with gentle emphasis, before she could make assumptions, "I'm not agreeing to be a bodyguard."

Her stomach bottomed out. This felt too much like losing, and by God, she did not lose. Determination stiffened her spine. "Tell me what it is you need." More money, obviously. She could swing that. "Designated time off? Better benefits for dependents?" Working around that would be trickier, but she'd figure it out.

Brand shook his head. "Truth is, Sahara, I can't see myself working for you."

Wow. Now that hurt. Peeved, she moved away from him to sit in the chair behind her desk. A power position.

She met his gaze without flinching. "I see." No, she didn't.

"You're too pushy." He smiled as he said it, taking away some of the sting of that nasty observation. "And too used to getting your way. You love being in charge, but then, so do I."

Never in her life had she been so offended. "Those insults are your way of telling me you don't like me?"

She rose from the chair again without realizing it, hands flat on the surface of the desk as she leaned toward him in challenge. "I got a very different impression."

"I like you," he confirmed, but then added, "because you're not my boss." He surprised her by mimicking her position until their noses almost touched over the middle of her desk.

She didn't know where to look. His eyes drew her, so dark they were almost black, and always filled with wickedness.

Then there was his firm mouth set in that small, teasing smile that did crazy things to her. High cheekbones, a strong jaw, a masculine nose...

And oh, what that straight-armed pose did for his biceps.

She inhaled...and breathed in the scent of warm, musky male.

It seemed imperative to put some space between them so she slowly straightened.

Brand's smile widened and he, too, straightened. "Coward."

"Oh no," she corrected. "But I have priorities that take precedence over...other things."

He went back to crossing his arms. "Over me, you mean."

"Nonsense. You are a top priority right now. I want you on the team."

"The agency isn't a team, Sahara. It's you dictating and others following orders."

She said through her teeth, "I'm the coach. I direct, encourage and—" *Bossed.* "—cheer. Rah-rah and all that."

He laughed.

Not with her, no. He laughed *at* her.

"Where did you work before you took over here?"

Was he genuinely interested or just trying to move past her obvious irritation? Not that she'd stay irate long. It was a waste of time. She was more about positive forward strides.

Or getting even.

For now she'd work on moving forward by answering his question. "Before Scott disappeared, he often had me involved with the business. I learned everything here from the ground up."

"Describe 'ground.'"

"All right." He probably thought she'd been pampered, placed in a high-paying position from the get-go. Nothing could be further from the truth. "When I was still very young, Scott let me sit in on meetings just to get a feel for things. When I turned eighteen, I worked as an attendant for the private elevator to his office."

Surprise showed in his eyes, but he covered it by asking, "Was there an armed guard even then?"

"You say it like it was the Stone Age." Feeling more confident, she again circled her desk but instead of getting closer to him, she moved to the wall of windows to look down on the Cincinnati traffic. "I'm thirty, so it was only twelve years ago. And yes, Scott always had top-notch security at the agency, including an armed elevator guard."

"But instead of the guard escorting clients up to his office, he had you do it?"

"Yes. The guards were stationary, one at the main floor and one at his office."

Brand joined her, standing close at her back so that

his stirring scent enveloped her. "I bet they got an ear-ful before they ever reached your brother."

Dear Lord, was that a blush she felt on her face? She didn't embarrass easily—except that he'd nailed it per-fectly. How many times had Scott remonstrated her for being too pushy?

"Sahara?" Brand prompted.

She wished she hadn't worn her hair in her usual clas-sic updo. With her nape exposed, the heat of his breath sent swirling sensations to riot in her belly.

Brazening her way through the awkward moment, she flapped a hand and admitted, "I might have been a little nosy."

"And a little opinionated?"

"Maybe just a smidge." His closeness made her edgy, so she again moved away, very casually in hopes that he wouldn't know he had her on the run. "After that job, I was a lobby receptionist."

"Fired from the elevator job, or was it a promotion?"

Damn him, did he really have such a low opinion of her? Maybe he *didn't* like her. That was something she'd never considered. She got along great with the other bodyguards who were all friends with Brand.

Or…did they feel the same way, too? Did they humor her in person while resenting her the rest of the time?

Disliking that possibility, she paused near her desk and, doing her best to keep the frown off her face, said, "A lateral move, actually."

"Uh-huh. Did Scott tell you that?"

Scott had told her to quit harassing the clients—but she didn't feel like sharing that part. Although, seeing Brand's expression, she'd bet he already assumed as much. He seemed to know her too well.

Better than anyone else, in fact.

"Scott told me he wanted me to experience every facet of the business."

"But you were never a bodyguard."

She took pleasure in saying, "Yes, I was."

Now Brand frowned, and she loved how intimidating he looked. He'd make an ideal bodyguard if only he'd realize it.

"Bullshit."

She tsked at the crude language, her idea of a reprimand. "Scott taught me to shoot. I'm actually pretty good at it."

"I've never seen you practice."

"Here, with my employees? Of course not." She had to maintain some mystique. "Scott owned his own range elsewhere and now it's mine."

"Where?"

She smiled. "It's private."

He countered with "Protecting a client isn't always about shooting."

"No, it's mostly about intelligent decisions, good planning and quick thinking." She let her gaze dip over him. "It's one reason I thought you would do so well at the job."

"Me, yes. But you?" His long strong fingers circled her upper arm. "You're brilliant, Sahara, so no problem there."

The assurance that he didn't consider her stupid would have been nice, except that the moment he'd touched her, her thinking faltered. So did her breathing. And her heartbeat.

"I've never known anyone with a quicker mind than you," he went on. "But when it comes to strength?" He lightly caressed her arm. "Physical strength, I mean. Does a woman like you, a woman who's always manicured and polished, have any?"

Just that simple touch, his warm fingers brushing over her bare skin, *on her arm*, and her priorities got all mixed-up.

At five-eight, she wasn't exactly petite, but Brand still stood half a foot taller, and next to his chiseled bulk, she felt downright dainty.

Oh, this wouldn't do. Sahara cleared her throat and made herself stare up into his eyes. "Brute strength? I'm definitely lacking."

"Didn't say you were lacking. In fact, I'd say you're just about perfect, but not strong enough to tangle with someone intent on causing harm."

"When someone is smart enough and quick enough, there is no tangling." She gave him her best smug smile and pretended her knees weren't weak. "I worked for three different clients. One job was glorified babysitting for a three-year-old while authorities tried to find a failed kidnapper."

Brand's expression softened to real concern. "The child—"

"She was okay. Her father, Mr. Drayden, chased off the masked man before he got away with her."

"Thank God."

Sahara agreed. "Drayden wouldn't rest until he knew who the man was and why he'd tried to kidnap his daughter, and was assured he'd remain behind bars."

"Did they ever get the guy?"

Sahara wanted to turn away, but that would be too revealing. "Yes. I shot him."

After the briefest pause, Brand clasped her other arm, too. "Tell me what happened."

"The sick bastard wouldn't give up. In his second attempt, he crawled in her bedroom window. He…had a knife. So I killed him." More brisk now, she explained, "He'd helped install the security system so he knew exactly how to shut it down. He claimed the girl was his, that he'd slept with Drayden's wife. She denied it of course, and to his credit, Drayden believed her. That turned out to be a good thing because they found out the psycho had made the same claim about three other children. Apparently he fixated on kids and convinced himself they were his even though he'd never touched their mothers."

"Damn."

His hold was soothing, but the last thing she wanted from him, from *anyone*, was pity. "The little girl, Mari, screamed from the gunshot, but she never saw the body. Soon as the guy hit the ground I scooped her up and got her out of the room, telling her it was just a loud noise." Sahara could still remember the thin arms clinging so tightly to her neck, the shaking of that small body and the soft sobs after the scream.

Until that day, she'd never thought about having children of her own. She missed Mari a lot.

"How long were you on assignment with the family?"

"Two months. But the time flew by since I mostly played with Mari." She twisted her mouth. "Afternoon tea with a G.I. Joe, a stuffed bear and a Barbie. Oh, the scrapes Barbie and Joe got into. The bear and I would just watch in amazement."

Brand grinned. "You know, I can almost picture it,

you in a tiny little chair sipping out of an empty plastic teacup with an audience of toys."

"Good times," she said, then tipped her head. "Can you see me killing a man?"

After briefly locking on her eyes, his gaze moved over her face and settled on her mouth. "Yeah, I guess I can. If it came to protecting someone you cared about."

Well, that was something anyway. "I had a shorter assignment with a twenty-three-year-old. I was only a year older than him and he had some serious misconceptions about the role of a bodyguard."

"How so?"

"I spent more time fending him off than protecting him. He got impossibly grabby."

Brand went back to scowling. "Your brother allowed that?"

"I didn't tell him! That would have been like admitting I couldn't handle the job, and it was an important one. He was a movie star's son being hassled by a radical group that opposed the star's last movie. Apparently, they didn't understand fiction versus reality. They wanted to drive home their point by making his son miserable anytime he ventured into public. You'll understand that it was all confidential so I can't give names or details."

"Sure. Tell me the part where you knocked the punk out."

She grinned. "We've already surmised that I'm not physically powerful."

He agreed by saying, "You should have quit."

"I couldn't. Scott chose me for the job because I was close enough in age to blend in. The boy didn't want his friends to know he had a bodyguard. Guess it dented his macho pride or something."

"First, he's not a boy. At twenty-three, he's a man. And second, I hope you dented the hell out of his pride."

That was one of the nice things about Brand: he had a similar mindset to her and they often agreed on things. "Of course I did. We were at a club with his friends. He kept trying to force me to dance with him. I knew where that would lead with the octopus, so I refused. I could keep an eye on him from the bar, but he wouldn't take no for an answer. He grabbed my wrist and wouldn't let go."

Expression darkening more by the moment, Brand asked, "What did you do?"

"I tripped him to the ground. That made him mad and he grabbed for me again."

"To do *what*?"

She shrugged. "I didn't want to find out, so I grabbed two fingers and twisted enough to break them."

"Ouch," Brand said with smiling satisfaction.

"He raged and decided it was time for us to go—with my wholehearted agreement. I had visions of the whole assignment going to hell, but it took an uptick when we stepped outside and the same group I was supposed to protect him from was there to mob him. That got him moving quickly to get in the car. On the way, I had to… ahem, assault a man who tried to drag my client back out of the car."

"Assault him how?"

"With my knee." She struck a pose, showing the knee she'd used and drawing Brand's undivided attention to her exposed leg. "In a place where no man wants to get hit."

Dragging his focus back to her face, Brand winced for real. "I gather that worked?"

"Like a charm." At least that night she hadn't shot anyone. "When Scott heard the whole story, he tore into the client and his father, and got me a bonus with an apology from the boy."

"Man."

"Man-boy," she compromised. "The third assignment was just a matter of escorting a local politician to and from a speech. It went off without incident."

"How come you never mentioned any of this before now?"

"Why would I?" She rarely discussed her background with anyone, because those stories all centered around her missing brother and left her grieving the loss anew. "My history with the agency has nothing to do with the reasons why you should sign on."

He turned speculative. "And you've been all about getting my agreement."

"Yes." She gave that a quick thought and asked, "Does knowing my history make you more inclined to—"

"Not really." Gaze intense, Brand slid his hands up her arms to her shoulders. "You've always amazed me, with or without the history report."

As he leaned closer—to kiss her, she was sure—she said desperately, "Work for me."

Without a smidge of regret, he said, "No," and then his mouth was on hers, his lips pressing, his tongue touching until she opened.

The second she did, his tongue slid in and she melted against him.

God help her, it was incendiary.

FROM THE DAY he'd met her, Brand knew it'd be like this. Sahara Silver with her classic bone structure, her sharp wit, her beautiful blue eyes and slender body, was almost too stunning.

He meant to keep his hands on safe ground, but then, he hadn't meant to kiss her either. Without really thinking about it, his palms slid over her shoulders and down her back, feeling the soft cashmere of her short-sleeved sweater, the firm resiliency of her flesh beneath.

She had expensive taste in fashion and always looked like a million bucks. She loved sugary pastry, but far as he could tell, she never gained a pound. No matter the company she kept, be it fighters, senators or twisted criminals, she was always comfortable.

She had no problem pampering herself, and no problem taking charge of any situation.

She tasted good, and felt even better.

But kissing her was a dumb move because Sahara wasn't for him.

She wanted him, yes—to work for her.

She'd chased him—to get his agreement. For her, the hard-core campaign to win him over hadn't been personal.

He couldn't question her participation in the kiss, especially with her hands locked in his hair keeping him close, but when it came down to it she would always choose her brother's memory, and thus the agency, first.

The sexual attraction was secondary for her, and that made it not enough for him.

If his friends Leese, Justice and Miles didn't work for her maybe he'd take what he wanted before walking away. But that could end up complicating things for the guys who had left fighting for Body Armor, and he couldn't do that to them.

Sahara pressed closer, her breasts to his chest, her belly to his dick, and logic nearly flew the coop.

He lowered his hands to her perfectly shaped ass, toned from the sky-high heels she favored—heels that made her long legs look even more amazing. Scooping her closer, he rubbed her against him, then stifled a groan.

Two seconds more and he'd be hard.

Ending the kiss wasn't easy, not with her tongue dueling with his and all those soft, sexy sounds escaping her. He gentled her, slowed her down and finally freed his mouth. Hoping to make it less abrupt, he kissed a trail over her stubborn jaw to that sensitive spot just beneath her ear.

Subtle perfume vied with the natural scent of her fragrant skin.

She tipped back her head.

Unable to ignore that invitation, he teased damp kisses along her throat before drawing her head to his shoulder. He returned his hands to her upper back, moving up and down to soothe her.

Against her temple he said, "I'm sorry, Sahara. I shouldn't have started that." But he wasn't sure anything could have stopped him from tasting her. "This isn't the time or place to get carried away."

Awareness drew her back and she stared at him in shock, her blue eyes wide and vague, her lips—now slightly swollen—parted.

Brand smoothed a tendril of thick, light brown hair that had escaped her pins. "You okay?"

That got her stepping quickly away. "Yes, of course."

She brushed her palms against the tight material of her skirt over her thighs. "It was only a kiss."

For some reason, it annoyed him that she downplayed the impact. "A kiss that had you crawling all over me, and you damn near yanked out my hair."

Her eyes widened even more...and then she laughed. "We did get a little carried away."

"A little," he agreed, still nettled. Could she really be less affected than he was? Or was she hiding behind her usual cool persona?

"I'm fine." She reached up to remove his sunglasses, then stroked her fingers through his hair. "But did I hurt you?"

Her touch ignited him all over again. *Dangerous.* He'd known that about her within minutes of their first introduction. Catching her wrists, he lowered her hands—but then couldn't let go.

And she didn't pull away. After a long look, she said, "We could...discuss this more tonight."

Hell of a suggestion, but he'd damn near lost it in her office with Enoch just outside the door. If he had her alone, no way in hell would he be able to keep his hands off her. So he shook his head and explained, "I'm meeting the guys at a bar tonight."

One slender brow arched up. "*My* guys?"

Did she think she owned them? "If you mean Leese, Justice and Miles, yeah, they'll be there, but arriving at different times. I think Leese is between assignments, right? And both Miles and Justice should finish up for the day in time to join us."

"Us?"

"A half-dozen other fighters, some of their wives. You've met most of them."

She nodded. "Will you be going to that quaint little hometown place, Rowdy's?"

Damn it, did she plan to crash the party? Actually, how the hell did she know about Rowdy's? He thought about asking her, but decided he'd be better off getting out of there. "That's the plan, yeah."

She waited, but when he said nothing more, she briefly looked wounded before giving him a cool smile. "Have fun then." She went back behind her desk and turned on the monitor to her PC in clear dismissal. "Do let me know if you change your mind."

"I won't." But he didn't like being dismissed. "My sunglasses?"

As if she forgot she held them, she looked at her hand in surprise. "Oh sorry." Nonchalant, she leaned forward, offering them to him without getting up, her attention still on the monitor.

Proving he had a perverse streak a mile wide, Brand let his fingers slowly graze hers as he took the glasses.

Her startled gaze flew to his face, but she only grinned, once again in full control. "Wicked, that's what you are." She fluttered her fingers at him. "Thanks for stopping by."

And she went back to staring at the screen.

Left with nothing else to do, Brand walked out. That meeting hadn't gone as planned, but then nothing with Sahara ever did.

He knew he'd done the right thing.

So then why did it feel like he'd been kicked in the chest?

CHAPTER TWO

SHE WOULD NOT feel dejected, Sahara promised herself as she walked through the lobby toward the parking garage exit. Her heels clicked on the marble tiles and she smiled automatically at every friendly face she saw.

Anita, the lobby receptionist, stood to ask, "Done for the day, Ms. Silver?"

"I am, yes." She liked Anita, so she stopped to ask, "How's the weather out there? Still raining?"

"Storming, unfortunately. Do you need an umbrella?"

"I'll go from the garage here to my garage at home, but thank you. What about you?"

"I'll make a mad dash into my apartment, but I have a raincoat with me."

"So you're not worried about melting either?"

She laughed. "I like rain, actually. Always have."

"Same here. A good storm leaves everything fresh." Sahara buttoned up her lightweight coat and pulled up the collar. "Be careful driving then."

"You, too, Ms. Silver."

She waved as she stepped away.

Other employees spoke to her, all of them friendly and familiar but still respectful. For her, Body Armor was a business with a family vibe. After all, she'd practically grown up here. Being sixteen years older than her, Scott had taken over raising her while their parents traveled the world. She'd always known she was an unpleasant surprise for them, but she'd never doubted Scott's love.

The agency was all she had left of him and being here, surrounded by people he'd hired, protocols he'd put into place, contacts he'd built, made her feel closer to him.

Brand was a distraction, the first to consume her since she'd taken over the agency, and that scared her a little. She had to shake it off. She was not a woman to brood.

So he'd kissed her senseless, then made it clear that he didn't want her to join him for the evening. Men were fickle. She'd been dealing with them long enough that it shouldn't have bothered her.

But…she'd thought her men, *all* of them, liked her as more than a boss. They had an easy camaraderie. She'd spent time with them outside of work and they'd never seemed to mind. She liked to think she'd been helpful when it came to various problems they'd encountered.

Holding her purse strap over her shoulder, she pushed through the security doors to the parking garage. Her black Mercedes-Maybach, looking much like all the other black sedans in the garage, sat in isolated splendor in her private spot.

The spot reserved for the boss.

The spot where her brother used to park.

Stop it. Melancholy doesn't suit you.

She could have used a driver, as she often did. But tonight she'd wanted the solitude of a quiet drive home.

The storm raged and she pulled onto the road cautiously. At only 7:00 p.m., it looked like midnight, dark clouds obliterating any light. There wasn't much traffic, and even driving more slowly, she neared her home outside the city within twenty minutes.

She could see the keyless entry gate for the long private drive when suddenly an SUV pulled crossways into the road, blocking the way. She slowed, the sense of danger overwhelming her. Headlights shone in her rearview mirror as another black SUV approached and that vehicle, too, pulled across the road.

Well, hell. Her doors were already locked, so using the automated voice control, she called Leese Phelps.

He answered with a lot of noise in the background, so she assumed he was at the bar already. "Hey, Sahara."

"I probably have thirty seconds at most," she said quickly and with, she hoped, admirable calm. "With my driveway in sight, two cars blocked the road. There are three men from each car approaching." Her throat tightened. "They're wearing masks."

"Jesus."

"I do believe I'm going to be taken." At least she hoped that was the case, that they wouldn't murder her outright.

"Keep your doors locked." She heard the urgency in his tone. "I'm on my way and I'll call the police to meet me."

"You won't make it in time. Until this is resolved, you're in charge."

"Damn it, Sahara—"

"You know the protocol we used with Catalina. Enoch has the details—" She froze as one big man stood in the pouring rain beside her car, his face and body hidden in black. She couldn't even make out his eyes through the water dripping along the window.

Then he reached inside his jacket.

"Sahara?"

She ignored Leese's demand, her heart pounding in

fear…until the man slapped a photo of Scott against her window.

"Sahara!" he said again, his voice pure gravel.

"No police," she insisted. She'd take no chances spooking men who might have information on her brother. Leaving her car running, the call open, she shoved open the door and stepped out. "You know Scott? Where is he?"

Blue eyes, now more visible as she stood before him, narrowed in satisfaction. He wrapped a meaty hand around her upper arm. "You're going to tell me. Let's go."

BRAND IGNORED THE woman trying to get his attention with touches inappropriate for a public space. He ignored, too, the snickers of his amused friends as he drew back the pool cue to take a shot, effectively forcing her away.

He wanted to win the game, but he didn't care about female company right now. The leggy brunette who again tried to hug up to his side was cute enough, definitely stacked enough, but he couldn't drum up an ounce of interest.

He sank two balls on the table…just as her hand came around the front of his jeans, seeking balls of a different sort.

"Jesus," he muttered, catching her wrist.

"Stop playing hard to get."

He scowled at her. "Actually, honey, I'm not playing."

When Leese charged into the room, all but grabbing Miles and Justice, a sick feeling dropped into his gut. Brand thrust the cue at the pushy woman and, a few steps behind, followed his friends through the bar. He saw them talking as they went out the front door and into the storm, but through the throngs of people milling about, he couldn't hear their conversation.

He'd seen the alarm on Miles's face, though, and the rage on Justice's.

Only seconds behind them, he stepped outside and found them standing huddled together under the overhang, Leese talking fast.

He heard, "Sahara was taken. She knew it was going to happen when two cars blocked the road she was on."

Shoving his way into their throng, Brand demanded, "Where?"

Leese spared him a glance. "In front of her house, or very near it."

Someone had taken her. Every fiber of his being rebelled against the possibilities. She couldn't be hurt. *Please, God, don't let her get hurt.*

Justice bunched up like a junkyard dog and growled, "Tell me what to do."

"I don't fucking know," Leese said. "Right before she stopped replying, she insisted on no police. I heard her mention Scott to the men, six of them, so one of them must have said something, though I didn't hear any of them speak. I'm heading over there now to see if I can pick up a clue."

"I'm going, too," Brand said.

"You don't work for her," Leese reminded him.

Making it perfectly clear, Brand said, "I don't give a fuck. I'm going." When his cell rang, he and Leese were still engaged in a stare-down so he ignored it.

Justice gave him a shove. *"It could be her."*

Given the way things had ended between them, he seriously doubted that, but Brand dug the phone from his jeans pocket and glanced at the screen. He didn't recognize the number so he answered with a curt "What is it?"

Sahara's voice came through, along with a lot of static. "I have to make this very brief. I've been taken by some men who seem to think I know where my brother is."

His heart tried to escape his chest. *Her brother was dead.* Everyone knew it except for Sahara. With a touch of his thumb he switched her to speaker. "Where are you?"

"We're still driving, and I have no idea where we're headed."

"Can you see anything?"

"No windows." Someone in the background gave an abrupt order and, sounding annoyed, she added, "I'm told, since I can't give them Scott's whereabouts, I could instead have one of my men bring a ransom. Apparently the same amount Scott owed them."

Fury rippled through every muscle in his body. "I'll come get you."

"Yes, I was hoping that you would, Leese."

Leese? Did she not recognize his voice?

"The men know the agency well, including all my bodyguards. I'm sure they'll recognize you when they see you so please don't try sending the police instead. There are to be *no police*. Do you understand? Promise me."

Knowing now that she wasn't alone, Brand said, "I promise." He pictured some psycho next to her, manipulating her, *forcing* her to detail those terms, and rage worse than he'd ever known churned inside him.

There was some fumbling through the connection and suddenly a deep voice said, "Listen up, Phelps. Come alone and don't try anything or your boss is not going to have a pleasant time with us."

The man thought he was Leese, so he'd go with that. "Tell me when and where, and how much to bring. I'll be there."

Miles, Justice and Leese stared at him in strained silence. The storm raged around them with flashes of light that crackled across the black sky, and ground-trembling booms of thunder.

But it was nothing compared to his personal turbulence.

"Soon," the man said. "Repeat any of this to the cops and I'll gut her slowly—after enjoying her a bit."

"Touch her," Brand warned, *"and you're a dead man."* The call ended before he could say more.

Blood pumping fast, Brand clutched the phone and looked at each of his friends. He hoped like hell someone knew what to do.

"I'll rip him apart," Justice growled quietly.

Brand knew that when Catalina, one of Leese's clients—a woman he ended up marrying—had been in serious danger, Justice had been Sahara's personal bodyguard, protecting her against the threats that had spilled over to them all. Since then, Justice still felt overly protective toward her, even though he, too, would soon be marrying.

"He thought I was you," Brand said to Leese, trying to make sense of it.

Proving why he was top dog at the agency, Leese said, "Sahara either put in the call or gave them the number, and she sure as hell knows the difference between us. She said something about the men knowing all her bodyguards, that they'd recognize you—me."

Miles said, "It was a tip. She wants a face they *won't* recognize to show up."

"I assume so," Leese agreed. "That way, when I go to deliver money, the other, unknown person will have a chance of getting to her."

Brand ran a hand into his hair, then tugged in frustration. "She's never let up on trying to hire me to Body Armor. Hell of a way to lock me in, though."

Justice looked murderous. "You don't want to do it, fine. I'll go incognito."

Miles scoffed. "Like anyone would mistake a behemoth like you?"

True enough, Brand thought. Justice was enormous. "It was just an observation, Justice. No way in hell am I passing the buck." Even if Sahara hadn't singled him out, he'd insist on it.

After all, she'd called *him*.

"If she's hurt," he said, tortured by the thought but unable to obliterate it, "if one of those bastards even touches her—"

Leese interrupted his growing threat. "You're not trained, Brand. My best guess is that Sahara wanted me to find someone else who can fill in, but she didn't specifically mean you."

Digging in, Brand repeated, "I'm doing it." Leese and the others didn't know that he and Sahara had something personal going on, despite his efforts to the contrary. And he wouldn't tell them. They were Sahara's employees and if she wanted them to know, she'd do the telling.

But that didn't mean he'd let them cut him out. The way he saw it, Sahara had reached out to him, and by God, he'd be there 100 percent.

"You don't know how to shoot—"

"I've been shooting since I was fifteen."

That gave them all pause. "You have?" Miles asked.

"Are we really going to discuss my past right now?"

"No." Leese turned away with purpose. "We can ride together."

"To where?" Brand asked, even as he followed into the downpour.

Speaking loud over the storm, Leese explained, "In one breath Sahara put me in charge until she's back, and then she mentioned Enoch."

Soaked through to the skin, Miles and Brand climbed into the back seat of an agency SUV. Leese got behind the wheel and Justice rode shotgun. As they buckled up, Brand asked, "Enoch?"

"Respect him a lot," Miles said. "But he's an assistant, not a bodyguard."

"He's a hell of a lot more than an assistant to Sahara." Leese glanced at each mirror, then pulled onto the rain-washed road. "Remember when Catalina was taken?"

Justice said, "I'll never forget it."

"None of us will," Brand said, though he'd been involved only peripherally.

"We found her because Sahara had planted a GPS device on her." He paused as he switched lanes, then continued with "I think she has one on herself, too."

Brand gripped the seat behind Leese. "She said so?"

"She reminded me of the 'protocol' for Catalina. At first, I didn't understand, but it's starting to come together. I assume Enoch knows how to track her."

Justice already had out his phone. "I'll call him now."

Miles withdrew his phone as well. "I'll notify the others why we booked. They're going to wonder, especially since our cars are still there."

Brand hated feeling ineffectual, but while the others all seemed to know what to do, he hadn't a fucking clue. He kept picturing Sahara, her attempt to look blasé at what she saw as his rejection.

Fuck, it *had* been a rejection.

Of the job…and of her personally.

But not for the reasons she thought. He wanted her, too much in fact. More than she wanted him, obviously, since she would always put the agency first.

"I got hold of Armie," Miles said as he put the phone away. "He's letting the others know. They'll head over to her place to ensure her car is safely off the road."

Armie, like Brand, was a fighter but not a bodyguard, but as a close personal friend to each of them, he'd do what he could. "They know where she lives?" Brand asked.

"They followed us there when Catalina was threatened."

He'd missed a lot, Brand realized. Maybe too much. It pissed him off.

"Enoch is meeting us at Body Armor. Poor dude is frantic." Justice pocketed his phone again. "He and Sahara are close."

"She's special to everyone who knows her," Miles said.

Brand almost groaned. Special? Hell yeah, she was, in too many ways to count. From the time his friends had signed on at Body Armor, Sahara had been after him to join up, too. For too long now they'd engaged in a game of enticement and resistance—Sahara enticing and him resisting.

If it was just the job, no problem.

If it was only the strong physical chemistry, he could

probably fight that, too, despite the fact that Sahara personified sexy in a classy but still touchable way.

It was more than that, though. Sahara was the whole package, a gorgeous woman with an enormous heart and a real head for business. She knew what she wanted and she went after it without reserve.

She'd wanted him…but he'd turned her down. And now men had her—

Miles nudged him.

Lost in his thoughts, Brand glanced up and caught his friend's frown. "What?"

"Take a breath. If you're going to do this, you need to get a little control."

"I am controlled." Hell, that was one of the major ways that he and Sahara clashed. She wanted all the control, always, in every situation, but then so did he.

"You look ready to erupt."

Shaking his head, Brand shoved the rage deep inside and locked it down. He'd get Sahara back, then he'd destroy the bastards who'd taken her. "I'm fine."

"It can't be you," Leese said from the front seat, "because you don't know what you're stepping in to."

"Like you do?" Brand didn't get annoyed. It didn't matter what reasoning Leese used, he wouldn't change his mind. "You can't tell me that rescuing your boss from kidnappers is part of your normal workweek."

"No, but each one of us has dealt with similar situations."

"We're tried and tested," Justice said. "You're not. God only knows the number of ways you could fuck it up, and Sahara will be the one hurt."

Miles was the only one not giving him shit. "Fact is," he pointed out, "Sahara called Brand, and she made it

clear that the goons who have her would recognize us.
Even if we can trace her, who's to say they won't spot
us and kill her for it?"

"No," Justice insisted.

"She called me." Brand drank in a deep breath of
humid air. "Plus you're all married—"

"Not me," said Justice.

"You will be soon enough."

Justice couldn't deny that, and it had him growling
again. Maybe, like Brand, the lack of ability to fix this
problem ASAP left Justice frustrated.

But Justice didn't have the knowledge that he'd parted
ways with Sahara under less than ideal circumstances.
That was all on Brand and it was fucking well eating
him up, adding to the need to *do something.* "Tell me the
plan and I'll see that it happens. But understand this—
I'm going after her and that's it."

"Let's get to Body Armor and see what we're dealing
with." Leese drove aggressively despite the rain. "After
that, we'll make some quick decisions."

Along the way the men called their significant others.
Their low voices were intimate, except for Leese, who
spoke via the speaker through the car's Bluetooth.

"Dear God," Catalina said, her worry plain. "Poor
Sahara. She has to be frantic."

Logical assumption, yet Brand couldn't picture her
being anything other than her usual cool, in-charge self.
That, too, could be a problem. He reminded himself that
Sahara was intelligent. Surely, she wouldn't provoke her
kidnappers.

"Please be careful, Leese," Catalina whispered, "and
please bring her back safe."

"You know I will."

Each of the women knew and cared about Sahara, so Brand had no doubt they'd all shared those sentiments.

Enoch was in the lobby waiting for them when they arrived. He'd already assigned extra guards on the building, not only on the ground floor but also as lookouts on the upper floors. "If there's surveillance on the building, we'll know."

"Smart move." Leese led the way to the elevator and they all rode up to Enoch's office. He had his computer on and immediately showed them what he'd found. "She's not far from her house, only about forty-five minutes."

They each stood behind Enoch, leaning forward to see the screen. "They're not driving anymore?" Miles asked.

"Don't appear to be. The GPS has her stationary for about five minutes or so."

"Looks like she's in the slums," Justice complained.

"The program can't show me exactly where," Enoch explained. "But if you get near the area you should be able to pick up her signal on this cell phone." He handed it to Leese.

Brand took it from him.

No one said anything about it.

"I have access to some funds," Enoch explained. "But I doubt it'll be enough to pay off kidnappers."

"Let's wait and find out how much ransom they demand, then we'll decide what to do."

The waiting went against the grain for all of them, but until they got that call, it was all they could do.

"If Sahara was here," Enoch stated, "she'd ask me to get coffee, so that's what I'm going to do. All of you, make yourselves comfortable and I'll be right back."

THE VAN BUMPED over rough ground, taking her farther and farther away. No one spoke to her, but the four men riding in the cargo area continually watched her.

She pretended not to care and merely looked back, making note of what she could. Even sitting, their height was discernible, and under the dark sweatshirts and jeans, she could guess their weight.

One man had pushed up his sleeves and she saw that he was freckled. Another had darker hands, as if he spent a lot of time in the sun.

The man who appeared to be in charge was the only one not eyeballing her. He spent his time on his phone, not speaking but definitely perusing something.

When the van stopped, he pocketed the phone and moved to crouch in front of her.

"Give me your hands."

Sahara glared into faded blue eyes. "Why?"

His answer was to roughly grab her, jerk her arms forward, then hold her wrists while another masked man wrapped them in rough rope.

Clearly, they'd never done this before because with a little wiggling, she'd be able to pull free. What good that would do her, she didn't yet know. If she remained in the van with six men, two up front and four guarding her, she may as well be hog-tied.

For now, though, she held still and merely muttered, "I scare you that much?" She tsked. "And here I'm so much smaller."

His hand came up to clasp her throat, not tightly but in clear warning. "You have quite a mouth on you."

"Quite a brain as well." Defiant, she stared at him. *I will not let them cow me.* "What do you know about Scott?"

Disgusted, he let her go with a slight shove and sat back against the metal wall of the van.

Sahara said, "You know something, obviously. I want to know what."

The big man waited, watching her, and finally shrugged. "Do you believe your brother is dead?"

"No."

He sat forward again. "Have you had any contact with him?"

"No."

With a note of frustration, he asked, "Then what makes you think—"

"Somehow, if he were truly gone, I'd feel it."

The freckled guy barked a laugh. "Female logic."

She snorted. "Male logic would be an oxymoron, wouldn't it?"

"Shut up," the leader said.

The two men in front got out, closing their doors seemingly without fear of being heard. That told her that they must be someplace isolated…or perhaps they had a way of sneaking her out of the van without anyone noticing.

Seconds later the doors at the back of the van opened.

Sahara could see they were inside a large garage or warehouse. Dim, smelly and cold.

Three of the men climbed out. The leader, bent over in the confines of the van, took her arm and said, "Let's go."

For once her heels were a hindrance. With her hands tied, she couldn't use them to help her gain her feet. He solved that dilemma by dragging her on her butt toward the doors.

"Brute," she accused.

"I didn't drag you by the hair, did I?"

No, and she didn't want to prod him to it either.

When another man reached in, the boss said, "I've got her," and everyone else backed off.

Sahara realized what he meant when he stepped down, then hauled her out and over his shoulder. With one muscled arm he pinned her legs behind her knees, and with the other...

Dear God, he had his hand spread wide over her behind!

She reared up, using her bound hands to brace against his back. "So a kidnapper, and a perv, too?"

The swat he landed on her cheek stung, but she didn't cry out. She just gritted her teeth and, as he possibly intended, kept quiet.

He carried her as if she weighed nothing, going down concrete stairs and into a smaller, colder, darker room. Along the way her hair spilled loose, draping down to cover her face. She also lost a shoe, but the man paused to pick it up. He turned a corner, careful not to smack her head on the wall, and went down more stairs.

Her heart started to pound nervously and her mouth went dry.

Someone turned on a light and she saw that her prison was even worse than she'd suspected. Very small, maybe eight feet square, all concrete.

She did not want to be alone here, but as he set her on her feet she quipped, "How quaint."

The big man actually laughed.

Then he surprised her by bending down, clasping her ankle and helping her to step back into her shoe. From his kneeling position, he looked up the length of her body.

Grateful for her coat, which still covered her, Sahara tried to feign confidence. It wavered a lot when he came back to his feet, lifted her chin and gently brushed her hair out of her face. Sahara jerked away, but he only grabbed her upper arm and finished running his fingers through the unruly tresses, finding two pins still caught in her hair and pocketing them.

So maybe that wasn't about inappropriate thoughts, but rather he didn't want to take the chance that she'd know how to pick a lock.

She did, of course, but whether or not a hairpin would work depended on the lock.

Around them, she realized the others were working, turning on an overhead light—and blessedly, an electric heater. She moved closer to it, holding out her hands and trying to stop her shivers.

A cot was set up in the corner. It looked clean with a folded blanket and a pillow on top. One of the men added an extra blanket. Did they expect her to sleep here?

She hated that possibility.

"We realized after we had it arranged that you, being female, might find it too chilly."

Clearly the freckled guy had some notions about "females." In this case, since she *was* cold, she let it go.

When he continued to look at her, she said, "Thank you?" and he nodded in satisfaction.

Every second of this kidnapping got more and more bizarre.

Other than the cot, she noticed a portable toilet in the farthest corner, with a roll of paper on the ground beside it. *Oh, no and no.*

"Who are you people," she demanded, "and what do you ultimately want?"

Ignoring her question, the boss said, "It's time."

Her heart again stuttered. They would leave her here alone now?

But no, apparently only the boss would go, because he sent a penetrating look to each of his cohorts. "No one touches her, understood?"

They nodded.

Then looking at her, he said, "That rule is rescinded if she tries anything."

Oh, that didn't sound good. "Define 'try anything,' please." If she breathed, would that be provocation to jump her? "May I sit on the cot? Could I move the cot closer to the heater? May I have my purse back?"

"You're a smart lady. I'm sure you'll figure it out." He started to go, but then paused. "No, you can't have your purse. Not yet anyway."

The freckled guy clutched it, as if he held the prize.

Sighing, she watched the leader go back up those stairs and wondered how long he would be. For some insane reason, she felt marginally safer with him nearby; since he'd been the one doing all the talking, she felt she knew him a little better.

The rest, other than Freckles, were unknown quantities. They could be rapists, murderers—or just plain insane.

Predatory gazes tracked her as she circled the room, inspecting it. Other than the heater, the portable potty and the cot, the room was empty. She saw no other electrical outlets, so she went over to the cot and, using her knee, nudged it away from the wall. She bent, put her hands against the rickety frame and began scooting it toward the heater. Thanks to the metal legs on concrete, it loudly screeched as if death was near.

Two men came forward and, without a word, lifted each end. They carried it toward the heater. One of them, with a questioning look, waited.

It was in her nature to test the limits, so she said, "A little to the left please."

They obliged.

"No, a little to the right now."

Again, they did as she asked without comment.

"Perhaps a tad farther back—"

The cot hit the floor with a clatter and the two men walked away to stand with the others.

She smiled inwardly and said with sugary sweetness, "Thank you so much."

All five of them nodded.

Hmm... There was an odd gallantness to their behavior in direct conflict with hardened criminals. Testing that, she sat on the side of the cot and tried to look dejected.

Time ticked by in utter silence. Only the occasional sound of someone shifting position intruded.

She let out a sigh. In the smallest voice she could manage, she asked, "Am I going to die?"

Someone—she wasn't sure who, since she didn't look back—said, "Not if you follow orders."

Well. They certainly weren't ruling it out. Hopefully, Leese had understood her subtle message and was already at the office with Enoch. The tracking device could be easily positioned in her clothes or jewelry. For now, she'd made it part of her necklace. She prayed they wouldn't take that from her—if it would even work down in the bowels of the building.

She stood to pace. Her heels made a distinct clinking noise against the concrete. It wasn't just the feminine style of stilettos that she loved, it was the sound the heels made that really did it for her. The cadence helped her to focus.

She'd deliberately called Brand instead of Leese. If she'd had more time to consider it once they thrust the phone into her hand, she might have come up with another solution. But the boss man had already explained that he studied up on all her guys and had files on each of the bodyguards, new and old. That meant she had to take them by surprise somehow.

They wouldn't have anything on Brand since he wasn't part of the agency. At least, she hoped they wouldn't. He'd been there a few times, most recently that very day. But then, clients came and went, too, as did delivery people. For all they knew, Brand wasn't anyone special.

She knew better.

Brand Berry was her own personal temptation, and that made him special indeed.

Dragging him in to things kicking and complaining wasn't really her style, but then neither was losing.

Would he come after her?

She honestly didn't know and wasn't sure if she wanted him risking himself anyway. Circling the room again, she thought about what she'd say to him, what he might say to her—

"Sit down," one of the men said.

Another added, "Or at least take off those heels."

With a toss of her hair, she continued to pace. "If I'm dying anyway, I might as well suit myself."

She heard the footsteps as one of the men started forward with a snarl.

Then the boss man's voice intruded with "Back off," as he bounded down the steps.

"She started it."

Sahara turned with disbelief. "Grade school complaints? Really?"

A hard hand clamped around her arm and the boss said near her ear, "Quit pushing your luck," while propelling her toward the cot.

She couldn't keep herself from asking, "Or what?"

He pulled out a big shiny blade—and effectively stole her bravado.

CHAPTER THREE

SHE SHRANK BACK as he brandished that knife—then let out a thick breath when he only cut away part of the knot holding the ropes around her wrists.

Resisting the urge to rub the abraded skin, she asked, "Just to be clear, you're *not* going to stab me?"

"No. But if you can't contain yourself instead of needling my men, I'll take away all of your clothes and tie you naked to the cot."

As far as threats went, that was a doozy. To cover her horror over such an idea, she grumbled, "I'd freeze."

An arrested expression showed in his eyes seconds before he laughed. "You're entertaining, honey, when you're not provoking." He spun her around and, without a lot of finesse, jerked away her coat.

"Wait," she protested, trying to hold on to it. "I really will freeze and I promise not to—"

He tossed it to one of the others and said, "Check the pockets." Then he eyed her up and down. *"Behave."*

She had to swallow twice to get her heart out of her throat. Rather than agree with his edict—because she really wasn't sure she *could* behave—Sahara crossed her arms. The small room had already warmed considerably, so everyone would see it as a defensive move and she knew it.

"Nothing in them." The man handed the coat back to her, but when she only glared, he dropped it on the bed.

The boss extended a hand past her and Freckles brought him her purse. He upended it on the cot, then pawed through everything. A comb, her cell phone, a bag of M&M's, a small tin of aspirin, a tampon—he balked at the sight of that, then balked again at the pack of condoms.

Pale blue eyes slowly pinned her.

She shrugged. "I'm nothing if not prepared."

He stared a moment more, then asked, "Did you leave your keys in the ignition?"

"Please. My car has a keyless ignition." She gave him a look of haughty indignation for thinking she'd be so foolish. "The key fob is in an inside zippered pocket."

He opened it, his large hands clumsy against the small accessory. Her keys went in his pocket along with her cell phone—not that she'd expected to keep either. It'd be great if they at least left her purse with her.

"This?"

"Makeup remover cloths. Never know when I might need to do a touch-up." She unbent enough to reach for the purse. "Allow me, before you destroy something."

He gestured in a be-my-guest way, but said, "Any tricks at all, and you won't like the results."

She glanced up and saw two men with guns trained on her.

Definitely no trust at all. Opening another pocket, she retrieved her lipstick and mascara, with a small vial of perfume. The last pocket, on the bottom of the purse, held a power bank and extra cord. "In case my phone dies."

He took everything, squeezed every inch of her purse

to ensure nothing else was inside, then dropped it on the bed with the things he hadn't confiscated.

Considering how he'd just manhandled her purse... "What did you do with my car? And if you say you torched it and shoved it off a cliff, I'm going to be really pissed."

Amusement curled one side of his mouth. "It's parked at the end of your driveway." He eyed her askance. "Know a lot of cliffs around the city, do you?"

She waved a hand. "I meant that metaphorically." She gave him her own shrewd look. "How did you know where I live?"

His gaze hardened. "We know everything about you."

Well. That was alarming. "You've been following me for a while?"

He reached out and smoothed his thumb over her cheek, freezing her with the alarming gentleness. "Get comfortable, Sahara. It's going to be a long night."

Now she clutched at him. In bold accusation, she said, "You're leaving me here alone—" she stabbed a finger toward the others "—with *them*?"

All she could see were those pale eyes, but they definitely softened. "You'll be on this side of the locked door, and the guards will be on the other. Stay quiet, stay still and they'll have no reason to disturb you."

A little desperate, she blurted, "But I'm hungry."

"You have candy." He gestured at the M&M's on the cot.

"I need real food! I worked all day, straight through lunch in fact, and was going to eat dinner as soon as I got home."

Under the tight mask, his jaw flexed. He turned to

one of the men and said, "Go rustle up something. Make it quick."

The guy literally bolted from the room, taking the steps two at a time.

Glad of the slight reprieve, she sat on the cot and sighed again. "How much did you ask for?"

He knew exactly what she meant and replied, "Half a million."

The quick answer threw her. "Really? How did you come to that number?"

"Why not? You've got it."

She had it, yes, but it wasn't lying around like petty cash. Was poor Enoch scrambling, trying to figure out a way to get the funds together?

Or more likely, Enoch and her men were coming up with a daring and romantic play to get her back without giving the villains a single dime.

She liked that theory better. "So because I have financial security, you figured you'd rob me of it?"

"We're not robbing *you*. Scott's the one who cheated us out of it."

"By *dying*?" she asked, incredulous. No other conclusion came to her because her brother was an honest, honorable man.

Snorting, boss man sat beside her. "You don't believe that any more than I do." His massive thigh pressed against hers and she felt the heat of his body all along her side.

"No, I don't." Trying for subtlety, she inched away. "Tell me why *you* don't believe it." She needed some reassurance, damn it.

He gazed down at her. "You don't know your brother very well, do you?"

Insulted, she half turned to face him. "I know him better than anyone!"

"If you did, you'd know that whole death scene was a setup."

The words wrought a visual in her mind, choking her more than a fist could. Over sixteen months ago, her brother, Scott, and his then-girlfriend had gone out on his yacht on a beautiful sunny afternoon—and never returned. The Coast Guard found the yacht floating at sea, the deck covered in blood, his blood and hers…but no bodies.

Most people believed they were murdered and thrown overboard, but Sahara had never bought into that theory.

As if her love could keep Scott alive, she *refused* to believe it. She'd hired a PI and had had him on retainer ever since then.

"I hope that's true," she whispered. "I hope he devised the whole thing for some reason."

As if she were a puzzle to be solved, the guy angled his head, his gaze searching hers. "You wouldn't be pissed, would you? Even though all this time, you've thought he was dead?"

"All this time," she corrected softly, "I've believed he was alive and that eventually he'll come back to me."

After a few seconds of palpable pity, he patted her thigh.

She promptly removed his hand—or tried to.

He wasn't really cooperating; actually, his hold tightened.

Then luckily, her food arrived—a sandwich in a sealed plastic lunch bag, chips and a can of cola.

Her mouth watered. "Manna from heaven."

That got her another strange look—from most of the

men, really—but she didn't care. She ate when nervous, and God knew, she had plenty of reason to be nervous right now.

"Where'd you get the food?" Were they close to a deli? A grocery? He'd only been gone a few minutes…

One thick shoulder lifted. "I'd packed it for later, in case I got hungry."

"And you gave it to me?" She put a hand to her heart in dramatic appreciation. "Thank you. That's…well, I'd say it was sweet, but after all, I am your victim. Still, I'm grateful the plan isn't to starve me."

Given the sheepish bent to his head, she imagined her makeshift hero was blushing. He might've shuffled his feet at any moment if the boss man hadn't given an aggrieved sigh, snatched the food from his cohort and thrust it toward her.

She took the plastic-wrapped food and the cola, looked for a place to set them, didn't see one, and instead put the cola on the floor. So that she could eat in private, she shooed them away while opening the sandwich bag. "Go on. Do your business so I can get out of here."

"You," boss man said, "don't give the orders."

"But I'm so good at it." She bit into the sandwich, hummed at the taste of bologna, cheese and Miracle Whip, chewed and swallowed. "It wasn't a surprise to me, you know. That I could take over Body Armor and enjoy running it. I've always been an on-point, decisive person. Scott knew that. I only hope he'll be pleased with the changes I've made."

There was a general round of grumbling over that, as if they were personally offended over her interference in the agency.

She raised a brow, considering them. Men who disliked women in business…or something more? Perhaps it *was* personal to them. But why?

Had they worked at the agency?

She mentally jumped on that possibility, especially since it made more sense than anything else. If she could only see them, but their masks covered everything, and in some cases even shadowed their eyes.

Did they expect her to recognize them? She hadn't fired anyone, so they shouldn't have any grievances against her.

But what if Scott had…

"Get going," boss man ordered, sounding perturbed.

She tried to study each of them as they went up the stairs. Maybe something in their postures would trigger a memory, or if any of them had an unusual stride…

Rough fingers again lifted her chin.

This one particular kidnapper had a nasty habit of touching her far too often. She let him know it with a glare.

In answer, he stepped closer, until his big feet were braced around hers, leaving her unable to shift away.

It gave her the perfect opportunity to land a painful knee to the groin…but she didn't dare.

"Two guards will be outside this door."

Hmm… She said, "Yes?" in a way that sounded like a flippant *"So?"*

"Don't be stupid."

"Oh please. I am *never* stupid." She lifted away from his hand and, trying not to look intimidated, took another bite.

He didn't back up. "I'm leaving orders for you to be tied *and* gagged if you give them any problems."

At least this time he didn't threaten to take her clothes. She found some consolation in that.

"I'm in a dungeon," she complained. "What problems could I possibly cause? Now be nice and allow me to eat."

Shaking his head, he muttered, "Un-fucking-believable," and joined his mates. A second later she heard a heavy door clang shut, then the unmistakable sound of a bolt sliding into place.

The four walls tried to close in on her. The silence all but throbbed.

A little creeped-out, Sahara ate a chip, wondering what to do next. It was so silent in the concrete room, the sound of the chip crunching seemed absurdly loud.

After that last threat, they probably thought she'd wait quietly.

Unfortunately for them, patience definitely wasn't one of her virtues.

BRAND ZIGZAGGED IN closer to the building, pausing every so often and surveying the area with the night-vision binoculars Leese had given him. Under a lightweight jacket he wore a utility vest with Justice's Glock in an inside pocket; in another was a knife along with a Taser, nylon cuffs and additional ammo that Enoch had taken from their inventory.

The Body Armor supply area was more like an arsenal, with multiple weapons in a locked room next to the shooting range, where bodyguards practiced against targets.

Miles's voice burst into his brain straight through a wireless over-the-ear headset. "You there yet?"

"Yeah." He saw some activity, four guys coming

out, barely visible beneath dirty security lights. They kept their heads down, but black masks dangled in their hands. "Four men."

"What are they doing?"

"Scoping out the area. Wait…they went back inside but I hear an engine." He stared hard at the dark gap visible in the crumbling brick building. Seconds later, headlights came on and a white van pulled out. "They're in a white van." He read the license, repeating the numbers to Miles.

"Sahara said six, so there are at least two more still in there. Were you able to make out their faces?"

"No. The building looks abandoned and there's only one light. This whole area is gone, everything shut down. Other than some junkies in the alley and a vagrant passed out on a stoop, I didn't see anyone at all."

"It's after ten," Miles said, meaning that they'd had Sahara for over three hours already. "If they're leaving now, it might not be for long since the exchange isn't supposed to happen until midnight."

"Maybe they want to go over the location again."

"That's exactly what Leese is doing. They're liable to run into each other."

"Let him know." Brand lowered the binoculars. "I'm going in."

"They could be coming right back."

"All the more reason." No way in hell would he leave Sahara in there any longer than necessary.

Miles didn't argue. "I'll get hold of Leese and let him know, but keep the line open."

"Will do." Miles was nearby, positioned at a higher vantage point, there if necessary and to hell with being recognized.

Justice would tail Leese, far enough away not to be seen but close enough to get to him quickly if needed.

Enoch was back at the office, able to track Sahara up to a point if the cell failed to pick up the signal.

The storm had finally let up, leaving everything sodden, bringing with it a deep chill. Brand hadn't changed clothes so he was still in jeans and running shoes but now he had the vest and concealing jacket over his T-shirt.

"And, Brand? If you find there are more than two guys, don't do it alone."

"I can handle two." Hell, the way he felt right now, he could handle four. "If I need help, you'll know it."

They said nothing else as Brand made his way from alley to alley, shadow to shadow. As he ducked into one building, rats scurried behind him. He knew he shouldn't rush, but thinking of Sahara, what she might be going through, ate him up. He had to put that from his mind or he'd charge hell-bent into the building and damn the consequences.

He wasn't worried for himself. He'd die for her if that's what it took.

But he wouldn't risk her.

By the time he slipped through the same open garage door that the other men had exited, he'd regained his methodical control. Oppressive blackness filled the space, with little light penetrating from the street and a dank cold that sank into his bones.

Somewhere in this miserable hellhole, they have Sahara.

Using the night vision on the binoculars, he silently, stealthily, explored for ten minutes without finding any signs of her.

Knowing the others could return at any moment, frustration mounted…until he heard a man's muted laugh.

Senses on high alert, he followed the sound, glad now for the rubber soles. The sounds echoed, making the noise hard to trace, but when the laugh came again, followed by low conversation, it led him to a heavy door, thankfully open, then to stairs and another door, this one partially closed.

Brand peered through the narrow crack and saw two big men talking in front of yet another door—that one bolted.

"Those fucking heels she wears. Goddamn, they're hot." One man cupped a hand over his crotch. "You saw what they did for her ass while she paced?"

"Am I blind?" His friend chuckled. "Not that an ass like hers needs any help. If she wasn't so fucking mouthy, she'd be perfect."

"I like the idea of gagging her. She wouldn't be so hoity-toity then."

The other guy checked his watch. "Give her a few more minutes. She won't be able to stay quiet for much longer and then we can do as we please."

A snort, then, "Are you out of your fucking mind?"

"You heard what he said."

"Yeah, and I know the threat was for her, not an excuse for you to paw her."

Fury rose up. Brand wished like hell one of them would have used a name, but they were too busy fantasizing over ways to torment Sahara.

He knew in his gut that she was behind that locked door.

"Maybe if this rolls out as it should, he'll let us have some fun with her before—"

Going for the element of surprise, Brand left the gun in his pocket and instead stepped into the small space, taking the men off guard.

They both gawked at him.

"Be glad you didn't gag her, or you'd already be dead." He landed a hard right against the first bastard's nose, making him stagger back against the wall, then immediately kicked his friend in the face. He went down stiff, out cold.

Now with his nose streaming, the other creep tried to draw his gun. Brand had heavy fists and he enjoyed using them, in the cage, sure, during a competition.

But especially now, against a man who took pleasure in threatening Sahara.

He battered the man mercilessly, and it still didn't expend the rage inside him. When the man slumped, unconscious, he finally let up, but turned to deliver more punishment to the first guy, who was just starting to rouse.

He held him by his shirt collar. "If I find a single bruise on her, I'll come back and tear you apart." Before the fool could say anything, Brand smashed his fist to his face and the goon's head lolled on his neck.

Moving quickly, he retrieved the nylon cuffs and restrained both men with their arms behind their backs. Then he used the bigger cuffs to hobble their legs together. Lastly he checked them both for weapons, his movements efficient and without regard for any further discomfort he caused them.

When he finished, he stopped and listened, but heard nothing.

Heart punching in dread, he slid the bolt on the door

and swung it open. More steps led down—how fucking deep were they hiding her?

The lack of sound sent fear burning through him. If Sahara was down there, she wasn't moving, maybe not even breathing. He went down the steps, his gaze searching the barren room—and finally located Sahara to the side of the stairs, crouched down as if preparing to attack.

The stark concentration on her beautiful face cleared beneath incredible joy. "Brand! You came."

Seeing that smile did crazy things to his pulse.

Her hair hung loose around her, longer than he'd realized it would be. She'd taken off her shoes and had them next to her. Her coat was off and under her to protect her from the cold floor.

She'd hiked her narrow skirt up to midthigh.

Seeing the mess around her, he asked, "What are you doing?"

"Quietly disassembling this small electric heater to see what parts I could use to defend myself."

She still held a jagged piece of metal, folded to form the shape of a knife. To protect her hand, she'd wrapped something shiny and lavender around her makeshift handle. The weapon looked wickedly deadly—if she knew how to use it.

He assumed she did.

Maybe he'd done those men a favor, disabling them with their guts still intact.

He didn't see any tools, so he asked, "How?"

"I used the rim of the cola can to loosen the screws, then I took off the back cover. My shoe made a nice hammer and I—"

"What's wrapped around the handle?"

"My bra." Her chin lifted. "I didn't want to cut myself."

Of course, his gaze went to her breasts beneath the soft cashmere of her sweater. Yup, braless. He inhaled slowly through his nose.

"I was going to hunker over here and when they started down, I'd be cutting ankles. Maybe tendons—"

"Damn." *Gruesome*. Brand shook his head. "Tell me later." He held out a hand. "Let's go." Unwilling to risk the others returning, his top priority was getting her safely away from the area.

She stood with the electrical cord in one hand, the piece of metal still in the other. "You disabled the men guarding me?"

"Yes."

She quickly re-dressed, shaking out her coat and putting it on, hitching her purse over her shoulder and stepping back into her shoes.

"I don't know how the hell you walk in those things." And yeah, the way they stretched her legs and shaped her ass was something no red-blooded man would miss.

"I like them." She sent him a look. "You don't?"

Choosing not to answer that, he said, "Hurry it up."

She nodded and picked up the metal shiv again. "Okay, but I need to interrogate one of the men."

"No time for that." When she finally got close enough, he attempted to take the modified weapon from her. "You don't need this." Her resourcefulness amazed him, but it wouldn't be effective against armed men. "Here on out, I'll see to your safety."

Resisting, she stuck the cord in her coat pocket, switched the metal blade into her right hand and took his hand with her left. "That's so sweet of you, but I'll hold on to it just in case." Then she tried to take the lead.

Brand's immobility pulled her to a halt.

She glanced back, questions in her pretty eyes. Aggrieved, he moved around her.

When they stepped through the doorway to the landing, they found the two men still slumped, their bruised and battered faces red with their own blood, their hands and feet locked together.

Sahara stopped to stare. "Oh my. You managed all that rather silently."

Now was not the time for her to schmooze him. "Let's go, Sahara."

She ignored that order. "I was hoping once I got them unmasked, I'd recognize them, but now... I'm not sure their own mothers would know them."

"Do worms have mothers?" He tried again to get her going.

She tried again to pull free. "I told you, I need to question them." She nudged the closest man with the pointy toe of her shoe but he didn't rouse. "Is there water anywhere that I could throw on them?"

Brand clasped a hand to the back of her neck and leaned close, his gaze boring into hers. "We are going," he said succinctly. "Now."

Eyes flared with disbelief, she asked, "Are you threatening to *choke* me?"

He tightened his hold the tiniest bit, but she still looked only curious. "What I'm doing is getting your attention."

"Very rudely." She tried to shrug him off but he didn't let go. He knew he wasn't hurting her, but getting her on board with the rescue was imperative.

Scowling now, sparks going off in her eyes, she said, "You forget that I'm the boss, Brand. I give the orders."

He took grim pleasure in saying, "You forget that I don't work for you." When she started to speak, he cut her off. "We're leaving here. You either walk or I carry you. Up to you."

Her jaw loosened. "You wouldn't dare."

"Count of three, honey."

"I have a weapon!"

"That you wouldn't use on me, but if you think I couldn't take it from you, you're wrong." He started to scoop her over his shoulder and she backed up fast, almost tripping over the downed men.

"Be careful before you stab yourself!"

"If I do, it'll be your fault."

"Sahara," he ground out.

"Okay, okay!"

Brand turned, her hand once again caught in his, and got her moving. The dim light at the small landing faded as they maneuvered back to the main entrance of the garage, forcing Brand to use the binoculars. "Careful," he said, guiding her around some fallen equipment of some sort.

No answer.

They went up the next flight of stairs.

Still nothing.

Shrugging, he decided that Sahara's sullen silence afforded him the opportunity to share details. "Leese is headed to the exchange site, but then so are the other goons who took you. If they see him, they're going to want the ransom—a ransom he doesn't actually have. Once I get you out of here I'll contact him and the others, and they can move in to try to round up your kidnappers. Then you can grill them all you want."

"I didn't know that," she said, and then with more accusation, "*You* should have told me—"

"I shouldn't have to explain when your life is in danger."

"I wasn't worried about my life," she said in a small voice. "But you have to know I'd never willingly risk Leese."

Yeah, he did know it. Just to tweak her temper, he asked, "You'd risk me, though?"

"Don't be silly. You'd already pulverized those men and we'd have heard others before they reached us."

"They didn't hear me."

"Because you're stealthy, just as I knew you'd be. Admit it, you're made for this job. Why, I bet—"

"Keep your voice down." Used to her numerous, tireless pitches, Brand cut her off. "Everything echoes in here and we don't want to draw attention from anyone on the street. It's not exactly the suburbs."

In a whisper, she asked, "Did you see anyone out there?"

"No. Just the four who drove off."

"I think that's all of them." When she almost tripped, he caught her up against him. For just a moment her body pressed to his, the soft swells of her breasts reminding him that she'd removed her bra.

To make a handle.

For a shiv.

Holding her turned his voice gruff. "Those shoes are a hazard."

"Quit picking on my shoes." Her hand slid up and over his shoulder, then to his nape, where her fingers played with the ends of his hair. "If you weren't dragging me through the dark, I wouldn't stumble."

For the sake of his sanity, he said, "Let's try this." He shifted her around behind him. "Hold on to my jacket and follow exactly in my footsteps."

"Yes, sir."

He wouldn't mind hearing that much deference in bed. "Don't let go, Sahara. I mean it."

"I'm holding on, now get going."

The urge to remind her who was in charge nearly got the best of him, but he beat down his inner caveman and led the way. Just as they were reaching the large garage door that would lead them outside, he saw headlights approaching from the distance.

"Shit."

She snuggled close to his back and breathed, "Do we hide or make a run for it?"

"Both." He steered her quickly to the opposite side of the room, pulling her down with him behind several crates, deeper into the shadows. He wanted to put an arm around her, but keeping his hands free was critical.

"It'll be okay," she whispered.

As if in slow motion, he turned his head to see her. Crouched on those impossible heels, her improvised blade back in her hand, she watched the entrance.

Un-fucking-believable.

And impressive. His Sahara had guts. Because he couldn't resist, he pressed a small kiss to her forehead. "Don't attack unless I tell you to."

She nodded.

"I mean it, Sahara."

He saw her white teeth when she flashed him a smile. "I know."

As the headlights grew brighter, he explained, "Once they go down the first flight of stairs, you're going over my shoulder and I'm running out of here."

"Nope. I can run."

"Your heels will make too much noise and you could shred your feet if you try it barefoot."

"Oh." She gave it some thought. "Second time today I've been over a shoulder, and I have to tell you, I don't like it."

Someone else had dared to? No, he'd have to think about that later or he'd be destroying someone for daring to touch her.

Suddenly Miles spoke through the earpiece. "This has all been enlightening, but don't forget I'm here, okay?"

CHAPTER FOUR

THE INTRUSION OF his friend's voice took Brand off guard.

Shit, he had forgotten—but no way in hell would he admit it. "It's under control."

Sahara glanced at him. "What?"

"I'm talking to Miles. He's been with us the whole time."

She gasped, then hissed low, "He heard you threaten me?"

Brand found her hand—clenching the bra-covered handle of her weapon—and gave it a squeeze, his way of requesting her patience.

Miles cleared his throat. "You'll be able to get out?"

One way or another. "Probably."

"I'm nearby," he said. "If I hear anything I don't like, I'm coming in."

"Leese?"

"He and Justice are on their way back."

Brand felt compelled to remind Miles. "Sahara doesn't want police involved, so unless you know there's no other way—"

"Got it."

Sahara said, "Thank you."

He gave her one more squeeze, then told Miles, "They're here. Not a word, okay?"

"Understood."

The driver backed the van in, and even the red tail-lights were bright enough to give them away.

Brand pressed farther away, taking Sahara with him. He didn't know how she managed it, but she didn't make a sound and she didn't topple off those heels.

Conversation preceded the men from the van, and they sounded very disgruntled.

"It's a hell of a trip to make twice."

"When you're running things," the biggest of the men said, "you can fuck it up all you want, but I don't like to take chances. Now we know that we'll only be able to leave one guard here with her because everyone else will be needed to cover all the entrances."

"We'll have to turn right back around to get there by midnight and get set up," another mentioned.

"You had something better to do?" The big guy, still wearing a mask, left the van with a box in hand. The open door kicked on the interior light, and Brand saw that it was a cardboard carrier for a bag of takeout and two colas.

Unfortunately, the men still wore their disguises, the fanatical pricks.

"I have better things to do than cater to her," the friend grumbled. "That's for sure."

"She's only had a sandwich. Feeding her won't hurt anything." He slammed the door.

So the head honcho was disgruntled, was he?

"You're too soft on her."

That muttered complaint must have pushed him too far. Holding the food box in one hand, he used the other to slam his cohort up against the side panel. "When," he growled, "did I ever say we'd abuse her?"

"You didn't, but—"

"She's a means to an end, a way to get what we're owed." Clenching a fist in the complainer's shirt, he jerked him forward, then slammed him back again, pinning his forearm across the other man's throat. "That's all she is. Now you can either get on board, or get the fuck out. What's it to be?"

"He sure as hell isn't leaving," another man said. "We're either in this together, or we're all out."

The one being strangled under the muscular arm rasped, "I'm in. Jesus. Let up."

Seconds ticked by, three, four—and finally the boss shoved away. He flipped on a flashlight and stalked off, the beam bouncing ahead of him.

The remaining two men, the one who'd fucked up and the one who insisted he stay in, stared at each other.

"He's soft on her," the half-strangled dude insisted.

"Maybe, but one thing's for sure, you better keep your fucking mouth shut because either way, he's touchy when it comes to her." He loosened the mask to scratch at his neck, then turned to leave.

His friend followed.

A million thoughts went through Brand's mind, especially the supposed "softness" the head honcho felt for Sahara, but Brand knew they'd only have seconds to go so he shoved them all aside for now. He had to time it perfectly so that they weren't close enough to hear him running out, but hadn't yet reached the downed men to know they'd lost their bait.

He could practically feel Sahara's trepidation. "Stand, slowly," he whispered. He held her arm and helped her to do that. Then he took that freakishly wicked weapon from her.

Getting accidentally stabbed was not on the agenda.

"You'll get it back when we're clear," he breathed into her ear, then, "Ready?"

"Yes."

He tucked a shoulder against her middle and silently lifted her, his arm around her thighs to help balance her. Lifting the binoculars, he checked the path he'd take. Night-vision goggles would have been nice, but they weren't available in the Body Armor inventory.

Later, he'd talk to Sahara about that.

He let the binoculars drop back to his chest and eased out from behind the crates. "Once we hit the street, I'm going fast."

In answer, she grounded herself by clenching her hands in the waistband of his jeans. "Don't worry about me. Just get us out of here."

Brand strode silently toward the opening. A moon-lit night would have been welcome, but the scent of the storm still hung thick in the air. His feet had just cleared the garage when he heard the chaos behind him.

Needing no more incentive than that, he ran flat out, first up the street, then into an alley so that he cut through to another street, then into an empty building, across the floor and back out to another alley. He paused, listening, but the sounds were distant now.

"Put me down, please."

He did, letting her slide the length of his body, his hands going from her warm thighs to her shapely ass, to her small waist. He told himself he wanted to make sure she wasn't hurt.

His dick told him he was a liar. "You okay?"

"I think you broke a rib, but otherwise I'm fine."

Brand coasted a hand back up her body until he found

her throat. He curved his hand there, using his thumb to tip up her face. "Did I really hurt you?"

"No." Her hand covered his. She stepped closer. "May I have my shiv back now?"

Insane, but Brand smiled. Crazy, unpredictable, cool as a cucumber Sahara. "Do you actually know how to use it?"

"Stab," she whispered, "and twist."

He grimaced. "Yeah, that'd work." He gave it to her, then said, "Stay right here. I'll only be a second."

"It's dark and I hear rats."

So there was something she feared? "They won't bother you."

"I'll skewer them if they do, but hustle up."

Tunneling his fingers into her hair as a guide, he bent and took her mouth in a firm, quick kiss.

Before he did anything else stupid, he edged toward the front of the building. Holding very still, he listened, but didn't hear anything.

Miles said into his ear, "The van just sped away."

Damn. "All of the men?"

"Two were carried out, but yeah, there were six of them."

"Sahara is going to be pissed."

"Somehow I get the feeling you'll talk her around."

Hearing the note of humor in Miles's voice, Brand said, "Fuck off."

Moving right past that, Miles asked, "She's not hurt, is she?"

"Hurt? She was planning a massacre." Ready to get her to safety, he added, "We'll head to the corner of South Street and Garfield. You can pick us up there."

"Dicey area. Watch yourself. I'll head back to get the car and be there in five."

Brand returned to Sahara. She was right where he'd left her, eating M&M's out of her purse. When she heard him coming, she asked, "Brand?"

"Yeah."

"Have you eaten? Because I'm starved."

Would she ever cease to amaze him? He knew she had a hundred things on her mind, all of them more important than food. Then again, she was a pragmatist, especially when it came to basic needs.

Her no-nonsense approach meant she'd be doubly disappointed to know she couldn't question anyone, so he ignored the mention of food and broke the bad news. "I'm sorry, honey, but the goons took off."

She absorbed that in silence, then slammed her weapon against a rickety wall. "I *told* you I should have interrogated those men!"

He caught her shoulders before she could begin pacing. "They were carried out, so my guess is they couldn't have answered your questions, no matter how you tortured them."

"Oh, they'd have talked," she promised in an evil voice.

Brand grinned again. "You're scary, you know that?" He kissed her once more, a little longer this time. "Mmm. You taste like chocolate."

"It's the candy."

He went in for a deeper taste, and damn her, she let him. When he pulled back, she breathed, "I wanted to hold you so badly, but I have M&M's in one hand and this trusty dagger in the other, so—"

Later, he promised himself, then shook his head because he couldn't seriously be thinking about going down that path. Everything Sahara did ultimately ended up back at the same place—with her need to find a brother who was no longer alive.

For hopefully the last time, he took her *trusty dagger* from her and led her through the crumbling building and out to the street. At least the air was fresher here, even if everything dripped from the storm. "We have to meet Miles a few blocks up. It's a nasty area so if anyone shows up, for the love of God, get behind me and let me handle it."

"Like a knight in shining armor?" She sighed. "So romantic. It's almost like you were born to be a protector."

He huffed a laugh. "You never give up, do you?"

"When I want something this much? No."

If she wanted *him* that much, he'd be flattered. But she wanted another employee and that was a whole different game.

They made it to the corner without incident. It was a little busier here, more bustling with traffic passing and a few places lit up: a bar, a convenience store, a gas station. He watched as Sahara buttoned up her coat, tied the belt and turned up the collar.

Her long hair curled a little from the stormy humidity and she looked so damned sexy, so sweet, all he could think about was having her.

It was in part due to the adrenaline dump. Back in the day he'd been a regular street brawler and, to be honest, he'd loved it. But his mom hadn't, and so he'd gotten his shit together, went legit and made it to the SBC.

That was all up in the air again, though, and odds were, he'd have to quit after the next fight.

But not yet.

And not to be Sahara's underling.

"I'm cold."

"Is that a hint for me to warm you up?"

"Could you?" Without waiting for an invite, she stepped in to him, her cheek against his chest.

Feeling her shivers, he held her closer, his free hand wrapped in her hair. "How come you never wear it down?"

"Because I'm the boss."

She said it like it made perfect sense. "Bosses can't have long hair?"

"Bosses have to look controlled."

Trying to figure her out, he asked, "And the clothes you wear?"

"They're my expensive, professional, classic I'm-in-charge-and-I-know-it clothes. Perfect for a shark."

She sounded sleepy, and that automatically led him to thinking about her going to bed. At her big mansion. Alone. "Tired?" he asked.

"A little, but I need food before I rest." Keeping her chin on his chest, she turned her face up to his. "Do you feel like eating?"

A loaded question, especially with the way she looked at him. Did she mean to put carnal images in his head? Whether she did or not, he got a distinct visual of her on her back, her long legs over his shoulders while he stroked her with his tongue.

"Brand?"

Damn it, now she sounded breathy but he couldn't tell if it was exhaustion or interest.

Bottom line, if she wanted company, he'd be company. "Sure. Where do you want to go?"

"My place."

Her place? Oh hell no. Trying to be reasonable, he said, "I was under the impression that the kidnappers know where you live."

"Clearly, but once I'm locked inside they can't bother me."

"They've already bothered you."

"Yes, but there's nowhere more secure than my home." She walked her fingers up his chest. "And you can ensure I get inside safely, right?"

Be alone with her in that mausoleum? With her braless, her hair down and the caveman testosterone still pumping hard through his bloodstream? Bad idea. "Sahara—"

"Look, isn't that Miles now?" Once she spotted him, she straightened with relief. "Thank goodness because, much as I hate to admit to a weakness, I'm ready to crash." As if he didn't already know it, she heaved a heavy sigh and said, "It's been a trying day."

What an understatement.

And what a woman. Sahara would always be a handful...but then, Brand had very big hands.

He was incredibly pissed—and also impressed—to the point where he couldn't reconcile the two emotions. He sat in the back of the van with his downed men, ready to finish them off the second they came to.

Carrying them out hadn't been easy, not up those stairs. Sahara...carrying her had been a pleasure. She was a shapely thing, slender and toned but still soft in all the right places. And she smelled good. It had taken great resolve on his part not to turn his face against her hip and...

"They're coming around finally," Olsen said.

Ross gave him a dark look and he went silent again.

Olsen had a problem keeping his mouth shut. No one was supposed to talk to her but him. He, at least, hadn't underestimated her.

Much.

But Olsen, with his ideas on the weaker sex, couldn't stop his blathering. It's a wonder Sahara hadn't flayed him alive.

Ross had no doubt that if she'd decided to, she'd have found a way.

When the man closest to his outstretched legs groaned, Ross gave him a nudge. "Think carefully before you say anything. One fucking lie and I'll throw you out to the street where you can die without being a pain in my ass."

Not taking the threat to heart, he groaned again.

Ross sat forward. "Tell me she didn't do this to you."

The groan mixed with a laugh. "No. A man…he came in to get her."

Ross relaxed, but only a little. Of course, Sahara hadn't done all that damage. The lady might have brass cojones and plenty of ingenuity, but she didn't have the bulk and muscle needed to demolish grown men. "And what the fuck were you doing? Jacking off?"

"Talking to Terrance."

Uh-huh. "So you two geniuses were so lost in conversation, you didn't hear this guy come in?"

Terrance struggled onto his side. "Didn't hear a sound, Ross. Then suddenly he was there." Gingerly, a hand to his nose, he sat up. "I think it's broken."

"You think?" Ross eyed the grotesque swollen flesh that used to be Terrance's nose. "Your nostrils damn near touch your ear. Yeah, Sherlock, it's broken."

Olsen shook his head. "Figured it was a man. I didn't

think that skinny lady could do all that damage, but Ross wasn't so sure."

Ross slowly turned his head to glare at Olsen. "You haven't yet figured out that she somehow signaled the guy who came for her?"

Olsen looked struck. "Signaled him?"

"How the hell else do you think he found her?"

Andy, too, managed to sit upright. "I didn't recognize him as one of her bodyguards, but the bastard sure knew how to fight."

"There wasn't any *fight*," Ross snapped. "He wiped the floor with the two of you."

"I got taken by surprise with a kick to the face," Terrance defended. "I don't remember much after that."

"And you?" Ross asked Andy. "Your face is so fucked, I barely recognize you."

With only one eye open, Andy complained, "I don't remember shit either." He moved his tongue in his mouth, then spat out a tooth.

Ross gave a disgusted laugh. "So this guy just materialized out of nowhere and started destroying you both?"

Terrance glanced at Andy.

Andy, looking a little alarmed, tried to frown but Ross caught the look.

With throbbing menace, he asked softly, "What did you do?" Fury brought him slowly forward. "Did you touch her?"

"No." They were both quick to deny.

Then Terrance, maybe seeing a way to deflect the anger off his own head, admitted, "We were talking about her, though, and I guess he overheard."

Even softer now, Ross asked, "What did you say?"

Holding his ribs, Terrance scooted until he could sit

with his back against the side of the van. "I just pointed out how hot she looked in those heels."

If he hadn't been so pathetically abused, Ross might've hit him again. Yeah, she did look killer-hot in the heels, but they knew his rules.

Sahara Silver was off-limits—and damn it, in his mind, that included fantasizing over her.

After touching the bridge of his nose and wincing, Terrance added, "Dumbass over there was running his mouth, though. I'm guessing that's why he got the worst of it."

Andy did look a mess, more deliberately worked over. Not a spot remained on his face that wasn't bruised, swollen, split or bloody. It was a wonder he could speak at all with his lips so fat. Even his ears were mangled. Given how gingerly he moved, he'd taken plenty of body blows as well.

Ross didn't care. He didn't have an ounce of sympathy.

"What were you saying, Andy?"

"Nothing." He must have thought better of that, and explained, "Same shit as Terrance."

Ross waited.

As the tension grew, Terrance put his head back and closed his eyes. The other men looked away. Andy shifted—and groaned.

"Jesus H. Christ, Andy. Just spit it out," Olsen snapped. "You're making everyone uneasy."

Sullen, Andy stared at his feet. "I made a joke about gagging her."

Unaccountable rage gripped Ross. "And?"

"I just said she'd be perfect except for her mouth, and I joked—*joked*, Ross—about checking on her so I could gag her. I knew she wouldn't be peacefully sitting down there, waiting like you told her to, and you did warn her what would happen if she didn't behave. I figured she was up to something, and I guess I was right, wasn't I? Somehow she called that prick and—"

"Did you actually touch her, Andy? Did you lay a single finger on her? Even get *close* to her?"

All of the men stared at him, aware that he just might snap if—

Terrance said quickly, "We never even opened the door, Ross. It was just talk, that's all."

Gradually, Ross got his shit together. He was making a fool of himself over her, but damn, he'd been studying her for so long, he felt like she belonged to him.

Being with her today, having control of her while also being her protection, had affected him in ways it shouldn't have.

Means to an end.

That's what she was, what she had to be. Allowing himself to feel anything else was beyond stupid. It didn't matter that she was gutsy and fearless, refined despite the circumstances, bold and intelligent... He clamped down on all those wayward thoughts.

Means to an end, goddamn it.

Forcing himself to sound reasonable, Ross said, "She had no way to call anyone from the basement."

"So she *was* down there behaving?"

Olsen snorted. "Hell no. She took apart the heater. Parts are missing. I'm guessing she made a weapon." He grinned, seeing the surprise on Andy's and Terrance's faces. "If her boyfriend hadn't stomped on you, she might've done it herself."

"He's not her boyfriend," Ross said, his voice deliberately devoid of inflection. "She doesn't date, not since Scott went missing."

"Not a bodyguard, not a boyfriend," Terrance said. "Then who was he?"

"I don't know." That fact really pissed him off. "But I intend to find out." *No,* he silently promised her, *we're not done, Sahara. Not by a long shot.*

And the next time I get you, I'll make damn sure you don't get away.

BRAND TRIED NOT to look as uncomfortable as he felt standing in Sahara's grand foyer. Far as he was concerned, it was a terrible idea, never mind that she had a locked gate and a high-tech security system. She shouldn't be alone, period. But she'd ignored all his arguments, damn it, and the other guys hadn't been any more successful.

He suspected it was her pride insisting she stay in the house; she wasn't a woman who'd easily show her fear. He knew it, he understood it, but Jesus, he hated it.

Now, after unsuccessfully trying to convince her to at least bring in the cops, the others had left.

"No," she'd asserted. "This is personal. They know something about Scott. I'm going to handle it my way, so get used to it."

Her way, for the remainder of the evening at least, was to pretend she hadn't been taken hostage.

Her car, which probably cost more than some houses, had been parked in the end of the driveway just as, she claimed, the kidnappers had promised. She'd wanted to drive it up to the front door herself, but the men had outvoted her on that.

Once Miles had done a full sweep of the car, Justice

drove it up to her garage. Of course, they'd wanted to take turns standing guard, but Sahara refused that, too. They all had upcoming assignments to prep for, and she felt safe in her own home, so they'd only hung around long enough to ensure she wasn't too upset—ha!—and that no one had tampered with her house.

Brand would stay with her—she'd agreed to that much—but the guys didn't like it. They trusted him, but as they'd said, he wasn't a bodyguard. Still, he assured them that he wouldn't let anything happen to her, and he intended to make good on that promise.

The keyless entries, one at the street that opened wide arched gates, and another at the end of the long lighted private lane that secured the main entrance, were still set.

If anyone without the passcode had tried to intrude, alarms would have gone directly to a security company.

Showing no residual effects from her adventures, Sahara stepped out of her shoes, wiggled her toes, shrugged off her coat and hung it on a coat tree. The enormous shiv she placed at the bottom of the stairs.

"What," he asked, "do you plan to do with that?"

"I'm partial to it now, so it'll probably reside in my bedroom."

With her bra still used as a grip for the handle?

She gave him a tentative smile. "Come on."

Brand wasn't sure if he should remove his shoes as well. His running shoes wouldn't hurt the polished marble floors, but then again, what did he know about the protocol for a mansion?

Without him having to ask, Sahara answered by hooking her arm through his and leading him to the kitchen.

He felt the full curve of her breast against his upper arm and it kept his body humming with tension.

Any other woman and he'd have already checked the invitation to see how far it extended. But not with Sahara Silver, owner of Body Armor, self-proclaimed shark.

The kitchen was something out of storybooks, momentarily distracting him once she let him go. He turned a full circle taking it in. "Damn." The detailed ceiling was its own work of art. One end boasted a sectional couch under tall windows, a center island held plenty of bar stools and at the other end was the thick wooden table that could seat six.

"Grab a seat. Do you want something to drink while I throw together a meal?"

Yeah, he wouldn't mind the whole bottle. Maybe it'd help him get through this bizarre night. He shook his head as he pulled out a chair at the table. "I'm good."

"Coffee then." On bare feet she went to a massive refrigerator and retrieved several things, including chicken fillets. Going on tiptoe, stretching those sexy calves, she got down a bowl and dropped the chicken inside, then poured in Italian dressing, dashed in some other seasonings, and used a fork to stir it around. Next she set her oven, then washed her hands and got the coffee started.

She seemed to do it all with planned movements meant to best utilize her time and streamline all processes.

Nothing new in that. Sahara was one of the most efficient people he'd ever met.

After grabbing a cookie from a big round jar, she joined him at the table, watching him while she nibbled. She held it out. "Want a bite?"

He shook his head. "What are you cooking?"

"Italian chicken, baked potatoes and salad."

Hell of a meal to "throw together" after midnight. He lifted a brow. "Dessert first?"

"Oh, honey, a single cookie could never be dessert." She popped the rest in her mouth, left her seat to poke at the chicken with the fork, then got out a dish and prepped it with butter. "How hungry are you?"

Starving…but not for food. Every time she went on tiptoe, he had the burning urge to run his palms up the inside of her thighs. The movement of her breasts under that soft sweater kept drawing his attention, too. Her nipples were just tight enough to be visible—and to make his mouth water.

She looked over her shoulder in a provocative way—deliberately or not, he wasn't sure. "Brand?"

He met her gaze with a piercing stare, *very* deliberately. "I would have been fine with a sandwich."

Blue eyes lit up. "Something fast and easy, huh?" Her mouth curled. "Not my style." Looking away from him again, she washed two potatoes, then put them on a plate and into the microwave. "Although, this meal is pretty quick and not all that difficult."

Brand was still pondering her "fast and easy" comment, knowing he might be fast with her, but not easy. No, he wanted to claim her. He wanted that bad. "I get the feeling you're teasing me, Sahara."

His tone alerted her, and she turned to face him. "Maybe a little. You always resist easily enough."

Not tonight. "Trying to see how far you can push it?"

She braced her hands behind her on the counter, which pushed out her breasts. One leg bent, her gaze sultry, she said, "I'm curious. Aren't you?"

He already knew his breaking point, and he was damn

near it already. Smiling just to confuse her, he asked, "So how long is this meal going to take?"

The oven dinged and she turned away. "Thirty minutes."

He watched as she got everything in the oven. She ate another cookie while putting together a salad, and then she set the table, leaning close to him, brushing against him.

She was really feeling frisky tonight—or was it something more?

When she started to move away, Brand caught her arm. Her skin was soft and warm, her bones delicate, but the woman had iron in her blood and a will made of titanium.

Brushing his thumb over the silken skin inside her elbow, he asked, "Is this your way of reacting to the evening?"

A flash of uncertainty filled her blue eyes, then cleared behind a big grin. She put a hand to his chest. "One of the most appealing men I've ever known is in my kitchen, and you want to dissect my mood?"

That evasive nonanswer only made him more determined. "Yeah, I think I do." He tugged.

Of course she resisted his efforts.

And of course he won the small battle.

She either overestimated her strength, or underestimated his.

Sahara ended up sprawled in his lap, a sexy, squirming armful. As he worked to contain her, he asked, "Easy or hard, Sahara?"

Her eyes flared wide and her lips parted.

Cursing himself over his unfortunate wording, Brand briefly looked away. When she again tried to scramble free, he locked his arms around her and pinned her with his gaze.

Being so close, he saw the thickness of her lashes, how her pupils dilated—he even felt the warmth of her faster breaths.

Her gaze dropped to his mouth.

Fighting his way out of the cage with the number one heavyweight would have been easier, but he managed not to kiss her. "We're going to talk about what happened tonight, especially what happened while you were alone with them."

"We are?"

He saw no reason to repeat himself, so he merely waited.

Proving she wasn't on her A game right now, she cracked. "There's nothing much to tell. They said Scott owed them money and they were getting it back by ransoming me."

That sounded true—but no way was it the whole story. "You said someone put you over his shoulder?" Even though he'd done the same thing, it infuriated him to imagine it.

"The boss man," she confirmed with an indignant nod. "The one in charge. He warned the others not to bother me, and they didn't. Shoot, they hardly spoke to me. But he explained a few things."

"About Scott?"

"No, just...the rules."

Something in her expression, in the way her voice dropped, alerted him. Opening his hand on her back, he soothed a path up and down her rigid spine. "What rules, honey?"

She stared at him. "You're comforting me?"

"Something like that."

"Oh." Suddenly she tucked herself closer, her cheek against his shoulder, her hand sliding up his chest. "This is nice."

Drawing out her name like a warning, he said, *"Sahara."*

"I really don't want to talk about it. Nothing happened, I promise."

Brand tunneled his fingers into her hair, then tugged her head back. "I know you better than that." He wanted her trust. He needed her to know that she didn't have to be the boss every minute of every day, not with him.

Her searching gaze bounced back and forth over his. "You have really thick, dark eyelashes, Brand. Did you know that?"

"Sahara—"

"And all this sexy stubble," she said, reaching for his face.

"Enough." Brand tilted out of reach. "You're going to tell me what happened to you, so stop trying to distract me."

Groaning, she whacked his shoulder. "You're not normal, damn it! Why can't you just take what I'm offering—"

His mouth covered hers in the most expedient way to silence her annoyance. She immediately sank against him, all the vibrating agitation draining from her slim body.

Perfect.

Too perfect.

Bordering on dangerous…and wasn't that absurd given the situation they'd just escaped?

CHAPTER FIVE

IT DIDN'T TAKE long for Brand to realize he'd made a strategic mistake.

Clutching at him, Sahara adjusted her position, taking his tongue when he went in for a deeper taste, then giving her own as he tried to retreat.

Her low sound of pleasure made him throb, especially when she twisted so her breasts more fully met his chest and her bottom squirmed over his lap, or more specifically, over his thickening erection.

Whoa, a boner right now would be wholly out of place.

Easing up by slow degrees, Brand kissed the corner of her mouth, her stubborn jaw, the sleek column of her throat.

She was so soft and fragrant everywhere. He could get drunk on the scent of her skin, on the feel of her against him, on the taste of her mouth and the sexy sounds she made...

More prominent than his need, though, was her reaction to his questions. She was usually so forthright that her avoidance now worried him.

Pressing her head to his shoulder, he drew a few deep breaths, giving them both time to recover before asking, "What rules?"

Still limp against him, she muttered, "God, you're stubborn."

Her hair felt like silk through his fingers. "If we're comparing…"

"We're not." She huffed, but didn't try to get away. "If you must know, I bluffed through most of my nervousness. I didn't want them to know that I was concerned so I acted like they were nothing, less than nothing."

That didn't surprise him at all. Sahara could be terrified, and she'd show indifference. "Pride?"

"In part, sure. But I also wanted to find out what I could about Scott, so I kept pushing."

Like she often did with him. Only he wasn't a kidnapper, and they both knew he'd never hurt her.

Seconds ticked by before she softly added, "I was told to behave or I'd be stripped naked and tied to the cot."

Motherfucker.

"Obviously I couldn't let that happen."

She couldn't have stopped them—and that's why she'd been making the weapons. He gathered her closer, proud of her, impressed and overwhelmed with the need to protect.

Forget beating the shit out of the guy; he'd kill him instead.

She whispered, "It frustrates me that in some ways women are weaker than men."

When it came to possible rape, she meant, and he wanted to crush her closer still. "I'm sorry you went through that."

"Even that vile threat wouldn't have been so unsettling, except…well, I don't know if I imagined it or not, but he seemed to…" She gave it some thought. "*Like* isn't the right word, but then neither is *want*. It's hard to explain and I might be way off base but I think he…"

When she curled a little tighter against him, Brand said, "I've never known anyone as smart and intuitive as you. Whatever you're thinking, I'd bet a championship belt that you're dead-on."

She pushed back to see his face. "Really?"

"Really." Sahara always packed a sensual punch, but now, with her hair loose and her eyes vulnerable, she could bring him to his knees. "You have great instincts, honey."

Her teeth worried her plump bottom lip before she gave it up. "He admired me, Brand. Now isn't that bizarre?"

"No. I can't imagine any man *not* admiring you."

"I…" She closed her mouth, opened it again and finally said, "Thank you."

"You're welcome." Seeing that she was a little more relaxed, he asked, "How could you tell what he felt?"

"The way he'd look at me as if I'd surprised him, and the way he'd smile at me. I even made him laugh a few times, and not necessarily on purpose. He constantly warned off the other guys but then he'd touch me when he shouldn't, when there was no reason to. Like sitting so close that his thigh was against mine." She shuddered.

To keep her talking, Brand suggested, "Maybe he wanted to play on your helplessness."

Umbrage brought her brows together. "I was never helpless."

No, she probably hadn't been, at least not in her mind. Unfortunately for her, not everyone shared her delusions. "You were a woman alone with six armed men."

"I guess, but it never really felt like they meant me

harm, not really, and that's why the main guy's attention bothered me. You know, I'm the first to admit I'll dive into a battle of wills, but for him it was more than that. I couldn't gauge him, couldn't figure out his intentions, and that made him more dangerous."

"It bothers you that you backed down?"

Again indignant, she asked, "Who backed down? I bided my time wisely and at the first opportunity, I made a weapon." Under her breath, she muttered, "No one is getting me naked without my explicit permission."

So damn fearless. It was a serious discussion, and still the corner of his mouth twitched into a near smile. "You were as prepared as anyone could be." He didn't stop himself from kissing her again, softer this time. "For the record, Sahara, you impressed the hell out of me."

She tried to lean in for yet another kiss, but they both knew where that would lead. He controlled himself, and her, which suited him, but was something she disliked.

Getting her back on track, he asked, "So the man who threatened you is the same one who carried you?"

"Yes. He didn't let anyone else touch me at all. He barely allowed them to look at me. While we were still in the van, he'd tied my hands—not very well, but I didn't think it'd be prudent to pull my hands free right in front of him. That would have just gotten me tied more tightly, and who needs that?"

"Smart," he said, to cover the burgeoning rage. If Sahara hadn't been so savvy, if she'd been more intimidated, what might have happened to her?

For all her brass, she was a soft, very feminine woman. The thought of anyone handling her roughly, tying her, threatening her, burned like acid in his blood.

"Having my hands tied made it difficult to stand up

once we needed to leave the van, especially in the heels I favor. So he dragged me on my behind to the doors, got out and hefted me over his shoulder."

"Like I did?"

She cast him a disgruntled frown. "Well…not as gently."

"I'm sorry—for both times."

Her hand went over his shoulder to his nape, and her fingers started a slow tease over his fevered skin. "It was necessary when you did it, but if I ever see *him* again, I'll make him sorry."

"Yeah?" Her words were a distinct contrast to her touch. "What will you do?"

She opened her mouth—then suddenly sniffed the air and scrambled off his lap. "I have to turn the chicken, and in ten minutes it'll be time to eat."

Another avoidance?

Brand didn't know if it was because she couldn't think of anything dire enough, or because she already knew what she'd do and she didn't want to shock him.

With Sahara, it was probably the latter.

As THE NIGHT wore down, Sahara wasn't sure what to do. So far, none of her efforts had moved Brand. It was like smacking her head against a brick wall, unproductive and painful.

He'd enjoyed her dinner, giving her a lot of praise and eating every last bite.

"Another cookie?" she asked, sipping her coffee.

"Two's plenty for me. You made them yourself?"

"Yes."

"You're an amazing cook."

He'd already said that a few times. "Why do I get the feeling you're shocked?"

He smiled lazily and shrugged. "You said it yourself that you're a business shark. Seems like overkill to be Suzy Homemaker, too."

That made her laugh. "I'm not. I mean, I could be." She was pretty sure she could do anything she set her mind to, and if she did it, she'd damn straight do it top-notch. "I've enjoyed cooking, but cleaning—not so much."

He looked around again. "I guess you have a crew who keeps this place in order?" As he said it, he stood and headed to the sink with his dishes.

"What are you doing?"

"My share of the cleanup."

"So gallant." She popped the last bit of the cookie into her mouth then pitched in.

Anything was better than calling it a night.

As they worked, she deliberately brushed against him. He acknowledged her efforts with a satisfied and very male smile, but nothing more.

She could probably strip naked and he wouldn't give in.

She wiped off the table while he dried the baking dish that couldn't go in the dishwasher. Any second now he'd walk out, and she wasn't ready for that.

When she would be ready, she didn't know, but it definitely wasn't tonight.

Sidling up next to him at the sink, she made another effort to keep him around. "Brand?"

He looked down at her, watching her rinse the dish-cloth. "Something on your mind, Sahara?"

So many things. If she told him she was nervous, that she didn't want to be alone, he'd stay. Unfortunately, she couldn't bring herself to utter the words. They'd make her feel weak, and worse, they'd make her look weak. "Would you like to see the rest of the house?"

"I was going to ask."

"You were?" Well, damn it, if she'd just waited...

"This place is so huge, how do you know everything is still locked up?"

"Good security system." She rethought that real fast and added, "But it can't hurt to check, right?" After drying her hands, she gestured. "This way."

As they went around the interior, she tried to take her time, showing off artwork and things her brother had specifically chosen, but Brand seemed more interested in the security system and the keyless locks on the doors.

"Everything is well lit," she pointed out, after they'd gone through the library, two studies, a gallery, a guest room, kitchen, dining and breakfast area, a formal living room, and a cozier entertaining room.

"What's through here?" he asked, poking his head into a suite of rooms.

"Technically those are service quarters. My brother used to keep a full staff around." She shrugged. "I prefer my privacy so now that I live here, I just have a cleaning crew that comes by once a week."

He gave her a funny look, then took the lead going downstairs. "Where's your bedroom?"

"My rooms are upstairs."

"You use more than one bedroom?"

"Well, there's my bedroom, my changing room, sitting room, bathroom—"

"Got it."

Did he think she was bragging? Yes, wealth was something she'd taken for granted, but it wasn't something she had to have to be happy. Because she wasn't afraid to work, she couldn't see herself as a pauper, but neither was she a snob who needed so much luxury. "You know the house belonged to my brother, right?"

"Yeah." Brand got to the bottom of the stairs and headed straight to the back of the main room to the large double doors that opened into the backyard. "You ever think of selling it?"

Appalled by that idea, she scowled at him. "Of course not."

He glanced at her.

"I would never willingly part with anything of Scott's."

Nodding, he turned back to double-check the locks, examining them in detail. "Justice cleared these as secure?"

"He did." Justice had stayed with her before as her personal bodyguard, using rooms on the main floor. Out of all of them, Justice had a special knack for understanding alarms and the best way to wire a system.

Moving on to a window, Brand kept his back to her. "Leese said that he's stayed here, too?"

"Yes." Once, when necessary, Leese and Catalina had used the rooms in the basement.

Brand went to the right, and she followed. "Most of that area is used for storage. There are no windows, so no way for anyone to break in."

He did a cursory glance through each room anyway, before backtracking and going to the far left where a pool table and other games filled a large section.

Watching him prowl around did funny things to Sahara, making her think of things she never had before.

Like how nice it'd be if she weren't alone.

Trying to summon up some of her notorious poise, she opened the guest bedroom. "This is the room Leese and Catalina used. There's an attached full bath, a sitting room with a PC, and a bar with a sink and microwave."

"All the comforts of home."

She inhaled, worked up her best I'm-in-charge smile and said, "Does that mean you'd like to stay for a visit?"

"I'm definitely staying."

Crazy reactions happened inside her: elation, uncertainty...*lust*. Having Brand in her bed would go a long way toward helping her forget the horrible day and night.

She licked her lips, trying to decide what to say next, then decided to hell with it and asked, "You want to stay down here? Because, Brand, it's awfully far away—"

"Exactly. Too far away." He approached, his dark gaze assessing her, making her think she might get another kiss—or more.

He only took her hand. "Let me see your rooms."

That sounded like a euphemism to her, and in her mind, she gave a mental fist pump into the air. Finally, Brand was giving in. Once she got him in her room, nature could take its course.

Going for serene confidence instead of triumph, she said, "Sure," and got them on their way.

Racing would be too obvious, so she forced herself to a measured stride.

It wasn't easy. Brand dwarfed her with his size and she thrilled at the contrast, her thoughts jumping ahead to how his weight would feel over her, the heat of his skin and all those delicious muscles...

"You're quiet."

She cleared her throat. "Just thinking." *And getting myself turned on.*

The staircase was wide enough for them to go up together, still hand in hand, back through the house, and then to the double staircase that split her large foyer and led upstairs.

She picked up her manufactured shank from the bottom step, holding it in her free hand. Looking toward her discarded shoes in the entry, she decided to leave them rather than release Brand; she could get the shoes tomorrow.

She smiled at him and started up, her heart already galloping in anticipation.

They were on the third step when he said, "I can use the rooms Justice had. That's only one floor below you."

Sahara froze. It took her brain a second to compute what she'd just heard.

Rejection *again*. Damn it, when would she learn?

Maybe it was the buildup, thinking he'd finally be hers, but she rounded on him in the grip of unreasonable anger. "You want to sleep *on a separate floor*?"

He stared down at her. "It's not about what I want, Sahara. It's about what makes sense."

Disappointed, infuriated—*despondent, damn him*—she tried to snatch her hand away. "Great idea!"

The blasted man held on.

She stopped tugging and through her teeth, said, "Let. Go."

His thumb rubbed over her knuckles. "Sahara—"

On the verge of losing it, and knowing she couldn't do that in front of him, she hissed, "Let me go right now! I don't need you to inspect my rooms. They're fine. The house is fine. I'm *fine*." Liar—but her personal turmoil was no longer any of his business. "The security is the best money can buy, so I don't really need anything at all. Since it'll be morning soon, you should probably just go on home." Mortified that her voice broke there at the end, she spun around and dashed up the steps, her shank swinging at her side.

"Be careful," he yelled. "If you fall you're going to stab yourself."

"Go to hell!" She reached the landing at the top of the stairs and, still running, went to the left, farther down an unlit hallway and then right through the open door to her bedroom. She slammed the door shut and locked it, sealing herself into the dark interior. She rested her forehead against the cool wood.

Emotions welled up, too many of them to count, too varied to define a single one. Things she didn't want to feel bombarded her.

She left the lights off. A large mirror hung behind her dresser, another full-length mirror beside it. Not only did she refuse to let Brand witness her pathetic upset, she didn't want to see it either.

Breathing hard, fighting off idiotic tears, she made her way to her bed by rote and sat down with her blade across her lap. "Stupid," she mumbled to herself. "So stupid."

A second before she heard the sound, she sensed the movement behind her. All the air whooshed out of her lungs.

She leaped off the bed and swung the dagger at the same time, colliding with jarring impact against something solid.

"Jesus, Sahara."

Oh dear God. She knew that voice and it terrified her. "Don't you dare move," she threatened, keeping her tone strong despite her terror. "I'll cut your head off, I swear I will."

To the side of her, in the darkness, her kidnapper asked, "Will you now?"

"Yes." She quickly rolled over and off the bed away from him, sweeping out with the blade as she did so, thinking she'd feel a hard hand grab her wrist or ankle at any moment and then what would she do? Panic raced through her until her feet were again on the floor.

No one touched her.

Slowly, as silently as possible, she backed up until her shoulder blades touched the door frame next to her dressing room.

The door was open when she always kept it closed. A cool evening breeze wafted in around her.

Had he somehow come in through the window?

What if he'd brought the other men with him? They could all six be in her room with her! She wouldn't stand a chance.

Why had she so stubbornly insisted on coming home?

And what the hell had happened to her security system?

Eyes wide, she tried to see through the darkness. She might bump into one of them any second now…

No, she told herself. *Stay calm, keep your head and think.* She couldn't count on Brand hearing her, not from a floor away—if he had even stayed after she'd ordered him to go.

Please, she silently prayed. *Please, Brand, still be here.*

She needed a way to gain the upper hand. If she knocked over something—a lamp or a chair—perhaps Brand would hear it.

But what if he didn't? She'd be giving away her position. She needed to see the bastard, to know where he was.

An idea occurred to her.

Holding the blade tight in her right fist, she used her left to feel for the light switch just inside the dressing room.

It clicked on silently.

Since the room was behind her, the sudden bright light didn't blind her.

Her intruder wasn't so lucky. The glare hit his face and he flinched, lifting an arm.

He stood only a few feet from her!

She'd known his voice, and now she recognized his size, but it was the first time she'd seen him without the disguise. Big, with sandy-brown hair and those light blue eyes, some might call him handsome, but the aura of menace chilled her blood.

Sahara struck out and he ducked, reaching for her at the same time. The blade cut into his arm, slicing just below his elbow, making him retreat.

She quickly sidestepped and, taking an aggressive stance with the blade lifted at an angle over her shoulder, she threatened, "Reach for me again and you'll lose the arm."

"With that flimsy thing?"

"That's not my blood ruining the area rug."

Looking down he saw the trail of red and, amazingly enough, moved to stand on the hardwood instead. Closing a hand over the wound to try to stanch the drip, he assessed her. "You made that from the heater, didn't you?"

"Yes."

"And you brought it to your bedroom?"

Good thing, she thought, but said only "I've grown fond of it."

His mouth didn't move, yet she could almost swear he was amused. The last thing she'd wanted to do was entertain him.

Those blue eyes she already knew so well stared into hers. "Next time I get you—and, Sahara, I *will* get you—I'll remember just how ingenious you are."

Back to the threat of tying her down naked? *Not happening, buster.* "Why?"

Surprise lifted his brows. "Why what?"

"Why will you get me again?" She backed up another step, resisting the urge to search the rest of the room for the others. She had a gut feeling he'd come alone. "If you want money, I'll pay you. Just tell me what you know about my brother."

This time he smiled openly—and it was scary-mean. "You want to know about Scott? Sure. He's not the saint you paint him to be."

"No, not a saint," she agreed. "But he is an amazing brother." She hitched her chin. "What did you do for him that he'd owe you money?"

"A job. And he double-crossed us."

"Doesn't sound like him."

"Sounds *exactly* like him," he insisted, then added, "the bastard."

Sahara growled and hefted the blade high. "Insult him again and I'll gut you from neck to groin."

Awe held him captive. "You'd actually try, wouldn't you?"

"There'd be no 'try' about it."

His now-familiar gaze slowly touched all over her, from her tumbled hair down to her bare feet then back up to meet her eyes. "You're magnificent," he breathed. "I hope you know that."

His twisted admiration frightened her even more. She was debating what to do, how to get out of this conundrum, when a knock sounded on her door. "Sahara?"

Brand. She'd forgotten all about him and now, during her moment of distraction, the big bruiser shot in and grabbed her around the waist, taking her down to the bed in one hard dive.

He immediately pinned her wrists to the bed, stared into her eyes a split second, then swooped down and ground his mouth against hers.

What was he doing?

Brand was right outside the door, and he wanted to *kiss* her?

She struggled to twist her face away, but the pressure was so hard she couldn't maneuver. Instead, without a single thought for the consequences, Sahara sank her teeth into his lip.

He reared back—and she yelled, *"Brand!"*

Something hard hit the door, splintering wood.

The big man hastily rose with his fingertips touched to his bleeding lip. "You need some discipline, and I'll be happy to give it to you." He smiled. "See you soon, Sahara."

It took her a second to realize she could again grab her blade, but he'd already gone back through her dressing room and presumably out the window—not that she'd check.

She had no intention of facing him alone again.

Another loud crack brought her back to her senses. Oh Lord, Brand was about to destroy her door!

"Brand, wait!" Shaking all over, she raced over, saying, "Let me unlock it."

"Do it *now*."

The second she unclicked the lock, Brand charged in so hard and fast that the door bounced off the wall. His gaze swept the room and, seeing nothing, he stalked into the closet, the bathroom and finally the dressing room.

Inching up behind him, Sahara said, "I guess he managed to come in through the window."

"He?" Brand searched the large room as he went through it, but it was obviously empty. "Who are we talking about here, Sahara?" Fifteen feet square with one wall of windows, blinds up and mirrors on the other walls, there wasn't any place for someone to hide.

"The bastard who kidnapped me."

"You're sure?"

A makeup vanity sat before the open window, now pushed askew, her plush white chair on its side, some of her makeup spilled to the floor.

"Yes," she whispered. "I'm sure."

Hands braced on the sill, Brand leaned to look out the window. "Other than the screen on the ground out there, I can't see shit."

"The lights are out?"

"No, but he must've already reached the shadows."

She held the weapon tighter. "How did he get in, anyway?"

Brand rubbed the back of his neck. "My guess is he climbed that tree. But was the window locked?"

"Yes. It always is. And there are alarms…"

He turned on her. "We have to call the police."

She wrapped her arms around herself. "You know I can't do that."

He reached her in three long strides, his hands clasping her shoulders. He started to say something, then his eyes narrowed. "Your mouth is bleeding."

"What?" She reached up, then remembered and, after tossing the dagger to the bed, stalked away to the bathroom. "Not my blood. When he kissed me, I nearly bit through his lip."

Brand stiffened. "He *kissed* you?"

When she shuddered, he softened his voice. "Sahara—"

Revulsion had her racing to her bathroom. At the pretty pedestal sink, she turned on the hot water and quickly rinsed her mouth, then loaded her toothbrush with toothpaste and scrubbed.

To have wanted Brand so badly, then have that animal assault her—

"Hey." Brand closed his hand over hers. "It's okay, babe."

"I'm not your babe." She spat and rinsed, then rinsed again and, feeling the need to flee, tossed aside the toothbrush. "You," she accused, pushing past him, "didn't want any part of it."

"It?" he asked, rinsing her brush and shutting off the water before following close behind.

"Me." She gestured up and down her body, still moving away. "Don't pretend now that you—"

He caught her arm and spun her around so fast she slammed up against his broad chest. Though his expression looked fierce, he spoke gently. "Shush, please."

Incredulous, she snarled, "You expect me—"

"I'm so damn sorry." He sounded agonized. "You shouldn't have been alone."

Sahara wanted to throw up her hands, but Brand

held her upper arms, making that impossible. "So help me, Brand, if you feel guilty because someone was in here, instead of feeling guilty because you rejected me, I might just use my shank on you."

He kissed her forehead. "I don't feel guilty," he whispered. "I'm fucking furious."

Oh. He didn't really sound furious, though...until he spoke again.

"I want to kill that bastard for daring to touch you. I want to kick my own ass for letting you run off like that when I should have checked this room. I finally realized that, but I was too late."

"You showed up in the nick of time," she reminded him.

As if she hadn't spoken, he growled, "I'm especially pissed that I needed to stay with you instead of going after him."

"Going after him? What would you have done? Climbed down the tree?"

"Yes, and probably a lot faster than he managed it."

Refusing to take blame for holding him back, she tried to shove away. "Hey, I never told you not to—"

He gave her a shake, interrupting her angry outburst. "And don't ever accuse me of not wanting you. You're smart enough to know that's bullshit. I *always* want you."

Okay, now he both looked and sounded enraged, but then, she wasn't exactly composed herself. He'd said so much there, Sahara wasn't sure where to start. She tackled the easiest part first. "I won't let you kill him. I need him to answer questions for me."

His jaw loosened, then clenched tight. "You can't be serious."

She wasn't done. "And in case you're confused on the matter, you don't *let* me do anything. I came upstairs because I wanted to. It was never your choice to make. I was pissed and I made a decision. Turns out it was the wrong one," she had to admit. "Coming home at all was apparently wrong. But that's on me, not you."

Staring up at the ceiling, Brand appeared to count to ten.

Far as she was concerned, he could count to a thousand and it wouldn't change anything. "What do you mean, you want me?"

His jaw flexed.

Poking him in the chest, she asked, "Why the hell would you turn me down—tonight of all nights—if you're as interested as I am?"

A little more time passed before he got around to answering. "We need to prioritize, okay? I have to let the guys know what happened. You have blood on your floor—"

"I cut him when he tried to get grabby."

Brand gave a low groan, landed a quick kiss on her mouth and continued. "Plus we have to leave here. Somehow he got past your touted security, so no way are we staying."

"Agreed." She eyed the blood on the floor with distaste. "I think he ruined my rug, but it should clean off the hardwood." She frowned. "I've never dealt with blood on hardwood before so I'm not certain."

"I'll clean it." His hands kneaded her shoulders. "Do you want to change clothes before we leave?"

She had blood on her shirt. "Yes."

He stared into her eyes. "Do you need any help?"

"Did you want to have sex?"

Taken aback, he asked, "Now?"

Sahara pushed free of his hold. "If you're helping me change clothes, then you're damn right, now."

His chest expanded on a deep breath. "I was asking if you were too shaken—"

"I'm not." Why she took her fury out on Brand, she couldn't say. She only knew she wouldn't be whiny again. Anger was preferable to that. "Give me five minutes." Not about to enter the dressing room, she went into her closet and closed the door to change in private.

She heard Brand say, "Take all the time you need, honey," in a very understanding way.

Damn him. Not since Scott's disappearance had anyone treated her with kid gloves. If Brand didn't stop, she'd end up crying, after all, and then he'd really feel the brunt of her anger.

CHAPTER SIX

IT WAS THE first time Brand had ever seen Sahara really dressed down, and he could barely look away.

Somehow, the faded skinny jeans and soft blue sweatshirt made her more beautiful, and even sexier.

By the time she'd stepped out of the closet, he'd almost finished cleaning the blood. Because she'd said she'd do it herself, he'd waited for her protests. She'd surprised him with a mere sound of frustration before marching into the bathroom and closing that door much as she had the closet door.

Shutting him out.

He deserved it after he'd screwed up so badly, not only by hurting her feelings, but by failing to ensure her safety.

Sometimes he forgot she had feelings, she could be so mercenary in her efforts.

Maybe if she'd acted a little more upset over her abduction, and been a little less on the make, he could have kept his priorities straight.

When next she'd emerged, it was without her makeup and with her hair loosely braided.

He'd been struggling with a powerful surge of lust ever since.

While Justice, Miles and Leese investigated different areas of the break-in and assault, Brand kept his eyes on

Sahara. It bothered him that she'd gotten so quiet, sitting alone on the steps, her thoughts hidden.

The urge to promise her...*everything* kept his focus unwavering.

Part of it, he knew, was his inner caveman getting to play dangerous games of rescue. He understood now why his friends liked this security shit so much. For an alpha male, it fed a very basic instinct. A larger part, though, was Sahara herself. Being with her kept him on his toes, and in the normal course of things she gave as good as she got.

Today had not been normal, and seeing this softer, more susceptible side of her only made her more appealing.

She wasn't the in-control business shark as much as a woman who needed and appreciated his help.

The various facets to her personality fascinated him. He admired her strength, and was drawn to her softness.

Taking care of someone else hadn't been on his agenda. Hell, he'd been struggling with unexpected responsibilities already.

With Sahara, it was different because she was different. He relished the chance to care for her.

Brand was just about to join her on the stairs when Justice returned from his investigation of the security panel. "Could the kidnapper have known Scott well enough to know your passcode?"

On the bottom step of the right staircase, her arms around her knees, Sahara shrugged. "I don't think Scott would have given those codes to anyone, but I can't say for sure. Why?"

Brand considered sitting with her, but she'd been giving him "don't touch" vibes ever since the attack. "You think that's how he got in?"

Leese, who'd just stepped in after searching the yard, said, "He might've used the tree to leave, but I don't think he climbed it to get in. That first branch is too high to reach, even with a jump, and the tree is too wide to shimmy up."

Sahara snickered. "How do you know? Did you try it?"

Leese had no qualms about sitting with her. In fact, he took the step above her then put a hand on her shoulder.

Miles leaned against the newel post next to her. "Climbing out of your window to the tree and jumping down from the last branch wouldn't have been too hard. But I agree with Leese. He got in another way."

Justice nodded. "I'm thinking he came in right through the front door and then reset the alarm system. When you didn't show up alone, he hid—and it paid off." He said the last as an accusation aimed at Brand.

Brand started to reply, but Sahara beat him to it.

"Brand doesn't work for me, and he hasn't had the same training as you three." She shook her head. "No, this is on me. I'm the one who insisted on coming here."

"He should have gone upstairs with you," Justice stated.

Sahara lifted a brow. "Once I made up my mind to go upstairs *alone*, do you honestly think he could have stopped me?"

Not as abrasive as Justice, Miles said, "Stopped you, no. That'd be like trying to stop a stampede. But he still should have gone up with you and checked the room first."

This time Brand cut off Sahara before she could reply.

"I agree." He knew he'd fucked up. "Believe me, it won't happen again."

Snapping her head around to glare at him, Sahara reiterated, "You do not work for me."

He held up a hand. "So we think the guy got in the front door. That has to mean he had the codes." Keeping in mind her desire to withhold her personal background, he said, "Sahara told me about another case where a guy who had installed the system had everything he needed to break in."

"That was different," she said. "Scott changed the passcode after the installation." And with that, she shoved to her feet and sashayed off into the kitchen.

Brand watched her go, specifically the sway of her perfect ass in the snug-fitting jeans. *Damn.* The lady had a body that looked great no matter what she wore.

And if he ever got to see her naked...

With conflicted thoughts, he turned back around—and caught all three of his friends staring at him with varying degrees of interest.

Was he supposed to do a trick? Irate, he asked, "What?"

Steely-eyed, Leese asked, "Are you working for her or not?"

He was still struggling with that decision. "Probably not."

"Make up your mind already—" Justice said, heading off to join his boss "—or hit the road. She doesn't need indecision on this."

Brand wouldn't allow anyone to push him away from Sahara. "Not happening."

Justice pivoted with a frown.

"Let it go," Miles said to Justice.

As the only one of his friends who knew why Brand

might leave MMA, Miles probably had more patience to wait for his final decision.

When Justice subsided, Miles lifted a brow at Brand, asking, "You two involved?"

Define involved. Drawn to each other? Definitely. Constantly butting heads? All the time. Smothering in sexual chemistry? God yes.

Brand shook his head. "Not yet sure about that either." None of them would accept that so he went on without pause. "But I do know she shouldn't be alone."

"I'll be with her," Justice said. "You just go on home and figure out your life or something." He strode away for the kitchen.

Brand stared after him. He could understand Justice's confusion since he didn't know all the facts, but he'd only put up with so much before he'd lose his temper. "Why the hell is he so pissy about this?"

"He hasn't shaken off his stint as her personal protection." Leese, too, started for the kitchen. "I have no idea why you're even thinking about leaving MMA, but I suggest you make up your mind. Just know that if you stay, it's a commitment until this is wrapped up. No waffling in and out."

"I don't *waffle*, damn it."

With a roll of his eyes, Leese disappeared into the kitchen.

Miles waited to chime in until there was only the two of them. "You have some tough choices ahead with the SBC and your fight career. I know that. The thing is, you can't be part of the setup then just bail if things here aren't yet resolved. No one is going to accept that, least of all Sahara." Then Miles left him, too.

Sahara was like the Pied Piper—where she went, the others followed.

Alone in the foyer, Brand grumbled and looked at the door…but he knew he wasn't going anywhere.

His friends were right—it was past time he made a decision. A lot depended on Sahara. Talking to her, gauging her reaction, was key. He couldn't do that if he walked away now. If he stayed, if he insisted on being the one to protect her, they'd have ample time to talk it out.

Ample time for other things as well, and that was a concern. He could keep it together, but he had a feeling that dissuading Sahara would take all his wits and then some.

After a deep breath, he joined the others.

He expected to find Sahara devouring more cookies, but instead she stood by herself at the window facing the side yard, watching the sunrise.

As if she'd only been waiting on him, she faced them all, offered up a wan smile and said with her usual sass, "If you boys are done playing, I need to get to the office."

No one else seemed surprised by that except Brand.

"You're going in today?" he asked with disbelief.

Sahara gave all her attention to her employees.

Justice said, "I'll hang around and reprogram your codes."

She nodded. "Thank you."

"And I'm going to call your landscaper to get that tree trimmed," Miles said, "then I'll do a general inspection to see if there are any other weaknesses."

"I appreciate that."

"I'll go to the office with you." Leese leaned back against the counter. "You saw him this time, right? That means we have some work to do."

Sahara nodded. "I could use your help as I go through all of Scott's old associates to see if I recognize him among them."

Irritated with them all, Brand said to Leese, "She needs to sleep." And then to Miles and Justice, "She can't stay here even if you do get things buttoned up. The bastard got in once so he might be able to get in again."

She gave him a long look. "Shouldn't you be training for a fight?"

"It's months away." And despite what he'd told her, he didn't yet know if he'd be fighting. He had a lot of conflicts to iron out.

"Ah." Saying nothing more, Sahara paced away from the window.

Brand blocked her. "I think you should stay with me."

She blinked at him. "With *you*?"

"Yes."

Justice coughed. Miles laughed.

Showing some sense, Leese shuffled everyone out of the room.

Soon as they were alone, Brand moved in closer to her. Seeing the exhaustion, the wariness and her confusion, he cupped his hand to her face and gently repeated, "Stay with me."

She drew in and released a slow breath. After glancing toward the doorway where the others had left, she whispered, "I'm only a little shaken, but I—"

"Shh." He brushed his thumb over her soft, full lips—and then he replaced it with his mouth. He'd meant to indulge in a single peck, a way to let her know that she didn't have to explain to him, and then he'd get her agreement.

But Sahara never did anything half-measure.

With a small, hungry sound, she fit her slim body to his, sliding her hands up his chest to his shoulders and then to his neck.

That's all it took.

Brand gathered her closer, his arms around her, his head tilted to the side so he could deepen the kiss, explore her mouth with his tongue, coax her tongue into his mouth—

"Ahem."

Shit. It took him a second to get a grip, then he turned so his back was to Justice, effectively hiding Sahara. "We'll join you in a second, Justice."

"Only a second, huh? Looked more involved than that to me. Maybe I should start calling you Speedy?"

"Justice," he warned.

"I wasn't gone that long. You two must've really jumped into it, huh?"

Sahara, being unlike other women, laughed.

No embarrassment for her.

Peeking around Brand, she said, "You're hilarious, Justice."

"He has his moments," Brand agreed. Unfortunately, this wasn't one of them.

"Yeah, well, I'm sorry to interrupt." He eyed Brand. "Sort of. Thing is, we all agreed that you should leave at the same time as Leese, so…is that going to be any time soon?"

"Yes, very soon," Sahara promised. "While I get changed, would you please call Enoch and ask him to have my brother's suite at the agency cleaned out and prepped? He knows my eating habits, so I'd like for him to arrange groceries as well."

Brand had no idea what she was up to now. "Why would you—"

"It makes perfect sense for me to stay there," she said in a rush before he could even finish his question, "but I'd rather not deal with the memories right now."

"I'll take care of it," Justice promised her.

"Scott's belongings should be put in storage, but the women's stuff can be donated somewhere." In dismissal, she added sweetly, "Thank you, Justice."

"Sure thing." Cell phone already out to call Enoch, Justice exited the kitchen.

Brand couldn't hold back the amazement he felt. "Nothing rattles you, does it?" She hadn't been in the kitchen worrying as he'd thought. Not Sahara. No, she'd taken some quiet time to plot her next step.

He couldn't imagine anyone ever taking her off guard.

"I'm the woman who raced upstairs in a fury, if you'll recall. I was plenty rattled."

Actually, she'd raced away so he wouldn't see her upset and he felt guilty as hell about it. He knew he'd hurt her feelings when that had never been his intent.

"Rattled, huh?" Giving her the excuse, he smoothed his hand along her thick braid. "I'm surprised you'd admit to it."

She faked a stern frown to go with her dire warning. "Ever repeat it and we'll have a problem."

"Your secrets are safe with me."

Still kidding around, she flared her eyes wide. "Wow, what a promise. How do you know I won't unload on you?"

"You could," he said with sincerity. "I wouldn't mind."

She patted his chest. "Yes, well, I refuse to be a wimp, so don't hold your breath."

Covering her hand with his, Brand said, "You can trust me, Sahara." If she'd rather stay at the agency suite, fine, but he'd figure out a way to stay with her.

"Trust you to make me nuts," she muttered.

"Sahara—"

"I need to change for the office and pack some things for my stay in the suite. Are you still playing guard dog?"

"I am." Except that he wasn't playing.

"Excellent." Putting her small, soft hand in his, her grip firm, Sahara led him out of the kitchen and toward the stairs. To Leese, she said, "I'll be ready to go in ten minutes."

"Hey, Speedy," Justice called after him.

Vexed, Brand glanced back.

"Protect her this time."

Brand flipped him off, but then also gave a nod. He'd protect her all right.

Today, tonight and for the foreseeable future.

BRAND LEFT AFTER she and Leese were in the offices. Sahara wasn't sure what to think about that, but she pretended to think nothing at all. In front of everyone, he'd kissed her forehead, told her he'd see her again soon, then just walked away.

Soon could be later in the afternoon, later in the week or at the end of the month. She just didn't know.

Should she have accepted his offer to stay with him?

No. That would smack of being needy, which would undermine her authority in a big way.

She could have invited him to stay with her instead, but again, needy. The thought of spending the night alone in her big house had given her chills. Unfortunately, the idea of being alone in the suite wasn't much better. At least she knew the agency was protected; no one could get past the 24/7 security.

Except…people once had.

They'd shot her guard, grabbed Enoch and nearly killed him, then gotten to the suite where they'd attacked Leese and Catalina. At the time Catalina wasn't yet Leese's wife, but they were already well on their way to being more than a client and her bodyguard.

Thank God, Leese was a lethal, highly trained machine who'd made the attackers regret the decision to intrude.

It'd be best to put that horrid breach in security from her mind. Since then they'd tightened up all entry points. She'd be fine. She believed it, so she just had to find something else to occupy her mind. Given that she was anxious to dig into the files of her brother's known associates, she had plenty of distractions at hand.

She was at her desk, coffee beside one elbow, the shiv she'd made at the other, painstakingly going through each file and cross-referencing them with any photos she could find, when Enoch opened her door.

"He's ba-aack."

Sahara straightened. For one startling second, she thought Enoch meant her kidnapper. Then she caught his smile and, clearing her throat, asked, "Who?"

Sliding into the room and closing the door behind him, Enoch said, "Brand Berry."

"Oh?" Sooner than she'd expected. "I thought he'd left for the day."

"Apparently not." Enoch's smile turned knowing. "Care to share?"

Actually... She hopped up from her chair and skirted her desk. "What do you think of him?"

Without hesitation, Enoch said, "Big, capable, confident."

All true. Sahara added, "Plus smart, attentive, motivated."

Enoch nodded. "The emotional in a nice physical package equals just what you need."

That gave her pause. "You think I need someone?"

"Sahara," he chastised. "You know you've been one of my favorite people for a very long time."

"Ditto." She and Enoch had met prior to her brother's disappearance, and they'd immediately hit it off. She'd leaned on him after Scott came up missing, and when she inherited the agency shortly after that, she'd asked him to be her assistant.

Best decision she'd ever made, and that was saying something because she didn't make bad decisions.

She'd grown Body Armor, shifted the focus, given it more clout, more *sex appeal*—and through every change big and small, Enoch was there helping her to make it a seamless transition.

"You're also one of the strongest people I've ever known. More independent even than Scott."

"Really?" Crazy how much that flattered her.

"Once Scott made the business successful, he went about enjoying that success."

He said that like an accusation. "I enjoy the success."

"No, you always push for more, and that's fine. Your single-minded drive is a big part of who you are. But you shouldn't forever go it alone."

"I have you."

"Always," he vowed. "But you should have more than

just a friend. I want to see you loosen up a little. *Live* a little." He softened his voice. "Share yourself."

Enoch made it all sound perfectly normal, not at all needy. "You know why I don't date."

"That was a long time ago."

She nodded. Sometimes it felt like a lifetime had passed since the last guy tried to charm his way into the family finances. "Scott always weeded out the users, the men only after my wealth, but now…how can I tell what a man really wants?"

"Oh please." Disgruntled, Enoch frowned at her. "I respected Scott a lot, you know that. But he was sometimes wrong—especially when he assumed anyone attracted to you was only after your money."

It didn't happen every time…just often enough that she stopped trusting herself. She'd been born into money, and was left a healthy inheritance that Scott had expanded exponentially. Money had never been one of her worries—except when it came to knowing which was the bigger draw, her or her wealth. "I *am* filthy rich, and that's a powerful lure for a lot of people."

"You think the money is so important that a man can't really see you?" He scoffed. "Have you looked in a mirror lately? Trust me, any guy with blood pumping through his veins sees *you*. And even if he's not interested in…romance, he's bound to admire you, respect you, and—"

"Like me?" She often wondered.

It was one of the things she appreciated most about the fighters she'd hired, as well as their close friends. They were friendly to her, but so down-to-earth, capable and self-sufficient, thoughts of benefiting from her wealth never entered their minds. If anything, they seemed to forget she had money and influence.

Enoch's scowl grew darker. "Of course they like you. You're beautiful, witty, honorable and, well…" He flapped a hand. "Apply all those accolades we already gave to Mr. Berry because you have them as well."

"Not his strength."

With a snort, Enoch said, "I'd match your cunning and determination to his physical strength any day. And that's the beauty of it—he's a good counterpart to your personality."

"I would like to know him better," she admitted. "Only he won't let me hire him."

"Ha! If he worked here, he'd have grounds for sexual harassment charges in no time. You—" he emphasized "—are as nuanced as a tsunami when you want something…or someone."

In most cases, she saw no reason for nuance. Propping a hip on the desk in her favored position, Sahara idly swung one foot, her shoe dangling off her toes. "I guess that could be a problem, at least until he gives in."

Enoch shook his head in exasperation.

"But if I can't hire him, then how should I—"

Squaring his shoulders, Enoch said, "Sleep with him."

That bald statement coming from her circumspect and very proper assistant caused a smile to tug at her mouth. "Sleep with him to get to know him?"

"For you, it'd be the most expedient way."

Obviously, she wasn't averse to the idea, but to hear her friend instructing her… "Enoch, you're blushing."

In a low voice, he confided, "I feel like a pimp."

Sahara laughed. "Not a pimp, but as my best friend

and an irreplaceable assistant, you more than anyone can advise me."

"Then out of concern, let me say: be yourself with him."

"I'm always myself. Who else would I be?"

He bent a stern look on her. "Sahara."

Mimicking him, she replied, "Enoch."

He rolled his eyes. "You've taken the role of boss to heart. You know, you don't always have to be the one in charge, the strong one. Sometimes it's nice to delegate— or even to lean on someone else."

No, she didn't want to do any leaning. "I delegate to you all the time."

"That's not what I mean and you know it."

"Fine. I promise I'll try to be myself." Feeling impulsive, she gave Enoch a hug. He was smaller than her, and in no way resembled the ripped fighters she'd hired as bodyguards to ramp up the agency's sex appeal. But he didn't need physical stature to be one of the finest people she'd ever known.

While they were involved in this mutual exchange of respect and admiration, she pressed him back and asked, "How's Tina?"

Surprise blanked his expression. "You know about her?"

"My number one guy starts a torrid affair and you think I'd miss it?"

He sighed. "It is rather torrid."

Delighted for him, Sahara grinned.

She'd always known of Enoch's keen intelligence and aptitude for organization, but in the last year, she'd discovered new depth to her friend.

His loyalty to her, to all innocents, had enabled him to

endure terrible abuse—to the point that the thug who'd taken him thought that he had choked Enoch to death.

Thank God, Enoch had hung on.

Remembering that awful time, and how close she'd come to losing someone else she loved, weakened her composure. Her throat felt thick and her eyes got blurry. Squeezing him tighter, Sahara said, "She's a lucky woman."

He patted her back, and since he always saw through her, asked, "Are you sure you're okay?"

Sahara nodded and concentrated on not letting the tears fall. "Yes, thank you."

Proving his value, Enoch didn't press her. "You're welcome. If you need anything, please let me know."

He'd been more attentive all morning, constantly checking in on her without actually hovering. He'd even brought her an iced and decorated donut with her coffee. "You're the best, Enoch."

"I'll look for proof of that in my next raise." After winking, he opened the door and announced, "She'll see you now, Mr. Berry."

On his way in, Brand said, "You really have to quit calling me that. It makes me feel like I should be in a suit or something."

Enoch laughed. "All right, I'll drop the formality." He leaned close to Brand and said sotto voce, "Take care of her."

"I plan to."

Exasperated, Sahara said, "I don't need anyone to—" The door shut before she could finish her protest. "I swear he does that on purpose."

Brand was smiling when he turned to her, but the smile slipped. "Hey? You okay?"

She devoured him with her gaze. He looked freshly showered and shaved, and he'd changed into another pair of jeans, this time with a black Henley that fit snug to his wide, hard shoulders, his solid chest, and then fell loose around his tapered waist and flat abs.

Trying for a brisk tone, Sahara asked, "Why does everyone keep asking me that?"

"Maybe because you've been through hell, had your life threatened, got mauled by a lunatic, haven't had any sleep and possibly got false hope about your brother."

No, it wasn't false. She wouldn't believe that.

Arms crossed, weight shifted to one hip, she countered, "Are you okay?"

"Me? Yeah, I'm fine. Why?"

"Well, let's see." She propped her hip on her desk again and crossed her ankles in a negligent pose. "You went through nearly everything that I did, you also haven't had any sleep and your friends are heckling you because I didn't play the good little girl and ask the big protective fighter to check my bedroom for danger."

Wearing a crooked smile, he approached. "That sounds like a private fantasy or something."

"Perhaps, but I'll reserve it for someone who's willing to play."

The smile firmed into a straight line. He didn't stop until he had her shoulders clasped in his big hands and she had her head tilted back so she could stare into his dark eyes.

"I wanted to talk to you about that."

Her pulse jumped. "About playing?"

"Somewhat." His thumbs gently caressed her tensed muscles. "I want to stay with you."

In case he'd forgotten, she said, "I'm staying in the suite here."

"I know."

And he still wanted to stay with her? When he'd left, she'd thought… But here he was, back again, and she so badly didn't want to be alone.

Yet being with Brand and not touching him would be impossible, and despite her promise to Enoch, Brand didn't seem like a willing participant to his suggestion.

When she didn't say anything, Brand asked, "It's a regular living space?"

"Yes. Scott used it sometimes for entertaining, but mostly for convenience, especially when he had the house built, and then later when he wanted it remodeled. Leese and Catalina stayed there when she was first a client and it wasn't safe to move her. It's on the top floor of the building, fully furnished and entirely secure."

Nodding, he said as if he expected her agreement, "I have my overnight bag in the car."

So he'd gone home, showered, changed and packed… to be with her? Going for honesty, she admitted, "I would enjoy the company."

"Great."

"But I'm not sure it's a good idea."

"You staying alone isn't a good idea. Me staying with you is the right thing to do."

So obligation motivated him, not interest? Damn the man for keeping her confused. She sidled away from him, her hands on her hips. "I don't see how it can be right when you only tease me."

He ran a frustrated hand over his head. "Sahara…" Abruptly he changed his tone to sound more reasonable.

"Come on, honey, you know you didn't really want sex after just being kidnapped."

She lifted a supercilious brow. "I wanted it then and I want it now."

Brand hitched his chin with doubt. "Right now?"

"Well…" She looked back at her *hard* massive desk, then at the small, but softer sofa against the wall. "I mean, not exactly this second. I'm not sure my office is private enough for that."

New heat entered his eyes. "Your office would be plenty private enough, I promise."

That put all kinds of vivid sexual images into her mind. She took in a slow breath and nodded. "All right."

"But," Brand said with exaggerated patience, "you haven't had any sleep, you've been through a shit-ton of upset and now you're worried about Scott again. Don't you think it'd be better to give yourself a chance to re-coup?"

No, not when she'd wanted him even before the kidnapping. "I'm always worried about Scott and I'll stay worried until he's back home with me. I've never needed much sleep, and I'm already over what happened." The last was a huge lie, but what she needed most was the unique closeness of intimacy. Enoch knew it, so why didn't Brand? "If you're still tired, a little traumatized maybe, you should definitely go home and rest up."

Brand shook his head. "You make 'rest up' sound very wussified."

She gave a delicate shrug. "If the description fits…"

He stepped closer, a new edge to his demeanor. "Do you always use insults to get your way?"

Now that he pointed it out, she felt like a bully. "Usually only with you, and it still doesn't work." She sighed. "I'm sorry."

"My ego isn't that fragile, Sahara. You don't need to apologize."

Throwing up her hands, she snapped, "Then I guess I should just give up?" She really hated that idea, but she hated throwing herself at him and being repeatedly rejected more.

Indulgent, Brand said, "I'd rather you didn't."

Okay, hold up. "You've got more mixed signals than a virgin on prom night."

He grinned. "What I'd like you to do is recognize that you're a little off balance. That's why you're coming on even stronger than usual, and using insults. Am I right?"

She gave a very grudging "Maybe."

"Allowing yourself some time to come to grips with everything isn't a bad thing. I promise it doesn't make you a wuss."

"Are you coming to grips with it?" She waited for his denial.

He surprised her by saying, "I think so. Even though I'm sure you'll be safe here, I know I want to stick closer to you, to see for myself that you're okay."

His admission gave her a small thrill. "That sounds awfully involved for someone who doesn't want involvement."

"Never said I didn't want to be involved."

"Then—"

"But there's a small problem, honey. See, you take the whole boss gig to heart even though I don't work for you. You need to learn to separate that once you leave the office."

Did she do that? Yes, probably.

"You're a boss," he said. "But that shouldn't define

you. You're also a sister, a friend…and a very sexy woman."

He looked at her so intently, as if willing her to understand.

Hanging on to that *sexy woman* compliment, she said, "I can try to separate things." She had promised Enoch, after all. "It's just that I'm so good at being a boss." And maybe not so great at the other things. "Ask anyone who works for me."

"Maybe they say that because they *do* work for you. Let me remind you again: I don't." He slid his hand up her throat, his long fingers curling around to her nape and his thumb tilting up her chin. "I'm also good at being the boss."

Sudden insight sent her brows up. She had no qualms challenging him. "So this is about the big macho fighter being too insecure to take orders from a woman?"

"More insults?" When she scowled, a dangerous smile curved his mouth. "I'd say it's about you being afraid to be a woman."

Absurd! She started to jerk away, but suddenly his other arm locked her to him. That didn't stop her from struggling.

"Can't bear to hear the truth, Sahara?"

Far as challenges went, he nailed it. She stopped levering away and instead thrust her face up close to his. "I'm not afraid of anything."

He chuckled at her bravado. Actually *chuckled*!

Furious over his galling amusement, Sahara could think of only two ways to wipe away his humor.

Her knee could land home in a very sobering way.

The other option would be… She kissed him.

Or more like she attacked his mouth.

When he leaned back to avoid the assault, she followed, her hands now fisted tight in his shirt, high against his collarbone. She nipped his bottom lip, sucked it into her mouth, licked over it, and then, sealing her lips to his, she explored the damp heat of his mouth. She loved the slick texture of his strong white teeth, his velvet tongue, and she especially loved the low growl he gave in reaction.

Abruptly, he stopped retreating and instead adjusted his hold.

The hand around her nape tipped her head farther back so he could take the lead. His other hand scooped down to her behind and pressed her against him, their bodies perfectly aligned for a tantalizing fit.

It was a battle of wills, each of them trying to take control...until Brand backed her up so that her thighs bumped into her desk. Proving his strength, he scooped her up one-handed and sat her on the edge.

Against her lips, he said, "Open your legs."

Never one to give in easily, she asked, "Why?"

"I want between them."

Oookay. That sounded enticing. He still firmly clasped her nape, making it impossible for her to look away. He saw everything she felt, probably read in her eyes everything she considered. Just to throw him off, she smiled...and slid her knees apart.

"Good." He pushed up the slim skirt she'd changed into, then widened her legs farther by stepping between them.

The denim of his jeans felt rough against her inner thighs.

So did the free hand he traveled up the inside of her knee.

The sensation of his calloused fingertips firm on her

sensitive flesh, along with the probing force of his dark brown gaze, made her eyes heavy.

As if he knew it, he whispered, "Keep them open." To ensure he had her attention, he brushed his knuckles over the crotch of her silken panties.

Like a bolt of lightning, the touch sizzled all along her nerve endings, making her gasp and bringing a flush to her skin.

"So hot," he whispered, still idly stroking. "I'd like to make you wet, too."

She was getting there pretty quickly already.

When Enoch's voice came through the intercom, she jumped.

"Mr. Delamore is here, Ms. Silver."

Brand slowly withdrew his hand and, with attention to detail, carefully straightened her hair, when she hadn't even realized it was mussed. "Mr. Delamore?" he asked with more than idle curiosity.

"Prospective client." Her voice trembled as surely as her limbs. Wishing it wasn't so, she explained, "We had an appointment."

"Tell Enoch to give you three minutes."

Nodding, she started to stand, but Brand shook his head. "You can reach the intercom."

Another challenge, and this one was harder to meet because she felt like warm gelatin. She reached out a hand for the intercom button, was still a few inches away and ended up leaning back on an elbow, practically sprawled on her desk—with Brand standing between her legs, his hands holding her hips.

Trying to steady her voice, she touched the button and replied, hopefully in her usual no-nonsense tone, "Apologize for the delay, but I'll need five more minutes."

"Yes, ma'am."

The deference Enoch adopted for clients usually struck her as funny, but not this time. When she started to rise, Brand leaned into her, balancing himself on his outstretched arms at either side of her shoulders.

"I told you three minutes."

Rather than fight the inevitable, she relaxed her spine and accepted that, in this instance, Brand had won. "I'll need two extra to recover."

His attention was focused on her mouth. "One more kiss then, before I let you get back to work."

"Yes." She'd love one more kiss. Or a hundred more, even.

"First, though, tell me you're okay with me staying the night."

Blackmail? He knew how badly she wanted that kiss. "Will there be more teasing?"

"That's up to you." As soon as he said it, he took her mouth in a kiss that left her gasping. She found herself flat on her back, his body meshed with hers from the junction of her legs all the way up to her breasts.

She'd never look at her desk the same way again.

Smiling down at her, he promised, "We'll discuss teasing, and more, tonight."

Damn him, how did he recover so easily? Still breathing heavily, she nodded. "Okay."

He tenderly cupped her face. "What time will you finish up?"

"Seven."

"And you won't be leaving the office?"

She shook her head.

"Promise me?"

If he worked for her, she'd take him to task for that.

But as he forever pointed out, he wasn't yet an employee so she only said, "I don't lie." Not over something so trivial, anyway.

He pressed his mouth to hers one last time, then straightened, bringing her up with him and helping her to her feet. "I'll be back here before seven, then."

So he was leaving again? "Where are you going now?"

His fingertips grazed her cheek. "Leese is going to show me around. If you need me, I'll be nearby."

She liked how often he touched her, *how* he touched her, how he looked at her... Then what he said sank in. *Leese was showing him around?* For what reason? "Are you considering—"

"We'll talk tonight."

With her heart punching, she watched him walk out.

She couldn't wait for the opportunity to get some answers. But for now, knowing he'd have to pass the wealthy and snobbish Mr. Delamore amused her as she imagined the much smaller man's reaction to Brand's rugged, intimidating presence.

Mr. Delamore. She probably only had a minute left, so she darted into her attached bathroom and straightened her clothes, tidied her hair once more and repaired her makeup.

Unfortunately, there wasn't a thing she could do about the aroused flush to her skin.

Not yet. But tonight she'd have Brand all to herself. They'd talk...and then she'd explain to him how it had to be.

CHAPTER SEVEN

"HELL OF A SETUP." After going through the on-site gym with state-of-the-art equipment, not only for a workout but also to hone specific skills, Brand didn't think he could be further impressed.

Then they reached the shooting range in the basement.

It appeared to run the length of the building with at least twenty stalls so that a group of people could practice shooting at the same time. An electric target retrieval system made it easy to trade out for new targets when practicing with different guns. Bullet berms cut down on ricochets, and rubber-padded walls cut down on noise.

Leese walked him to the selection of weapons, manned by two attendants who made sure everything went back to where it belonged. "Damn near any firearm you can imagine is available for practice shooting. You can't take them out of here, but we come in early, sometimes stay late, to keep sharp. It gives me a chance to see how other guns feel. I prefer a 9 mm semiautomatic to a revolver, but I'm proficient with .40 and .45 caliber semiautomatics, too."

Brand nodded. "I've shot just about everything there is, from a small .380 to the Dirty Harry .44 Magnum." He grinned at Leese. "My dad—" actually his uncle "—has always collected guns. I grew up on fifty acres, and shoot-ing cans off a fence was a daily exercise."

"Is he still collecting?"

"Yeah." During his last visit a week ago, his mom had practically force-fed him her special chocolate cake while his dad had showed off three new "treasures." "Mom says he has an accumulation, not a collection, because most of them aren't worth all that much. He started with the rifle he used as a kid, then inherited a few pieces from his dad and it went on from there."

Grinning, Leese asked, "Is he a survivalist?"

Brand laughed. "He could be. I mean, if Armaged-don came, Dad's someone you'd want in your corner. But he doesn't have an underground shelter and he's not hoarding canned goods or anything like that. Mostly he just likes to know that he could make it if the power grid failed."

Leese led him to a selection of earplugs, safety gog-gles and target ammo. "How come we've never met your folks?"

Unwilling to dwell on the deeper reasons, Brand went with the surface excuses. "They live in Kentucky. I get down there every month or so, but Mom was in a car wreck a decade ago, broke several bones, hurt her back and now she has some trouble getting around."

"Damn, that's rough."

Miles came down the steps just as they were ready to start up. "Took the tour, huh? What do you think?"

"It's pretty awesome."

"An understatement," Miles said. "Blew me away when I first saw everything. And so far the jobs have been terrific. Plus Sahara works with me so that I don't have to be away from Maxi too often."

Maxi was Miles's soon-to-be-wife, and in fact, they would probably beat Justice and Fallon to the altar. After Fallon's very sheltered and secluded upbringing, Justice was determined to make up for all she had missed. The big lug made it his life's mission to wine, dine and woo his fiancée. Since Fallon, who was no longer insecure, beamed with happiness, they all figured Justice—at least in this instance—knew what he was doing.

"When's the wedding?" Brand asked.

"She's still remodeling the kitchen, so who knows?" Miles smiled. "She wants the wedding on the farm."

Since Maxi had inherited the property from her grandmother, it had a lot of sentimental value. Miles had worked it out—with Sahara's help—so he could be a bodyguard, and live with Maxi there.

"We're all going out there next Sunday to build a ga-zebo by the pond," Leese said. "Want to join us?"

Brand asked, "Will Sahara be there?"

Miles shrugged. "Not sure it's her thing, you know?"

Two days ago, Brand would have thought the same. But not now. "Text me your plans and I'll ask her. If she's not interested, she'll say so, right?"

They both stared at him.

Miles was the first to crack, grinning widely. "A-ha. So you two *are* involved. I knew it."

He didn't mind saying "Maybe. I'm still figuring it out."

Leese asked, "So are you going to join the agency?"

"I'm not sure about that either. I can't see me being involved with my boss, you know?"

Leese chuckled. "That'd be different, wouldn't it? Especially with a steamroller like Sahara."

Exactly. Brand rubbed the back of his neck, then admitted, "I have other things to consider, too."

"MMA?" Leese guessed.

"Yeah. There are some…family issues I have to figure out."

"If I can help, let me know, okay?"

That was nearly identical to what Miles had told him. Damn, he had good friends. "Think you could show me the suite before I head up there with Sahara? I'd like to get an idea of the layout."

They knew now that he'd be staying the night with Sahara. Only Justice had complained, mostly because he'd rather be the one to guard her. They all respected her a lot, and more than that, they were fond of her.

Steamroller or not, Sahara was a very endearing woman.

To Brand, she was also sexy as hell.

Ross Moran walked through the posh club to a private meeting room in the back. Loud music vibrated against his skull and rattled in his chest. Strobe lights pricked at the periphery of his vision.

He fucking hated clubs. The monotonous techno beat, the writhing press of too-warm bodies, the overt sexuality. He liked seduction. He liked the *hunt*.

Give him a quiet dinner, an idle walk in the park, a secluded boat ride on the river any day over the chaos of a club's let's-hook-up atmosphere.

Sahara didn't like clubs either. In all his research on her, he hadn't found any instance of her indulging in the singles scene. No, she was more about business meetings, business dinners and swanky business parties.

The woman was all business—but he planned to change that.

One way or another.

Without knocking, Ross turned the doorknob and entered the room, his gaze sweeping over the occupants and the exits, gauging the situation in a single glance.

About what he expected: decadent perversion.

In the mere seconds it took him to make that assessment, a thick, no-neck goon moved to block him. Big mistake.

Ross landed a heavy punch to his gut and, before the man staggered back, easily took the gun from his hand.

"Call him off," Ross ordered, "before I do real damage."

Alarm flashed in the eyes of US District Attorney Douglas Grant. He clasped the narrow hips of the young lady grinding over his lap and shrugged off the other who stood at his side, her tongue in his ear.

"It's fine," he said quickly to No-neck, who'd already recovered only because Ross hadn't wanted to maim the lesser man for attempting to do his job, and Grant knew it. To the others in the room, he said, "Leave us."

One suited guest stood with prudent speed and made a beeline for the door, veering off only to move cautiously around Ross. Another refined fellow, more curious than wise, was a little slower but still gave him a wide berth.

The women, stripped down to their lingerie to show off enormous fake boobs and skinny butts, appeared too young for such world-weary expressions.

Ross opened his wallet and pulled out a few hundreds, passing them over to the girl still straddling Grant's lap.

"Sorry," Ross explained, "but I need at least a half hour."

Grant sputtered, "But…"

One dark look silenced him. "Thirty *private* minutes."

"I already paid!"

"You can afford it." He winked at the woman. "You'll share that, right?"

She slipped away from Grant and, eyes pretending interest, smiled at Ross. "Of course, baby. We work together and share *everything*."

Instead of that enticing him, as she'd no doubt planned, Ross felt pity. No woman that young should ever be that desperate. It wasn't like Grant, at almost fifty, carrying thirty extra pounds and blessed with a loose jaw, had anything to draw a lady other than his political power and bank account.

But then, for some women, that was more than enough.

He briefly wondered what Grant had planned for the evening. A threesome with guests watching? Sick prick. Maybe that's how he kept his stature, by lording it over the underlings.

He had plenty of vile friends who encouraged and enjoyed his activities. Some more than others—which is how he'd first gotten involved with Grant.

Ross took the woman's arm—as much to keep her from getting too close as to get her out of the room. Glittered lotion covered her skin, and now his palm. The sickening scents of cheap perfume and cheaper alcohol assaulted his nostrils. Her friend, looking more than a little baked, followed along in a stumble.

Fake bodies and paid-for compliance had never been his thing.

His appetites led more toward real women, with soft natural curves stacked around strength of character and a confident attitude. Yeah, that's how he thought of Sahara Silver. Loads of attitude, haughty independence, an angel's face and a sinner's body.

Perfection, that's what she was. Bending her to his will would be the sweetest satisfaction. He'd accomplish it gently, but firmly. And she'd end up loving it.

After minimal insistence, he got the ladies out the door, then turned with a smirk. "Damn, Grant, you're the embodiment of irony." As the DA, he was supposed to clean up shit like this, not contribute to it.

"It was a private moment," Grant growled.

"With two suck-ups and lackluster protection as your audience? Twisted." How such a high-profile social climber managed to skirt the inevitable scandal amazed Ross. "Wasn't it you who hired me to get rid of your niece's boy toy? Is she still mourning his early demise?"

"Shut up," Grant hissed, his gaze frantically searching every corner of the dim—and empty—room. "There are cameras everywhere."

Ross laughed aloud. "So having a couple of teenagers grind on you is okay, but no mention of your *business*?"

Grant half came out of his seat before thinking better of it and sinking back to the chair. "What do you want, Ross?"

He approached the table, pulled out a chair and sat to skewer Grant with his gaze. "You owe me, Douglas. I'm here to collect."

Color washed out of the older man's face. Voice

lowered to a strained whisper, he asked, "What do you mean? I paid you."

"To do various jobs, yes. But not to lie for you." As a special job for Grant, he'd run off a whiny little shithead who, according to Grant, was "using his *niece* to try to blackmail his way into a fortune." Ross suspected the young man had to go for a very different reason.

When it came to Grant's niece, the apple didn't fall far from the tree. They were both sexual deviants.

Grant assumed he'd killed the punk. Ross preferred to make him disappear a different way—by scaring him out of town and making it clear he might not survive if he ever came back. Contact with the niece was strictly forbidden.

The nitwit had understood and vanished without a trace.

Shortly after Ross had accomplished his mission, they'd discovered that an undercover cop had been investigating the shithead for some serious drug peddling.

Overall, it seemed that Ross had done the punk a favor.

Fresh alarm filled Grant's bugging eyes. "The truth would have destroyed us both!"

Again, Ross shrugged. "I could have protected myself without covering for you." Especially given he hadn't murdered anyone. "Hell, I probably would've gotten a grand plea bargain."

"That," Grant warned, "would be more difficult than you think."

No, Ross knew it'd be near impossible to sink Douglas Grant, given all his old-family connections, which was why he'd gone along with the dual alibi that saved Grant's ass and in the process, gave him useful leverage. "I went the extra mile for you, Douglas, and now I need you to do the same."

Grant looked like a cornered rat.

"Stop sweating. All I need is for you to throw a ritzy party, invite a certain special lady and include me on your guest list."

"You can't kill a woman at my house."

That assumption annoyed him. "I'm not going to kill her, damn it. I just want some time with her." Time to win her over without her feeling threatened.

Skeptical, Grant asked, "Who is she?"

"Sahara Silver."

"From Body Armor?" Grant shook his head. "She wouldn't attend. Doesn't like me, you know."

"I heard she actively *dislikes* you." Didn't surprise Ross. He knew Grant operated more as an inside man for the wealthy than a defender of justice. His Sahara wasn't like that. No, she'd go to war to protect an innocent. He admired that about her. Hell, he admired *everything* about her. "You'll have to pitch it as a way to patch up the conflicts."

"A party," Grant mused. Then he said with enthusiasm, "You know I don't mind entertaining. You should have said right off that's all you wanted."

"Not all." Pulling a small notebook from his pocket, Ross slid it across the table. "To Ms. Silver and anyone else who asks, I'm an upstanding fellow, someone you know well. I've jotted down the details of our association. Learn it. Don't fuck it up. We'll go over the more recent dates now to ensure we're on the same page." Ross couldn't make up a story until he knew where Grant had been.

Grant toyed with the notebook. "Mind telling me why you're doing this?"

Ross gave him his coldest stare. "You know better than to ask."

Fresh terror pushed Grant back in his seat, but when Ross made no move toward him, he relaxed again. "This doesn't sound bad at all. Throw a party, and fuck over that bitch, Sahara Silver." He chuckled. "I call that a win-win."

The ignorant bastard was too busy laughing to dodge Ross's fist. And damn it all, he knocked him out. Actually, he knocked him out of his chair, too.

Ross stared down at the crumpled body on the floor, a purpling bruise already spreading over his jaw. He really needed to get a handle on his territorial instincts where Sahara was concerned.

Seeing her at the party would help, having the opportunity to speak with her, just be near her... He couldn't wait to witness her expression when Douglas spun the carefully created fairy tale about their association. She'd realize that she couldn't fight him, and then she'd realize the truth.

Eventually, she would be his.

EVEN THOUGH HE'D already learned every inch of the suite during his tour with Leese, Brand paced around, going from one room to the other.

He had to keep moving, otherwise he'd dwell on Sahara taking her bath. A "relaxing bubble bath" she'd said. As it was, his overactive libido kept picturing her stepping out of those sexy high heels, unzipping that slim-fitting skirt and slowly pushing it down over her shapely hips, then unbuttoning that silky blouse, one button at a time, until that, too, landed on the glossy tile floor.

Had she left her hair pinned up to keep it dry, or let it down so that it floated around her breasts in the water?

He drew a strained breath and went to stand before the windows overlooking the Ohio River. Lights on barges sent ribbons of colors to dance over the surface of the water.

How long was she going to be in there?

He withdrew his phone and again checked the time on the screen. Hell, wasn't ninety minutes long enough?

He remembered that his mom, after her injury, would stay in the tub for an hour. But that was to treat her aches and pains, not just to soak.

Thinking that gave him an awful idea: did Sahara have any aches and pains?

She'd finished work a little after seven—late, in his opinion, especially considering how early she started. Instead of retiring to the suite then, she'd insisted on getting restaurant food, which had left him divided. He wanted to get it for her, but that would leave her alone, and taking her out of the agency left her susceptible to an attack.

Luckily, Leese answered when he called. He told Brand to go ahead and take her with him—as if either of them could have stopped her if that's what she wanted to do. Then Leese spoke with Sahara, who very reasonably agreed that it wouldn't hurt to have one of the guards from the agency follow behind at a discreet distance.

It didn't surprise Brand that everyone in her employ appeared to adore her. They wanted to protect her, not because she was the boss but because they cared.

Sahara was that kind of person, the kind who got involved, who listened, who understood. She valued everyone who worked for her, from the maintenance crew to the bodyguards to her personal assistant—and they all knew it.

Leaving the window, Brand strode down the hall, pausing by the bedroom door. She'd left it open, but had closed the door to the connecting bath. On the nightstand next to the bed was the weapon she'd made. She'd replaced the bra around the handle with some other material.

The real surprise was that she hadn't taken it into the bathroom with her.

Shaking his head, he surveyed the room.

He'd expected her to choose the master bedroom, but instead she'd put her things in the guest bedroom. He assumed the idea of using her brother's room left her uncomfortable.

Or maybe she figured Scott would return any day now, and she didn't want to intrude on his space.

It was damned heartbreaking, the way she clung to hope.

He checked the time on his phone again, then went through the bedroom to the bathroom door. "Sahara."

No answer.

After going out for food and eating it in the suite, combined with her extended bath, it was now past ten o'clock. They were supposed to talk about their relationship...*and didn't he sound just like a chick?* Disgusted, he rapped his knuckles against the door. "Sahara?"

Nothing.

She had to be exhausted. It was too late now for an in-depth discussion when most of all she needed sleep.

But her silence bothered him.

He couldn't think of any injuries she'd had, but what if she hadn't told the whole story about her kidnapping? What if that bastard had hurt her?

She could be in there quietly crying.

The possibility twisted his guts.

And thinking of possibilities...had someone gotten to her? Was he stupidly waiting for her and she was already—

He tried the doorknob, felt it turn and half opened the door, keeping his gaze averted from the tub.

The large mirror on the opposite wall made the effort useless.

Ah, hell.

Arrested by the sight, Brand went still, barely even breathing.

Lying boneless in the tub, hair pinned up in a soft, messy way, eyes closed and not enough bubbles left in the water to conceal her, Sahara dozed. The waterproof earbuds explained why she hadn't heard his knock.

One hand rested limply over her belly, the other draped the edge of the tub. She had her right leg stretched out, her left slightly bent. The water, edged with small bubbles, lapped around her shoulders, her pale breasts and the tops of her thighs.

In his mind, he'd pictured her naked many times, but his imagination hadn't done her justice.

His blood pumping hot and fast, he turned away from the mirror to face the tub.

An erection strained the front of his jeans.

What to do? He couldn't let her continue to doze in the bath. She needed to be in a bed. She needed real, restful sleep.

What she didn't need was him coming on to her tonight.

Would she be embarrassed if he woke her? Who knew with Sahara?

Either way, he still had to do it.

Glancing around the glamorous bathroom, he saw her wet toothbrush on the side of the sink, the towel she'd set out…but no clothes. She'd already put away her things, so he left her long enough to go to his own bag, took out a clean T-shirt, then stopped in the bedroom and turned down the bed.

As prepared as he could be, he returned to the bathroom.

She hadn't moved.

The situation sent heat throbbing through him. He'd wanted plenty of women, and had had plenty of them, too. He'd experienced convenient attractions and mind-numbing lust.

He'd never known anyone like Sahara. He'd never before dealt with the things she made him feel.

Mind made up, he set aside the shirt, then crouched beside the tub.

God, she was beautiful. And so fucking sexy.

He smiled, because she was also autocratic.

Seeing her like this, though, with her makeup gone and her face utterly relaxed, was a revelation. Her lashes—paler without the mascara—rested on her damp cheeks. The heat of the tub had flushed her skin. Tendrils of golden-brown hair clung to her neck and shoulders.

No woman could be more appealing than her.

"Sahara?" He brushed his knuckles over her dewy cheek. "Come on, baby. Wake up."

Shifting, she drew in a deeper breath through her nose, then settled again with a sigh.

Brand fought the urge to look anywhere other than

her face. "Sahara." He cupped her cheek. "Honey, you need to wake up."

Her eyes popped open, so blue and definitely dazed. "Brand?" She frowned, then removed the Bluetooth earbuds. "What are you—"

A second later, realization hit and her eyes flared.

Forestalling any panic, Brand stood and opened the towel. "Time for bed."

Bemused, she sat up, her gaze glued to his.

Poor choice of words. "I had no idea what you sleep in, so I just brought you one of my shirts." He waited, showing extreme control by not looking at her body.

Still visibly confused, she stood. "I usually sleep naked."

Water sluiced down her body, and Brand knew he was starting to sweat.

"I'm sorry I passed out." A yawn cut her off as she stepped out of the tub and into the towel. "I'm more tired than I realized."

"Even superheroes need rest every now and then." He wrapped the towel around her.

She reached for the edges of the towel and started to step away.

Voice low and rough as gravel, Brand said, "Let me."

Their gazes held, until she shrugged. "This is so odd. Not at all how I planned things."

Yeah, not even in the same universe as his plans either. "I want to take care of you, Sahara. That doesn't mean you can't do it yourself. Doesn't mean you're weak." He opened the towel again to begin drying her. "Just means I want to."

Nervous fingers tucked a wet lock of hair behind her ear. "No one's ever—"

"Good." He kissed her forehead. "Now just relax."

She smiled lazily. "No problem with that. I think I was out for the night. If you hadn't woken me, I might've still been there in the morning."

Had she done that before? Given the hours she kept, it wouldn't surprise him.

He dried her as quickly as he could, yet when he glanced at her face, her eyes were closed again, her head lolling. "Hang on, honey."

Keeping one hand on her elbow, he reached for the T-shirt and tugged it on over her head.

Standing passively, for once not trying to take over, she murmured, "It doesn't bother you that I'm naked."

She didn't say it as a question, but rather a statement, so he replied the same way while feeding her arms through the sleeves. "Doesn't seem to be bothering you either."

"Tomorrow I might be embarrassed." Sleepily, she slumped against him. "Promise you won't ever tell anyone."

Arm around her, Brand led her toward the bed. "You don't ever have to worry about that, not with me."

"I know."

When he lifted the covers, she crawled in, turned on her side away from him and let out a lusty sigh.

"Get some sleep."

She mumbled something vague and faded away.

For far too long Brand stood there beside the bed, feeling things he didn't understand, before he convinced himself to turn out the lights and walk away. He left the door slightly ajar.

Since she didn't want to sleep in her brother's room, he didn't either. After a quick shower in the other bathroom, he crashed on the couch. Wearing only his boxers, one arm stacked behind his head, he stared at the ceiling and watched the shifting lights through the open windows. It took him a long time to get to sleep when all he really wanted to do was join Sahara.

Dawn had turned the sky a grayish pink when he awoke to a sound. At first he didn't move, not physically anyway, but his senses sharpened on high alert. He breathed slow and easy, listening.

There, he heard it again.

It was a sound that struck terror in a man's heart.

A sniffle, a catch of breath…

Sahara was crying.

He didn't think about whether or not she'd want privacy; there was no way in hell he could stop himself from going to her.

The door remained as he'd left it, slightly open, but thanks to the closed drapes the room was still dark. "Sahara?"

A sudden stillness, thick with dread, filled the air. "Go back to bed, Brand."

Not on your life. He heard the tears in her voice. "What's wrong?" Even moving closer, he could barely make her out on the bed.

"Nothing," she whispered. "Sorry I woke you."

Sitting on the side of the mattress, he reached for her shoulder. "Honey—"

"*Please* just go. I promise you, I'm fine."

He couldn't leave her, but grilling her right now wasn't the right thing either. "Scoot over."

Stunned, she half turned toward him. "What do you think you're—"

"It's barely dawn and I'm still tired." He crowded in,

spooning her, dragging her close against him so he could hold her tight. "Isn't this nicer?"

His heart beat ten times before she grudgingly said, "Yes."

He waited for her to relax, all the while willing himself not to get hard. A tough request after seeing her naked, touching her body and God, the way her ass fit against his groin...

He just held her for a while, but he knew she hadn't gone back to sleep. Because she was still upset? It gnawed on him, the need to console her.

Keeping his voice low, he said, "Odd that you didn't mind me seeing you naked, but you're defensive over a few tears."

"I've been naked before."

But she never cried? He hugged her. "You definitely have no reason for modesty. I mean, I tried not to look, but I'm only human."

Her fingertips teased over the forearm he had draped around her and pressed between her breasts. "I'm glad you looked."

Yeah, that wasn't going to help him keep a boner at bay. "If I'd have known that, I would've dumped the nobility right off." At least her voice sounded steadier. He kissed the top of her head. "Will you tell me why you were—"

"No."

He should let it go, but he couldn't. "Sahara..."

With more weariness than heat, she said, "I had a dream, okay?"

His thoughts scrambled. "About the kidnapping?"

She shook her head. "About Scott. I...miss him."

Even as he wished for a way to comfort her, he resented how much of her time she wasted on a ghost. "I know you two were really close."

She fell silent, then finally said, "Really, I'm sorry I woke you."

Brand squeezed her. "Stop apologizing to me."

"Okay." She thought for a second more, then suggested, "You could help me forget the dream."

Temptation gnawed at him. She'd only had around six hours of sleep, and he'd probably gotten four. "You need to be at work in just a few hours."

"Takes me less than half an hour to get ready."

"Damn, so you *are* Wonder Woman? I always suspected."

Her sharp elbow came back, landing against his abs.

Just for fun and to play along, he faked an *Oof* even though it hadn't hurt.

He heard the smile in her voice when she said, "That's for insinuating that all women primp too long in the bathroom."

"Pretty sure that's a basic fact of life." This was nice, he decided, lying in the dark with Sahara, teasing, playing.

Getting ridiculously turned on.

"Brand?"

"Hmm?"

"I'm saying yes," she whispered, "if you'll only ask."

So she'd felt his erection, obviously. He wanted her, very badly, but trying to think of what she needed most, he said, "I think we should talk about your brother." He waited for her refusal.

Instead, she said, "I've wondered what he'd think of you."

"Me?" The idle way her fingertips teased over his

skin drove him to distraction. He kept imagining them elsewhere, making it tough to concentrate.

"Scott was good at reading people." She turned to face him, still close, but now with her breasts against his chest.

And he hadn't forgotten, not for a second, that she wore only the shirt.

No panties.

Now with those teasing fingers on his chest, she asked, "Have you ever been seriously involved with a woman?"

It felt like a trap, so Brand tried to think of the right thing to say.

She saved him by adding, "I was once or twice, with men, I mean, until Scott met them and realized what they were really after."

Brand went still, absorbing that hit, then erupted with anger.

In one smooth move he flipped Sahara to her back and loomed over her. "What the hell is that supposed to mean?"

Eyes wide in the dark, she asked, "Which part?"

"Damn it, Sahara." He kissed her, which seemed to be his go-to move for every emotion she made him feel—anger, lust, humor, worry, sympathy...always a kiss to resolve it.

Her small, cool hands slipped up his chest to the tops of his shoulders, gently kneading. "What are these muscles called?"

"What? My traps?"

"Mmm, traps."

"Trapezoid. Why?"

"They're delicious."

"No," he said more to himself than her. "Don't start seducing me."

"But you're already between my legs."

He caught his breath, well aware of every inch of her that touched him. "Believe me, I know. Let's both ignore it for just a minute, okay?"

"Only a minute?"

"Maybe two." He kissed her again. "What do you mean that Scott figured out what the guys really wanted?"

"They were after connections. Financial and social. One of them had tried to get backing from Scott and failed, then he met me—"

"And probably fucking well fell in love."

"Well, that's what he claimed. But he hadn't told me about his efforts with Scott, which did seem suspect, right?"

"He probably got one look at you and forgot all about Scott."

She laughed. "You're very sweet."

No, he was very hard. He knew how badly he'd wanted her from the jump, so how could any other man be different? "You broke up with the guy?"

"Yes."

"You loved him?"

"I guess not, not really. I liked him a lot, though, and I thought he was 'the one.' Good thing Scott knew better."

Brand would really like to go back in time and have five minutes with her asshole brother. "Who was the second guy?"

"A farmer. I mean, I figured a farmer wouldn't have any connection to Scott, you know?"

"Let me guess. Scott managed to dredge up something shady?"

"Don't say it like that," she chided. "He was looking out for me. He always had my best interest at heart."

Brand nearly groaned. "So what was wrong with the farmer?"

"The farm was failing. I loved it, but he wanted out. Getting to my money would have been a big boost and made the transition for him much easier."

"Did he tell you that?"

"He said we'd start over somewhere else, that between my money and what he'd make from selling the farm, we'd be in great shape."

"Sounds reasonable to me." Not that he'd ever touch a single cent of her money—especially now that he knew her perception of it.

"When Scott told him my inheritance was protected—"

"*Scott* told him?" He got angry all over again. "You didn't tell him yourself?"

"I would have, but Scott met him and explained, and that was the end of that. He left mad and never contacted me again, which was all the proof I needed."

"I'm not buying it."

She drifted a foot up the back of his calf, making him tense all over. "That's because you're a really nice guy."

"Odds are the guy was pissed, and insulted, and you never bothered to talk it out with him because Scott had you somehow convinced cold cash was more attractive than you are. And in that, honey, he was wrong."

With a tiny bit of uncertainty, she asked, "You really think so?"

"Yes, and if you're wondering what the lure is for

me, it's your attitude, your brass, your brains, your sexy body, your beautiful face, your confidence, your—"

Laughing, Sahara wrapped her long, slim legs around him. "You're good for my ego."

"Your ego should be huge." He'd always thought it was. She'd coasted through a kidnapping as if she'd taken a walk through the park, but she was still so damn hurt over her brother's indiscreet method of "protecting" her. Damn the man. "Just so you know, I have zero interest in your money."

She drew his mouth down to hers. "Do you have interest in me?"

"I'm going to be insulted if you tell me that isn't already obvious." To prove his point, he nudged his straining erection against her smooth belly.

"Very obvious...that you're interested in sex."

"Sex with *you*, Sahara Silver." Hell, he couldn't resist her any longer—in fact, he could barely remember why he'd been resisting. Something about complications...that no longer seemed so important. Anything they had to work out, well, she was more than worth the effort.

Sahara was with him, she trusted him, she wanted him, and he was done being noble. Giving up the fight, he settled fully against her. "How could I be interested in any other woman when you're the most unique, challenging, infuriating—"

"Hey, I liked the other compliments more!"

Brand opened his mouth on her throat. "Delicious." He nuzzled his way down to her breasts, dragging the neckline of the big loose shirt along the way. "Fragrant." Lathing his tongue around the nipple he exposed, he whispered, "Sweet."

"Better," she breathed. She sank her fingers into his hair, holding him close. "FYI," she whispered, "I didn't pack condoms."

Brand smiled up at her. "I did."

CHAPTER EIGHT

Sahara wasn't a timid woman, especially when it came to sex. She had no problem giving direction, stating what she liked or didn't like, when she wanted something more, softer or harder, when slower worked better than faster…or vice versa.

With Brand, she didn't say a single word because he already seemed to know.

Repeatedly, in between tantalizing touches all over her body, he came back to her mouth. He kissed her as if she were precious to him, then consumed her with his lust, alternating between gentle and hungry, reverent and feverish.

She couldn't get her bearings. All she could do was *feel*.

His hand swept down her waist to her hip, back up again and over her breast. He seemed to be learning her, relishing each curve or hollow he found.

Just as busy touching him, Sahara explored every taut muscle in his neck, back and shoulders, down to his bulging biceps, and back up again. His skin was so sleek and hot, his hair cool and silky.

He kissed her again, his tongue stroking deep as he moved against her in a full body caress.

Liking that too much, she tightened her legs.

Brand kissed his way to her ear. "Let's get rid of this shirt."

He didn't wait for her agreement, was already lifting her as if she weighed nothing, and whisking away the shirt. He handled her as easily as he would a rag doll, and at the moment, she felt just as boneless.

Now, with her naked, he reached past her for the nightstand.

For a split second, she thought he was getting her dagger and wondered why. But no, he only grabbed the remote and parted the drapes so that dawn spilled in, filling the room with a pink glow.

"Better," he said as he slowly settled back beside her. Balanced on a forearm, he looked her over, studying every part of her in minute detail, even her feet. "You're fucking perfect."

A silly smile cut through the haze of need. "Flatterer."

When his broad hand settled over her belly, she lost the humor. He rested his hand there, not moving it except to coast his thumb back and forth over her skin, teasing her, ramping up her anticipation.

"Let's talk for a minute."

He had to be kidding. She dropped her head back to the pillow with a groan.

"It's pertinent," he promised, then leaned down to kiss the top of one breast. "I'd like to make an agreement."

That she wouldn't get overly involved? No, she couldn't do that. She was already far too fond of Brand, far too fascinated and too desperate to have him, and—

"You know I have an issue with you being my boss."

Her eyes popped open. Definitely not what she expected. Cautiously, she said, "Yes?"

"I've been thinking about this, and how we can make

it work." He bent to her breast again, this time softly, leisurely drawing in her nipple until her legs stiffened, her back arched and a low moan sounded from her lips.

Sitting back again, Brand stared at her breasts, lightly blew on her now-wet nipple and said, "You can be as bossy as you want—when you're in the office or talking to your employees."

With her heart still pounding, she said, "Gee, thanks, but I don't need your permission to—"

"Hush." He drew her nipple back into the heat of his mouth, and this time lightly grazed her with his teeth. "I'm agreeing that I don't mind that commanding side of you, but while you're with me, I think you should experience the other side of things."

The oddest rush of excitement coursed through her. She did her best to shake it off. "I'm not sure—"

"Just listen for a minute."

She frowned over what sounded like a command, but she kept quiet.

Pleased, Brand smiled at her. Almost as a reward, he pressed his hand downward until he cupped his palm over her sex, his long rough fingers curving into her most sensitive flesh. The touch was so stirring she nearly gasped.

Keeping his gaze locked with hers, Brand scrutinized everything she felt, each small reaction, then he continued. "I will never do or say anything to undermine your authority at the agency or with my friends who work for you. But at the same time, whenever we're around my friends, it needs to be clear that we're in a relationship, and I don't mean employer and employee."

He'd inferred so much, she licked suddenly dry lips.

His hand being *right there* made it difficult to think. "Will we be in a relationship?"

"You're naked under me." His fingers probed, parting her so that his middle finger could press barely inside her. "You're getting wet." He lightly swirled that intruding finger. "I'd say we already are."

Around a gasp of pleasure, Sahara thought, *Oh good. A relationship.* Now if he'd only get on with it. "So not just sex?"

"With you? No."

She liked the way he said that, as if he couldn't help himself from getting involved—especially if they were to be intimate. She accepted that she was already far too drawn to Brand, so it was nice to know she wasn't alone. "You won't be mean, will you?"

He raised his head, his expression concerned. "Do you really have to ask?"

She gave it some thought—not easy considering what he did to her—then shook her head. "You wouldn't be."

"No, I wouldn't." He withdrew his finger, only to slip back in with two, this time going deeper. "But I will enjoy taking the lead."

"In bed?"

"Definitely." He kissed her, longer this time, his tongue stroking into her mouth in the same rhythm as his fingers.

Loving the taste of him, his heady scent, she clung to him, her hands reaching as much of him as she could. He really needed to lose the boxers so they'd both be naked.

When he ended the kiss, she started to tell him so, but he didn't give her a chance. "In bed, and any place outside of your work."

Outside of work could cover a lot of ground. She wasn't sure about committing to that.

Brand insisted. "Tell me you agree."

Damn him, his fingers were still again. "I think this level of teasing falls into the category of being mean."

"Then agree," he said, grinning at her. "I know your word is good, but keep in mind, honey, you can call it quits anytime you like. You won't be permanently locked in." As he spoke, he pressed his fingers deeper, curling them so they touched in just the right spot to shoot sensation through her body. As if that weren't enough, he brought his thumb into play, slicking up and over her clitoris. The dual assault stole her thoughts, her breath, even her will to deny him.

She lifted into the touch, whispering, "Agreed."

Proving he'd gotten what he wanted, Brand stopped teasing and instead went about devastating her. His mouth latched on to a nipple, sucking strongly. His fingers found a rhythm that quickly drove her to the edge. She felt him hard against her hip, with the boxers still between them.

Pleasure grew in an ever-tightening coil. Heat built in pulsing waves. She gasped every breath, desperate for release…then groaned as the climax washed through her. Brand released her breast to lift up, watching her as she bowed and twisted. She squeezed her eyes shut, her lips parting on a low cry.

"Beautiful," he murmured, but he didn't let up.

Just when she thought she couldn't take anymore, he left her.

Standing beside the bed, he said, "I'll be right back. Don't move. Not a single muscle."

Sahara leaned up to look at herself. Legs sprawled,

skin damp…damper between her legs. She went flat again with a sigh. Was this part of his plan to take charge in bed? Did it matter?

"Yeah, sure." She didn't think she had the energy to do much moving anyway.

He walked out, but was back seconds later with a condom. She turned her head to watch him, but otherwise remained boneless.

Holding the packet in his teeth, his gaze burning hot on her body, he shucked off his shorts.

Finally. And damn, he looked fine, as amazing as she'd imagined, maybe more so.

Naturally, she'd never been with anyone who *wasn't* attractive. She had standards, and while intelligence and kindness might rank at the top, being physically appealing was important, too. Yet, she'd never been with anyone so finely honed, with muscles cutting everywhere, across his shoulders and chest, down his abs, through thick thighs and strong calves.

His movements were fluid, his strength flexible. He paid no attention to his body, and she couldn't look away.

A fighter, ripped and ready to engage.

With her.

Sahara touched a hand to her throat, nearly overcome with anticipation. Her skin tingled, and her heart started pounding all over again. She felt the pull of excitement in her nipples, her stomach…and between her legs.

Dark hair sprinkled his upper chest then bisected his body in a narrow line, swirling around his navel, then cutting low again to frame his erection. Even that part of him was enough to steal her breath.

As she stared, he wrapped a hand around himself and stroked once.

"I like how you look at me."

Her attention shot to his face. His incendiary dark gaze bored into hers.

"I knew fighters had sex appeal," she explained. "It's why I was so keen on hiring them for the agency."

His gaze narrowed. "You've thought about the others the same way?"

Unable to keep her gaze off his body, she shrugged. "I suppose I have, in a mercenary, detached way."

He stepped closer, both hands now dangling at his sides, the condom held between two fingers. "Explain that."

"I knew they'd be good for business, that I could exploit their employment in a way to play up the sex appeal angle." Her eyes briefly locked with his. "Sex sells."

His body tensed even more—which really only further delineated all those beautiful muscles.

Knowing what he really asked, she explained, "But I never thought about sleeping with any of them. I never considered what they'd look like naked beside my bed, with a condom in hand, preparing to have sex with me."

His chin tilted up. "That's the truth?"

A laugh teased from her. "So you not only think I'm too bossy, you think I spend all my time fantasizing about my employees?" She laughed at him. "However do I manage to get so much done?"

After a brief consideration, he tore open the condom packet and rolled on the protection. "I'd rather you not think of them at all." Properly covered, he pressed her right leg farther away from her body and settled over her. "Especially not now."

Heaven, feeling his weight press her down. "You're

the one who always wants to talk. And I did just have a splendid climax, so I'm feeling rather—"

He slid into her in one hard thrust, then balanced on his elbows over her. "Feeling what?"

No, she couldn't engage in idle banter, not now. She swallowed, and managed to whisper, "Filled."

"And hot?" He pulled back, his gaze on her face, then drove in hard again. "How about hot?"

Her body bowed with renewed pleasure. She nodded. *Very hot.*

"And wet?" he asked as he cupped her breasts, holding them together so that with each idle thrust, his chest brushed her nipples.

"Yes." Even as she said it, she felt a rush of liquid heat.

"Hot and wet," he agreed, his tone sultry as he ground himself against her. "For me."

"Yes," she said again.

"Say my name, Sahara."

"Brand." Her fingertips sank into the firm muscles of his shoulders. Her blood rushed, already racing toward another release. *Amazing.*

"Put your legs around me and hold me tight."

She did, hooking her ankles over the small of his back. "Kiss me." She needed his mouth.

He stared down at her.

"Please."

He very briefly brushed his mouth over hers. "You're not the boss right now, so you need to make it a pretty request."

Ohhh, she liked this game. Lifting her lashes to stare up at him, thrilling at the look in his dark eyes, she said, "Brand, kiss me, *please.*"

He obliged without comment, ravishing her mouth, riding her hard, his rough hands still holding her breasts and now his thumbs pressing her nipples…

She came in a sudden explosion of pleasure, putting her head back and crying out. With him inside her, it was even more intense, more powerful.

Brand whispered, "That's it, that's it," kissing her throat, lightly biting her shoulder until he, too, stiffened and groaned out his release. He kept his face against her, but gradually his hands softened on her and his thrusts slowed.

He rested against her.

Still throbbing with acute pleasure, Sahara smiled. From the moment she'd met him, she'd felt the chemistry and known sex between them would be incredible.

What she hadn't expected was the warm glow of contentment—and a strangely disturbing proprietary need.

She wanted Brand to be hers.

And he just wanted to be the boss.

AFTER FINISHING HIS shower in minutes, Brand pulled on his casual clothes and started coffee in the kitchen, along with breakfast. Though she'd taken a marathon bath last night, Sahara lingered in the shower.

He'd have to remind her of what he'd said earlier: women took forever getting ready.

While he cooked a healthy breakfast that would also satisfy her sweet tooth, he called Leese.

His friend answered with "Everything okay?"

Everything was stupendous. He felt good, better than he had in months. "Yup. I was just checking in. She'll be down to the office soon. Anything happen that I need to know about?"

Leese laughed. "You definitely sound in a better mood. Should I ask?"

He grinned. "Probably not."

"Ah, gotcha. It's odd as hell, but whatever. Long as she's guarded. Too often she has more courage than caution."

"So overall, you're glad I'm with her?"

"Sure. I mean, I'm not blind to the way she looks, and you aren't working for her, so...no problem, right?"

"Right." For Brand, it was so much more than Sahara's appearance, but he wasn't in the habit of baring his soul. "Have any of you found out anything else?"

"Sorry, no. Sahara's been going through Scott's acquaintances, hoping to recognize the guy who broke in to her house. But she's the only one who saw him."

"I got an idea of his size, but yeah, when they returned from meeting you and Justice, the fucks still had on their masks."

"Paranoid or duly careful, who knows? Anyway, Justice is sure he got in through the front door, so there has to be a tie somewhere. If we can figure out who he is, we can deal with it."

The shower shut off and he knew Sahara would emerge soon—maybe sooner still if she knew he had food for her. "Even though I'm not working for her, do you mind keeping me in the loop?"

"Not if you do the same. It'd be better if she didn't go anywhere alone, so if you have to leave her, let me know."

He didn't plan to budge, but he said, "Got it." After he disconnected, he checked the meal then went to the bathroom door. He could hear the whir of a blow dryer. After a rap of his knuckles, he said, "Breakfast in five— or will you still be primping?"

The door opened. Wrapped in a towel, one hand holding a round brush in her hair, the other holding the blow dryer, Sahara asked, "What breakfast?"

He couldn't resist kissing her. She tasted minty and her skin smelled luscious. "Warm raspberry vanilla coffee cake, and strong coffee."

Her eyes lit up. "Oh my God, amazing sex followed by delectable food. Be still my heart." This time she went on tiptoe to kiss him, and promised, "I'll be out in five."

Just to prompt her, he said, "Yeah, right. I'm betting half an hour, at least."

She stuck her tongue out at him, used her heel to close the door, and he heard the blow dryer come back on.

Grinning, he went back to the kitchen and did a quick job of setting the table. He poured two coffees, set out creamer and sugar, and then removed the coffee cake.

Fragrant steam filled the kitchen area.

He'd just gotten out a knife to cut it when Sahara came breezing around the corner. She carried her shoes and her hair swung loose, but otherwise she looked as put together as ever.

"Under five," she boasted. "You owe me an apology for doubting me."

She wore a slim-fitting above-the-knee tan dress with elbow-length sleeves. It hugged her body in all the right places, and now he knew exactly what that body looked like, the scent of her skin, how she responded.

Unable to resist, he put a hand on her waist and drew her in against him. "I like your hair down." Golden brown, thick, silky soft. He'd like to feel it drifting over his skin.

Over the tops of his thighs. He tamped down on those thoughts.

"Thank you." Her mouth twisted. "I just didn't have time to fix it, but honestly, it only takes a few minutes for me to put it up so I still would have made it on time." Moving past that, she sniffed the air. "That smells amazing."

He lifted her face for a kiss, appreciating the fact that she wore no lipstick. "Take a seat and I'll serve you."

"Such a gentleman," she teased, perching that sexy ass on the edge of the chair and putting on a pair of heels. Her movements were feminine and somehow arousing.

Down, he told his dick. Much as he enjoyed the private time with her, he was determined not to interfere with her work, and that meant helping to ensure she got to the office at her usual hour.

The second he set the plate in front of her, she dug in, then hummed her appreciation. "Sooo good."

The look on her face stirred him again. It was getting ridiculous, the over-the-top way he reacted to her. "I'm glad you like it."

"You know I enjoy pastries in the morning."

"Not a pastry," he pointed out. After she'd taken another bite, he said, "It's actually healthy since it's made with a lot of grains."

"No way."

"And low calorie."

"That proves it. You're a magician."

A crooked smile tugged at his mouth. "Because I can make food taste good without dumping in a pound of sugar?"

The heated look she sent his way nearly destroyed his resolve. "Cooking is just one of your talents." She sipped her coffee and made more sounds of appreciation. "So I know this might be awkward, but I need to know—will you be here again tonight? You did mention a relationship and I'm hoping it comes with more of these amazing benefits."

"I'll be here."

She nodded. "And tomorrow?"

"Tomorrow, too."

She grinned. "You're so agreeable, should I keep pushing?"

"No, you should finish eating so I can walk you down."

That had her face falling. "You're leaving?"

"Wasn't really planning on it, but I don't want to be in your way either."

"So you have the whole day free?"

As soon as she asked it, his cell rang. After glancing at the screen, he growled, "Maybe not."

She started to ask, but then her cell rang, too, only she'd left it in the bedroom. She grabbed another quick bite then rushed down the hall to retrieve it.

When she returned a few minutes later, he was still on the phone, and she didn't offer him privacy, so he turned his back on her. "Becky," he said into the phone, his voice strained, "the PT is necessary, so stop giving everyone a hard time."

Becky, his *mother*, said in a slurred voice, "This blockhead doesn't understand that I'm in pain. I want him fired."

He sighed. Odds were the very qualified physical therapist would quit, given Becky's impossible nature.

"You're not in a facility, you have around-the-clock care and you're getting better. Why can't you just be happy with that?"

Her voice rose to a screech. "You expect me to be happy? You dump me here and just wash your hands of me, like—"

"Like you did to me?" When he'd been only five.

She whined, "I did you a favor and you know it."

Yeah, he knew it well.

"Come and see me, Brand. Pleeease."

For him, her voice grated like nails on a chalkboard.

"You know I'm not supposed to get upset. I'm not supposed to be depressed or sad. But you make me so damn angry and so sad all I can do is cry!"

Every nerve ending in his body rebelled, but damn it, he didn't know what else to do. "Fine. I'll visit later."

"When?"

"I don't know yet, but until then, do what the therapist tells you." He disconnected before she could say anything else.

Dreading it, he slowly turned to face Sahara. She was back in her seat, eating the last crumb off her plate and making no pretense of not sympathizing with him.

"Stop it," he told her, grabbing up his coffee and finishing it off. He didn't want her pity.

Instead of responding directly, she told him, "Leese won't drink coffee."

"Leese is a fanatic about health. He's the one who taught me that recipe."

Sahara nodded. "I just like sweets, but Catalina survives on junk food. Or rather, she used to. These days Leese does most of the cooking and he's managed to convince her that good-tasting food can be good for her."

Relieved that she didn't press him, Brand said, "She still indulges in the occasional pizza, cheese coney or fast-food burger."

"Mmm," she said. "Cheese coneys, with the steamed hotdog, the chili, all that cheese on a bun…"

"So you're a fan, too."

"Hey, a girl's gotta live."

They smiled together.

Then Sahara ruined it by saying, "I'll go with you."

He knew exactly what she meant, and refused without a second thought. "No."

Supremely confident, she finished her coffee and stood. "Well, I say yes because later in the week, you're going to want to go with me and turnabout is fair play, right?"

"Go with you where?"

Hip out, she smiled at him. "District Attorney Douglas Grant is having a little party Saturday and I'm invited. Naturally, I declined, because Douglas is not only a pig, he's also crooked and I dislike him very much. But he promised that he had a good reason for inviting me, that he hopes to make peace between us and in fact, it's suddenly his fondest wish to work with me instead of against me." She flipped back her hair. "So I agreed."

"Jesus, Sahara."

"I assumed you wouldn't want me to go alone." She carried her cup and plate to the dishwasher, placing them inside. "But of course, I have no problem doing that if you have other plans."

As she straightened, Brand took her arm and turned her into him. "We're not at the office."

Those crystal-blue eyes sparkled. "So?"

"So, I want you to behave." He had long arms and he

only had to bend a little to slide a hand up the back of her thigh—under her dress.

Her eyes went heavy. "What are you doing?"

"Ensuring I have your attention."

"You have it."

He cupped the bottom of her cheek, barely covered by tiny silky panties. "Then stop trying to provoke me."

"Is that what I was doing?"

Giving her a stern look, he slipped one finger over the crotch of the panties. With her dress scrunched up in the back, he arched her toward him, easy to do with the heels she wore.

Fighting a grin, Sahara bit her lip.

He loved seeing her like this, confident as always but game to play, amused and turned on. "You were trying to manipulate me again, but we had an agreement and you will stick to it."

She nodded.

"Better." Hell, it was all he could do not to grin as well. She looked so adorably obedient, as only Sahara could. "You shouldn't be going to a party, *but*," he said, emphasizing the word before she could voice her ready complaints, "my part of the bargain was that I wouldn't interfere with work. So we'll go——"

She said a happy little "Yay!"

"——but you'll be careful, and by that I mean you'll stay where I can see you." He didn't trust this sudden party, or the smarmy DA who wanted to make peace. The timing was off, coming on the heels of her being kidnapped. "I'll want to know more about this Douglas Grant person."

A little breathy, she said, "I can tell you all about him on our way to your visit today."

He wasn't taking her anywhere near his mother. "Not happening."

She heaved a sigh. "You're going to be so annoyed with me."

"Because.?"

"Because I have resources, and if you go without me, I'll figure out where, and then I'll follow."

"No—"

"And while I know that's not following the letter of our agreement, I hope you'll forgive me." She put her arms around his neck and rested the side of her face against his chest. "You promised me that we're in a relationship, and that's what people in a relationship do: they support each other."

"I don't need support." Yet he tunneled the fingers of his free hand into her hair and, with his other hand still under her dress, held her closer.

"Maybe," she whispered, "I should go with you because *I* need the support."

That didn't make a bit of sense, but Brand kissed her forehead and, as usual, gave in. "All right. But I promise you're going to regret it."

MIDWAY THROUGH THE DAY, after she'd gone over a hundred photos and still hadn't seen her kidnapper, Enoch stuck his head in the door.

"Mr. Wallington on line one."

She blinked up from her study of computer files and saw why Enoch hadn't simply used the intercom. The blessed man carried in lunch.

"You're too good to me."

"Not possible," he said, sliding a sandwich and soup

from Panera in front of her, along with a frosty green tea. "Your favorites, so eat, okay?"

"Not a problem. I'm famished." It had been too many hours since she'd eaten that divine treat Brand had made for her. If she'd been thinking, she'd have brought the rest to work with her. Actually, after she finished lunch, she could probably sneak up to the suite to—

"Don't forget you have an appointment in twenty minutes."

She barely choked back her groan.

"And two more after that." Commiserating, Enoch said, "I'm sorry, but the next few hours will be hectic, which is why I really do hope you'll eat."

"You have my word." She picked up the phone and clicked line one as Enoch exited the office. "Good afternoon, Justice."

Skipping a greeting, he said, "Did you schedule landscapers at your house?"

Startled, she picked a piece of turkey off her sandwich and replied, "No, of course not."

He cursed, got himself together and growled, "They were here. They not only trimmed everything, but butchered your tree."

"My tree?"

"The one we'd already cut back so no one else could use it getting in or out of your house. Well, there's no chance of that now. It's a bare trunk damn near to the top!"

She sat back in her seat, thinking. "The landscapers come often, but they always tell me first. They can't get through the gate otherwise."

"I was here," Justice said, "looking things over."

"Looking things over?" she repeated.

"We agreed—"

"We *who*?"

Picking up on her incredulous tone, he paused. "Leese, Miles and I. We figured we'd take turns stopping by, making sure no one was around...looking things over."

"I see." And no one had thought to discuss this plan with her? Did Brand know? Did they all think her too frail for details? "Why wasn't I told?"

"I figured Leese would tell you," he said fast. "But he got held up today so I guess he hasn't had a chance."

Ah, so they weren't protecting her from the plans. That mollified her—a little. "You let in the landscapers?"

"They came in behind me. After Miles called them yesterday, we knew to expect them, but since someone had gotten in here, I figured I'd watch them anyway, just to be sure, you know?"

"And?"

"They did a terrific job. The grass is cut and edged, the bushes shaped, the trees trimmed. I had no reason to think they weren't legit until I saw what they did to the tree. And if you didn't tell them to do it, then what the hell is going on?"

"I don't suppose you got photos of the men?"

"No."

She sighed. "Well then, I really have no idea. But I have appointments starting in—" she checked the clock "—fifteen minutes, and I need to devour my lunch. When I get some free time I'll call the landscapers and find out if it was in fact them, and if so, why they butchered my tree."

"Yeah, you do that. I'm going to get hold of the others."

"Justice—"

"I'll catch you later, Sahara." And he ended the call.

Grumbling, Sahara took a big bite of her sandwich. She had a feeling it hadn't been the landscapers at all, but who would sneak onto her property, do the job of well-paid landscapers...and then destroy her tree?

CHAPTER NINE

WHEN SAHARA TOLD him what happened, Brand wanted to turn the car around and cancel the trip to see Becky. Any excuse would do, but this one had meat, had legitimacy.

Unfortunately, Sahara refused.

"I've been looking forward to it. If you cancel, I'll feel obligated to go back to the office, and I swear my eyes are crossing from searching through so many files and matching names to photos. Give me a good old-fashioned confrontation any time."

Brand tightened his hands on the steering wheel. "Who do you want to confront?"

"No one, now. But I would have certainly questioned the phony landscapers if I'd been there. Unfortunately, I've been denied that opportunity."

Thank God for small favors. "Why the hell didn't Justice get some photos if he was skeptical?"

She shrugged. "He wasn't, because he had no reason to be, not until he saw that they'd nearly cleaned my largest tree of all its branches. Not only did they take off every branch that could lead to my window, they cut away any that came close to the roof."

Had someone taken further steps to protect her? Or was there something else in the works?

Whatever was happening, it wouldn't hurt for him to

keep her away for a bit. He checked the rearview mirror again, but still didn't see anyone.

Given how Brand felt about Becky, the visit with her would be brief, so he decided on a detour. It was only five, but keeping Sahara busy until bedtime would probably be a good thing. "Do you have to be back right away?"

"No. I can be free for the rest of the evening." She traced a fingernail up his forearm to his biceps. "What did you have in mind?"

Brand laughed. "Not that." At her fallen expression, he added, "At least until later. For now, I thought I'd squeeze in another visit." For vague reasons that he didn't want to analyze, he'd like for his mom to meet Sahara, and vice versa. "What do you think?"

Leaning her head back against the seat, she gazed at him. "I'm at your mercy."

He liked the sound of that. "Give me a sec." He pressed the hands-free function on his steering wheel and dialed up his mom. When she answered, her voice was so gruff he knew he'd probably caught her napping.

"Brand, honey, how are you?"

Beside him, Sahara perked up.

"I'm good, Mom. I'll be down your way to see Becky and thought I'd stop by for a visit first."

"We'll be here. I have a meat loaf in the oven, so bring your appetite."

Sahara grinned.

"I'll have a guest, Mom. That okay?"

After an expectant pause, she said, "Of course," with a tinge of excitement. "Who is it?"

"Sahara Silver. You're on speaker, so you can say hi if you want."

Sahara sat forward in happy animation. "Hello, Mrs. Berry. How are you?"

Though the mistake was understandable, Brand corrected her. "She's Mrs. Hodge."

"Yes, sorry, Mrs. Hodge. I'm so excited to meet you."

Another long pause, and then, with curiosity but no censure, she asked, "You told her?"

"She's going with me to meet Becky, too," Brand explained, as if that was why she knew.

Sahara sent him a look. "Actually, he told me a while ago."

"He did? Hmm, that's very…interesting."

"Mom," he warned. "Don't make a big thing of it."

"No, of course not." Then sweetly, "Hello, Ms. Silver. Please, call me Ann."

"If you'll call me Sahara."

"Such a beautiful name."

"Thank you."

"How do you and Brand know each other?"

"Some of his friends work for me at my security agency, Body Armor."

Sahara didn't mention that she hoped to have him work for her, too, and he appreciated that.

His mom didn't know the demands her sister made of him, and he didn't plan to tell her. If he did, she'd feel obligated to alleviate the burden, when it wasn't hers to bear.

Raising her sister's son had been more than enough.

He could still remember the day Becky had dropped him off on his aunt. He'd been five years old, already loved Aunt Ann and was excited to stay with her. Where his own mother was often absent, and grouchy when she was around, Aunt Ann showered him with attention and affection. He'd cherished the time with her.

But it was still a rude awakening as the days with her turned to weeks, and the weeks to months.

He was young, but not so dumb that he didn't realize he'd been given away.

Once he asked Ann about it, everything changed. She stopped trying to shield him from the truth and instead embraced it, telling him that he was the greatest gift she and Uncle John had ever received. She'd said that from now on, he was hers and she'd never, ever let him go.

That was the day he started calling her "Mom."

For the next half hour, the women chatted without his input, discussing everything from the weather and meat loaf, to life in the country versus cases at Body Armor.

Finally, his mom wound down enough to ask him "How long before you're here, honey?"

"We'd just gotten on the road when I called. Maybe another half hour or so, depending on traffic."

"I'll go tell John. He has a new gun to show you, so I know he'll be thrilled."

Brand laughed. "Okay. See you soon."

After they disconnected, Sahara said, "She's charming."

"I've always thought so." Charming, caring, concerned and everything a mother should be.

"Who's older? Ann or Becky?"

"Becky by two years." His mother might have been the oldest, but Ann had always been the responsible one.

"What does she think about Becky being back in your life?"

That's where it got tricky. Brand shrugged, trying to sort out the deceptions. "I haven't told her the extent of it. She's territorial where Becky is concerned, a feeling leftover from when I was a kid and Becky would occasionally threaten to come into my life. More than once Ann had to bail her out financially so she wouldn't disrupt everything."

"Ann told you about that?"

"No." He laughed. "She did everything she could to protect me from my mother. But I'd catch pieces of conversations between Mom and Dad." He glanced at her. "My aunt and uncle."

"I know," Sahara said gently. "And I understand. Though they might be your aunt and uncle by blood, they *are* your parents in every other way. I'm sorry I got confused. I promise it won't happen again."

"Don't apologize." He, better than anyone, knew how messed up it was. "It's like a freaking Jerry Springer episode. My aunt is my mom, my mother is nothing at all…" Except a responsibility he didn't want, a guilt trip he didn't need.

"If that were true," she said, "you'd refuse any contact with her."

He shrugged that off, refusing to make too much of it. "I'd take pity on anyone. But the fact is, if I don't help Becky, she'll be back at Mom's, expecting her to take care of everything."

"So you'll take care of her instead?"

Yes, but not for Becky's sake. Brand took the exit from the highway, his tension mounting. "Don't saint me, okay?"

"Oh, I would never do that."

A reluctant laugh pushed away the frustration. "Got me more in the sinner category, huh?"

"You've got a bit of the devil in you, yes. But then so

do I. Together we should have loads of fun, don't you think?"

At the worst of times—like on a trip to see Becky—Sahara amused him. "You could be right."

"Of course I am." She glanced down at her shoes. "You know, it occurs to me after speaking with Ann, I probably should have changed clothes."

"Why? You look great."

"Yes, but your parents have so much property. I'd like to see the creek, and the tree house you and your dad built when you were ten, and—"

"Whoa." What the hell? Had he totally zoned out while they were speaking? Apparently so. "Mom told you about that?"

She tipped her head. "About many things. Weren't you listening?"

"Guess not."

She jumped tracks, asking, "How far is Becky from your Mom's?"

"Twenty minutes or so. We'll head out after dinner, okay?"

"Whatever you want, Brand."

The way she grinned gave him pause. Yes, Sahara amused him. She also kept him on a keen edge of lust. And when she smiled in that certain way, he had no idea what to expect…but he knew he had to be ready.

SAHARA LOVED EVERYTHING about Brand's childhood home. Even while eating a truly delicious meat loaf dinner with homemade mashed potatoes, gravy, applesauce and green beans, she couldn't stop looking around. Exposed ceiling beams ran the length of the living room/dining room combo, with rustic hardwood floors throughout. Mostly leather furniture in a buttery soft beige filled the room, with the exception of a cozy stuffed chair in a pretty multistriped pattern that she assumed Ann used.

Ann was a delight. She had Brand's dark eyes, but her hair, in a cute sideswept style, was much lighter than his golden brown, almost blond, even. She wore very little makeup, but didn't need it with her dark brows and lashes, and her clothing was as pretty and comfortable as her home. Jeans, a loose flowing top in rose and cowboy boots.

"This is delicious," Sahara said for the third time, making Brand's dad laugh.

"I love a girl who knows how to eat."

"No problem there," Sahara assured him. Holding a flaky biscuit, she gestured to the living room. "Do I assume that the amazing cook is also the talented decorator?"

Ann flushed with pleasure. "Oh stop. This old place is about comfort."

"And style," Sahara insisted. "Everything is perfectly balanced and coordinated, functional and beautiful. It takes a real gift to pull that off."

Brand smiled at Ann. "She's right."

"Here now," John said. "You two keep filling her head and she'll get to thinking she's too good for me."

"Never that," Ann promised, and she blew her husband a kiss.

Brand cast a look at Sahara. "Never mind them. To this day, they're always flirting. At least with you here, I assume it'll only be flirting and nothing more."

Laughing, Ann swatted him. "Stop! What will she think of us?"

"I think you have a beautiful relationship, one to be envied." Sahara smiled. "This is what a family should be. Thank you for allowing me to join you today."

Brand sat back, a thoughtful expression on his face, and watched while his parents gushed at her. She saw cynicism in his small smile, as if he thought she'd just worked everyone.

It was true, she was good at winning people over, especially when dealing with prospective clients. But in this instance she hadn't spoken a single insincere word, so she lifted her chin and ignored his scrutiny.

"Did you leave room for dessert?"

Brand answered his mother for her, saying, "She always has room for dessert, isn't that right, Sahara?"

Was he baiting her? Let him. "Absolutely." She stood when Ann did and began collecting the dishes.

"Oh no." Ann tried to shoo her back to her seat. "You're our guest. Please—"

"I can't," Sahara insisted. "It would wound me. Ask Brand. He knows I'm not an idle person."

"Gospel truth," Brand said. "But why don't both you ladies relax and I'll clear the table?" He stood and took the dishes straight out of Sahara's hands.

"Excellent idea," Ann said. As if she'd been hoping for a chance to get her son alone, she added, "And while you do that, I'll make coffee to go with the dessert."

"I can make coffee," Brand said.

"Don't be obtuse," his dad remarked. Then he said to Sahara, "Ann makes the best pineapple upside-down cake. I hope you like it."

"How could I not?" Soon as mother and son left the room, she continued her conversation with John. "So Brand tells me you're something of a gun aficionado?"

"Have quite a collection," he said with a nod. John was a big brawny man without Brand's height, but he was like an excited kid when it came to his weapons. "You want to see?"

"I would love to see, thank you. Do you think we have time before dessert?"

John, already pushing back his chair, nodded. "When those two get to yakking in the kitchen, it could take hours. They won't miss us."

Sahara seriously doubted that was true, but she was anxious to better her acquaintance with Brand's dad. On the way to his study, which, he explained, was converted from a guest bedroom, she got to see more of the house.

Everything was picture-perfect and she easily imagined Brand growing up here, how he might have used the old tire swing in the tree out front and probably put his shoes in the cubby by the front door... She even visualized him and his "mom" having long, meaningful chats in the kitchen before he left for school.

When they passed one bedroom, she stopped to stare. "Don't tell me. This was Brand's room?"

Beaming, John stepped back and looked into the room with her. "He got tall quick and we had to get him a big bed. Storage on the ceiling, too, since he was into just about every sport there is."

Sahara could hear the pride and she mentally added "tossing ball with his dad" to her list of childhood delights. "So he was always an athlete?"

"Naturally strong, naturally fast."

"Naturally cocky?"

John grinned. "Not *too* much."

"Just right. I agree." The headboard and one side of the king-size bed butted up against walls. A navy blue corduroy spread rested over checked sheets and two fluffy pillows. From the walls, and yes, the ceiling, hung everything from a hockey stick, skis, baseball bats, mitts, oars and even things she didn't recognize. The room should have felt crowded, but instead it felt... loved. "He had a terrific childhood, didn't he?"

"We tried to give him the best we could."

She turned and, on impulse, gave the older man a hug. "You succeeded."

"Here now," he said, his beefy hand patting her back. "What's that for?"

"Just a thank-you." She stepped away, feeling ridiculously grateful, but damn it, Brand had gotten the childhood she hadn't. While his pseudo parents had loved him to the hilt, hers had chosen to jet around the world. If it hadn't been for Scott—

No, she wouldn't go down that morose road right now, not when she was having such an amazing time learning Brand's history. "Let's see those guns."

"And rifles," he said, once again hustling her along.

CARRYING THEIR COFFEE, Brand and his mom found Sahara out back with his dad, poised in her heels and form-fitting dress, with a lever-action Winchester rifle, the butt of the stock braced against her shoulder. He already knew she was aiming for a target a good distance away, because it was the same target he'd shot with his dad a thousand times.

"Is she any good?" Ann asked.

Brand smiled. "At everything." An odd sort of pride swelled inside him. If he was a betting man, he'd put his money on Sahara nailing a bull's-eye.

"She has good form," Ann noted. "Gotta say, I've never seen anyone shoot dressed like that."

She was fucking gorgeous, but he only nodded.

"She's beautiful, Brand."

Knowing his mom fished, Brand said without inflection, "That she is."

When Sahara fired, she didn't flinch, not from the sound or the kick. She lowered the rifle muzzle toward the ground, gave a serene smile and started talking to John—who stared at her in stupefaction.

Yup, Brand knew that look: she'd nailed it.

For another twenty minutes, Brand stood there with his mom, watching as she went through several other weapons, guns and rifles alike.

As Brand had said, she was good at everything.

John, more astonished and impressed by the moment, asked, "Are you any good with a knife?"

Brand called out, "She's great with a homemade dagger."

Knowing what he meant, Sahara tossed back her head and laughed.

"A dagger?" John asked, now confused.

"More like a shiv," she explained. "Out of necessity, I made it from a small metal heater."

Brand joined her in the tree-shaded yard. "With a bra for a handle grip."

Giving him a sly look, Sahara remarked, "That does seem to be the part you remember best."

Earlier, he'd thought she might be schmoozing his folks just as she'd often schmoozed him, though he couldn't imagine an endgame in that endeavor. Now, he realized she was just having fun. Truly enjoying herself.

It seemed surreal that a wealthy, high-powered boss

of an elite security agency could mix and mingle with a country-dwelling middle-class couple. But she managed it, not only with ease, but with verve and pure, unadulterated pleasure.

In her expressive clothes, patented updo and sky-high heels, Sahara fit in. He was starting to think she'd fit in anywhere she chose, because she was that good, that comfortable in her own skin and with her own sense of self.

Brand hated to break up the fun; he especially hated to take her to Becky next. It'd be like going from a party to a funeral.

But she'd insisted.

So after they'd devoured their dessert and half a pot of coffee, Brand announced that they had to go.

His mom hooked her arm through his. "You'll bring her back?"

Sahara, close enough to hear, put her hands together as if praying, even pretended to whisper a silent prayer around her smile and a wink.

He laughed. "Probably, but not too often. It's a drive and she works long hours."

"Next time," Sahara said, "I'll dress more appropriately and then John can show me the creek."

"I could show you all the awards Brand won," Ann offered.

Brand rolled his eyes. "Those were from high school, Mom."

"I'd love to see them," Sahara assured her.

She probably would. So far, Sahara had shown a keen interest in anything that pertained to him. He wasn't used to that. He'd had plenty of relationships, some more important than others, but he'd rarely had anyone who focused on his background. Usually the interest was his career in MMA, and the person he was now.

Not the boy he'd once been.

He had to admit, he was just as interested in her past, especially this infatuation she had with her brother and the delusion that he was still around.

SAHARA WAS IMPRESSED with the very cute apartment Brand had arranged for Becky. On the ground floor, it boasted an efficiency kitchen, one bedroom and bathroom, and a small sitting area currently filled with a fully remote hospital bed. Sliding doors opened to a small patio with a padded lounge chair and table, lush plants, and a view of a pond.

In the hospital bed, Brand's birth mother scowled at her.

Clearly, the woman was still ailing. Her hair was lank and unstyled, her skin pasty and loose as if she'd recently lost a lot of weight, which she probably had. Her eyes were dull and lifeless. She clutched at a sheet, keeping it tucked over her thin body.

After quick, awkward introductions, Becky had requested—or more like demanded in a grating whine—that Brand go to the grocery for her. She wanted all sorts of things not readily available in the supplies he'd stocked. Even though her caretaker had also been to the store, she claimed the "stupid woman" hadn't gotten the right things.

Brand tried to get Sahara to go with him.

She'd opted to stay behind.

Reluctantly, he'd left her.

"So," Sahara said, moving to look out the patio doors. "The apartment is beautiful."

"It's a box, not much bigger than a tomb."

"Nonsense." Sahara's smile never slipped when she turned to face the woman. "It's cheerfully decorated and just the right size for one person. Brand thought of everything, even making sure you had easy access for some fresh air, or the restroom."

"I can't do any of that on my own."

"But your caretaker said—"

"That stupid woman doesn't know anything."

Without invitation, Sahara sat in the chair beside the bed. Brand had explained all the complications from Becky's initial cardiac arrest. Little by little, her body had failed her and she'd almost died. A blood infection, kidney failure, repeated seizures…it had been very touch and go before she finally turned a corner.

There had still been weeks in the ICU, in addition to the month she'd already spent there. The medical costs would be astronomical.

She knew Brand was taking care of therapy, and supplying a home since Becky claimed to be homeless.

According to the caregiver, Becky needed to be doing more on her own. Staying in bed was not a cure, but could add to new complications—like pneumonia. Unfortunately for both Brand and Becky, she didn't want to move, didn't want to exert herself and didn't show any appreciation for what Brand had given her.

"You're on the road to recovery now," Sahara said firmly, "so it's just a matter of physical therapy, proper nutrition and strict adherence to your prescribed meds."

Becky narrowed mean eyes. "Are you accusing me of abusing my meds?"

Most definitely. Sahara continued to smile, and instead of taking the bait, she said, "You look a lot like Brand. Same color hair and eyes."

"He got nothing from that loser who fathered him."

Curious over that comment, she asked, "What does Brand think of his father?"

Becky snorted. "Never met him, since I'm not sure which loser fathered him." Then she sneered. "And don't you dare judge me. I was young and dumb and I know it."

Sahara denied any judgment with a shake of her head. "You said he got nothing from his father, so I assumed—"

Lifting her chin, Becky stated, "You said it yourself, he looks like me." Under her breath, she muttered, "Though he probably wishes he didn't."

"He has to be pleased with his looks. After all, he's gorgeous."

"The smug bastard knows it."

Sahara stiffened, and now her smile felt sharp. "*Bastard* is such an old-fashioned insult for a child who had no choice in the decisions his mother made."

"Don't you—"

"And smug? Please. Brand is generous, obviously." She gestured around the apartment. "And also kind." She looked pointedly at Becky. "In fact, I'd call him damn near perfect."

"You want to marry him, don't you? You're after his money!"

Sahara laughed. When Becky's face turned red, she laughed even more, but managed to say around her amusement, "Better! At least now you have some color in your cheeks."

"Shut up!"

Unperturbed, she said, "You know what, Becky? You're a pretty woman. Even looking wretched from your illness, I can see it."

She sank into the bedding, the sheet to her chin. "I can't help looking wretched, as you put it. I almost died."

"Yes, there is that." Sahara studied her. "Would you like me to arrange for a personal stylist to visit you here? Someone to do your hair, your nails, maybe give you a pedi and a facial? Wouldn't that be lovely? Of course it would. Every woman likes to look her best, and nothing improves a woman's outlook like being pampered. After all you've been through, it would be refreshing, right?"

Becky eyed her, wanting to complain, but also interested. "I can't afford anything like that and Brand would never—"

"It will be my treat." She beamed, waiting for a response.

Suspicion narrowed Becky's eyes. "Why would you do that for me?"

Choosing honesty, Sahara said, "You're miserable, and that makes it more difficult on Brand." She shrugged. "It's as simple as that."

"So you *do* want to marry him."

Leaning forward, touching Becky's arm, Sahara said, "If you tried for a year, you'd never be able to understand me or my motives, so please don't tax yourself."

"Then explain it to me."

"I'd rather not." She stood, looking around the space again. "This would be so much nicer without the hospital bed in here. I mean…it's a *hospital bed*. That's enough to depress the hardiest spirit." Becky was not hardy. Indulgent, yes. Filled with self-pity, definitely.

"I'm sick," Becky growled.

"Yes, I know." Sahara surveyed the room, mentally taking measurements. It was a small space, made smaller by the bed. "Perhaps a soft padded love seat and a pretty lounge chair in a fresh, feminine pattern. Wouldn't that be nice?"

"Yes," Becky admitted, unsure where Sahara was going with the conversation, and afraid of giving up another freebie. "But this is what Brand gave me."

Brand had given her an expensive hospital bed? So remarkable. "You asked for it, I presume?"

"Because I'm *sick*," Becky reiterated again.

"Yes, I know," Sahara said for what felt like the tenth time, "but you can surely walk from the sofa to the bedroom, right?"

More confusion clouded Becky's face. "Why bother to get out of the bed when I don't feel like doing anything?"

"Nothing at all? That's too bad. I thought to offer a shopping trip also, perhaps to get some clothes that better fit you until you regain the weight you've lost. But if you can't even get from this room to that one—"

"You would take me shopping?"

"Yes." Pleased that Becky had taken the bait, she continued. "I noticed some nice trendy places local to here. We could find you some flattering yet comfortable outfits for when you go out to the patio. Perhaps some long flowing skirts and soft sweaters." She looked out the sliding doors and saw a man by the pond playing with a dog. "The neighbors would be so shocked with your new appearance…especially any men."

Becky sat up in the bed, her thin shoulders a little straighter. Trying to be shrewd, but without adequate ability, she said, "It would maybe help me to make the effort if I had something fun like that to do."

"Then I'll endeavor to create some fun."

Becky looked like a child, hopeful yet wary. "What will Brand say about—"

"Brand doesn't tell me what to do." Well, maybe he did…when she wasn't at work, although he hadn't really pushed that agreement yet. She shrugged. "If you're concerned, don't tell him."

"Hair and makeup he might miss. Even some different clothes. But he'll notice if I have new furniture."

"Eventually." She grinned. "But by then, you'll already have it, won't you?"

Still skeptical, Becky said, "Okay. Not that I really think you'll do it. But I'll play along."

"Excellent." Sahara pulled a pen and two business cards from her purse. She slid one under the notepad on Becky's side table. "That's in case you need to contact me." Then she asked, "What's your number?" After she'd written it on the back of the card, she returned it to her purse. "I'll be in touch shortly."

They finished in the nick of time, because Brand returned, arms loaded with the specific items Becky had demanded, and more.

He put everything away, telling Becky where to find it, then went one further by asking her if she needed anything before he left.

"You're going already? You just got here."

"I'll try to come again soon," he said, without any enthusiasm.

"I don't want to be alone," she whined.

Sahara's brows went up. Not once had Becky whined

while Brand was gone. "It's my fault," she offered. "I'm out of time for the day."

Becky flashed her a frown.

"I enjoyed our visit while Brand shopped for you. Are you sure there isn't anything we can get you before we go? Maybe you'd like to sit in the recliner outside? It's still sunny."

"It's getting too cold."

"Nonsense. I'll tuck a blanket around your legs." Not giving Becky much of a chance to argue, Sahara stripped away the bedclothes and helped her to her feet. Near her ear, she said, "You need to start getting your strength back."

Becky groused and grumbled until Sahara had her settled in the lounge chair on the patio, slippers on her feet, a quilt tucked around her. She even got Becky a sweet tea over ice, and a few magazines to look at, then put her phone beside her.

"Now, just relax and enjoy the air and think about getting better so you can have some fun."

Brand had stood back, arms crossed and expression enigmatic, until Sahara mentioned fun.

"Rehab comes before fun, and Becky, I expect you to start doing what the physical therapist tells you."

Sahara patted his arm. "She and I have already discussed it and she's going to cooperate to the best of her ability. Isn't that right, Becky?"

Refusing to look at either of them, her face set in mulish lines, Becky nodded.

Brand softened, saying, "I'll try to check up on you next week."

"Why not Saturday?"

"Sahara has a dinner party."

"So a party comes before—"

Interrupting, Sahara said with heavy innuendo, "Just think how surprised he'll be with your progress, Becky."

Hinting that she'd have the makeover by then did the trick. "Yes, he will be." Becky picked up a magazine and thumbed through it. "So what about Sunday?"

"We're helping friends build a gazebo."

Because she hadn't known that, Sahara said, "We are?"

"Maxi wants one by the pond and I told Leese we'd join them. All the guys will be there."

Warm pleasure spread through her, making her smile extra bright. "I'd love to."

Brand tucked a wisp of hair behind her ear. "You know anything about building gazebos?"

She lifted her chin. "I'm intelligent enough to learn."

He grinned. "I have no doubt."

With a sound of annoyance, Becky said, "So I won't see you this weekend. Fine. Have fun doing other stuff. Whatever."

Brand didn't move. "You're welcome, Becky."

Rolling her eyes at the prompt, she twisted to see him. "I already said thanks."

"No, I don't think you did."

Screwing up her face, her tone sour, she said, "Thank you for taking care of your mother who almost died."

Since he'd gotten his way, Brand smiled. "You're welcome." He took Sahara's arm and guided her away.

Sahara was thinking that mother and son were more like adversaries who'd called a very temporary truce. While Becky might not be his mom, Brand couldn't enjoy having such a strained relationship with her. In the long run, she didn't know if she could help, but she'd give it her best try by giving Becky a new focus.

The second they were in the car, Brand asked, "Okay, what was that about?"

After just touting her intelligence, Sahara played dumb. "What's that?" Unfortunately, she wasn't that great of an actress.

"You know what I'm talking about." He put the car in gear and pulled out of the lot, not once looking to where Becky sat on the patio. "What surprise do you have planned for me?"

After rolling down her window, Sahara waved to Becky. The woman ignored her, keeping her nose in the magazine. She sighed. "If I tell you it won't be much of a surprise, now will it?"

He didn't press her, but he did warn, "If you're thinking to try to reconcile me with Becky, don't bother. I'm doing my duty, but I'm not doing anything more."

Sahara didn't care about duty. She cared about his feelings. She cared about his life.

She cared about him—far, far too much.

CHAPTER TEN

BRAND DIDN'T LIKE the evasive way Sahara got her phone from her purse and checked for messages.

"Sahara?"

"Hmm?"

She was definitely up to something. "I'm telling you now, don't get involved."

In a huff, she lowered the phone and glared at him. "Do you think you could try trusting me just a little?"

"No. Not with this."

Appearing hurt, she paused and asked, "Do you trust me with anything else?"

He wanted to reassure her, but this was too important to leave open to interpretation. "I trust you to keep your word."

One slim brow arched. "My word?"

"We had an agreement—and honey, we're not in the office, and not around your employees." Brand spared her a quick glance. "That means I'm the boss."

Silence filled the interior of the car, then he felt her hand on his shoulder.

"Do you have some orders for me, sir?" Her fingers trailed down his arm, off his arm and onto his leg. She curved her hand over his thigh, fingertips dangerously close to his junk. "Something you'd like me to…do?"

Forgetting all about his mother, Brand accused, "Tease."

"I enjoy teasing you." Her nails lightly scraped over the denim at his crotch. "Don't you enjoy it?"

"Yeah." He enjoyed it a lot. Holding the wheel tight and keeping his gaze on the road, he said, "Maybe you should save the teasing until we're home in bed, though."

"It's a long drive." Resting her head against the seat back, her smile in place and her gaze steady on his face, she withdrew her hand. "Maybe I'll just tell you what I'd like to do to you, instead."

"I'm game." Hell, he was already half-hard.

Sahara wasn't one to do anything halfway, and the woman was far from reserved. She boldly detailed her seduction, what she'd like to do to him, how and where she'd do it, leaving out nothing.

By the time they got to the agency, Brand could barely think for wanting her. Sahara's brand of foreplay nearly torched him.

Yet he still noticed the man standing across from the parking garage, half in the shadow of a shop overhang, his demeanor watchful—until he spotted Brand. Then he became more alert.

Briefly, their gazes held as Brand drove past, but short of stopping in the middle of the road, Brand had no choice but to turn into the garage. As he did so, he glanced into the rearview mirror—and saw no one.

"What?" Sahara asked, giving up her lurid description of where she would kiss him. She twisted to look back through the rearview window. "What's wrong?"

"Probably nothing," Brand said. "I saw...someone. He seemed to be watching the agency."

Frowning, she said, "Describe him."

"Hard to do. Tall, wearing a hoodie. He was mostly in shadow, away from the lights."

"I don't see anyone."

"Yeah, he disappeared after I spotted him." *Or after he spotted us.*

"The man who kidnapped me was enormous. As big as you."

"This guy looked a little shorter. I'd say six feet tall or so."

Sahara lost interest. "Not our guy, then."

Brand wasn't convinced, so he stayed aware as they entered the building, pausing to speak to the guard. Much as he'd like to get hold of the bastard who'd taken her, he'd rather not do it with Sahara present.

He'd feel better once he had her secure in the suite.

They stepped inside, and as he locked the door, Sahara was busy shedding clothes. He turned and found her stripped down to her bra and panties.

She had a thing for fine lingerie, and looked fucking gorgeous in it.

"In a rush?" Brand asked.

"After all that teasing?" She reached back to open her bra, then dropped it over a chair with her clothes. "Aren't you?"

"Yeah," he murmured, letting his gaze move over her. With her hands up to free her hair, she looked even more slender. But she had an inner strength that left him awed.

Standing there against the door, Brand toed off his shoes, bent to remove his socks, then stripped off his shirt. Watching Sahara, he moved to the couch and sat down. "I remember every word you said, everything you promised."

"Mmm." She smiled as she came to stand before him. "So do I."

"Take off your panties."

"You're still wearing your jeans."

Yeah, they'd stay on a while longer—at least until he got her off. After all the verbal foreplay, he didn't trust his control, but he could see in the flush of Sahara's skin, the tightness of her nipples, that she needed release.

Her teasing had teased her also.

"Take them off, Sahara."

She hesitated, but only for a second. "So I'm to be naked while you're not? Does that mean you plan to touch me?"

"It does."

Her smile warmed. "I can handle that." She peeled off the tiny strip of lace she called underwear.

Brand patted his thighs. "Come here."

When she started to sit on his lap, he stopped her, using his hands to guide her over his thighs so that she straddled him instead. With his hands on her narrow back, he bent her toward him—and latched onto her left nipple, sucking strongly.

The pleasure was so keen, she almost lurched away.

He enjoyed saying, "Stay still."

"Brand," she moaned.

"Shh." He switched to the other nipple, sucking, licking, leaving it as ripe as the left. He liked the way Sahara squirmed, the little sounds she made, how her fingers clenched in his hair.

Kissing a trail to her throat, he murmured, "I love how you taste." He drifted his hands down her back to her hips, rocking her against the ridge of his erection beneath worn denim. Once she caught his rhythm, he went back to touching her, kissing her. He curved both hands over the globes of her ass, kneading the firm flesh. "Will you like how I taste?"

Arrested, she shuddered and said, "Should I find out?"

"Yeah." *Hell yeah.* "Sounds like a plan." Holding her arms just above her elbows, he eased her back and off his thighs, then urged her down to her knees.

Looking even more excited, Sahara said, "Now you'll take off your jeans?"

He shook his head, slumped into the couch, and stretched his arms out along the back. "You can unzip them."

Sahara licked her lips and smiled. "This feels like a challenge." Her fingers touched the snap to his jeans. "I like it."

He liked it, too, especially the part of seeing Sahara on her knees in front of him, naked. Brand tried to relax, but every muscle in his body tensed as she opened the snap and slowly, agonizingly drew down his zipper.

Being the diabolical woman that she was, she leaned down and nuzzled against his stomach, her fingers playing over his erection. When he shifted slightly, she quickly opened the material and freed him from his boxers.

Her small hands encircled him and she pressed a soft kiss to the head.

Brand nearly groaned, but he enjoyed the game too much to give it up this quickly. "Stroke me."

With a sly smile, she whispered, "Yes, sir."

Damn, she was even better at the game than he was. He'd never survive—especially when her grip tightened and she started a slow, firm stroke up and down his length.

He pressed his feet hard to the floor, bracing himself against the pleasure.

Her breath teased over him, and she asked, "Okay if I kiss you now, too?"

Taking in her tumbled hair, the heat in her beautiful blue eyes and the rosy glow to her skin, he nodded. "As long as you use your tongue."

God, she did. With a throaty purr, she licked around him, her tongue hot and wet, and then slid her lips down and over him, taking more and more until she closed her mouth on him.

Unable to bite back the groan, Brand tangled both hands in her hair and drew her closer.

She braced her hands on his upper thighs, her head bobbing slowly as she made him insane. His lust churned; the need to release burned inside him.

He kept one hand cupped on the back of her head, and with the other, he reached under her to find her breasts. She was so soft all over, so sleek and sexy... Deeper and deeper she took him until he knew he couldn't hold back any longer.

"That's enough."

"Mmm," she said against his dick, so that even the small murmur felt like a hot caress.

"Sahara." It wasn't easy since he really didn't want to stop, but he got her mouth off him when he said, "I want to be inside you."

Lifting dazed eyes, she stared at him. "But I could—"

"No doubt. But not this time." He caught her upper arms. "Come up here." Shoving his jeans lower, he completely freed himself, then found his wallet and the condom inside it. He handed it to Sahara. "You do the honors."

Smiling, she flipped it a few times, then tore it open with her teeth.

He enjoyed watching her, the way her thick hair swung down around her face when she bent to the task, how her breasts moved, the flex of her nimble fingers. Letting her put the rubber on him was its own form of sweet torture.

"Now," he growled, at the end of his control. "Ride me."

Excitement sparked in her eyes. "Oooh, that sounds more like me being the boss again." She came up to her knees, one hand holding him, and started to sink down.

Brand clasped her hips. "Slowly." At the same time, he leaned in and gently caught her nipple with his teeth.

Gasping, she stroked him against her wet heat, but he held her so she couldn't rush things. By small degrees, her body slid down his length and when finally she held all of him, he kept her still, further teasing.

"Brand," she moaned, her inner muscles squeezing tight. *"Please."*

Seeing her like this, so needy, wanting him so badly, satisfied something deep inside him. "Okay."

The second the word left his mouth, Sahara kissed him hard and began rolling her hips. Brand helped her, guiding her, lifting into her, faster and harder, deeper, and when she tipped her head back and cried out, he joined her.

God, it was good. So good.

He was still trying to catch his breath when Sahara collapsed against him, her cheek on his chest, head under his chin, body lax.

He couldn't imagine anyone being more compatible with him in bed. But then, on a very basic level, he'd always known the sex would be incredible.

Today, though, she'd shown how nicely she meshed
with his folks, too, while still staying true to herself. Sahara didn't try to fit in. She didn't have to.

She was perfect as is.

SAHARA AWOKE THE next morning with a nudge from
Brand. She stretched, yawned and opened her eyes to
see him standing there in boxers, beard shadow and
holding a cup of coffee.

How could a man look so good? She smiled. "Good
morning."

Brand handed her the coffee in bed, then asked,
"What did you have planned with Becky?"

Wow. So she'd managed to distract him last night,
only to have him jump right back to it first thing in the
morning? She glanced at the clock. It was only seven
fifteen.

Unlike many people, she woke sharp, so she sipped
her coffee, then said, "I promised to take her shopping."

A black scowl marred his handsome face. Mouth
tight, he bit out, "No."

"Now, Brand—"

"I told you not to interfere."

Uh-oh. He sounded far angrier than she'd expected
him to be. Trying to explain that she'd been acting in
his best interest wouldn't work. Currently, he didn't look
receptive to any explanations. It's why she'd chosen to
admit to the shopping trip she'd planned, but not the
makeover.

She could find a way around shopping…

"I'm sorry."

Standing away from the bed, his face set, Brand
folded his arms. "Why do I have trouble believing that?"

Easy enough to answer. "Because I'm headstrong and usually determined to get my way." Placing the coffee on the nightstand, she swung her bare legs over the side of the mattress. "Please believe me that I'd never do anything to hurt you."

His hand slashed through the air. "It's not about hurting me."

Of course it was. Men like Brand didn't want to discuss emotions or feelings, but she knew his mother's betrayal had cut deep. How could it not? Gently, she promised, "I won't take her shopping."

Reluctantly, his gaze went over her body. "It's fucking unfair of you, Sahara. How can I argue when you look like that?"

Relief took the knots out of her stomach. "I was hoping you couldn't." She brushed back her hair and tried a tentative smile. "We have forty-five minutes before I have to be at work."

He groaned—then took the two big steps necessary to reach her. "I need ten."

"That works for me." She'd have to really rush it, but she'd manage.

"God, you make me nuts."

Before she could reply to that, Sahara found herself thoroughly kissed, her body stroked all over, and then Brand bent her over the edge of the bed and took her hard and fast. Her fists grabbed the sheets, anchoring herself as pleasure pounded through her.

More than that single sip of coffee would have been nice.

But sex with a scruffy, hard-bodied hottie? That beat the hell out of coffee as a wake-me-up any day.

Precisely ten minutes later, her body still humming,

Brand carried her into the bathroom and set her on her trembling legs.

Leaning against the door frame, he asked, "Anything I can do to help?"

"You've done enough," she promised him.

He smiled. "I'll warm your coffee."

"Thank you." She took a two-minute shower, brushed her teeth and was rushing through eye makeup when someone rang the doorbell.

She stalled.

At the same time that she realized it had to be Leese, Miles or Justice, it hit her that she and Brand had left their clothes thrown all over the entry.

Oh crap.

Dashing out of the bathroom, she shouted, *"Wait..."* then slipped to a halt on the polished floor when she saw all three of the men standing inside the door.

Looking around.

Brand followed their gazes, and an "oh" expression hit his face. He shrugged an apology to Sahara and, pretending it didn't matter, said, "Come on in. Sahara is scrambling to get ready for work. We're running a little late today."

Brand had pulled on fresh jeans and a casual black button-up...that he hadn't yet buttoned. He hadn't yet shaved either, but his hair was damp, so she assumed he'd caught a shower as well.

When the silence penetrated, she tore her gaze away from Brand and found the other three staring at her. "What?"

Justice cleared his throat. "You look nice with your hair down."

"That's what I told her," Brand said. Then bold as you

please, he walked over and gave her a kiss. "I'll put on more coffee. Why don't you guys come into the kitchen so Sahara can finish up?"

"Wait," Sahara said. "They're here for a reason, right?"

"I don't know." Brand looked at them. "Something up?"

Leese shook off the stupor. "Yeah, actually. We have something to share."

"Should have waited until she made it to the office, though," Miles said. "I told them that, but did they listen?"

"Apparently not." Sahara strode around the living room snatching up articles of clothing—including her bra and panties, which, thankfully, were with her dress over the back of a chair rather than on the floor. She planned to wear the same shoes, so she stepped into them. "Give me thirty seconds before anyone says anything. And, Justice, would you let Enoch know I'm going to be a few minutes late?"

"Sure thing."

"You're the best." She hustled down the hall to the bedroom, dumping the clothes inside. Going into the bathroom and bending at the waist, she flipped her hair forward, secured it with a band, and then twisted it around to form a casual chignon. She slipped in earrings, gave her makeup one last look and joined the men.

Brand was looking at something on Leese's laptop and she gasped. "You started without me!"

Brand pulled out a chair for her and handed her coffee. "It's photos from the security cam at your house."

"It dawned on me," Justice said, "that I might find some footage of those landscapers."

"Did you?" She hurriedly gazed at the laptop. All she saw was the back of a head.

"That's the thing." Leese crowded in next to Brand and rolled several photos past the screen.

Sahara frowned. The back of a head, back of a head, arm up blocking the face, head down and turned away and another back of the head. "It's almost as if they knew where the cameras were and avoided them."

"Exactly." Miles helped himself to coffee. "Every shot's like that."

"The big question, then, is do you know them?"

She shook her head at Justice. "It's hard to judge body size, but I don't think it's the men who took me. None of them are big enough to be the main guy, and the others just seem wrong."

Brand said, "You transferred those photos to her?"

"Yeah. They'll be in her files, waiting for her." Leese closed the laptop. "I sent them to you, too, Brand. The two of you can maybe enhance them, blow them up a little, whatever."

Justice finished his coffee. "You coming to the office now?"

She glanced at Brand. "I'm ready." But what would he be doing for the day? "What about you?"

"I have some errands to run. I'll be back in time for lunch if you're free."

Just that easily, he brightened her morning. Amazing that the idea of lunch with a man—a man she'd slept with last night and again this morning—could make her so happy. "Come with me to the office and we'll ask Enoch."

At the office, the other men splintered off, Miles and Leese with assignments, Justice with time to hit the range and work out. After Enoch told her she had time for lunch at noon, Brand still followed her into her office, waiting until Enoch finished going over the day's appointments for her.

Once they were alone, Brand said, "About that party this Saturday."

"You've changed your mind? You don't want to go now?"

"You leap to the oddest assumptions."

It didn't seem all that odd to her. Brand had been furious about her making arrangements with Becky—and he didn't even know the whole of it. "Sorry. What about it?"

"How fancy will it be?"

A new thought occurred to her. "If you need me to buy you a suit—"

His finger pressed to her lips. "One, I own several suits. Two, even if I didn't, I sure as hell wouldn't let you buy one for me. Three, I just need to know if we're talking dress casual, a suit or a tux."

Sahara stared up at him, waiting for him to remove his finger so she could reply.

Instead, he traced her lips, then bent to kiss her. It was a brief, gentle touch, and it stole her breath away.

"What's it to be?" he asked.

"Do you own a tux?"

He grinned. "No, but I know how to rent one."

She smoothed her hands over his shirt. He looked very handsome in the black shirt, a brown cargo jacket over it. He still hadn't shaved, but she liked the rugged look on him. "I'll certainly dress up, as I suspect most of the women will." She loved dressing in her finest clothes. "But you'll be fine in either dress casual or a suit. Up to you. Douglas Grant wears suits every day as the DA, so for parties he's usually pretty casual. When it comes to the men, I wouldn't be surprised to see some of them in jeans."

"I'll find some middle ground, then." He brushed his thumb over her cheek. "You're going to be here all day?"

"Yes. But eventually I'll need to get back to my house to pick out my clothes and shoes and jewelry."

"I'll go with you for that."

"It should be fine now—"

He cupped her face. "I'll go with you."

"All right. I'd like that."

After one more touch of his mouth to hers, Brand stepped away. "See you for lunch."

Oh, how she loved the progress with her relationship.

She watched Brand leave, then moved to her desk and called for Enoch. He'd be able to locate a stylist willing to do a house call for Becky.

After she got that done, she'd fit in some online shopping. If she couldn't take Becky to the stores, she'd have to bring the stores to Becky.

One way or another, she was determined to help Brand.

And to do that, she had to help his mother to get on with her life.

THE LAST FEW days of the week went by in a happy blur. Brand had lunch with her twice, and each night they enjoyed dinner together. Between them they came up with meal plans that were both delicious and semihealthy. Brand hadn't yet committed to a fight, but neither had he committed to Body Armor.

She was a little afraid to press him, which was totally

unlike her. Her true nature was full-steam ahead, but for the first time in her life, she felt...tentative.

Her time with Brand was *so* good she didn't want to rock the boat.

Of course, when he saw his mother, the boat might not only rock, it could capsize.

The stylist had visited Becky and done an amazing job. Her hair had stunning highlights and a new cut that better suited the shape of her face. Her new makeup showcased all her best features, features she shared with her son, like her dark eyes, long lashes and high cheekbones.

In the middle of an important meeting Sahara had gotten first one text, then another and another, all of them selfies from a very pleased Becky. The clothes had arrived, too. Becky was disappointed that they couldn't go out to shop, but still overjoyed with what Sahara had chosen for her. In one of the photos, Sahara could see that Becky wore a new outfit.

Sahara knew she had good taste, and she was a decent judge of character, so she'd pegged Becky as someone who would react positively to gifts that showed off her figure and made her feel more like a desirable woman.

Not that she'd discuss it with Brand. No, a son wouldn't want to think that way about his mother—especially a mostly estranged mother.

She was determined that she'd visit with Becky again, but first she wanted to enjoy her hectic weekend.

She'd just closed out her computer when Brand stuck his head in the door.

"Enoch said you were done for the day."

"Enoch is always correct," she replied, already coming out from behind her desk. She paused to stretch her aching shoulders. "I've finally gone through every contact I could find associated with my brother."

"And?" Brand turned her and began gently kneading the tensed muscles in her neck and shoulders.

Sahara tipped her head back, eyes closed. "Nothing. I couldn't find a single man who even resembled my kidnapper."

"I'm not sure I like you referring to him as yours." Brand kissed the side of her throat.

"I didn't mean it affectionately, but I'm very invested in this. Territorial, maybe. I want to find him. I want revenge."

"And you want to know what he knows about your brother."

"Exactly." She needed to know. It was always there, chewing on her peace of mind. *How could Scott have any association with a vile kidnapper?*

"You're getting tense again." His fingers carefully pressed deep, working her, almost forcing her to relax.

"You're good at that." She twisted to see him, eyeing the trim beard he had now. She liked it. "You're good at everything, aren't you?"

He smiled. "If we take this upstairs, I can show you just how good I am—with a proper massage."

"Proper, huh?" She groaned and collapsed back against him. "Tempting as that is, I have to go to my house tonight. I need to get my party clothes for tomorrow."

"All right. I can take you there now."

She beamed at him. "It's like having my very own hot chauffeur, who's also a sexy roommate and a kick-ass bodyguard."

"I'm a jack-of-all-trades." As she went to get her coat

and purse, he added, "It's starting to rain and the temps have dropped. Want me to warm up the car?"

"Thank you, but it's not necessary." She turned up the collar. "We'll go from the parking garage to the garage at my house. It'll be fine."

On the way out, Brand called Leese to let him know their plans. "Just to be on the safe side," he said. Brand still wasn't convinced that it was just a bystander who'd locked eyes with him a few days ago, or that it hadn't been the kidnappers at the house pretending to be landscapers.

Sahara didn't think it was, not after studying the security cam photos and seeing no resemblance to the body types. Still, she appreciated Brand's caution. In so many ways, he'd make an ideal bodyguard, his instincts already perfectly aligned for the job.

As usual since the kidnapping, Brand stayed alert to their surroundings, even on the drive to the house. All looked quiet as they drove in, but then, the guys had taken turns randomly stopping by to check on things. Anyone watching the house would have realized that Sahara wasn't there, and it was well scrutinized for intruders.

When they stepped inside, Sahara glanced around in surprise. Somehow the house felt even bigger...and emptier.

Brand peeled off his jacket, laying it over the volute at the bottom of the handrail. "I still can't believe you live alone in this place."

"I know." Her heart beat a little faster when she looked up the long stairs and at the dim landing at the top. "I used to feel completely safe here, but after being in the suite, this place feels… I don't know." She shivered and said, "Vacant."

Brand slipped his arm around her. "You were attacked in this house. It makes sense for you to feel differently here now. You won't be here alone. Not for a very long time." He got her moving. "Not until you're ready."

Was Brand already looking for an end date to their relationship? She hoped not, but even if he was, she wouldn't return here. She'd stay in the suite…which would also feel empty without Brand in it.

How had she gotten so attached to him, so quickly?

She leaned against his side. "Don't ever tell anyone, but I'm a little spooked."

"I'll be right here with you." He kissed her temple. "And honey, you know it's okay to be human, right? No one expects otherwise."

"I do," she admitted. "I expect a lot of myself. And usually I can deliver." If Brand weren't with her, would she make herself go through the house alone? Maybe. But she was glad she didn't have to.

It didn't take her long to choose a dress, find shoes and a wrap to match, then locate complementary jewelry.

When she opened the jewelry case disguised as a mirror on the wall, Brand whistled.

"That's a lot of bling."

She grinned. "Scott gave me most of it. Birthdays and Christmas and stuff like that. Some of it is older, handed down through the family. And a few pieces I bought myself."

"That's a handy place to hide it all."

She gestured at the standing jewelry case, as tall as her dresser. "I have a lot of other pieces there, but the expensive stuff is better kept out of sight." She picked

out a ruby-and-diamond choker with matching drop earrings. After she'd placed everything in a small carrying
case, she said, "I'm ready if you are." More than ready.
With the oddest feeling of being watched, she was anxious to be on her way.

Brand took the case from her, holding it in one hand
and taking her hand with the other.

RAKING A HAND through his hair in frustration, he turned
away from the small camera. "I don't like it." An understatement: he fucking well *hated* it. "She's entirely
too close to him."

His cohort shrugged. "What do you have against
him?"

"For starters, I don't know him, and that's unaccept-
able. I want every detail you can dig up on him. Everything from his friends and family to his favorite candy
bar. Start with a criminal background check, his job and
his bank account. How much money does he have, where
does he spend it, how does he spend his leisure time."

"I'll get started on it tomorrow."

"Tonight. I need to know something about him before
she goes to the party." He rubbed his chin and turned
back to the camera, watching as she and the big man
left the foyer. "I need to know what I'm up against—
and how best to get rid of him."

CHAPTER ELEVEN

SEEING SAHARA'S DRESS on a hanger did not prepare him for seeing it on her. The long red dress hugged every curve and hollow of her body in a way that made his blood thicken.

The slinky material dipped low between her breasts, showing off a lot of cleavage, then fed into a cinched knot that emphasized her narrow waist. A split on the left side cut up to midthigh. Silver heels made her legs even longer.

She'd worn her thick brown hair down, but tucked back on one side, which showed off the jewels in her choker and earrings.

As he pulled her Mercedes into the designated parking area for the party, he made note of the area, of other people heading in and of the impressive house.

Not as impressive as Sahara's, but still, a mansion.

These were her people, her peer group, and she'd fit in while he didn't even want to.

Brand glanced at her again. She sat serenely, legs crossed, looking out the window.

Every man in the place is going to want her.

How could they not? No woman could be as impressive as Sahara Silver. He wasn't a man who suffered jealousy, but if he could—without looking like an ass—he'd steal her away so no other man could ogle her.

A valet appeared in front of the car, intent on parking for him. Brand refused. When Sahara gave him an incredulous look, he explained, "I need to know where the car is, and I need the keys on me so we can leave if necessary."

She puzzled over that. "You honestly think something will happen at a party? At the DA's house?"

"Let's just say I'm not sure it won't." He had a bad feeling about it, and when it came to Sahara's safety, he wasn't willing to discount any concern.

Brand found a spot at the end of a line of cars that would leave an opening for a hasty exit. It meant they had to walk a little farther to the house, but the rain had stopped before morning and there were plenty of stone paths to use.

Two attendants, who remained in the lot with flashlights, watched in confusion as they left the car. Brand asked the closest man, "You'll be here for the duration?"

"Yes, sir."

"Can I count on you to ensure no one comes near her car until we return?"

He looked even more confused. "Uh…yeah. I'll watch it."

Brand handed him a hundred and said, "Make sure it doesn't get blocked in, too."

Eyes a little wider, he said, "Yes, sir."

Sahara smiled at the second guy, who clearly didn't appreciate being left out. "There's another hundred in it for you when we return."

He grinned. "Yes, ma'am. I'll be here."

She hooked her arm through Brand's. "I have a strong need to be fair."

"Understood." They entered through the front of the

house where two security guards checked names. These men, too, gave Brand curious looks, but Sahara's smile never slipped and since she made it clear he was her guest, they ushered them in.

"How many people are here?" Brand asked. As Sahara had said, he saw men in suits, others in work-casual clothes, and a few wearing jeans and Polo shirts.

In his black pants and button-up, with the collar open, he fit right in. Clothes-wise, anyway.

"Probably a hundred or more," Sahara said. When someone offered to take her wrap, she shook her head and instead draped it over an arm. "Douglas heats the garden area out back, and utilizes a game room downstairs. I assume anywhere we go, it'll be this crowded."

"So where do you want to go?" He didn't like standing in the open, especially with Sahara turning heads.

"Come on." Keeping her arm in his, oblivious to all the men watching her, Sahara propelled them forward, past several rooms, to a bar set up in a wide area where many couples danced to a live band. "Drink?"

Brand told the bartender, "Cola."

Smiling, Sahara said to him, "Party pooper." She took a glass of wine.

When a casually dressed man approached, Brand stiffened. The man paid no attention to him at all and went straight for Sahara, his face lit with an enormous grin. "You came! I'm so glad." He clasped her bare upper arms and drew her into an embrace.

"Of course I did. I'm a woman of my word." Sahara dodged his kiss by leaning into Brand. "Douglas, I'd like you to meet Brand Berry. Brand, this is District Attorney Douglas Grant."

Douglas blinked as if someone had just materialized, proving he hadn't even noticed Brand.

Brand slipped his left arm around Sahara, but extended his right hand. "Beautiful home you have."

Shaking off his surprise, Douglas accepted the gesture with a firm but friendly grip. "Yes, thank you. Brand, is it?"

Brand nodded.

"You two are…together?"

Why the hell did he have to look so shocked? Brand grinned to hide his insult and said, "I'm doing my best."

Leaning forward, Sahara confided, "His best is *amazing*."

"I see. Well I…" He looked beyond Brand, frowned, then turned back again. "You like the house, huh? I prefer the Hamptons. We have a quaint little cottage there… Well, you know nothing is that small in the Hamptons, not in the best areas—"

Sahara chimed in with "Isn't that your father's property, Douglas?"

"Yes, well…" He cleared his throat with a frown. "I don't get away often enough to bother buying my own. When I do find time for a vacation, I enjoy it there." After that rambling explanation, he said, "Why don't I show you around?"

Since Brand wouldn't mind seeing the layout, he nodded. "All right."

Before they could take two steps, Douglas added, "Sahara, I see Lisa looking for you. Stay and visit, and I'll bring Brand right back to you."

No, Brand didn't like that idea at all. "I'd rather—"

"She'll be fine. Though it's been a while since she

visited, Sahara already knows her way around. Isn't that right, Sahara?"

"Yes, it's been a good long while since I visited." She sipped her wine. "I didn't think to ever return."

Douglas's smile grew brittle. "I'm glad I could persuade you."

"Curiosity," she explained with a small shrug. "I want to hear all about your willingness to work with me."

Presumably it was Lisa who suddenly embraced Sahara, saving Douglas from having to reply. The woman was already talking a mile a minute. Douglas's wife? Brand wasn't sure, but Sahara did seem to genuinely like her.

He resisted Douglas's efforts to lead him away, and with an apology for interrupting Lisa, leaned in to say near Sahara's ear, "Stay here, okay?"

"Of course."

"*Right* here," he emphasized, his voice still low, his gaze holding hers. "I don't want to have to look for you." In a place this packed, he'd have a hell of a time finding her.

She put a hand to his jaw, brushing her fingertips over his growing beard stubble, then went on tiptoe to whisper, "I'll stay in this room, but watch Douglas. He's a snake."

Brand briefly put his mouth to hers. "You look so hot." And with that, he turned and left with Douglas, pressing through the crowd.

This was going to be the fastest tour in history.

Or so he thought.

Douglas waxed on about every room until Brand was ready to abandon him over the excess of details. They were on the upper floors, going through an elegant library that, according to Douglas, held a bunch of first editions that amounted to quite a collection, when a stacked blonde joined them.

Wearing a short black sleeveless dress and heels as high as those Sahara favored, the woman brushed back her long loose hair. She was a little on the voluptuous side, but in all the right ways.

Brand hoped she was there to interrupt the tour.

Red lips smiled when she spotted Douglas, but then her gaze transferred to Brand. She looked him over from head to toe the same way a dog ogles a meaty bone. "Douglas," she cooed, without looking away from Brand, "you're needed in the garden."

"Problem?" Douglas asked.

She shrugged a bare shoulder. "Some debate that only you can decide, apparently, but don't worry, I'll tend to your guest."

Smiling, Douglas said low, "I just bet you will," and then in a normal tone, "Brand, meet Chelsea Tuttle, daughter to my wife's dearest friend and a member of one of the most influential families in the state. Chelsea is like a niece to us. We're very close."

Brand nodded, uninterested in family dynamics when he'd rather be with Sahara. "I should go."

To Chelsea, Grant stressed with strange emphasis, "Brand is here with Sahara Silver."

"Oh really?" Gray eyes widened with mock surprise. "Sahara is here?"

"Downstairs," Brand said, wondering if everyone knew Sahara. "And since the tour is over, I believe I'll join her."

"Nonsense." Chelsea latched onto his arm. "I'll finish showing you around." She dismissed Douglas with a glance. "Go tend to your party. I'll handle this."

As if he'd been ordered by the president, Douglas smiled and walked out.

Brand decided to follow. "Thank you, Chelsea, but I better get back." He attempted to free his arm.

She held on, even leaning closer so that her perfume filled his head and her boobs rested against his biceps. "Sahara does hold a tight leash, I know, but surely she can manage without you for a few minutes more."

Irony at its finest, since it was Chelsea who wouldn't let go. "You know her well?"

"I hired her agency once, back when her brother ran things." Her other hand brushed his thigh. "She was underfoot even then, making a nuisance of herself."

"A nuisance?" Brand already disliked the woman. He stepped back, away from her wandering fingers. "If you really do know Sahara, you know that's not true. Whatever she does, she does better than anyone else could do it."

Chelsea leaned in again, and this time she more boldly caressed him. "Well, well, she has you smitten, doesn't she?"

Brand laughed even as he took her wrist and removed her hand. "If you mean I think she's amazing, then yes. Hell, she's the smartest, most beautiful woman I've ever known."

Chelsea blinked, at a loss for words. Unfortunately, it didn't last. "Maybe there are things about her you don't know."

There was nothing he wanted to hear from Chelsea Tuttle. "And maybe you're just jealous of her?" When she gasped, he added, "It's understandable, but still unattractive."

She was so surprised by the direct insult, he finally managed to free himself.

Unfortunately, as he headed out the door, she followed, and before he could make it down the stairs she'd plastered herself back to his side, determined to boldly grope him.

For some reason, that made him even more anxious to get to Sahara. He had a bad feeling about things. Concern spiking, he ignored Chelsea and lengthened his stride.

He needed to know Sahara wasn't in danger. He needed to see her *now*.

SAHARA AND DOUGLAS'S SISTER, Lisa, whom she hadn't seen in a year, moved to a quieter corner to speak. She remained in plain sight, just opposite of the busy bar. Still, she watched for Brand. He was so protective that she wouldn't be surprised to see him back in five minutes.

"You're smiling," Lisa said. "Does the happiness have anything to do with that godlike hunk you brought along?"

Odd how the sister could be so nice, and the brother be such scum. Sahara let her smile widen. "It has everything to do with him."

"Are we getting serious?"

"Actually," Sahara said, "I tried to convince him to work for me. He'd make an amazing bodyguard."

Lisa leaned closer to guess "But he refused because he'd rather get busy in bed? Nice."

Since that was so close to the truth, Sahara laughed.

"He's actually an MMA fighter, but he's thinking of retiring from that. Until he makes up his mind, though, I don't stand much chance of getting him to hire on."

"Hello, Sahara."

That particular deep voice, coming so close behind her, stole Sahara's breath. She jerked around—and came face-to-face with her kidnapper. At first, she merely gaped. How had he gotten in here? How dare he approach her so publicly?

Seeing him in a lighted room, in a comforting crowd, gave her a whole new perspective. Yes, he was still big, and she realized he could still be threatening, but freshly shaved, his sandy brown hair combed back, his suit stylish, he seemed less a monster and more a controllable man.

You can do this, Sahara. He wouldn't dare hurt you here.

For a few seconds her pounding heart kept her silent as they stared at each other, unblinking, her astounded and him pleased.

"What are you doing here?" she finally got out.

"You and I have unfinished business." His gaze moved over her, belying any menace in those words. "God, you're beautiful, even more than I realized."

Hoping for a few minutes to think, Sahara turned to Lisa—but she was gone, drawn away into conversation with a nearby group. Her thoughts scrambled as she tried to decide what to do, and a second later she felt a big firm hand clasp her upper arm.

That was alarming enough, but then warm breath said into her ear, "Don't run off. What are the odds of us meeting like this?"

She'd bet the odds were pretty damn good, since he'd

obviously kept tabs on her to know where she'd be and
when. Her entire body urged her to flee, but she wasn't
a coward and here, in this safe setting, might be her best
chance to question him.

That is, if she could get some moisture back into her
dry mouth, and tamp down on the internal trembling.

Bravado was her friend, and she turned back to him,
her gaze direct and her voice cold. "Get your hands off
me."

He slid his loosened hold down her arm in a slow caress that gradually allowed her fingers to slip free. Un-
disturbed by her rancor, he casually leaned a shoulder
against the wall. "I knew you'd be stunning tonight, but
I never expected—"

"You dare to come into the home of the district attorney?"

Rather than be alarmed by that disclosure, he flouted
polite societal rules by taking a deep swig of his beer
straight from the longneck bottle, his gaze never leaving hers. "You hoped to set me back on my heels, maybe
panic me a little, didn't you? Obviously, you don't know
that Douglas and I are old friends." He smiled. "We go
way back. We—"

"So this was a setup?" She had no doubt Douglas
Grant associated with unsavory sorts, being so sleazy
himself, but to invite one of those cohorts to a party?
No, he would never. The only thing Grant cared more
about than his twisted pleasure was his reputation and
power. He wouldn't risk those idly. "That's why Douglas
invited me, isn't it? It wasn't about him making peace
with me at all." She saw his surprise. "What do you have
on him? I assume you used blackmail?"

His gaze gleamed…with admiration? She wasn't sure.

Then he said, "Not much gets by you, does it?" in a way that confirmed he was impressed.

She waved it away. "I know Douglas, who and what he is. I should have thought of blackmailing him myself."

Suddenly the hulk straightened and held out his hand. "What do you say we start over? I'm Ross Moran."

Sahara ignored the gesture. "How do you know my brother?"

With a small smile, he let his hand fall back to his side. "He hired me for a job."

"When?"

One brow lifted. "Not long before the yacht incident, actually."

With a curl of her lip, she assured him, "I would have known if he'd hired thugs."

"I'm not a thug," he protested. "And yes, under usual circumstances, you probably would have known. This was private, though, and for a while, Scott and I were close." He gazed down at her. "Close enough that I knew all about you."

She found it very hard to believe that Scott had discussed her with a kidnapper.

Ross continued, saying, "Unfortunately, when things got…tricky, he tucked in his tail, ran away and refused to pay up. That's the truth."

Strange, but she believed him—at least that things had gotten tricky and that he hadn't been paid. Scott wouldn't have run away, though. If he avoided the mess, there was a good reason. "What job?"

"Like I said, it was private. So here, in the DA's house, is not the place to discuss it." Ross moved closer, suggesting huskily, "Have dinner with me, Sahara."

She did not like the way he said her name, almost savoring it. "Sure, when hell freezes over." Something occurred to her and she asked, "Did you twist Douglas's arm to get him to lead Brand away?"

"Brand?"

"The man who came here with me."

He lifted one thick shoulder. "You know how Douglas likes to brag. He was probably hoping to impress your *friend*."

So he'd been watching her since her arrival? Of course he had. She suppressed a shudder of disquiet and lifted her chin. "Oh, he's more than a friend."

Ross's attention dipped to her mouth. "Too bad for him, because I don't like competition."

Her eyes widened. Had he just issued a threat against Brand? She glared. "He has none."

Ross let that go. "I had hoped you would come alone. It would've been easier, but you should know, I'm not going to let anyone get in my way."

That was definitely a threat, damn it. She breathed more deeply, and leaned into his space to ask "You consider me stupid?"

He smiled, saying with admiration, "Far from it. I've never met a woman more clever than you, or more complicated. You look all soft and delicate, but I'm learning you have a backbone of steel."

"It surprises you that I'm a strong woman? Careful, Mr. Moran, your sexism is showing through."

He didn't deny it. "Most women want to be coddled. And call me Ross."

"I'd rather not. Our...association is going to be as brief as I can manage."

"Funny," he said. "I'm planning just the opposite."

If she thought too much about his plans, she'd lose her facade of nonchalance. "Tell me about the job."

"Join me for dinner."

She shook her head and offered a compromise. "You could come to my office."

He snorted a laugh. "Now who thinks who is stupid?"

"Oh, there should be no doubt what I think of you, Mr. Moran. Stupid is only the beginning of a litany of insults. After all, if Brand finds you here, he'll—"

"Kill me?" Ross asked, unconcerned.

"You're judging others through a very small prism of your own character. Brand is not a murderer. But he'll make you wish you were dead."

"Don't let it get around, but I'm not a murderer either." He smiled. "And so you know, I'm not as unskilled as my men. If you think he'd have an easy time with me—"

"Famous last words." She smirked. "He'd annihilate you."

Ross laughed. "Let me worry about that, and you just worry about how and when we'll get together to discuss Scott."

Sahara expected Brand back at any moment. Once he arrived, she'd lose her chance to ask anything about Scott, so she needed to change tactics. Insulting Mr. Moran had gotten her nowhere, and hadn't put the slightest dent in his annoying good humor.

She drew a slow breath and accused, "You're a cruel man, Mr. Moran."

"I can be." He eased closer, his gaze caressing her face. "But never to you."

So far, so good. "No? You kidnapped me, threatened me, accosted me—"

"Don't be dramatic," he said with a small smile. "It was just a kiss."

God, she wanted to slap him. "—and now you taunt me with info about my missing brother. I'd call all that very cruel."

"I need your brother to pay up. Using you to extort the money from him seems like the best option."

Even while trying to soften her, he *still* planned to use her!

Growing serious, solemn, he pledged, "Understand something, Sahara. No matter what our future holds, you have my word that I won't ever hurt you."

Insane. He was certifiably, undeniably, insane. "You threatened to hurt me," she reminded him.

He gave a slight shake of his head. "I threatened to strip you naked." His gaze became intent. The pads of two fingers brushed over her shoulder. "And tie you down." He drew a strained breath. "But I wouldn't have let the others touch you."

The others…yet he hadn't claimed *he* wouldn't touch her. She locked her jaw. "You don't think it would have hurt to be in such a vulnerable position? Let me assure you, it would have been horribly painful, *worse* than being struck."

He was silent a moment, his fingers playing over her skin, then he whispered, "I'm sorry."

Dumbfounded, Sahara shrugged away his touch and demanded through her teeth, "Tell me what you know about my brother."

"I'm not trying to tease you, Sahara. Whatever I say, you're going to have a million questions. But—" he added, before she could blast him again "—as an act of good faith, I'll give you the bare bones of what I know."

She subsided, waiting, letting her impatience show.

He cocked a brow. "You agree, no questions?"

Of course she'd have questions, but to get him talking she said, "Fine."

"Your brother suspected one of his clients of enslaving women."

"What?"

Ross rolled his eyes. "If you insist on doing this publicly, at least try not to draw attention to us."

"But—"

"Uh-uh. No questions." He watched her, and when she quieted, he continued. "The client wanted Body Armor to provide security during a special event. Scott felt like something was off, so in turn, he hired my men and me to discover what we could about the client and those on her guest list. He didn't put his own men on it because if we got caught, he didn't want it tracking back to Body Armor."

Ah, that made sense.

"Naturally, your brother was right. He always did have uncanny instincts."

"I don't understand—"

Ross put a finger to her lips. "Didn't I tell you there would be questions?"

Repulsed, she jerked her head away. "Don't touch me again or this conversation is over."

"End it anytime you want. Talking wasn't my idea anyway."

Damn it, he had her and he knew it. "Brand will be back soon. Can you please finish?"

"Please," he repeated thoughtfully. "I like the sound of that on your lips."

Her eyes narrowed. "I'm armed, Mr. Moran. Did you know that?"

He surprised her by throwing back his head and laughing. When he sobered, he teased, "Would you shoot me? Here in the DA's house?"

"Without hesitation."

"You know what? I believe you." His eyes, a paler blue than hers, still twinkled with hilarity. "Actually, there's not a lot I wouldn't put past you."

She didn't want to hear his bizarre form of flattery. "How much did my brother owe you? I'll see that you get paid in exchange for all the information you have." As much as it galled her to reward him in any way, she wanted to know everything, not just dribs and drabs.

After giving that some thought, Ross finished his beer and set the bottle aside. "I'll admit, getting paid had been my number one concern. Even after watching you, learning your patterns, learning *you*, I thought the money was the point. But once I actually met you…" To get his meaning across, he looked her over. "I'm not so sure."

"Don't be a fool." He'd *learned* her? What the hell did that mean? Everything he said made her more uneasy— and yet, against her will, she believed he was trying to be genuine. "Tell me what you know."

He touched her cheek. "Not kissing you is hard—"

"Don't you dare!"

"—but I wouldn't put it past your boyfriend to chase me through the house. He looks capable of embarrassing us all with his bad manners."

"What are you talking—"

"Word of warning—he should be more careful who he hangs with at parties."

What did he know about Brand? He'd gone off with Grant, so—

"I'll see you soon, Sahara." Ross quickly stepped around her and disappeared into the crowd.

Sahara put a hand to her chest to contain her thundering heart. What had spooked him?

She glanced up to search the crowd—and locked eyes with Brand. He stood across the room with a very curvy woman draped all over him. Since the woman was facing Brand, standing close and trying to get closer, Sahara couldn't see her well.

Brand wasn't exactly discouraging her. No, he was too busy mean-mugging Sahara.

Of all the nerve!

Fury hung around him like a cloud, as if he had the right to show his anger while he allowed some woman to nuzzle his ear?

He started toward her, and almost knocked over his admirer. As if he'd only just then remembered her, he peeled her clinging arms away and started forward again.

She clutched at him, doing her best to hold him back. Distracted, he tried to shake her off—without taking his gaze off Sahara. He literally dragged the woman a few feet before he finally shed her.

Sahara had a dozen questions lined up, but Brand didn't give her a chance to ask any of them.

As soon as he reached her, his voice pitched low and mean, he growled, "Who the hell was that?"

Her eyes widened at his harsh words, and she saw several heads turn their way. It wasn't easy to smile so casually. In a pleasant tone of voice, she said, "Don't you dare cause a scene."

"Tell me."

She lifted a brow. "I was going to ask you the same thing."

His eyes narrowed. "You want me to go first? Fine. I don't know and I don't care. Your turn."

His abrupt attitude was still drawing attention. Bracing her hands on his shoulders, Sahara lifted up to kiss his mouth and whispered, "Remove the scowl, Brand. I mean it. I work with some of these people." When she eased back, she saw that he still looked annoyed, but no longer ready to go on a rampage. "Much better, thank you."

His mouth moved in a very mean smile. "Start talking."

"I take it you saw Ross Moran?"

"Who?"

She wound her arms around his neck so he couldn't get away, and said with a careless smile, "He's my kidnapper."

Brand went utterly still, every muscle in his body taut and bulging as if preparing for battle.

"I've handled it," she promised. "So put your hands on my waist, kiss me and as soon as the party ends, we can talk."

Brand reached up and pulled her arms away. "This is one of those times where I'm going to be the boss, and you're going to listen to every word."

That he spoke so calmly reassured her. "This is a business party—"

"Party's over. Either we walk out together, right now, like a civilized couple, or I carry you out."

Her eyes flared. "You wouldn't dare."

Expression set, he reached for her—and she hastily stepped back.

A nervous giggle slipped out. Good God, she never *giggled*. "Brand!" she whispered. Secretly, she had to admit she liked his fierce determination to protect her.

As if he weren't being outrageous, he asked, "Would you rather walk?"

Oh, when she got him alone, she'd set him straight.

Or maybe kiss him. It was a toss-up whether she felt amused or furious.

"Yes." Her smile kept twitching in a bizarre way. "I prefer to walk." She started around him, but he pulled her back, lifted her wrap around her shoulders, then anchored her to his side.

"I am not a sack of potatoes," she complained.

"Trust me, honey, I know exactly what you are."

He forged a path through the crowd, sparing any niceties for those they disturbed, which left Sahara to say hastily "Excuse us" and "Pardon" several times.

Once outside, she tried to extricate herself from Brand's tight hold, but he didn't loosen up, not even a little.

Gaze constantly scanning the area, Brand trotted her off the grand porch, down the lighted stone steps and along the walkway until she protested, saying, "I can't keep up."

Slowing, he glanced down at her. "It's those heels."

She gasped. "Don't you dare compound this situation by insulting my shoes."

"They're not practical."

They were on a direct path to the car when from around the corner of the stone wall encircling the property, Ross appeared. "I like her shoes."

"You!" Sahara swung around to face him, dreading what conflict might now ensue. Her first thought was to block him from Brand. They didn't need a brawl on the front lawn to enhance the scene they'd already caused.

Before she could draw another breath, she found herself tucked behind Brand.

Bemused at how quickly he'd moved, she accepted that her intent hadn't gone quite as planned.

Peering around the blockade of tense muscle Brand provided, she saw Ross lift his hands in a supplicating way. "Call him off, Sahara."

"Do I look like I have control of this, you ass?"

Brand remained ominously silent.

Seeming unconcerned with Brand's dark mood, Ross said, "Now that we're out of the house, I thought I could warn your *friend* to be careful who he talks to."

It infuriated her that Ross continued to refer to Brand as a *friend*. *"He is more than that,"* she snarled, then gasped when Brand tucked her back behind him again. Protesting his high-handed treatment, she knotted her hands in his shirt…but because she didn't trust Ross, she didn't say anything that might distract him.

Believably lethal in tone and posture, Brand growled, "You have two seconds before I break your face."

Ross ignored that to say, "I'm not the one who was chatting up a lunatic."

"What is that supposed to mean?"

Ross opened his mouth to reply, and a whizzing sound cut through the air.

Sahara didn't immediately understand—until pieces of rock from the wall splintered a mere inch from Ross's shoulder.

She didn't have time to react; Brand shoved her down

and behind a tall decorative statue. It wasn't adequate to hide them both, but Brand again used his body to shield her.

"Jesus," Ross growled, touching a spot of blood on his face where the splintered rock had cut him. "You fucking shot at me?"

Sahara hissed, "I didn't pull a gun, you dunce."

"Then who?"

Brand said, "Stand there until he takes another shot, then we can figure it out."

That prompted Ross to swing up and over the wall, out of sight. Where he went, she didn't know and didn't care.

"Brand," she said as calmly as she could manage, "we have to move or you could be hit."

"Not yet." He kept one hand on her head, holding her down and against his chest. "Not until I know it's clear."

Arguing with him would be pointless; she could tell he wouldn't budge. Since the bullet had struck closest to Ross, she asked, "Leese, maybe?"

"No. He'd have told me."

"Then who?"

"No idea, but I don't like it."

When her phone dinged with a message, she tilted back to see him. They stared at each other for several heartbeats.

"Check it," Brand said, "but carefully. I don't want any part of you exposed."

She nodded and, maneuvering carefully, withdrew her phone. She read aloud the message on the screen: You're not a target. She glanced at Brand. "I don't recognize the number."

They didn't move. She could see Brand considering things, his frustration obvious. "Try texting back."

She thumbed in "Who is this?" but it wouldn't send. Disappointed, she said, "Not delivered."

"So someone can text you, but isn't accepting replies?"

"Apparently." It wasn't until that moment that she realized he held a gun in his hand. "Brand?"

Another text came in. She looked at it, and frowned. *Your boyfriend's not a target either. Get out of there before the police show up.*

Reading it himself, Brand blew out an exasperated breath. "How the hell am I supposed to trust that?"

The valet he'd paid came over, his expression confused. "Are you all right?"

Brand tossed him the keys. "Bring the car here. As close as you can get it."

"Uh...sure." He looked around, trying to find a reason for their behavior. Clearly he hadn't witnessed the bullet hit the stone. "Just a sec." Jogging off, he headed for the car.

"He thinks we're nuts," Sahara predicted.

"So do the rest of the people standing around gawking at us."

Sahara got her head lifted enough to see that they had indeed caused a stir. She surprised Brand, and herself, by laughing. It had been the most bizarre night...

"It's not funny, babe."

"It's a little funny," she insisted. "God knows Douglas will probably never invite me back to his home." *Not unless he's again coerced.*

Brand called Leese while waiting for the car. Short and succinct, he explained what happened, ending with

"Find out everything you can about Ross Moran." Leese was just as abrupt, apparently. Brand replied, "No, we don't need you here. I won't let anything happen to her. Yes, I'm sure." He pocketed the phone.

"Moran's probably gone by now, but Leese is on it."

Hoping to reassure Brand, she said, "He'll have a report for us by morning, I'm sure."

Leaving the engine running, the kid got out and held the door open, waiting.

It was the oddest thing, but the text she'd received reassured Sahara. Call her a fool, but she no longer felt at risk. Whoever had taken that shot hadn't been aiming at her or Brand, but had instead been warning off Ross. She didn't doubt that it had been a deliberate shot made to look like a near miss.

If it wasn't one of her men—Leese, Justice or Miles—then there was only one other person it could be.

Joy pumped into her bloodstream, making her almost giddy. She didn't care if they looked like fools, didn't care what impression the other guests got.

All she cared about was that Scott was apparently alive.

She wasn't ready to share with Brand yet. She'd talk to her PI first, see if he knew anything and she'd try to isolate the job Ross had mentioned to her. If he'd worked for Scott, there had to be a record somewhere.

But at this moment, what she really wanted was to be alone with Brand so she could show her appreciation for his caution—and ensure he hadn't done anything wayward with the woman who'd stuck to his side, a woman, she suspected, assigned by Ross, despite his denials.

What she didn't want or need was to hear Brand lecture her on unrealistic expectations. She knew everyone assumed Scott was dead.

She'd never believed it, and the text felt like proof that she was right. Who else would both protect her with gunfire, and reassure her with a message?

Peeking around Brand, she said, "If we go now, there's a group of people between us and the area where the shot probably originated."

Brand scowled at her. "You're enjoying this."

"No," she promised, trying to bank her jubilation over the text. "It's just amusing to see how we've disconcerted everyone."

"Fuck," Brand muttered, then with a quick glance to verify what she'd said, he stood with her and made a direct line to the car, being certain every step of the way to put his body between hers and possible danger, then hoisting her in from the driver's side and climbing in behind her. "Keep your head down."

Trying to follow that order wasn't easy, not in a long dress and heels. Soon as she got in the passenger seat, Sahara reached past Brand with the promised money for the valet's friend. "You'll give that to him?"

"Yes, ma'am."

The poor kid barely had time to get his arm out of the car before Brand slammed the door and drove off.

While she stayed ducked down as ordered, Brand sat erect in the driver's seat. "Aren't you worried about getting shot?"

"I'm not the one who was kidnapped or assaulted."

"True." Once they'd left the lot and gotten on a main street, Sahara slowly, hoping Brand wouldn't object, straightened in her seat. She smoothed her dress and tidied her hair. "You should know, Ross promised me he wouldn't hurt me."

His hands locked on the wheel so tightly tension rippled up his forearms, through his biceps and into his neck and shoulders. "You're on a fucking first-name basis?"

Her brows rose at his acerbic tone. "I wasn't nice to him, if that's what you're thinking. In fact, I was utterly rude." She shrugged. "It didn't bother him. He almost seemed to admire me more for it." Seeing Brand's expression darken further, she scowled, too. "Do *not* say that *F* word again."

Brand glared at her. "After all this, you're offended by a *word*?"

"It's unbecoming." She set her purse on the seat next to her and chafed her arms, chilled now that the adrenaline was wearing off. Her wrap wasn't sufficient to help. "However, I *am* offended that you had a groupie crawling all over you."

"You don't have to worry about that."

"I'll worry if I want to."

Incredulous, Brand took a corner a little too sharply. "The way your mind works is—"

"Amazing? Thank you. I'm able to compartmentalize. The danger is over now—"

"You don't know that."

"—and I'm more than ready to explain to you how much I disliked your treatment." Even though the Neanderthal approach had been a little thrilling, she couldn't let it slide.

"No."

"*No?*"

"We agreed that at times—especially times like this—I'd be the boss."

"I thought you meant in bed!"

"That, too, sometimes."

Her frown intensified.

"Tonight was dangerous, more dangerous than we expected. I did what was necessary and you don't get to complain about it."

Stunned by that, she half turned to face him. "That's bull and you know it! Most of your initial reaction to Ross Moran was jealousy."

"True."

She gaped at him. "You admit it?"

"Sure. We're in a relationship—we agreed on that, too, if you remember—but if it had only been jealousy, I'd have found the bastard and set him straight right then and there. Fact is, I wanted to do that. Bad." He rolled his shoulders as if trying to loosen the strain. "I put your safety above my personal, very territorial feelings and attempted to get you out of there, away from harm."

Huh. He'd admitted a lot there. She felt a warm glow expand. Tonight had been weird, but also somewhat magical.

Scott was likely alive and watching out for her, and Brand had just admitted to feeling territorial.

Under his breath, he added, "I didn't know the prick would follow us out, have the balls to approach you in front of me, to dare to warn *me* or that someone would take a potshot at him with you standing so close by."

Scott didn't take potshots. He was an excellent aim. "I think Ross felt safe because he'd somehow manipulated Douglas into backing him. Having a DA on your side could be pretty good insulation against ramifications."

"Maybe...but not this time."

"Meaning?"

"Whatever it takes, we're going to bury him."

Sahara frowned. She wondered if that was jealousy speaking again. "Not until I've found out what he knows about Scott." Then again, if her suspicions proved true, she wouldn't need Ross Moran at all—and Brand could do whatever he wanted with the brute.

CHAPTER TWELVE

ROSS WASN'T IN the mood to hear all the nonsense. Around him, his cohorts badgered, argued and complained. It was annoying as fuck. "Enough already. What's done is done."

Olsen, his unofficial second in command, sat beside him. "Just because you've gone soft on her doesn't mean the plan was bad. We still need our money, and she's still the quickest, easiest way to get it."

Ross shook his head. The bitter coffee he drank made his stomach burn. After the sleepless night he'd had, it was too early for this shit, too early to meet in an abandoned house, too early to be convinced that Sahara should still be a target.

And yet, at the same time, it was already too late for him.

He kept remembering the contempt in her beautiful blue eyes, her complete disdain when he mentioned grabbing dinner to talk. He'd thought for sure that she'd come along willingly to learn more about Scott. He'd have happily, ruthlessly, used her curiosity, and her love for her brother, against her.

But no, she was too sensible to fall for it. Even more troubling, she was already involved with a damned fighter who looked to be perpetually angry.

That burned worse than the shitty coffee.

Without inflection, hoping to discourage his nitwit cohorts, Ross said, "She's a lost cause." With any luck, the others would buy it.

Of course he didn't mean it, not when it came to his personal involvement, but they didn't know that.

"We disagree," Terrance said. "Once we have her, she'll pay up."

Ross shook his head. "She's too smart for us to catch her off guard again. She won't be left alone, not for a single minute."

The fighter stuck to her as if they were already married.

Except when he let Chelsea Tuttle grope him. *What the hell was up with that?*

Could it mean Sahara wasn't really all that involved with him? He'd been watching her for a while and she never dated. Somehow, while he'd been growing enamored during his surveillance, she'd been hooking up without him noticing.

Hopefully, it was only a hookup—and with any luck, her angry protector wouldn't bring more danger to her with his associations.

"So she has a man or two with her." Olsen shrugged. "Big deal. We can handle that."

"Those bodyguards of hers are ex-MMA fighters, not ill-trained street thugs. You saw what happened to those two." He gestured at Andy and Terrance, whose wounds hadn't completely faded yet from the beatings they'd received.

Terrance's still-swollen nose sat off center on his face, framed by two black eyes. A patchwork of mottled bruising, splits and lumps covered Andy's face. When he smiled, you couldn't help noticing the missing tooth.

Ross shook his head. "Whoever rescued her that day worked the two of them over as if it was his job—a job he loved." Ross was willing to bet it was her escort. That one certainly looked capable of inflicting all sorts of damage. Ross wasn't afraid of anyone, but Sahara's friend had given him pause.

"There are four of us," Olsen reminded him. "And you're the best at fighting."

Yeah, he'd convinced them of that. Beating any one of them wouldn't make him break a sweat, but that wasn't saying much.

Still, he put on his macho act and nodded. "I can handle myself, but I don't see the point in doing it. It'd be a waste of time because Sahara doesn't know where Scott is. That means we can't use her to make him pay."

Andy gave a huff of disagreement. "She knows, but even if she doesn't, so what? Body Armor is her company now, so she can damn well pay us."

"That was never the plan." Sometimes he hated dealing with imbeciles. "Scott owes us. Scott should pay." Sahara shouldn't have to pay for her bastard brother.

Besides, his pals were running short on patience and high on frustration. He wasn't sure he could control them and he didn't want Sahara in any real danger. If any one of them touched her, Ross knew he wouldn't be able to control his temper.

She was his. Somehow, he'd make it so.

Idly, Olsen turned his coffee cup on the scratchy surface of the thrift store table. "You didn't mind getting the money from her before."

Ross swiped a hand through the air. "That was just a gut reaction, a desperate grab to make it work." And an attempt to spend more time with her. "But it's not what we're about."

"Maybe it's not what *you're* about," Olsen said. "But I'm betting the rest of us feel different."

Ross twisted to face him, his anger dangerously close to the surface—and his phone alerted him to a message. Glad for the interruption, he withdrew it from his pocket and glanced at the screen. Money is in your apartment. Now leave her alone.

His eyes flared. *No fucking way.* It couldn't be...

Shooting to his feet, Ross held his phone out in front of him as if someone might jump out of it.

"What is it?" Olsen stood, too, his red brows scrunched together. "Problem?"

"No." The last thing he needed was the other three overreacting. Fear made them reckless, and that could be dangerous for everyone. Keeping the screen turned so no one else could see the phone, Ross texted back, Who is this?

The message wouldn't send.

Damn, he hated mysteries. Only one way to know the truth. Pocketing the phone, he said, "I have to go."

"Go?" Terrance asked. "Where?"

"Back to my place." His new place that no one should know about. If the money was there, that'd mean someone had been watching him closely.

Pair the text with the fact that someone had shot at him, and he was starting to think he'd finally found Scott.

It didn't bode well at all that Chelsea Tuttle had, on the same night, been cozying up with Sahara's date.

Damn. If Scott was around, he had to urge the others

to caution, so he paused in the doorway. "Someone is on to us. Watch your backs, okay?"

Terrance scowled. "What the hell does that mean?"

He couldn't confide in them, not until he knew for sure what was happening. "I just have a feeling."

"But what about the girl?" Andy demanded.

To appease them, Ross said, "You're right. We'll get her." At least if he had her, she'd be safe. "Give me a little time to work out a plan." And to figure out how best to protect her. "We can't afford to fuck this up again."

"When?" Olsen asked. "I'm getting damned tired of waiting."

Ross shook his head. "I'll be back in touch soon, and until then you should all lie low." If he found the money in his new place, he'd wait until he was sure he wasn't being followed, then he'd give them their shares.

He knew how badly they wanted the cash, but he saw no reason to get their hopes up until he was sure.

It could be a trap, and he could be walking right into it.

To settle things with Sahara, he'd take his chances.

BRAND DESPERATELY WANTED to get Sahara out of town for a bit. The trip this morning to visit Miles and Maxi would take them to the country in southern Ohio, very near the Kentucky border. That worked perfectly for him.

All through the night, he kept seeing again how Moran had dared to touch her in such a familiar way, as if he'd had the right.

He'd approached them without fear of repercussions—until someone had taken a shot at him.

The man was confident and unpredictable, and from

what Sahara had told him, he was obsessed with her.
That worried Brand.

Whoever had fired the gun complicated the worry.
He hated the unknown.

She'd talked to her PI last night, but the man claimed
he hadn't uncovered anything yet. Brand had seen her
disappointment, but it hadn't dented her unwavering determination. Every so often she smiled, as if over some
secret thought.

It worried him.

While Sahara had slept soundly tucked against him,
her delicate, manicured hand on his chest, her long hair
spilling over his arm, he'd lain awake going over various scenarios in his mind.

Why had her kidnapper tried to warn him? What had
he meant about chatting up a lunatic? Was he talking
about Douglas Grant?

Sahara's soft body heated his; her slow, deep breaths
had teased his skin. All of it had amplified his need to
protect her.

What he felt for this one particular woman defied
description.

Somehow, he had to unravel the threat, but that
seemed such a daunting task when Sahara herself refused to worry.

He closed his eyes, agonized over the idea of her
standing there with a kidnapper, asking for information.

It was a long time before he'd finally gotten a little
sleep.

Very early the next morning, when the sun had barely
risen, they got on their way. Justice followed along behind them, just in case. Since he was going to the same
place, the only inconvenience was getting up earlier than

he'd planned. Fallon, Justice's soon-to-be-wife, was with him, so he knew Justice would be extra vigilant.

Leese had already found plenty of info on Ross Moran. The man was mostly legit, working as a private investigator and, when necessary, extra muscle, but as proven with the kidnapping, he often went to extremes if the price was right. Upper elites hired him, like Douglas Grant, but that didn't rule out the scumbags. Unfortunately, he was no longer at the last residence listed, so it would require more tracking before Brand could get answers.

Answers he'd happily beat from the man.

They'd eventually find Ross, he didn't doubt it, and they'd start with questioning Douglas Grant.

The powerful DA might not appreciate the interrogation, but Brand didn't really give a damn. He was complicit in putting Sahara in danger.

Unfortunately, Sahara insisted on sending some of the older employees—the bodyguards she'd reassigned after hiring Leese, Justice and Miles—to visit Douglas. Those men, she claimed, were a different breed and better suited to putting Douglas at ease so he'd talk more freely.

Didn't matter to Brand if the man was at ease or not, but this was one of those circumstances where she was the boss, a damn good boss, so he bit back his complaints and trusted her to handle it.

In the seat next to him, looking fresh in skinny jeans, a long sleeve V-neck ribbed shirt that hugged her body and rubber calf boots, Sahara fretted—but not about her latest misadventures. "I don't see why we can't stop at the store. It's bad manners to go to a party empty-handed."

"It's not a party," Brand explained for the third time. "I'll be helping to build a gazebo. Maxi wants to feed us while we're there, she said so, and Miles stocked the cooler, too. It's their way of thanking us."

"I'm also going to help."

"Sure." He wondered if Sahara had ever swung a hammer. He imagined her driving a nail, and had to smile. Did she think the jeans and boots fit the part? He had to admit, she looked great in her version of weekend work-wear. He especially liked her hair in the thick braid.

He liked it even better loose.

He liked it most of all spread out on a pillow with him over her, each of them straining for release.

Switching gears, she said, "I keep thinking about Chelsea Tuttle. You're sure you weren't flirting with her?"

Over coffee that morning, she'd asked questions about the woman who'd come on to him at the party. Brand wasn't sure he'd ever forget the name, not after the way Sahara had reacted.

"I'm not a liar, honey." He glanced at her. "You didn't recognize her at first?"

"She's had a lot of work done." Half under her breath, she added, "Not all of it complimentary."

Brand held in his laugh. "She looked too young for plastic surgery."

"She is, but she's practically addicted to it. She's also obnoxious and full of herself, and very self-centered. Awful rumors have swirled around her for years now."

"What rumors?"

Sahara lifted one shoulder. "Perversions, money problems, indiscretions." She frowned. "Maybe that's what Ross was talking about when he approached us outside."

Brand was still pissed over her using the kidnapper's first name. "Perversions, huh?"

"It's said that she likes to watch."

"So, a voyeur?" He shook his head. "Not my thing, but it doesn't sound all that bad. My rule is to each his or her own, long as no one is being hurt."

She leaned toward him and said in a false, ominous whisper, "But people do get hurt—that's what she likes to watch."

"No way." He'd disliked Chelsea from the start, but she hadn't struck him as sadistic. Just obnoxious and too grabby.

Sahara nodded. "That's one of the rumors. She gets off on seeing other people humiliated, degraded and hurt. Normally I pay no attention to rumors, but if you'd talked to her instead of letting her lick your ear, you might have picked up on her cruel bent. She is *not* a nice woman."

"I didn't *let* her do anything, her tongue was never in my ear and we did talk, smart-ass. Just not very long." Brand gave her a look. "I wanted to check on you, and good thing, since *you* had a kidnapper breathing down your cleavage."

Sahara scoffed. "You talked, huh? About what?"

"Mostly you." Briefly, he wondered if he should tell her the whole truth, but then decided, *why not*? He liked her show of jealousy, especially since he'd been jealous, too. It wasn't like she and Chelsea would ever be friends. From what he'd heard so far, they were more like enemies. "She's not a fan of yours."

"Well, I would hope not. After all, I have morals, and she does not."

Brand smiled over that. "How do you know her anyway?"

"Her father contacted Body Armor to hire personal security for her during a big bash. Not uncommon for the wealthy, especially for Chelsea since her father considers her his precious little jewel." Sahara twisted her mouth in distaste. "Unfortunately, the agents came back saying they were the ones who'd needed protection—from her. She treated them as bought-and-paid-for slaves, which she figured included sexual favors."

Brand whistled low. "We're talking about the same men now retired to less high-profile details?" Far as he could tell, they were sticks-in-the-mud, suit-wearing uptight middle-aged snobs who might have been top-paid bodyguards at one point, but were probably more for show than results.

"Yes. Nothing about the men said *sexy and available*, but Chelsea didn't care. When they refused her, she carried on in front of them, enacting sexual games that they had to watch in order to stay close enough to protect her. Before you suggest it, no, they didn't enjoy it. In fact, the overall consensus was revulsion."

And he'd been alone with the woman? He should count himself lucky that she'd only tried to cop a few feels. "She was pushy," Brand admitted. "And she made it clear she didn't like you. But I never guessed she'd go that far."

"She's been entitled since the day she was born."

"So were you, but you're not pervy."

She sent him a brazen smile. "I can be pervy when the mood strikes me—and when the right man is available."

Brand scowled.

Laughing, she said, "I meant *you.*"

"Oh." Yeah, when it came to sex with Sahara, he was game 100 percent. "Anything you want, honey, anytime you want it, you let me know."

"Thank you. I think I will." She checked a nail. "So, what did the bitch say about me?"

Brand gave a short laugh of surprise. "Bitch, huh?" He really did enjoy her attitude.

"I know her better than you."

"I get that. So tell me, what happened with the men she hired from Body Armor? They told Scott what she'd done?"

Sahara nodded. "She'd been after Scott for a while so she was always on her best behavior around him. He never saw her more devious, cutthroat side. Mostly he considered her a spoiled princess type, but not really dangerous. She'd told Scott that yes, she'd flirted with the men after having too much to drink, but that she hadn't meant any harm. It came down to her perception against theirs, and Scott decided they'd only misunderstood. He didn't want to condemn her after one incident, you know? Men," she said in disgust. "They never seem to realize how lethal women can be."

Suddenly, Brand knew that Sahara had taken matters into her own hands. "What did you do?"

With a careless shrug, she explained, "She was doing her best to get the guards into trouble, and that really infuriated me, especially when Scott didn't one hundred percent side with them."

"You went against your brother?"

"I protected my brother…by warning her off." As if she thought he might criticize her for it, she rushed on, saying, "Scott had done the same for me plenty of times. He was always checking up on anyone I dated, so I just returned the favor. He seemed blinded to her true nature, but I sure wasn't. So I…had her followed."

"Wow," Brand said. Sahara's relationship with her brother was nothing short of incredible. To him, it sounded like they were close, but also adversarial.

And for sure, Scott overstepped—often.

Memories had her scowling. "I ended up with some juicy recordings of her in some very bizarre acts."

"Bizarre how?"

She huffed out a breath. "I'd love to give you every gory detail, but part of my deal with her was that I wouldn't expose her if she'd stay away from Scott. Let's just say the rumors are true and leave it at that."

He imagined Chelsea Tuttle causing harm and it turned his stomach. "One question, okay?"

"All right."

"Did she always have willing partners?"

Loathing hung heavy in her tone when Sahara replied, "Unfortunately, no, and that's where I drew the line. I reported her to the DA."

"Douglas Grant?"

"Yes. Because he knew her better than I did, and because I'd agreed not to expose her, I took Grant's word that he'd handle it."

"Since he told me she's like a niece to him, I gather he did nothing?"

"No, he didn't—the lying bastard."

Brand knew her well enough to guess. "You took matters into your own hands?"

"In a way. I told Chelsea that if I ever heard of her enacting her sick games on anyone else, or if she ever sought out my brother again, I'd happily destroy her. Publicly, financially and with some physical harm thrown in."

Yup, that sounded like the Sahara he knew and lo— Brand pulled up short on that thought. It was too soon, too many things were up in the air, and…the idea of caring that much unsettled him.

But he couldn't keep from touching her.

Reaching across the seat, he rested his hand over Sahara's thigh. "You're a hell of a great sister, Sahara."

"I wonder if Scott would agree." She covered his hand with her own. "So spill. What did the evil one say about me?"

"Well, it makes more sense now, but basically she said you were a nuisance at Body Armor."

"Of all the nerve."

She sounded only mildly insulted, so Brand guessed she'd been expecting something worse. "I shut her down."

"Did you?"

"Accused her of being jealous." He grinned. "She didn't take it well."

"I notice it didn't get her off you."

"No, I'm not sure anything short of a crowbar would have accomplished that. The lady was grabby."

"*Lady* is hardly an apt description. Just be glad you didn't go off alone with her. God only knows what would have happened to you."

Since he knew he could hold his own against a woman, no matter how devious or twisted she might be, Brand laughed.

They chatted for another twenty minutes while driving, until Sahara got out her phone.

"Who are you calling?"

"Just trying to reply to that text again."

He waited while she thumbed in a message. "And?"

"Still not received." She dropped the phone back into her purse. "It is *so* frustrating."

Brand wondered when she would mention her suspicion. He knew who she thought had sent that text.

After everything that had happened, damned if he wasn't starting to think it possible, too.

Instead of saying what she had on her mind, she went back to her nemesis. "I still say you looked awfully cozy with Chelsea."

"I was shaking her off and you know it. You're the one who let your *kidnapper* crawl into your space."

"I was trying to find out about my brother."

He kept silent, waiting.

"Brand?"

"Yeah?" The sun came out with a vengeance, glaring across the windshield.

"Can I tell you something?"

He slipped on sunglasses as he took the exit off the freeway. "You can tell me anything."

"Okay, then." She drew a breath. "I care an awful lot about you."

Not what he'd thought she would say.

As the words stroked over him like a warm caress, Brand slowly smiled. "Is that so?" He waited for further confirmation, then he'd tell her that he felt the same.

In a sudden rush, she said, "I also think my brother is alive, and in fact, I believe he's the one who sent the warning shot at Ross and then texted me." She ended that with a huge, beatific smile.

Damn, Sahara knew how to take him off guard. First,

she sidetracked him with the admission of how much she cared, and then brought him sharply back around with the speculation on her brother that he'd been expecting.

He took a left off the exit, noting how the scenery changed to tall trees and endless fields. The colors of fall were everywhere, making for a beautiful sight beneath the blue sky and bright sun. "That's a dangerous habit, honey."

"What?"

"Saying things that make my head spin while I'm driving."

"Why would your head spin? It makes sense. Who else would be protecting me if not Scott?"

So she didn't want to talk about her first declaration? Since he wasn't sure what to say in return, he let that go for now.

As to her brother, he tended to agree, but he wanted to hear her thoughts before he drew too many conclusions of his own. "Tell me why you're so sure it's him." If it turned out they were both right, someone would have a lot of explaining to do.

She turned to face him. "If Scott faked his own death, he had to have had a really good reason. If that reason still exists, it's possible he can't come forward yet, but of course, he'd want to protect me anyway. There's no way he'd let me be hurt if he could stop it."

Brand took yet another turn and the paved road narrowed to a rough gravel lane as it led to the inherited farm where Maxi and Miles now lived. "If you believe all that, then you also have to believe he knew that Ross Moran kidnapped you." And he had done nothing. "Why else would he worry about the man being near you, unless he knew he was a kidnapper?"

"Ross said he did a job for Scott and never got paid. If Scott didn't pay him, he had to have a good reason."

"So we can assume that he knows Ross personally." Scott would have known the danger existed, but he hadn't insulated Sahara from it.

In Brand's view, that was unforgivable.

For only a second, Sahara considered that. "Maybe Scott just found out about the kidnapping. Maybe—"

From a cornfield on the passenger's side, a beat-up truck barreled out, engine revving at breakneck speed.

Cursing, Brand thrust out an arm to pin Sahara back in her seat, then hit the gas, steering one-handed as he attempted to avoid a collision.

He didn't quite make it.

Deliberately, the truck clipped the back of her car. The wheels lost traction on the loose gravel. They fishtailed wildly, bumped in and out of the ditch before Brand brought the car to a jarring halt in the middle of the road.

He glanced in the rearview mirror; he knew Justice wasn't far behind, but he didn't yet see him.

The truck, engine still revving, filled his rearview mirror.

"Call Justice if you can."

Sahara, wide-eyed, scrambled to grab her phone. Her purse had spilled to the floor and it took her a frantic few seconds to locate it.

"Tell him we're riding like hell to the house, so if he doesn't catch up, that's why." Just as Brand finished, the truck lunged forward, spitting gravel and filling the air with dust.

Vaguely aware of Sahara talking low and fast, Brand stepped on the gas and sped away. He concentrated on staying ahead of the truck and on the country road, despite the sharp twists and turns.

Seeing a big curve ahead, he went faster, saying to Sahara, "Fuck this." They'd never make it to the house without another incident. He had to act now. "When I get out, you slide over behind the wheel."

"Brand!"

"Anything happens, you drive on. Do you understand me?"

"I won't leave you," she shouted, her tone panicked, her expression appalled.

"You will, because I can't do shit if I have to worry about you. Now promise me, damn it."

She drew a shuddering breath. "Okay."

He jerked the car to the side of the road, slammed it into Park and stepped out—his gun already in his hand.

The truck skidded around the corner. The driver spotted him taking aim in the middle of the road, and swerved in surprise before slamming on the brakes.

Brand fired. His first shot hit the grille of the truck. The second caught the hood and the third destroyed a tire.

To his surprise, the chickenshits immediately drove into a field in a giant U-turn and ran off.

Apparently a direct confrontation hadn't been on the agenda.

With the sunshine pouring through their windshield and highlighting both their faces, he'd gotten a good look at them.

They were the same men he'd pounded on when he'd found them talking about Sahara after locking her in a basement. Men who worked with Ross Moran.

So much for the bastard not hurting her.

He watched until he couldn't see the truck anymore, then turned back to Sahara's car. She was behind the wheel, the car in gear and her foot on the brake.

It reassured him that she had listened and was ready to react. Now he knew he could trust her to be reasonable when necessary. Keeping an eye on the road, Brand headed to the driver's side.

Sahara immediately put the car in Park. Eyes sparking and with a slight tremor to her voice, she climbed out, shouting, "Don't you *ever* do that again!"

Bemused, Brand murmured, "So much for being reasonable."

When she faced him defiantly, Brand sucked in his breath.

"Damn." Until that moment, he hadn't realized that she'd hit her head. A thin trail of blood cut down her forehead, across one eyebrow, then along her temple. It came from a swelling lump on the right side of her forehead. "You're hurt!"

Mouth tight, she blinked at him. "That sounds like an accusation." She thrust a finger at his chest. "I can't help it that my head bumped the window. It's fine."

"You're not fine, damn it." He pulled off his shirt and reached for her. "You're bleeding."

She took a swift step back. "Don't you dare soil your shirt! We're already going to be late getting to the party. I don't want you showing up shirtless."

Incredulous, Brand stared at her. Adrenaline still pumped through his blood, and he could barely focus around the rage burning through him. "It's not a party," he gritted out, "and we're heading to the hospital to have you checked." Again, he reached for her.

She bumped into the open door. Holding up a hand,

she said, "I have tissues in the car so I don't need your shirt, and we're *not* going to the hospital. If I tell you I'm fine, then I'm fine."

Brand lifted her chin, winced at the expanding bruise and made a decision. "I'm afraid I'll have to pull the boss card."

With a gasp, she asked, "To insist on the hospital? *No.*"

"We agreed—"

"I want to go to the party. I *really* do. Why can't you just trust me when I say that I'm okay?"

It wasn't a damned party, and she was hurt, but her blue eyes pleaded with him. He wasn't a big enough dick to insist when she'd obviously been looking forward to a day out.

Against his better judgment, he said, "You'll tell me if you start to feel sick, if your head hurts or if you get dizzy?"

"Yes, I promise."

He blew out a breath. "I do trust you, so if you say you're not hurt that bad, I'll take your word for it."

"Thank you." She smiled now that she'd gotten her way. "I actually have a first aid kit in the trunk. I just need a bandage or something."

Or something. "Remember, if you start to feel bad in any way, we're going."

"Sure. Whatever."

Thrusting a hand into his hair, he growled with impotent frustration. She was the most infuriating, unique, incredible woman...

Just then Justice came around the corner, saw them and pulled up at the side of the road.

He whistled when he got out. "Damn, Sahara. You okay?"

Happy now that she'd gotten her way, she all but sang, "Yes, of course," and went around to the passenger side to get the tissues while Brand opened the trunk.

"She bumped her head," Brand explained to Justice, watching as Fallon hurried to join Sahara. "I wanted to take her to the hospital—"

"And she refused." Justice nodded. "Yeah, Sahara isn't a wimp, but she is god-awful stubborn. It'd probably require a severed limb for her to willingly go."

Another surge of anger cut through him. "Probably. Help me keep an eye on her, okay?"

"You bet."

"Did you see the truck?" Brand found the kit and went around to the passenger side.

"Driving like a bat out of hell, one tire blown. I'd have given chase but—"

"You have Fallon with you."

"Yeah." Justice added, "Plus I wasn't sure what had happened with you two, whether or not you needed help."

While Brand used a premoistened antiseptic swab to clean away the blood from her face, Sahara detailed the "adventure" with enthusiasm. "I was so impressed with Brand's driving. He's as good as I am, and you know I don't give that compliment lightly."

Justice snorted. "You're a lunatic. I'm still traumatized from the time you decided we were being chased."

She grinned. "I thought we were."

"Bull. You just wanted to show off."

Her grin widened even more. "You could be right."

Brand had difficulty breathing, so he sure as hell couldn't grin. She was hurt, bruised and bleeding. The attacks were adding up. No one knew when the next might happen, or how much worse it might be.

How could she keep joking?

Fallon, Justice's fiancée, joined them, her soft eyes concerned. "At least you didn't get much blood in your hair."

"True. Good thing I'd put it in a braid." She looked down at herself. "Unfortunately, I did get some on my shirt, but it's dark so I should be able to rinse it out."

Already the bleeding had stopped, but Brand saw that the swelling was worse. "We need to get some ice on this."

"We're not far from the house," she said. "I'll take care of it then." She stared up at Brand. "Is it colorful?"

"Very."

"Is that why you look so grim?"

The urge to chase down the bastards and annihilate them scorched any efforts at being pleasant. "We were damn near T-boned on purpose, driven off the road and you got hurt. What do you think would have happened if they'd gotten to you?"

With a small butterfly bandage now on her head, she snuggled against him, saying soothingly, "I knew you wouldn't let that happen."

Did she really have that much faith in him—or was it that nothing ever truly rattled her? He couldn't say, but he crushed her close, uncaring that Justice rolled his eyes and Fallon smiled.

Against his chest, Sahara asked, "Is my car hurt?"

"Yeah, but it can be repaired."

"I know." She patted his back. "You recognized them, too?"

"The same bozos I stomped when I—"

"Rescued me." She leaned back to grin at him. "And this time was no less daring."

"Sahara," he said with exasperation. The last thing he wanted was for her to romanticize the whole thing.

She turned to Justice. "I wish you could have seen him step out to the middle of the road, legs braced apart, arms straight as he took aim. Very Dirty-Harryish." She shivered dramatically. "Made my heart pound, it was so sexy."

"Yeah," Justice said, giving Brand a hard whack on the shoulder. "I bet that's exactly how he wants you to describe it."

The irony in his tone made Brand's ears hot. "Fuck off, Justice."

Both Sahara and Fallon laughed.

With everyone being ridiculous, it was another fifteen minutes before they finally arrived at the house.

Fall was especially in evidence here. Maxi had inherited a small house on a beautiful piece of land, surrounded by an assortment of trees now displaying various shades of red, orange and yellow. Sunlight glittered through the leaves and off the large pond. Dozens of feral cats perched around the property, watching their arrival.

Justice had obviously called ahead because the crew had congregated to greet them. Miles already had an ice pack ready, and his fiancée, Maxi, led Sahara directly to a full lounge chair where she and Catalina, Leese's wife, insisted she sit.

Good luck with that, Brand wanted to say. He'd be willing to bet Sahara wouldn't stay down for more than a minute or two. The woman didn't understand her own lack of strength.

Catalina served Sahara a tall, cool drink. Together, the women huddled around her. They were a mix of styles, with Catalina's long light brown hair, blue eyes and casual flair for sloppy comfort, Fallon's shoulder-length dark hair and darker eyes with more tailored clothes, and Maxi's long blond hair and cutting-edge fashion.

And then there was Sahara, different from each of them, a self-proclaimed shark—who at the moment appeared overwhelmed.

Brand noticed the slightly dumbfounded expression on her face, and found his first smile. To Leese, he asked, "Was this your idea?"

Leese nodded in satisfaction. "I might've given the women a nudge, but you know how they are. It didn't take much."

"Nurturing," Miles said. "Every one of them."

All but Sahara. She was a caring person, but she wasn't much of a coddler.

He wondered how she'd be with kids. He recalled the assignment she'd had early on protecting the little girl. She'd kill for a child, no problem, and he knew she'd raise a daughter or son to be strong and independent. That was a lot, whether she was into kissing boo-boos or not.

"She'll tell any one of us to back off," Leese said, "but she tries to be nicer to the ladies."

Justice laughed. "I hadn't noticed that before, but you're right. Look at her taking aspirin from Fallon! If I tried that, she'd tell *me* to take them."

"Or ask you, in a very condescending voice, if you'd managed to hurt yourself," Miles said.

Brand watched her, how carefully she reacted with

the women, how stoic she was about her injury, and he knew he couldn't fight the inevitable.

He was in love.

It didn't surprise him; Sahara had been stealing his heart little by little ever since he'd met her.

The big question was what to do about it.

CHAPTER THIRTEEN

SAHARA FELT…NUMB. If the guys were trying to pin her down, she'd have already, gleefully, rebelled.

But it was the women, and she liked them all so much that she didn't want to inadvertently offend any of them by telling them to buzz off.

So while Brand and the other men were rapidly building a beautiful gazebo, she sat there like a useless lump in the lounge chair, cats all around her, an ice pack on her head, her drink constantly refilled, even a cushion under her feet…until she couldn't take it a second longer.

It was almost laughable that when she sat up and tossed aside the ice, all three women jumped toward her.

"Please," she said with a grin, "relax. You're scaring the cats." When Maxi inherited the farm, it came with dozens of feral cats, most of them not so wild anymore. Sahara hadn't been in the chair long before three of them had decided she'd make a comfortable place to snooze.

Of course, each of the other women also petted the felines. Maxi and Miles had gotten the animals spayed or neutered, vaccinated, and they were fed twice a day.

"You shouldn't be up," Fallon warned.

Sahara laughed. "Of course I should. I'm not great with idle time."

"But you're hurt," Catalina said.

"Not really. Just a bump." She stood and looked at

each of them. A gentle breeze stirred the colorful leaves in the trees, prompting several to twirl gracefully to the ground. She loved fall.

She didn't love being treating like an invalid.

"I appreciate the concern, I really do. I hesitated to say that you're overdoing the mollycoddling because I didn't want to sound unappreciative or something. Then I realized that just because you're women doesn't mean you're fainthearted. It doesn't mean your feelings are fragile, right? After all, you're strong women." She thrust up a fist in a sign of unity. "And as strong women, you know that being female doesn't make us more delicate than men."

"Actually," Fallon said, "I'm definitely more delicate than Justice."

Catalina snorted. "An elephant is more delicate than him."

Maxi laughed when Fallon swatted at Cat.

"But you're still just as strong," Sahara insisted.

"As Justice?" Fallon quirked a brow. "Not likely."

"She means emotionally," Maxi said. "And in theory, I agree. But when I was having all my trouble here at the farm, it was awfully nice to lean on Miles."

"And I'm sure he's leaned on you, too."

She shrugged. "Maybe. Most times he's so confident that he focuses more on protecting than any 'leaning.'"

Hmm. Sahara gave that some thought and realized that Brand was the same. He wanted her to lean on him, to let him protect her and care for her, but despite all the turmoil with Becky, he didn't reciprocate. He needed to talk to her about his feelings so she could show that she understood. Maybe once he did that, he'd understand her equal need to help, and then she could tell him the different ways she was trying to make Becky less of a burden.

Seeing that the women weren't understanding, Sahara sighed, then propped her hands on her hips. "My point is that I'm fine, and I want to think you're all grounded enough that you won't be offended when I say enough is enough."

They each watched her with varying degrees of concern.

It was so ridiculous, she almost laughed. "I'm going to give Brand hell, because if we'd stopped to get food and drinks, we might have missed those morons who tried to run us off the road." She'd already explained every detail of the attack to the women. They'd been duly horrified.

"Food and drinks for what?" Maxi asked.

"Here." When Maxi gave her a blank look, Sahara explained, "I didn't want to come empty-handed. I know that's rude, but Brand wouldn't stop."

"Oh please, you're invited guests! Besides, good friends are welcome anytime, no gifts needed."

Good friends. Struck by that possibility, Sahara asked, "You mean Brand?"

She shrugged. "Sure. And you."

Catalina chimed in. "I know you're the boss and everything, but you're still one of us."

"A significant other, she means," Fallon said.

Was she a significant other? "Brand said we're in a relationship."

"Duh," Catalina said. "Was that in question?"

"Justice said he's never seen Brand act like he does with you."

Maxi nodded. "Miles says that usually he's pretty

distant with women. I mean, not physically distant, but it's different with you. You two seem close."

"Connected," Fallon added.

Only a minute before, Sahara had been determined to join the men in building the gazebo. She'd wanted to hammer something, damn it. She'd wanted to prove she was strong and capable, not a woman who wilted over a bump.

Now, though, she decided she'd rather stay right where she was, chatting with the women. The conversation proved insightful. She'd love to hear more about how Brand was different with her from how he was with other women.

Mind made up, she reseated herself in the lounge chair, and even put her feet back on the cushion.

The cats took that as an invitation and curled up against her again, one on her lap, one against her hip, one by her knees.

It turned into a very enjoyable afternoon, different for sure, given the lazy way she sat around talking, but still very fun. She couldn't imagine a prettier setting. Even being overrun with cats, multiple birds flitted in and out of the trees. The day remained mild, sunny, with just enough of a breeze to tease over her skin.

Watching Brand work was never a hardship. She loved seeing the muscles in his back flex, how his biceps bulged, how those delicious abs tightened. Unlike the other guys, who sometimes got scruffy but eventually shaved, Brand sported the short, trimmed beard and mustache. Sahara found she liked the rugged look.

She especially liked the way his stubble tickled her skin when he kissed her in various sensitive places.

She had to admit, she had some serious hunks working for her. Each one of them was gorgeous in their own way, but in her opinion, Brand was by far the handsomest.

Around noon, the men came up to the house for food. While they washed up, Catalina grilled hamburgers and hotdogs, and Fallon and Maxi carried out trays of side dishes and drinks. Sahara was about to help with that when a message dinged on her phone.

Brand stood nearby guzzling water—shirtless. But then, all the guys were shirtless now. Most were barefoot, too, since part of the work on the gazebo required standing in the pond.

Brand looked her way as she got out her phone.

Given the stark expression on his face, she wasn't the only one concerned that it could be another anonymous text.

She unlocked her phone…and saw a photo from Becky. Brand's mother sat on her new love seat, and she looked so happy that Sahara was filled with pride.

"What the hell?"

She jumped when Brand took the phone from her limp hand. He had approached so silently, she hadn't been aware of him looking over her shoulder, and now dread filled her.

Trying not to appear as guilty as she felt, she said, "It's Becky. Look at her smile. I think her attitude is improving."

For far too long, Brand studied the photo in foreboding silence. Finally, his expression cold, he said, "I take it this was your doing?"

She barely resisted the urge to wince. "Which part?"

"All of it." His jaw clenched as he stared down at her. "The hairdo, makeup…the couch."

Oh, this wasn't going well at all. She swallowed down her unease and tried for a bright tone. "Well, I did lend her a stylist so she could refresh her appearance after her long illness. It always makes a woman feel better to look her best."

No reply.

Normally she could outwait the best of them, but this was Brand, and the guilt was coming on strong and fast. She glanced around and saw that everyone had clustered near the long picnic table piled with food—including the horde of cats.

Keeping her voice low, she said, "I wanted to help."

There was no understanding in his tone when he said, "I asked you not to get involved."

No, he'd flat-out *told* her not to, thus the guilt. "You said I couldn't take her shopping, so I didn't."

"Don't play with my words."

Worse and worse. "All right."

"She's not in the hospital bed." He glanced at the phone, then gestured with it. "She's on some froufrou love seat thing."

Sahara would have been offended by that description, but it was rather froufrou with the floral pattern and overstuffed cushions. "I, um…" Why was it so hard to say? Sahara stiffened her spine. "I bought it for her. I figured if I could get her out of the bed—"

"It wasn't your job to get her out of bed."

He didn't raise his voice, but she felt bludgeoned by his quiet anger all the same.

"Not my job, no, but I—"

"Anything else?" He continued to study the picture. "The clothes she's wearing?"

"I sent those to her…" Probably best to come clean,

she decided. "Five outfits in all, I believe, more if she mixes and matches them."

When his icy gaze finally came to her, he zeroed in on her bandaged head and his mouth flattened.

He was too subdued for the anger she knew he had to feel, the anger she could *see*. Suddenly it hit her why.

Slowly she stood. Guilty or not, she wouldn't let him treat her like a wilting flower. "Oh no, you don't. Don't hold back just because I got a bump on the head. I keep telling you I'm fine." She held out her arms. "If you want to blast me for overstepping, have at it. I won't break."

A strange, turbulent emotion narrowed his dark eyes.

He looked so explosive that she quickly added, "My only request is that you do so in private."

After a long, silent moment, he smirked. "Because you're the boss and you don't want your underlings to see you catching hell?"

Damn, he made her feel small. She lifted her chin. "Actually, because they're friends. At least I think they are. The ladies said we were, so I assumed—"

He laughed, but it wasn't a nice sound.

Before she'd met Brand, she seldom suffered uncertainty or angst over a decision. She'd always pushed forward with confidence.

Now, though, it seemed those unfamiliar feelings leveled her on a regular basis.

Yes, she had done things he'd asked her not to but it had felt right at the time because she knew, in the long run, it would help him.

Because she liked to face things head-on, Sahara released a slow breath and admitted softly, "Every time I turn around, I find myself in another impossible position with you."

Maybe it was the resignation in her tone, but Brand's gaze sharpened on her. "What the hell is that supposed to mean?"

She rolled one shoulder. "I wanted you to work for me, and I also wanted to date you. Big conflict, right?"

"You understand my position on that."

Yes—he thought she was too bossy, especially when he preferred to be the boss. "Then there's Ross Moran."

"He sent his buddies after you again today."

"I know." She was eternally grateful that they hadn't gotten to her, and that Brand hadn't been hurt. "But I still need to talk to him to get info on my brother, and you just want to annihilate him."

Agitated, Brand folded his arms. "He's still breathing, isn't he? I can show restraint when necessary."

She picked up a cat, holding it in her arms like a baby, taking comfort from its rumbling purr. "Now this." Her head started to pound but she didn't think it had anything to do with hitting the windshield, not when her chest also felt tight, and her throat was getting thick.

If she didn't know better, she might have thought she was choked up.

She kissed the cat's head, nuzzling the soft fur. "You won't give me a chance to explain, but I was trying to help with your mother."

"I told you to stay out of it."

"I know." It bothered her that she'd upset him. "The thing is, I'm not good at staying out of situations, especially not if I think I can help." She looked up at him, owning her flaws, admitting the truth. "I'm the type of person who is going to dive in. That's just me, Brand." And it would probably be one more thing he disliked. "I'm sorry."

He ran a hand over the back of his neck, checked that no one was close, then pinned her with a heated stare. "As long as my mother remains sour and difficult, I can resent helping her. But if she starts showing appreciation, then I'm going to feel like an ass for being so surly about it."

Her eyes widened. "You want to resent her?"

"After a lifetime, it's what I'm used to." He looked away. "And she doesn't deserve anything more."

"No, she doesn't." But Brand did. Softening her voice in deference to his mood, Sahara said, "I wasn't thinking about her when I decided to—"

"Interfere?"

Helpless to deny that, she shrugged. "Yes."

Hindsight was a bitch, but seeing things from Brand's perspective, Sahara had to admit that she'd badly miscalculated. She didn't blame him for being angry.

She again said, "I'm sorry." Truthfully, she didn't think she was a bad person, but maybe she had to do more introspection. She would better accomplish that on her own, away from outside influences.

Away from Brand.

She was just about to explain that to him when her phone dinged again.

Brand glanced at it and one brow climbed high. "Your anonymous tipster this time."

She squeezed into his side so she could read the message as well.

Don't go out alone. It's not safe. Trust no one.

"CRYPTIC BASTARD," BRAND GROWLED.

Sahara glared up at him. "That's probably my brother."

He didn't care if it was the pope. Sahara deserved a direct reply, not all this cat and mouse bullshit where neither of them knew what to think.

It enraged him when he thought of the danger surrounding her. She'd been kidnapped by a goon bold enough to approach her at an exclusive party, had shots fired near her and been nearly run off the road.

Brand had a feeling the danger was ramping up rather than receding, and it left him helpless to ensure her safety, especially when she appeared so cavalier about it.

That alone made him more disgruntled than usual, but add to that the text from his mother...

Sahara had made Becky smile.

How long had it been since he'd seen his mother happy? Probably...never.

Over the years, whenever she'd come by, it hadn't been to visit him but to squeeze money out of Ann. Most times, she barely noticed her son, and when she did notice him, it wasn't to share a soft word of affection or to show any caring. Not once had she given even a hint of regret for letting him go.

She'd seen him only as a tool she could use to her own advantage.

In fact, she'd never sought him out until her cardiac arrest. Then, with no one else that she could turn to, she'd suddenly remembered that she had a son.

He didn't like being bitter; it made him feel like the sulky, hurt kid he'd once been, yet he couldn't stop the corrosive resentment from eating away at him like acid.

Sahara had pampered Becky, when she wasn't the type to do that. She'd gotten Becky to smile, when Brand thought his mother didn't know how.

Sahara was fucking *friendly* with her, even though the woman had abandoned him.

Screwed up as it might be, that somehow felt like a betrayal.

He wanted to unleash his frustrated anger, but he was at a disadvantage. Despite the brave front she put on, Sahara was hurt and he didn't want to exacerbate her discomfort.

"Since you think this is your brother, I assume you'll follow his instructions and show more caution?"

She chewed her lip. "Scott could be in trouble. He might need me."

"Un-fucking-believable."

She scowled. "You know I don't like that word."

"I don't like you intruding into my private business, but that didn't stop you, did it?"

The careless insult made her wince, but a second later she squared off with him. Pointing at the phone, she snapped, "Then maybe you should remember that this is *my* private business."

Huh. She'd certainly turned that one around on him. "You're determined to get yourself killed, aren't you?"

Sahara snorted. "You keep thinking I'm an idiot when I'm not. I know how to make good decisions, and I will, but I don't need you or my brother dictating to me about when and where I go or what I can do."

So it wasn't just him she'd defy, but Scott, too?

A little floored, Brand stared at her. That wasn't at all what he'd expected. Sure, he knew Sahara defined independence, but he'd somehow gotten the impression she worshiped her brother and fell into line over his every request. "I would've bet money you did whatever big brother told you to."

She sent him a mocking smile. "Be glad that I don't, because if you read the text again, you'll see that he also ordered me to trust no one." She swept out a hand. "But I trust everyone here today, *you* most of all."

Her statement proved a balm, helping him to calm his anger. Suddenly he felt like an ass for his reaction over Becky. "If you mean that, then—"

She interrupted to say, "In return, you have to trust me to know what I'm doing." Caution crept into her expression. "That is, unless you're so mad about that business with your mother that our relationship is ready to crash and burn."

Oh no, he wouldn't leave her safety to anyone else. "You're stuck with me for now."

She scowled. "How long is 'for now'?"

Did she have to challenge him at every turn? Running a hand over his face, Brand knew he needed reinforcements, so he turned to the group.

"No," Sahara hissed, already guessing what he'd do.

As if he hadn't heard her protest, he called out, "Sahara got another text."

Heads lifted, frowns fell into place and as one, the small group started toward them.

Sahara shot him an accusing frown. "That was a dirty trick."

Brand cocked a brow. "You want to complain to me when you've been sneaking behind my back with my mother?"

"Well…" She relented. "Not if you put it like that."

"There's no other way to put it." She briefly closed her eyes, and Brand didn't know if it was from remorse or pain in her head. He'd feel a lot better about things if she would have agreed to go to the hospital. "We'll talk about it later."

"Thanks for nothing."

Now she was pissed? Well, misery loved company, Brand told himself. Eventually, they'd work it all out.

When Leese and the others reached them, Brand stepped back and watched the confusion, fury and insistence unfold.

Odds were, the guys wouldn't be able to curb her recklessness—but the women might.

He was counting on it.

HOURS LATER, A little sunburned but in better control of his temper, Brand let them into the suite. They'd gotten home without incident, but then, they'd formed a small caravan, with Justice and Fallon in the lead, Sahara and him in the middle, and Leese and Catalina in the rear. Everyone had been alert, wary of another attack, especially on the country roads.

Once they'd reached the highway, they'd all relaxed a bit while still remaining vigilant.

The others had followed them right up to the parking lot of the Body Armor agency, then waited until he and Sahara got in the door.

For her part, Sahara was subdued, which in itself was alarming since *subdued* wasn't a word normally used to describe her. He couldn't tell if she was angry, worried or if maybe her head hurt.

She'd been through so much in such a short time, and still didn't crumble. Under the circumstances, losing some of her sparkle was understandable.

"I'm going to take a shower," she said on her way past him.

Brand gently caught her elbow. She paused, but didn't face him.

"Hey. Are you okay?" He drew her around, and with two fingers lifted her chin so she had no choice but to meet his gaze. "Does your head hurt?"

She gave a brief, restrained smile. "Not really."

He coasted his fingertips along her delicate jaw. "Is there anything I can get you?"

For a second, she looked devastated, then she stepped against him, her arms around him and her head on his chest. Voice muffled against him, she asked, "Are you still mad at me?"

Never would Brand believe that it was his anger alone that had her so submissive. In most instances, Sahara would just fight back, not retreat. "My relationship with my mother is complicated."

"That's a nonanswer." She leaned back to see him again. "And like I already told you, my relationship with Scott is also complicated. Lately it seems my entire life is complicated. What if I wanted you to stay out of it?"

It struck him that her feelings were hurt. "You feel like I've cut you out?"

Disgusted, she shoved away and gave him her back, her arms hugged around her. "How can you cut me out when you've never let me in?"

"Now wait a minute." She was twisting everything around. "We're talking about you, not me."

"Always, I know." She looked over her shoulder. "I had to twist your arm to take me along to meet your parents and Becky."

He wanted to say he'd hesitated because he'd known she would interfere. But as she turned, the look on her face stopped him. "We've been a little busy, if you'll re-call. I couldn't see confusing things even more."

As if she'd hoped for something different, she briefly closed her eyes, then opened them again and forced a small smile. "Yes, it has been chaotic."

"Exactly." He started to close the space between them. Suddenly it felt like more than just a few feet.

Sahara stepped back, and that stopped him—just as she'd intended. After a deep breath, she said, "I'm not sure I can change."

He didn't understand her or this uncertain mood, but he knew one thing for sure. "You don't need to change."

"But we'll keep butting heads if I don't." She bit her bottom lip. "I don't know what to do."

For Brand, it felt like he was fighting for something very important, so he hoped he got the words right. And fuck the distance. He took two big steps to reach her and drew her against him. Hugging her, he whispered, "You don't need to do anything, babe. We're in a relationship, and sometimes that requires adjustment."

Her hands fisted in his shirt. "I'm not sure I like the idea of constantly having to adjust."

"Why not?" Her hair and skin smelled of the sun-shine and fresh outdoors. They'd gone from him being annoyed to her being distant—and yet he felt lust stir-ring. He couldn't be near Sahara without wanting her. With a grin, he said, "I've sure as hell had to adjust."

"You? Why would you have to?" Again she pushed back to see him. "You're perfect as you are."

A rueful laugh took him by surprise. "Perfect? God, Sahara, I'm so far from perfect, half the time I don't even know what I'm doing."

"You always know what you're doing."

He shook his head.

"And I used to, until lately."

"Until me?" Damn, he hated that idea. Brand cupped her face and bent his knees to look right into her eyes. "Let's agree that we've both blundered a little, okay? I know it's an uncomfortable feeling, but I'm not giving you up."

"You're not?"

"Hell, no." Set on convincing her, he took her mouth in a firm kiss. Sahara sank against him, returning the kiss with urgency. As he eased up, he whispered, "It's been a long day, so how about we draw some guidelines and going forward, we'll both do our best to stick to them."

Her eyes searched his. "And if we don't?"

She meant if she didn't, so Brand kissed her again. "Then we'll each try harder to understand."

Very slowly, a smile curled her mouth. "In that case, would you like to shower with me?"

CHAPTER FOURTEEN

SAHARA AWOKE BEFORE BRAND. She sighed as she nuzzled against the side of his broad, warm chest. Her right hand rested over a hair-dusted pec and, careful not to wake him, she let her fingers tease through the crisp hair.

He smelled incredible, a scent unique to Brand.

Even in sleep he held her close, his strong arm around her. Brand slept on his back, the covers down around his waist. She was on her side, tucked against him, one leg over his, the inside of her knee against his groin.

They were both naked.

Last night had been beyond amazing. Sahara didn't know if it was the excitement of the day or their personal conflict, but Brand had been especially attentive, leaving no part of her untouched. He'd been in a take-charge mood, a little dominant, and she'd loved every second of it. He had a way of issuing sensual orders that stole her breath and heightened her anticipation. Even before he'd thrust into her, she'd been on the verge of release, but he'd held back, content to watch her climax…then he'd made that happen two more times before he finally let himself go.

It was no wonder she'd awakened with a smile in place.

Even more important than the incredible sex was that Brand hadn't let her ruin things. He'd taken her doubts and somehow reassured her without letting her off the hook for meddling in his private business. Now, after a good night's sleep and a new perspective, Sahara was so glad.

They'd still have to talk about Becky, but at least she felt he'd listen to her explanations and maybe give her ideas a chance to work.

She also thought about his denial at being perfect. Without the glum attitude of yesterday, she could think about that more realistically.

Brand was right; he wasn't perfect.

Suddenly he stirred, his arm tightening around her in a brief hug before he even opened his eyes.

Sounding sexy and sleepy, he rumbled, "Good morning, gorgeous."

"Morning." She half crawled over him, her elbows on his chest. "Sleep well?"

"After the way you wore me out? Yeah."

"Me?" She gave him a laughing kiss. "I'm the one who was tortured with orgasms."

"Tortured, huh?" His lashes lifted and his dark, smoky eyes met hers. "I love watching you come, Sahara."

"In that case, feel free to do a repeat whenever you want."

His hands slid down her back to her bottom, and she quickly found herself completely over him, her legs trapped between his. "I don't suppose we have time this morning?"

She glanced at the clock, then let out a sigh of disappointment. "Lucky I'm the boss, because I'm already running late."

He lightly touched the bandage on her head. "I'm sure everyone will understand under the circumstances."

Sahara frowned. "I thought about what you said, and came to the conclusion that you're right."

Wariness entered his eyes. "About what?"

"You not being perfect." She gave him a quick kiss so he wouldn't be insulted. "Case in point is your insistence that a little bump on the head is a big deal. You know if it had been Justice, you wouldn't have given it a thought."

His gaze drifted down to her exposed cleavage, exaggerated by the way her breasts squashed against his chest. "Justice was a fighter. He's had plenty of head wounds and knows how to judge if it's serious or not."

"You think Justice has more sense than me?"

"Justice might act goofy, but he's not. Besides, this is about experience, not intelligence."

She gave that some thought, and decided to let it go. "You also accused me of being bossy, but I think you're even bossier."

He smiled. "When it comes to keeping you safe, you bet." He had both hands back on her rear, gently kneading. "And for the record, I like your bossiness. Your strength and independence are both sexy as hell."

Sahara reared up more to give him a look of incredulity. "You definitely made it sound like a complaint."

"For me to work for you, yeah. But not for this." He pressed a growing erection to her belly. "Not for a relationship."

"Oh." It was hard to concentrate when she felt him full and hard, throbbing beneath her. "Well, I think you're a little too autocratic."

"You would, since you like doing things your own

way without answering to anyone. But that's what relationships are, honey. Give and take."

"What are you going to give?"

He smiled. "How about we have this discussion over coffee?"

So what he'd give would require a whole discussion? "Count me in." She couldn't wait to hear it. "I'll get the coffee started and then meet you in the kitchen in fifteen minutes." She scrambled off the bed and headed for the bathroom without waiting for a reply.

When she emerged a few minutes later, her face washed and her teeth brushed, Brand was no longer in the bed. She pulled on his discarded shirt from yesterday and went to the kitchen to make the coffee.

Back in her bedroom, she chose an outfit to wear and quickly dressed, stepped into her shoes and contained her hair in a long, sleek ponytail fastened at the nape of her neck.

She applied her usual makeup in under five minutes, then headed to the kitchen. With smug satisfaction, she saw that she'd beat Brand in getting ready.

Yes, she was competitive, and whenever possible she tried to prove that she wasn't the stereotypical female who needed hours to prepare for her day.

She'd just filled her coffee cup when her cell phone rang. For a heartbeat she stared at it, then at the doorway to see if Brand would come charging in. He'd gotten decidedly protective about the anonymous messages she'd received.

He didn't appear, so she assumed he hadn't heard the ring.

Finally ungluing her feet from the floor, Sahara lunged forward and glanced at the screen. It was Enoch.

Anxious, she snatched up the phone and swiped her thumb across the screen. "Enoch, good morning. Everything okay?"

"Good morning, Sahara."

Recognizing something in his tone, she asked breathlessly, "What's the matter?"

He paused, then gave a short laugh. "I never could keep anything from you."

"Why would you want to?" Again, she looked to ensure Brand hadn't approached without her notice. She lowered her voice to keep from drawing his attention, in case he could hear her. "You're my bestie, Enoch. You can tell me anything."

"It's just that I'd prefer you not get your hopes up... or do anything crazy."

"It's about Scott, isn't it?" Her brother was the only topic that could get her hopes up, or make her do crazy things.

She hadn't yet had a chance to update Enoch on her weekend. She would have done that first thing this morning.

After doing a happy twirl across the kitchen floor, she said, "Tell me!"

"It *might* be Scott. I would have explained when you reached the office, but Brand usually escorts you down and then you have a meeting right after, so I figured I'd call..."

"You're killing me, Enoch." She felt like she might jump out of her skin in anticipation. "What is it?"

"Your PI called me. I didn't understand why at first, but he had a message to pass along and he was instructed that no one else should know."

"Meaning he didn't want to chance calling me directly?"

"Supposedly an order that came from Scott. But since the PI has never spoken with Scott, he can't say for sure, and that means you have to be extra, extra cautious. Promise me, Sahara."

"A message?" From the day her brother had gone missing, she'd had a PI looking for him. Every day she hoped for a clue, any clue, that proved Scott was still around. "What message?"

He spilled everything in a rush. "Someone claiming to be Scott called and said he'd been aware of the investigation for a while, and apparently had been dodging detection, but now he feels he has to reach out to you. He wants you to meet him tonight."

Already planning on how she'd make it happen, she demanded, "Where?"

"Promise me, first, or I won't tell you anything else. I need your word that you'll be careful."

"Of course. 'Careful' is my middle name."

"No," he corrected with exaggerated patience. "'Insanely reckless and impetuous' is your middle name. Especially where Scott is concerned."

Sahara squeezed the phone and frowned. "What is the message?"

Enoch groaned. "The person claiming to be Scott wants to meet with you privately. Just you and no one else. He said he doesn't know these new bodyguards you've brought on board, and you've all but retired the established guards."

Sahara went on defense without thinking about it. "The men I hired are *better* in every single way. It figures that Scott would second-guess me! Usually I concede to his judgment, but not this time."

"If it turns out it really is Scott, you can tell him all

about it. But my concern is that he wants you to come alone."

Since she totally believed Scott was alive and arranging to reconnect with her, she waved off Enoch's worry. "Where?"

Enoch sighed. "I don't know exactly, but he said it's where the two of you used to go to talk."

She didn't have to think about it at all; she knew exactly where he meant. "It's definitely Scott!"

"You know where he means?"

"Yes, of course." They'd often gone to the quiet spot near the river behind the privacy fence of her parents' property.

"Tell Brand."

"Are you nuts? Brand would flip out, and then he'd get all macho and protective and insist on going along, and since Scott doesn't know or trust him—"

"He should trust him because *you* trust him."

Unfortunately, her relationship with her big brother had never worked that way. She assumed he would always think of her as his little sister first, and a responsible, intelligent adult second. "I'm sure I can convince him, especially once he meets the guys, but until then—"

From behind her, Brand said, "Until then, you're going nowhere without me."

Sahara froze. Damn and blast, how had she forgotten to watch for Brand? She'd gotten so excited about seeing Scott again, about having his survival confirmed, that she'd been oblivious to everything else.

Through the phone, Enoch whispered, "Brand walked in?"

"Yes."

"I'll let you go."

He disconnected before she could stop him.

And still Sahara didn't move. She kept the phone to her ear, her thoughts rushing first one way, then another, as she tried to figure out how to explain.

Finally, deciding she'd just insist that she was the boss and this was her very personal business, she lowered the phone and turned to Brand with an artificial smile.

The smile vanished when she saw that he was on his own phone.

She heard him say "Leese? Can you get everyone together? Yeah, real important." His assessing gaze met Sahara's. "Your boss is planning to sneak out on her own to meet someone who may or may not be her brother." He nodded, his smile grim, and said, "My thoughts exactly. Right. I'll see you in an hour."

ENOCH GAVE HER a look of sympathy as she entered his office with Brand and found Miles, Justice and Leese all waiting. They stared at her with mixed concern and resolve.

"Don't you all have assignments?" she groused.

"Rearranged," Enoch explained. "Leese has ninety minutes, Miles and Justice have two hours."

"And Brand," she remarked in a saccharine tone, "has all the time in the world to butt in."

"That's what I'm willing to take," Brand said. "Your sarcasm."

Realizing that he'd harked back to the discussion they should have had in the kitchen, she made a face.

"And I'm willing to give you all the leeway you need—as long as you don't endanger yourself."

Which meant no leeway at all.

"In turn," he continued, "you could try a little trust."

Seeing no hope for it, Sahara nodded. "You know I trust you."

"Thank you." To Enoch, Brand asked, "Got a conference room ready?"

"This way." Enoch led the small troop down a hall to a private boardroom that featured a long table and ten chairs, a wall of windows overlooking the river, and a full coffeepot with cups, cream and sugar already set out.

Brand stuck close to Sahara, following her as she headed to the farthest end.

Disgruntled, she said low, "We were supposed to be talking about Becky."

"Why? You agreed to try not to butt in, and I agreed to be understanding if you do." Unlike her, Brand seemed to be taking everything in stride, and his inexhaustible patience made her want to scream.

He pulled out a rolling chair at the head of the table for her, then took the seat beside her as the others chose chairs nearby at either side.

She mean-mugged them, these men who worked for her—men she now considered friends.

They smiled back.

Damn it, they were all so wonderful, how could she stay annoyed? She knew they meant well, but they didn't understand Scott. He'd run off again if she didn't follow his directions to the letter.

As if he'd read her mind, Justice said, "Aw, buck up, buttercup. We won't chase off your brother."

"We can be subtle," Leese added. "You know that, right?"

"And in case it isn't Scott," Miles explained, "we need to be there. You're not dumb, Sahara. If you looked at this objectively, you'd admit we're right."

Brand leaned forward, his forearms on the table, hands clasped together and expression serious. "It'll be okay, babe."

The stiffness left her spine. Her life had been so much less complicated before these big, lovable lugs had entered it, but she knew deep down she wouldn't trade them for the world.

"Enoch," she said to her hovering best friend and ace assistant, "would you mind getting pastries to go with the coffee?"

He smiled in relief, recognizing the request as a return to the norm. "I already did. I'll see if they've arrived yet." He left the room with a new jaunt to his stride.

"We'll wait for him," Leese said. "After all, he's the one who got the message, right?"

"From the PI, yes," she said. "But I could just call him directly—"

"No," Miles said. "That might tip off whoever contacted him—your brother or someone impersonating him. We didn't all sneak in here just to blow the element of surprise."

"Right." She should have thought of that. "How did you sneak in?" Enoch had told her they'd come into Body Armor in a way that no one would know they had congregated. She had to admit, she was curious.

"Catalina drove," Leese said. "Anyone could see her dropping me off near the parking garage entrance, but they wouldn't have seen Miles and Justice, who were ducked down in back and entered low when I opened the back door to grab a jacket."

Sahara nodded. "Very sneaky. I like it."

"Sneaky," Justice growled, "is you trying to go off without us."

She held up a hand. "I've already rethought that and of course you're right. I'm positive it *is* Scott, but on the tiny chance that it might not be, I agree I should have backup."

"Well, hallelujah," Leese said.

She turned to Brand. "I probably would have come to that conclusion on my own, so please don't gloat."

"Wouldn't think of it." His phone buzzed and he withdrew it to look at the screen, quieted it with a touch of a button, then put it back in his pocket.

Suspicion bloomed. "Who was that?"

Brand shook his head. "Not important."

Before she could question him further, Enoch reentered with a tray of donuts, Danish and muffins. While he served coffee and the snacks, Sahara studied Brand.

She half turned toward him, asking quietly, "Was that Becky?"

He snorted. "After all you gave her, odds are she'd contact you before me."

Feeling culpable all over again, Sahara looked down at her hands. "Then who—"

"So nosy," he said in a mildly teasing tone, surprising her. "Actually it was Drew Black from the SBC."

Her gaze shot to his, apprehension getting a stranglehold on her. She knew that Drew Black was the president of the mixed martial arts organization Supreme Battle Challenge, or SBC as it was widely known. "What did he want?"

Brand shrugged as if it didn't matter. "I assume the organization want an answer about the next fight. I've been putting them off for a while now."

Her chest tightened. Sahara knew she could lose him

to the sport he loved, but lately, what he wanted mattered more to her than what she wanted.

Of course, Leese overheard. "Have you made a decision?"

Both Miles and Justice tuned in, waiting for his reply.

Brand looked only at Sahara. "The fight they want me to take is in Japan. I'd have to start training now to be ready, and there wouldn't be much time for anything else. Those two things combined made the decision for me."

Sahara frowned, paying little attention to the buzz around her as Miles, Leese and Justice weighed in, discussing the other fighter, the venue, even the payout in the contract. She wanted Brand to sign on as a bodyguard, but she didn't want him to skip anything important to him.

He'd already been struggling with his self-imposed obligation to Becky, and she'd only added to that burden.

She cut through the conversation to ask, "You're worried about me, aren't you?"

His dark gaze fixed on her. "Very."

Aware of the sudden fascinated silence, she chewed her lower lip. "I wouldn't want you to—"

"I know." He covered both her hands with one of his own. "I have a lot to consider, but there's time for me to decide. For now, let's figure out this thing with your brother."

THE MOST ALARMING PART, Brand thought, was that Scott—or someone pretending to be Scott—had chosen tonight to meet with Sahara. That made them scramble to create their plans.

Worse, it was dark as Hades down by the river where she said they were to meet. Not even the streetlamps reached, and with only a sliver of a moon and a few scattered stars, they could easily lose sight of her.

Brand, crouched down on the floor in the back of one of the agency's SUVs, said, "Park so your headlamps light the way and leave them on." He'd already disconnected the interior light so when he opened the door and followed discreetly, no lights would give him away.

With nervousness, or maybe excitement lacing her tone, she replied, "Okay. Good idea. I know my way, but still...there could be snakes out there. Or spiders, or—"

"You're afraid of spiders and snakes?"

"Not when I can see them, but I don't like the idea of stumbling into them in the dark."

"Yeah, I wouldn't like that either." Brand felt the surface of the road change as she drove off the asphalt and bumped over the rocky ground.

"I'll get as close as I can," she said softly. "But it's been a while since I was here, and that was always on foot. I don't think it's safe to take the car too much farther."

They'd driven an hour south along continually narrowing roads that followed the river. In the distance, Brand heard a barge horn echoing over the water.

"It's really foggy," Sahara whispered.

"We can cancel at any time," he said fast, hoping to encourage her to do just that. "Say the word."

"No. Foggy is probably good, in case anyone is looking for Scott."

"You have the mic in your pocket? We need to make sure the others can hear every word, too." The plan was for him to creep closer on foot, staying low in the dew-wet weeds and scrub bushes, while the others encircled the area, Leese on higher ground, Miles and Justice near the road, ready to close in if necessary. They'd gotten there earlier to find their hiding spots, to help avoid detection.

"I have it," Sahara promised him. "We tested it and retested it."

Enoch remained at the offices, monitoring the tracer tacked to Sahara's sweater.

They'd done all they could to ensure her safety, short of refusing to let her go, and he knew well that no man could do that. Sahara was a woman who understood the danger, weighed the risk to each encounter and made her own decisions.

She was a woman who loved her brother dearly and would probably face off with the devil to get him back.

Brand briefly closed his eyes. God, he hated that Scott had put her in this position.

She stopped the car. "I can see the river from here." She inhaled, then slowly blew out the breath. "Brand?"

"Yeah, babe?"

"I believe it's Scott, I really do. But at the same time, I'm so afraid that he might really be gone and that I'm just fooling myself, and that would be so awful—"

"Shh," Brand said, wishing he had the words to reassure her. He just didn't know. If it was her brother, he was a real dick for putting her through this. "You're the strongest person I know, Sahara. So strong, you leave me awed. You can do this, and however it turns out, we'll deal with it."

"Together?"

"That's sure as hell my plan."

Silence hung in the humid air, then she whispered, "Did you know I was falling in love with you?"

Jesus, she had a knack for startling timing. A new

rush of protectiveness surged through him, making his voice rough. "I was hopeful."

He heard the smile in her tone when she teased, "That was easier to admit than I expected."

"I'm glad. Soon as we get through this, I'll make a few admissions of my own."

She started to twist to see him.

"Don't," Brand warned. "If anyone is watching the car, they'll wonder who you're talking to." Was she stalling to work up her nerve? He imagined visiting the area with her brother at her side was vastly different from a late-night rendezvous under potentially dangerous circumstances. "I'll be right behind you, okay?"

"Okay. Brand?" She hesitated. "You be careful, too. I couldn't bear if you got hurt helping me."

"After what you just told me? You can bet my plan is to have you all to myself tonight in bed, and after I've exhausted you, then we'll do some talking."

"That sounds nice."

He heard an odd noise on the roof of the SUV and almost groaned. "Is that rain?"

"It's just drizzling. I have an umbrella, and I won't melt."

From his crouched position in back, he watched her stiffen her shoulders.

"It's time. Thank you for being here with me." She opened the door and stepped out, opening her umbrella before closing the door again, giving him no chance to say anything more.

Brand waited until she'd had time to go a few yards ahead, then he slipped from the SUV. Dressed all in black, he blended with the shadows. Midway across, he could see ribbons of light dancing over the surface of the river. Farther away, traffic hummed over a bridge.

This area, though, was nothing but rough bushes, rocks and crowded trees that shrouded the shore in darkness. He could barely see Sahara as she gingerly sat on a fallen log.

Her voice, soft and uncertain, carried to him when she whispered, "Scott?"

Ducking down behind a damp cluster of barren trees, Brand withdrew his gun—and a strong flashlight. If necessary, he could use the light to distinguish Sahara from anyone else.

They both heard the rustling of leaves as a body emerged from the right. Tall, dressed in a black slicker with a hat pulled low. Brand tensed.

Sahara shot out of her seat, the umbrella held limply at her side. "Scott!"

The intruder's arms opened and Sahara flew into them. Brand saw her feet leave the ground as the man hugged her hard, both of them oblivious to the rain.

Suddenly Sahara was sobbing, and Brand felt everything inside him clench in pain. He'd never thought to hear her cry like that, but now she wept with the same enthusiasm that she did everything else.

Her brother whispered, "Shh, shhh. I'm sorry, sis. So damn sorry."

Sahara slugged him, then shoved out of his arms. "They told me you were dead!"

"I know." He grabbed her in for another hug. "I had no choice, and I promise I can explain everything."

"You could have told me you were alive!"

"No, I couldn't tell anyone. I knew certain people would be watching you, and I'm sorry, hon, but you're an open book." He framed her face. "I didn't expect you to deny it, though, and to send a damned PI haunting my every step."

Sahara drew a shuddering breath. "You can come home now?"

"Not yet, but hopefully soon." Taking the umbrella from her and holding it over them both, Scott led her back to the log.

Brand had to keep reminding himself that this was her brother, a brother she adored, so he couldn't dismember the guy for making her cry.

But he wanted to.

"I can't believe it's raining." Scott sat with his arm around her, his head tipped to rest on the top of hers. "You're warm enough?"

She nodded, sniffled and dug out a tissue. "Yes. Where have you been, Scott?"

"Everywhere. Always on the move. Hiding." He stretched out his legs and heaved a sigh. "That night on the yacht… I was supposed to die." He touched his ribs. "The bastards stabbed me, but though it bled like crazy, it was only a superficial wound."

"Stabbed?" With new tears making her voice thick, she asked, "You're sure you're all right?"

He nodded. "I dove overboard before they could do more damage. It was so dark, you couldn't see past the yacht's lights. None of them knew anything about boating, so they kept watching the water where I'd gone in." He hugged her. "They didn't expect me to surface at the stern."

Sahara gasped. "The life raft!"

"You know I kept it strapped on the transom for easy access. They were excited, all talking at once, so they didn't hear me unfasten it. Even once I had it, I kept swimming away from the boat."

"You were bleeding?" she asked with a tremor in her voice.

"Yeah, and I don't mind telling you, every shark movie I'd ever seen kept playing in my head."

Asshole, Brand wanted to shout. *Why give her the gruesome details now?* She was already upset. Scott should be reassuring her, not adding to her nightmare memories.

"I was still pushing farther away when they started the motor and drove away from me. Then I inflated the raft and made my way to shore."

"You keep saying *them* and *they*. Who was it, Scott? Who did this to us?"

A gust of wind rode in off the river, causing the leaves over Brand's head to shudder, spilling more rain down on him. He swiped a hand over his face, determined to keep Sahara in his sights at all times.

He watched as Scott struggled with the umbrella.

"Let's talk in your car," he said.

She agreed, but just as they stood, all hell broke loose.

Two men exploded out of the bushes, guns in hand and shouting orders.

Brand started to lunge forward, but something solid hit him in the back of the head. He dropped to his knees, lost his hold on the flashlight, but maintained consciousness by a thread. The bastards had a strobe light and that, along with the shouting, added to the confusion. He could hear yelling, heard Sahara's distinctive voice cursing someone and then he heard a gunshot.

His heart went into his throat—until Sahara screamed, "Scott!"

She sounded equal parts panicked and pissed, but not hurt.

Knowing Leese, Miles and Justice were already on their way, Brand shoved to his feet. Through the wildly flashing light, he saw the men racing toward a small motorboat moored on the shore. In another bright flash he saw that one man had an arm locked around Sahara's throat, dragging her toward it.

"No!" He ran full tilt, stumbling twice because of the knock on the head, falling once onto the wet, loamy ground. He didn't stay down even when he heard Leese call his name.

The motor revved on the boat and it shot out to the river. Too many bodies filled that small boat, one of them Sahara's. He didn't dare shoot, not with her in the mix of the turmoil.

A gunshot sounded from the boat, and a second later he heard a snarled "Bitch!" along with the sounds of a scuffle.

"Sahara!"

"Take care of Scott," she shouted, the words muffled by the wind and rain.

"Scott's dead," someone said with a laugh.

"No," she screamed. *"Please..."*

The rest of her words faded away on the dark night.

Brand realized that he stood waist-deep in the frigid water. His heart felt numb, his lungs unable to get enough air.

Something bumped against his leg, and he looked down to see Sahara's mangled umbrella washing against the shore. His throat tightened painfully.

"Brand," Leese said urgently. "Come on. We have

to go. Enoch has a tracer on her. You know that. We'll find her."

Justice added, "But it's better if we don't wait."

Brand slowly turned, mud sucking at his feet. "Her brother?" he asked with ominous undertones.

"Coming around," Miles said. "He caught a bullet in the arm, just a graze, I think, but apparently he hit his head when he went down. I guess that's why the goons thought he was dead, why they left him and took her instead."

Fury carried Brand to where Scott Silver sat on the sodden ground, his back propped against the log, his head hanging forward.

Sahara's phone, still lit up, lay on the ground beside him. Brand picked it up and put it in his pocket. His heart started to pound in thundering beats.

With one hand, he hauled Scott to his tiptoes and rattled him. "You ignorant fucker! *Do you realize what you've done*?"

"I was careful," Scott muttered, wincing with the pain in his head and arm. "No one followed me, so they must have followed you."

Driven by blind rage, Brand cocked back a fist— and Justice captured it. Calm to the point of morbid, he said, "Stop and think, man. If you kill him, Sahara will never forgive you."

"You heard her," Miles said with his own measure of anger. "She's worried about the bastard. For her sake, we have to take care of him."

"I can take care of myself," Scott growled.

It required three deep breaths before Brand was able to open his fingers and let Scott drop back flat on his feet. He retrieved his fist from Justice, who gave him an apologetic whack on the back.

"His head, damn it," Leese said. "Go easy, will you. You saw him get conked."

"Butt of a gun, it looked like," Miles said. "Sorry we didn't get here quick enough."

"I'm fine," Brand lied…and immediately thought of how Sahara had said the same, how she'd stubbornly insisted it was so. Despite her denials, she was still hurt, and now unscrupulous bastards had her again. "After I get her back," Brand told Scott, "I plan to finish this."

"Suit yourself." Scott clenched a hand around his bleeding arm. "But we have to move now." As if he thought he could take charge of the situation, he started for the car, saying, "Tell me who has the tracer on her. How well do you know him? And how many cars did you bring? Jesus, it's no wonder you were—"

He squawked when Justice and Miles each grabbed one of his arms and practically threw him into the back of the SUV. Miles climbed in behind him. Brand followed.

Justice got in the front passenger seat and Leese got behind the wheel.

"What the hell is this?" Scott demanded, looking a little wary when Brand turned on the flashlight.

"Take off your coat." He located the first aid kit and opened it. For Sahara, he'd keep her asshole brother alive—for now.

"I don't need—"

Miles said, "No one gives a shit what you need. We're doing this for Sahara, so take off the fucking coat."

From the front, Leese said, "I'm calling Enoch now, so keep it down."

Silently, Scott struggled out of his coat. "I know Enoch. He has the tracer?"

No one replied, and no one moved to help him with his coat, but as he eased his arm from the sleeve, Brand saw the blood everywhere and quietly cursed.

Enoch answered on the first ring. "Everything okay?"

Leese said, "They got her, Enoch. We need to know which way to go."

"Oh God." Worry sharpened his voice. "Oh Jesus."

"Stop praying and give us directions," Justice ordered.

"I'm on it, I'm on it. Let me see…" The seconds ticked by.

Needing to occupy himself, Brand got out cleaning swabs, gauze pads and tape. His eyes burned and his guts churned.

She had to be okay. He had to have a chance to tell her how much she meant to him. She was…*everything*.

Every. Fucking. Thing.

If they touched her, if they hurt her, he'd—

"Okay," Enoch said, breathing hard. "They're on 71 heading toward 75. How long before you can be on the highway?"

"They crossed the river in a boat, so they have the jump on us. Maybe fifteen minutes or so, given traffic— once I reach the actual roadway."

Justice glanced over the seat. "Hold on. It'll be bumpy for a bit."

"Don't worry about us," Miles said.

Leese drove fast over the rough terrain, anxious to get them on solid ground. Every second felt like an hour.

"Take off the shirt," Miles said quietly.

Solemn, Scott did as directed.

"How bad is your head?"

"Mild concussion, probably," Scott said.

"I wasn't talking to you."

Brand glanced up as he scooted closer to Sahara's brother. "I'll live. Let's just concentrate on getting to her."

"We will, you know," Miles vowed. "Get her, I mean."

Brand nodded at Miles. "Call the old guys. See if they've found out anything from Grant."

"Douglas Grant?" Scott asked.

Again they ignored him. "And see if they've found a way to contact Ross Moran."

"I know how to contact him," Scott offered quickly. Everyone went still.

Scott cleared his throat. "I paid him, you know. Left the money in his apartment, then texted him and told him so. I figured that's why they were after Sahara, trying to get what I owed. I wouldn't have asked her to meet me if I didn't think that shit was already settled."

"How?" Justice demanded. "How did you find him?"

"I spent a hell of a lot of time tracking him down, that's how. He's key to exposing the bastards who tried to murder me."

"*Tried* being the operative word," Miles murmured.

Scott nodded. "Ross had done a job for me, but then I was attacked on my yacht and never got a chance to pay him."

Everyone went silent while Enoch gave more directions.

When he finished, Leese ordered, "Start explaining, and make it fast."

They now had something to go on. Brand couldn't think about anything else or he'd lose the fragile grip on his control. "I'll bandage while you talk." Examining Scott's arm gave him something to focus on besides his worry.

Miles held the flashlight. Neither of them reacted to the raw, ravaged wound in Scott's arm. Inch and a half wide, about three inches long, already blackened around the edges, it looked painful.

Knowing it would burn like hell, Brand swabbed at the blood, cleaning enough off around the damaged area so that the wrapping would hold.

Scott hissed in his breath, but held perfectly still.

"You need to go to the hospital—"

"Not until I have my sister back."

"—but no one is taking you there yet," Brand finished. It required everything he had not to blame the brother.

Still on an open line, Enoch asked, "You found her brother?"

"Yeah. And a whole shit-ton of trouble."

Enoch surprised everyone by gritting out, "Son of a bitch. I don't believe this."

Scott looked momentarily guilty, then rallied. "I have Ross's number. The bastard moved around a few times, but I found his new apartment. I left the money there that I owed him, then texted him to let him know. He should have found it already."

"You paid him everything?" Justice asked.

"Twice what I owed him, actually. I thought that would be the end of it."

"You thought your ass was finally safe," Miles accused.

"If that's all they wanted," Leese asked, "then who took Sahara today?"

"I recognized voices." Scott's face showed the pain he felt, physically and emotionally. "Not Ross's, but I definitely heard Olsen Winger. Maybe Terrance. There was so much chaos—"

"And that damned flashing light," Justice muttered.

Scott nodded. "They work with Ross Moran." Levering carefully to one hip, he dug the phone from his pocket, thumbed the screen and pulled up Ross's number.

Miles took it from him.

Scott started to object, but the dark stare from Miles convinced him to stay quiet.

"Let's not call him yet," Leese decided. "We need to get closer first. We don't want to push them into doing anything…rash."

Brand squeezed his eyes shut. No, they didn't want the bastards doing anything rash—like kidnapping her a second time, or shooting her brother. In comparison, rash could only mean one thing, but he couldn't contemplate that.

She had to be okay.

Trusting his friends to think clearly, to accurately gauge the situation, Brand busied himself by layering gauze pads on Scott's gunshot wound, then he wrapped and taped it down. "I have aspirin."

"I'll take three."

Brand handed them over. Inside, he felt like a bomb slowly ticking, the explosion getting closer and closer.

Enoch interrupted with more directions. "They're off the highway and driving through Darville."

"Never heard of it," Leese said.

"Just looked it up," Enoch said. "It's a dead little town, most of the businesses gone."

A perfect place to hide a victim.

Enoch went through directions for the exit to take, and then the roads to follow. Justice put everything in his phone to use GPS.

"Tell us if they stop," Leese said, speeding fast now that he was on wide highway. Luckily the traffic was low, which allowed them to make up some time.

In the distance, lightning shattered across the black sky. A few seconds later, thunder rumbled.

The storm matched Brand's turbulent mood. Sitting back against the wall of the SUV, he narrowed his gaze on Sahara's brother. "Now," he said, his voice evenly modulated to hide his rage. "Finish explaining."

CHAPTER FIFTEEN

SAHARA SHIVERED IN her wet clothes and bare feet. Why hadn't she dressed reasonably in jeans and boots instead of hoping to look her best when she reunited with her brother? It wasn't like he expected her to wear her classiest business outfit to a clandestine meeting at the riverbank. No, the choice of outfit was all her doing. She'd wanted Scott to have a good impression of her after all this time.

Her only concession to the weather and location had been a longer skirt, snug-fitting sweater and booties instead of stiletto heels.

The booties should have stayed in place, damn it, but somewhere along the way she'd lost one of them, maybe while getting dragged into the small boat. She had a vague recollection of a long scratch along the back of one calf and a solid crack to her elbow.

In the process of her second kidnapping, she'd also lost her umbrella and, unfortunately, her phone.

Worse, they'd taken her gun from her.

She blamed her stupid panic for that. If she hadn't seen Scott shot, hadn't seen him fall, she might have kept a cool head. Instead, blind rage had driven her and she'd jerked out the gun without thinking through the fact that three men surrounded her at close range.

The redheaded goon had backhanded her so hard

she'd nearly toppled out of the rickety boat. The blow was strong enough that darkness had temporarily closed in. It had been an easy thing for him to wrest the gun from her slack fingers.

Her face still stung. She was so damned cold that she appreciated the throbbing pain; at least it was something she could feel besides worry and stark, gnawing despair.

One guy looked back from the front seat. "Have you called Ross yet?"

The redhead who'd struck her in the boat and then tied her hands too tightly in the car muttered, "He's meeting us there."

Sahara cocked a supercilious brow. "Does he know why he's meeting you?"

For an answer, Olsen's frown deepened.

The driver leered at her in the rearview mirror, licked his lips and murmured huskily, "Ross won't object, not anymore."

"You'd be wise to leave her alone," Olsen said.

"Right before he left, he agreed it was a good plan to get her."

"*With* him, Andy. Not without him." Olsen slumped lower in his seat. "Don't fool yourself. When he finds out, he's going to be pissed."

Sahara memorized the names as they said them, and the faces now that she could see them. Eventually they would pay.

If she lived long enough.

She eyed Olsen. "So Ross is going to join us?" The more she heard, the more she thought Ross might be her best bet for surviving mostly unscathed.

Olsen spared her a glance. "You'd do best to keep quiet."

A tall order. She couldn't be quiet on her best days, so how could he expect it of her now, when she was so miserable that she really wanted them to be miserable, too?

If it was just physical discomfort, she could be all stoic and brave, no problem, but her heart ached, both for her brother and for the anguish she'd heard in Brand's voice as he'd shouted her name.

The two men she loved more than life…would she ever see either of them again?

Her gaze encompassed all the men. "I've heard of stupid, but this is off the charts. I almost feel sorry for you, knowing how it's going to end."

His tone taunting, the driver said, "Ross didn't want you hurt because he considered you more valuable if you weren't. But the rules have changed, sugar, and you're now free game."

Did he have to sound so anticipatory?

"You're a dumbass, Andy," Olsen snapped. "In case any of you failed to notice, Ross is sweet on her. If she hadn't tried to blow my brains out, I wouldn't have struck her. Ross is going to be furious and that doesn't bode well for any of us."

"I tried to kill you," Sahara said numbly, "because you shot my brother."

Terrance snarled over the seat, "You lied to us! You knew he was alive and that he owed us. But you—"

Olsen kicked the seat. "Shut up!"

They all seemed out of control, not at all like Ross, who had dictated with calm decisiveness. Sahara swallowed heavily, her fear very real. Ross had told her he wouldn't let her be hurt—but he wasn't here and these men seemed more than capable of hurting her in many, many ways.

She needed the upper hand, and she couldn't get it by cowering.

Turning her head, she glared at Olsen. He sat in sullen silence beside her. "Is it your plan to freeze me to death?"

"You'll be able to get warm and dry in a few more minutes."

Great. That meant the guys could catch up to her that much quicker. She worked up a believable tremor in her lips. "My arms are aching. Those wet ropes are tightening and I can't feel my fingers anymore."

His gaze narrowed on her. "Once you're inside, I'll retie you to the bed."

Uh-oh. Trying for mere curiosity rather than dread, she asked, "There's a bed?"

Andy again looked at her in the rearview mirror. "I'll help you take off those wet clothes. We'll have you cozy in no time."

She snapped, "Will you watch the road before you kill us all?"

He grinned suggestively and went back to driving.

Terrance, the passenger in front, scowled. "Who says you get to play with her?"

"I'm the one who took the worst beating from that gorilla who came after her. She owes me."

Sahara felt her nerves fraying. She drew up her legs and kicked Andy's seat. Hard. "He's not a gorilla!"

The car swerved dangerously, sliding on the wet road and damn near spinning. Olsen thrust out an arm to pin her in place until Andy got control of the car again.

Everyone was silent in shock.

Sahara, who'd half slid down the seat, struggled back up.

Olsen gripped her face in a hard hand. "Do anything like that again and you won't like the consequences."

"What will you do," she sneered as best she could, given how he squeezed her cheeks. "Kidnap me? Tie me up? Freeze me to death?"

Terrance laughed. "By God, she's got balls."

Olsen thrust her away. "She won't be so ballsy when I stick her in the trunk."

Sahara snorted.

He turned to her. "Naked. I'll stuff you in there naked—and I'll let Andy be the one to strip you."

Okay, maybe that quelled a little of her rebelliousness. But not all. "Ross is going to be furious. Did you know he visited me?" She lifted her chin. "We had a nice, friendly chat. He asked me out to dinner."

Another silent shock ballooned, then burst with a million outraged questions from all directions. She sat in smug silence until they wound down, then said with derision, "Oh, so you *didn't* know? Hmm. Interesting."

Olsen, being the closest, opted for the most intimidation—by pointing the gun directly at her. "Where did he visit you?"

"A party at Douglas Grant's house." She took pleasure in saying, "Do you know the DA? He's a pig, so I assume you're good friends."

Olsen looked blank.

Terrance jerked around over the seat to glare at her. "Why the fuck would he be visiting the DA?"

Sahara smiled. "Why, to see me, of course. He likes me." Her gaze coasted over all of them. "He's going to be so enraged when he sees how you've treated me."

"Fuck him," Andy said with venom, slamming his hands against the steering wheel. "We need to get paid!"

"We're here," Olsen said calmly. "Pull around back."

Sahara bent to see out the windshield, but until the headlights hit a stained glass window, she didn't realize they were at a church. *At least there shouldn't be a bed, meaning that had only been an idle threat.* "You've got to be kidding me."

"It's abandoned," Olsen said, already clenching one freckled hand around her arm. "Don't get any ideas about salvation."

She managed a credible laugh. "I bet you all incinerate the second you set foot on holy ground."

Olsen started to open the door, but it was suddenly jerked out of his hand, spilling him halfway out. Since he had a grip on Sahara, she got jerked across the seat.

The pressure on her tightly tied arms made her groan.

Ross Moran stood there, big, blue-eyed, heaving with fury. He seemed impervious to the rain drenching him, plastering his hair to his head, gluing his shirt to his broad shoulders. His fisted hands hung tense at his sides, and his scorching gaze went over her as she struggled upright.

Their eyes met, then his attention shot to Olsen. "Start explaining."

Sensing a change in her situation, Sahara asked, "Could I please get inside first? I'm soaked, freezing and I'd dearly love to have the feeling restored in my arms." After all, she couldn't run off into the night, during a storm, with her arms so tightly tied. She knew she wouldn't make it far.

If they'd remove the ropes and she could get her bearings, well then…

The blaze of anger on Ross's face settled into an inferno of quiet rage. He withdrew a large knife from a sheath on his belt and said, "Turn around."

Terrance protested, saying, "Ross—"

The knife pointed in Terrance's direction. "Shut the fuck up. I'll deal with you next."

Alarmed, he squeaked, *"Me?"*

Ross looked at Olsen and Andy. "All of you."

Trying to look brave, Andy stepped out into the rain, too—and promptly pulled up the collar to his jacket, already shivering. "We need our money, damn it."

"I got your fucking money, moron." Gently, Ross pressed her forward to better expose her hands. "Don't move." He sliced cleanly through the ropes.

"What do you mean, you have the money?" Olsen asked.

"Her brother paid it."

More questions exploded.

"Gentlemen, please." Sahara bit back tears as feeling rushed into her aching arms, up to her shoulders and into her neck. "Let's get out of this miserable rain."

Ross said, "The three of you go on in."

Olsen heaved a sigh. "Sorry, no can do, boss. She's got you bewitched, but what's done is done. We can't just turn her loose now."

"No," Ross agreed, "we can't." He scooped Sahara up into his arms, ignoring the groan she couldn't stifle.

Her entire body ached, and now more rain drenched her. "Please tell me this relic is heated."

"No," Olsen said, walking alongside them. "But we installed a heater. If you don't dismantle it, you should be warm enough soon."

Soon she'd be free, but she kept that to herself. She couldn't quite tell if Ross was with his comrades, or against them. His trite "no, we can't" bothered her a lot.

Then again, he wasn't a stupid man so he had to realize that taking a stand at this particular moment could get them both killed.

"I'm capable of walking."

"Barefoot?" He carried her easily, leaning over her to help shield her from the rain. "I can barely see where I'm going, but I've already discovered roots grown through concrete, broken glass and rocks."

Sahara peered down and saw that he was right. The puddles forming everywhere couldn't hide the treacherous path. Not that she'd thank him. He was the one who'd started this absurd campaign against her.

They went up rickety wooden steps that creaked under Ross's weight, then he dipped down to fit under a nailed board across a collapsing door frame and stepped into a dark vestibule. Dead vines had overtaken the crumbling plaster walls. Spiderwebs hung thick from the high ceiling.

When Ross stepped into the desolate little church, she found that very little outside light penetrated. Boards covered most of the windows, and grime coated those still unbroken. In one corner of the rectangular room, next to a toppled pulpit, a kerosene heater gave off welcoming warmth.

"Someone get a light. This place is crumbling."

"Got it." Terrance dug out a flashlight and turned it on. It flashed over every inch of the room in a disorienting light show. "Sorry, it's still on strobe. Let me... There." He adjusted it to a single beam that, when set atop a shelf, didn't quite reach all corners of the room.

Ross carried her past several pews, most of them rotting, broken or overturned.

Someone had stacked blankets on a still intact pew near the heater. Sahara saw the coil of rope and wanted to scream. Her wrists were raw, her arms and shoulders still protesting every movement.

Ross set her on her feet, murmuring, "Careful," when she wavered.

She straightened her spine and squared her shoulders, determined to hide her weakness. "I'm fine." She couldn't do anything about her shivers.

He tipped up her chin. "Before you come up with some harebrained idea of making a run for it, you should know that many of the floorboards are rotted. There are exposed nails everywhere, and several holes with jagged edges. Fall through and you drop all the way to a very dank, spooky basement. If you're not shredded on the way down, you're bound to break a leg when you land."

Lovely. Either put up with their mistreatment or risk mangling herself.

Then again, perhaps she had a third option. She looked Ross right in the eye and said, "I won't be tied again. It's horribly uncomfortable and as you just pointed out, it's not like I can run away."

Andy crowded close, sneering, "You're not calling the shots, lady, so stop your bellyaching and—"

Carelessly, without even looking at Andy, Ross straightened an arm and landed a fist to his face. Andy reeled back, landed against a kneeler, tripped and slammed awkwardly into a wall. Dust and cobwebs fell from the impact.

Ross stared at him, his expression demonic in the low, indirect light. "You're on thin ice already. Shooting off your mouth won't help."

Tension swelled within the church, so thick Sahara wondered that no one choked on it. Olsen and Terrance shared a look. Andy wisely clamped his lips together.

To Sahara, Ross said, "Andy's right. You're not calling the shots, but I see no reason to tie you. I also see no reason to keep you wet and shivering." He turned to Olsen. "You and Terrance stand by the front door. Andy, you stand by the hall exit."

With only a few grumbles, the men moved to do as ordered.

"Strip out of your wet things," Ross ordered, "and wrap up in a blanket."

Her stomach bottomed out at the suggestion. "No, thank you." Where were her men? Now would be a good time for them to catch up.

"You'll do it," Ross said, "or I'll do it for you."

Out of the corner of her eye she saw Andy grin, placated by Ross's implied brutality.

Suddenly Ross leaned close and grabbed the lapels of her coat, hauling her up to her tiptoes. Putting his face close to hers, he growled, "Do. You. Understand?" Then, more softly, he breathed, "Trust me or neither of us will make it out of here."

Her eyes widened. So this was part of an act, a way to dupe his men so he could help her? He'd moved his goons a fair distance away to ensure a modicum of privacy.

Taking advantage of that, Sahara murmured, "Allow me to play my part." She swung her hand up and around, determined to slap him hard.

Unfortunately, Ross caught her wrist, his expression incredulous. "You little hellcat," he breathed...almost with admiration.

Incensed that she hadn't gotten in one good crack, Sahara tried to jerk free.

Ross easily subdued her, flipping her around so her back was to his chest, then locking her close with his bulky arms. She tried stomping his toes, but he wore boots and she was barefoot. Head-butting him was out since she only reached his chest.

Andy hooted. Terrance snickered.

Quietly, Olsen said, "You already know you can't trust her, so stop dicking around."

Over her head, Ross asked, "Is he right, Sahara? Should I go ahead and strip you now? Or do you think you can behave?"

"That depends." Steamy heat rose from his body, alleviating some of her chill. "Will I get to undress in private?"

"In this room," he told her, "with everyone's gaze averted. That's as private as it's going to get."

"Then I'd just as soon keep my wet clothes."

He sighed. "Difficult to the bitter end." In the next instant, he stripped off her coat despite her squawking struggles, then his big paw settled on her shoulder, gently groping. His gaze landed on her breasts. "I suppose your sweater is dry enough. The skirt has to go, though." He reached for the side zipper.

Sahara slapped his hand, saying, "I'll do it!"

For a heartbeat or two, they stared at each other, her defiant, him amused.

"Spoilsport." He shook out a blanket, then held it up in front of her, stretched wide between the breadth of his long arms. "Good enough?"

Fuming, she gritted out, "Look away."

He laughed softly…and turned his head.

Unwilling to push her luck any further, Sahara unzipped and shimmied out of the sodden skirt. After being dragged through the river to the boat, everything from her waist down was drenched, including her panties, but no way would she remove them.

She dropped the skirt over the back of the pew, then took the blanket from Ross and wrapped it around herself toga-style, pulling one end to drape over her shoulder. Sitting in the corner of the pew closest to the kerosene heater, she tucked her feet up under the blanket.

That little skirmish had helped her to forget, for just a few minutes, the sight of her brother falling into the mud after the gunshot. She squeezed her eyes shut and put her head in her hands.

"Sahara."

She jerked her head up to glare at Ross.

He gave her a stern look that gradually turned into rage.

She didn't know what to think when he clasped her chin and lifted her face, turning it toward the dim light, his gaze searching. "How did you bruise your face?"

"I got in the way of your friend's fist."

He straightened with a slow menace that had Olsen saying, "She tried to shoot me! It was the easiest way to disarm her."

Sahara snapped, "You'd just shot my brother! Of course I wanted to shoot you. In fact, I still do."

Olsen huffed. "You see? She's nuts."

Fury got her off the bench. Her bare feet on the dirty floor sent a chill climbing straight through to her heart. "Don't think I've forgotten you, Olsen. You're the sexist pig who feels superior to women."

Olsen reared back. "What the hell are you talking about?"

"When you helped kidnap me the first time, I remember everything you said. I knew right then you were an insecure, ignorant—"

"That's enough." Ross forcibly pressed her back in her seat with a withering look that clearly said *cease and desist*.

"He started it."

"For the love of… Stay put." Assuming she'd obey, he turned away and said to the men, "Anyone else touch her, for any reason, and he'll be dealing with me. Are we clear?"

After a collective bobbing of heads in the affirmative, Ross wanted explanations of what had gone down.

Sahara could hear them explaining the chaos of the evening, how they'd intended to take Scott.

Ross clearly wasn't happy, especially since, according to what he said, her brother really had paid the money owed. Somehow, he'd gotten into Ross's apartment and left it there for him to find.

"Why didn't you tell us you got the money?" Andy asked.

"I wasn't sure if it was a trap. I didn't want to drag you all into it until I was sure no one had followed me."

Olsen nodded. "I remember you told us to watch our backs."

"I'd just gotten the text telling me the money was at my place. Even after I got home and found it, I kept wondering if Scott had men ready to close in on me—or on all of you, if I gave you away."

"You wouldn't," Terrance said with conviction.

"Of course not, but a lot of good it did me trying to

look out for you. Seems we might all be sunk anyway."
He rubbed the back of his neck.

"We found one guy hiding in the bushes, watching.
I clubbed him in the back of the head."

Brand! For an instant, pure terror gripped her. Then
she remembered Brand calling her name, racing toward
the boat.

Her pulse calmed as she realized he was okay. Injured, probably, but like her, he would recover.

Andy said, "It should have been easy, but instead of
raising his hands, Scott lunged toward me. I wasn't expecting that. I just…reacted."

"He's dead?"

With a shrug in his voice, Andy said, "Turned out
she had a small army with her. We heard them charging in, so I didn't stick around to take his pulse. He sure
dropped like a dead man."

In an effort to keep her heart from shattering, Sahara
concentrated on listening. Once her men rescued her, she
wanted to be able to give a detailed accounting to the
police. Assuming any of goons survived, the very least
they deserved was a long time in prison.

"How did you know he'd be there?"

Sahara was curious about that, too. She hoped they'd
keep talking, the longer the better, so her backup could
arrive.

Olsen said, "I was staking out the agency, seeing if
we'd have a chance to grab her since they missed her
on the road."

Ross straightened. "What do you mean?"

"Terrance and Andy. They tried to take her during a
trip south. She had that same bodyguard with her and
he decided to shoot it out with them instead."

Ross glanced toward Sahara. "I didn't know anything about that."

She stared back without reacting. Far as she was concerned, he'd started the scheme to get her, and that made him guiltiest of all.

As if unaware of the undercurrent, Olsen continued. "I didn't see her coming or going again. I guess they were being extra cautious after that. But I noticed a dude hanging around—"

"And it turned out to be Scott?" Ross guessed.

Olsen nodded. "He tried to conceal himself, wore a hat and sunglasses and loose jacket...but that's what drew my attention to him, you know? And then there was no mistaking him once I did look closer."

Sahara remembered Brand making note of a man outside the agency. She supposed Scott had been trying to look out for her, or maybe he just wanted to make sure she was getting along okay after his "death." If only he had trusted her...

"When I followed him to the river, I figured he was meeting someone, I just didn't expect it to be her."

Ross stared heavenward.

She seriously doubted any divine spirits were still hanging around.

"He'd been a sneaky bastard, hard as hell to find, so once I spotted him I wasn't about to let him get away again. He was extra cautious, but I remembered everything you taught us about tailing him, staying back and not doing anything to give myself away."

"And it obviously worked," Ross said.

Olsen nodded. "Scott got to the river and spent an hour scoping out the place. I was up on a rise, far enough away that he couldn't see me while Terrance and Andy got the boat. The plan was to grab him and force him to pay up."

"It was a good plan," Andy said, moving closer to her, propping a hip against one of the broken pews. "Until *she* showed up."

"She came alone," Terrance said. "Or so we thought."

"She's not stupid," Ross stated flatly, then his eyes flared and he turned to stare at her. Quietly, he said, "You're not stupid."

She released an evil smile. "No, I'm not. Far from it, actually." *Scott, please don't be dead.* She wondered at the time. Brand and the others should be arriving any minute now. She needed to warn them about the rotting floorboards so that no one fell through to the basement.

Not for a second did she doubt that they'd be coming for her. Thank God the tracking device wasn't in her phone or umbrella, since she'd lost those.

"Son of a bitch." Ross half laughed, then stood and glanced toward the door in expectation.

"What is it?" Andy asked. Alarmed, he grabbed Sahara's arm and jerked her toward him so roughly she stumbled off her feet and almost lost her blanket. "Did you hear something?"

Ross blew out a slow breath. "No." He glanced at the way Andy held her and how she scrambled to keep the blanket around her. "There's nothing there. Let her go, Andy."

"Bullshit." Gaze frantic, Andy jerked her to stand in front of him. "You're on it, aren't you, Ross?"

Terrance frowned. "You're losing it, Andy. Don't say shit you'll regret."

Olsen now stared at the front door, too.

Wrapping an arm tight around her waist and poking a gun into her ribs, Andy snarled, "This is a fucking setup."

Ross seemed to swell in front of her. "You little prick." He started forward with a determined stride. "You dare accuse me?"

"I'll shoot her!"

Ross froze.

From somewhere behind Sahara, Brand said, "Finger off the trigger or I'll gladly kill you."

She jumped, turned her head, and saw that Brand and Leese both stood there, grim-faced, their guns drawn and aimed.

Andy jerked around to face this new threat. He swung his gun wildly back and forth between the two men.

Taking advantage of his panic, Ross threw a meaty fist. Sahara ducked and the punch hit Andy right in the nose.

She heard the crunch.

Brand hauled her up and tucked her behind him.

Ross continued to pound on Andy, who put up a mild show of defense.

Amid the commotion, Terrance bolted out the front door, but he didn't get far. They all heard the scuffle in the vestibule, then Terrance got tossed back inside, his lifeless body breaking another hole in the floorboards so one arm and shoulder fell through.

Justice stepped in, a taunting smile in place.

"Wait," Sahara shouted, poking her head up from where Brand tried to shield her. "The floors are rotted! You have to be careful."

Justice backed up—and his foot went through the floor. He caught himself from falling completely, his arms splayed wide as he grabbed for the wall with one hand, and a table with the other. *"Damn."*

All hell broke loose—again.

Olsen withdrew a gun but Ross launched away from Andy and tackled him.

Leese muttered, "He's doing all our work for us."

After tucking Sahara down again, Brand said, "Your brother is okay."

It felt like the weight of the world lifted off her. Leave it to Brand to know exactly what to say. "Thank you."

Miles stepped through the door. "I suppose since no one else has tried to run out, all the action is in here?"

Leese looked to Sahara. "This is all of them?"

"Yes." Now that each of her men had joined her, she asked, "Where's my brother?"

"Out front," Miles said dismissively. "He was keeping watch with me—"

Which she took to mean that they didn't trust him, and Miles had ensured he didn't disappear again.

"—but now he's calling the police."

Was he too injured to join them? "He really is okay?"

Brand closely watched the fight between Ross and Olsen. "The bullet only grazed his arm. He hit his head when he fell, but he's fine." With that said, he stepped around the pew. "Stay down."

She nodded. "Okay." Looking over the edge of the pew, she watched Brand approach the brawl. He appeared far too serious and somewhat...wounded. There was a pinched look to his eyes and a tightness around his mouth.

She glanced at Leese.

He took his eyes off the melee long enough to wink at her.

They both turned back to see the action.

Wrestling Olsen flat to his back, Ross shouted, "Stop fighting, damn it." He pressed a forearm across Olsen's throat. "It's over. Let it go."

Olsen obligingly went limp, allowing Ross to wrest the gun from his hand.

"Andy was right," he said with bitter resentment around his great gulps of air. "You fucked us, didn't you?"

"Actually, he's in it as deep as you are." Brand snatched the gun out of Ross's hand and tossed it to Miles, who'd been about to help Justice get his foot out of the floor. "Maybe deeper."

Ross groaned. As he turned, he said, "I don't suppose you'd—"

Brand hit him hard enough to send him sprawling over Olsen again. Both men grunted.

Legs braced apart, shoulders bunched and fists clenched, Brand said, "Get up."

Ross looked past him to Sahara.

She laughed. "Don't look at me, you cretin. You brought this on yourself."

"I tried to help you!"

"After you made me take off my skirt."

Groaning, he shifted his wary gaze to Brand. "It wasn't like that, man. I wanted them to believe I was still on board with their idiot plans so I could—"

Brand hauled him up, which given Ross's size was no easy feat, and threw another punch.

Ross blocked it and took a swing of his own.

Big miscalculation, Sahara thought, when Brand took the blow, grinned and then landed several of his own against Ross, first hitting his face, then his gut, then his face again, ending with a kick to the sternum that sent him sprawling once more, this time to the hard, dirty floor.

With a sigh, she stood upright. "That's enough."

"I'm just getting started," Brand said.

"I'm sorry, but I can't let you do that." Holding tight to the blanket, she stepped around the pew and headed for Brand. "Not only will you destroy the rickety floor, but what Ross said is true. He protected me tonight."

"Tonight, but that doesn't explain—"

"He didn't know anything about them ramming us on the road, or this cockeyed kidnapping plan tonight," she explained. "If Olsen hadn't called him, he wouldn't even be here."

Sluggishly, Ross sat up. "A little late, honey."

Going tense all over again, Brand took a step forward.

Sahara grabbed his arm. "Brand, *no*." Then to Ross, she blasted, "Imbecile! Don't you know when to keep quiet?"

He touched his swollen mouth. "I'll start now."

Scott came through the door, one arm bandaged, a hand on the back of his head. "Too late. The cops are here and they're going to be real interested in everything you have to say."

Ross looked at him. "You and I have some private talking to do?"

Scott gave a mean smile. "I'm counting on it, you bastard."

"Me?" Ross pointed at Brand. "He's the one who was cozying up with Chelsea Tuttle."

Brand locked his jaw. "I wasn't, but what does that twit have to do with anything?"

Bemused, Scott said, "She's the one who hired out my murder."

CHAPTER SIXTEEN

SAHARA COULDN'T REMEMBER ever being so tired. After a lot of talking to the police, and then a visit to the hospital, the night had dragged on into dawn before they finally headed home.

At the emergency room, a physician checked her, Scott and Brand, but no one was seriously hurt. Scott's arm was cleaned and more properly bandaged. Luckily, neither Brand nor Scott had a concussion, but given their scowls, they both had killer headaches.

She got a tetanus shot after Brand noticed the deep scratch on the back of her calf from the rusty edge of the boat. One of the doctors found her a pair of scrub pants to wear. They were far more comfortable than the blanket.

Against her objections, Scott planned to spend the night at the house. She'd have rather kept him at the suite with her, where she could ensure he wouldn't disappear again, but then, he and Brand weren't exactly seeing eye to eye, so perhaps a little time was in order. In any case, she didn't have the energy to argue about it.

They would all meet up at the office at noon, hopefully better rested.

For a while there, adrenaline had carried her through, but as soon as they arrived at the agency, she crashed. She could barely get one foot in front of the other.

The night guards watched warily as Brand, with an arm around her, helped her to the elevator. To everyone they passed, Brand said, "She's fine, but it was a hell of a night. Sahara can explain tomorrow."

She'd made many friends at the agency, she realized. These people cared about her. That was nice.

Of course, she wouldn't be their boss any longer. She'd always known that when Scott returned, everything would change again.

Exhaustion kept her smile dim, but it was there.

Her brother was home.

Maybe she'd find a way to stay involved in the agency, but if it didn't work out, she was okay with that.

She had everything she needed.

Inside the elevator, she turned her face up to see Brand. His expression remained stark.

She touched his jaw. "Are you sure you're all right?"

If anything, his mood further darkened. "Yeah." He bent and pressed a firm kiss to her forehead. "Do you want a quick shower, or just to hit the bed?"

"Hit the bed," she said with an inelegant yawn. "I'm not sure I could stay awake for a shower."

Indulgent, he promised, "We'll shower together in the morning."

He got her inside the suite then removed her coat and his own before scooping her up and carrying her to the bedroom.

Her hair had dried in matted clumps, the rain had smeared her makeup, but they were both alive and that's what mattered. Thinking about all the close calls lately made her start to shake.

Brand methodically stripped her, pulled back the covers

and helped her into the bed. She wanted to protest the gentle treatment, but she honestly didn't have it in her.

She remembered the discussion of strength she'd had with the women. Smiling sleepily, she said, "I see what they mean now."

"Who?"

"Catalina, Maxi and Fallon." She snuggled into the pillow and closed her eyes. "Fallon insisted that Justice was stronger than her."

Brand asked, "That was in doubt?"

She heard one shoe drop, then the other. "We were mostly talking about emotional strength and independence. But Maxi said it's nice to lean on Miles." She opened her eyes and found Brand stepping out of his jeans and underwear. He tossed them into the pile with the rest of their discarded clothes. "Thank you for letting me lean on you."

He got into bed and curved around her, his chest to her back, his arms drawing her snug against him. "Thank you for trusting me."

She loved him, so of course she trusted him. "Brand?"

"Sleep, Sahara." He kissed her shoulder. "We'll have plenty of time to work out all the kinks."

She nodded. "Okay."

She was almost out when he whispered, "Don't ever scare me like that again."

She smiled…and faded into sleep.

BRAND WAS SO testy he almost didn't recognize himself. The bruise on Sahara's cheek had darkened. Combined with the cut on her temple and the scratch on her calf, she looked battered, yet she'd smiled at him as if nothing had happened.

After coffee, where she chatted in her normal way, they'd showered together.

She'd come on to him. She'd actually wanted sex before meeting everyone in the office.

Brand didn't know what to think about that, but he hadn't refused her. He didn't think he ever could.

Hell, he wanted her all the time.

The sex had been a little desperate, at least on her part, as if she needed the physical reassurance in order to face the emotional turmoil ahead. Aware of her injuries, he'd wanted to be careful with her, but she'd been frantic in her demands. He'd gotten her off first with his mouth, then again by sliding into her hard, the pace fast and deep.

Now she was dressed in her usual chic business attire with a formfitting dark skirt that made her ass look great, a cashmere sweater that fit her breasts to perfection and those I'm-the-boss heels. She'd left her hair loose and, other than the scrapes and bruises, she looked like a million bucks.

Like a very sexy million bucks.

As they headed to the office, she continued to chat, about nothing and about weighty decisions.

"I'm starving. I hope Enoch can rustle up some food, but maybe pastry first."

"Enoch is adaptable. He can manage anything you request."

"I've gotten used to the suite. I think if Scott plans to move back into the house, I'll just stay here." She glanced at him, brows lifted in inquiry. "You like the suite, don't you?"

"Sure." Was this her way of inviting him to stay? He

had his own place, too, but his apartment didn't hold any sentimental value. He could ditch it without a qualm.

"I wonder if they've made any other arrests yet."

"I imagine they took care of it last night." Scott claimed that Chelsea Tuttle had arranged his "murder." It wouldn't be easy to prove since she hadn't been on the yacht during the attempt. Considering that Douglas Grant, with all his influence and power as the district attorney, considered her a niece, implicating her might even be impossible.

Right before they stepped into the office, Sahara stopped her chatter and slipped her hand into his.

Brand paused. Seeing her vulnerable last night had been unsettling but he'd recognized it as an aftereffect of being utterly depleted both physically and emotionally.

Today she was back to her usual energetic self, an unstoppable force, a whirlwind...and yet she'd taken his hand as if she needed support.

She had it, of course. Always. But he couldn't shake off a niggling worry that something wasn't sitting right with her.

He could have lost her.

Pulling her around to face him, Brand cupped one hand to her warm, satiny cheek. "What's going on, baby?"

She gave him a wobbly smile. "I guess I'm just a little nervous."

"Sahara Silver, super shark?" His thumb teased over the corner of her mouth. "Nervous about what?"

She glanced around, saw that they were alone in the outer office and exhaled a big breath. "Everything is up in the air. Now that Scott has returned, what will I do?"

"Do?"

She laughed and dropped her forehead against him, hiding her uncertainty. "This is his business again. I swear, I'm happy to give it up to have him back, but I feel… I don't know." She leaned back to search his face, then admitted, "Lost."

"You're not lost when you're with me."

"*Am* I with you?" She stared up at him with near desperation. "I know my being the boss was a problem for you. Since I won't be anymore, maybe—"

Brand leaned down and kissed her. He'd meant it to be a firm smooch of reassurance, but instead he lingered, loving the taste of her mouth, loving everything about her. Against her lips, he promised, "Whatever you do, whether you're the boss or not, you won't be rid of me."

She bit her lip. "Do you mean for the near future, or just for right now, or—"

Enoch opened the door behind them. He seemed inordinately pleased, probably because Sahara finally had her brother back. "Everyone is in the conference room." He gave Sahara a huge, happy smile. "I already set out coffee and pastries. Anything else you need?"

"Even though it's lunchtime, I'd love a breakfast sandwich. Do you think you could have one ready for me as soon as we wrap up this meeting?"

"Of course. I'll call the deli that delivers. They probably have something."

"Thank you." She blew a lock of hair out of her face. "It was a really long day yesterday."

Enoch tilted his head, eyed the bruise on her cheek and nodded. "I'm sure." He glanced at Brand.

Brand shrugged. How could he reassure Enoch when he was currently so confused himself?

Gently, Sahara said, "I really am fine, both of you. I promise."

Just as gently, Enoch said, "I'm glad."

Would she be fine? Brand wondered. What if Sahara's brother ripped the agency away from her? Where did that leave her? What would Leese, Justice and Miles do if that happened?

He could understand Sahara's worry, damn it.

Scott stepped out of the room as they approached. His hair, the same color as Sahara's, hung damn near to his shoulders. His blue eyes were also like hers, only full of cynicism. Again, he opened his arms, and again Sahara hurried to him.

Brand let her go, then stood back. He didn't give them privacy by going into the conference room, but neither did he interrupt the moment.

Sahara squeezed him tight. "I can't believe you're finally back. I never gave up hope."

"I know." Scott levered her away, brotherly concern darkening his expression. "You're okay?"

"Of course." She rolled her eyes. "Why does everyone keep asking me that?"

He shook his head and said to Brand, "She likes to think she's invincible."

"Not really." Brand stared hard at her brother—and again had to fight the urge to pulverize him. "But she is the strongest person I know."

Sahara spun around to face him. "Really?"

Leave it to Sahara to like that compliment most of all. "Absolutely."

"She's tough," Scott said with pride. "I'll give you that." He looked around. "You changed everything, sis."

"Yes."

Brand heard the subdued hesitation in her voice, but Scott paid no attention. "It suits you."

Sahara took in his black thermal shirt, worn jeans and lace-up boots, and said, "Not sure I can say the same. This whole dressing down thing is a very different look for you. You do realize that all your regular clothes are still at the house?"

Scott grinned. "Somehow, I don't feel like a suit anymore. All this time I've gotten by with only a few pairs of jeans and a half-dozen shirts. It's a simpler way of life."

Sahara reached up to smooth his untrimmed hair. "I'll take your word for it."

His mouth quirked on one side and his gaze softened. "You're still a clotheshorse, I see."

Why did every damn thing he said sound like an insult?

"Of course." Sahara looked him over again, then nodded. "You know, I think the rugged look suits you."

Scott hauled her in for another hug. "Damn, but I missed you, sis."

"I missed you, too. So much." She touched his unshaven face. "Didn't you get any rest?"

"Actually, no."

"But why—"

"So impatient. I'll explain everything as soon as we get inside." He grinned down at her. "Come on. I have a lot to tell you."

"More than what we learned last night?"

"A lot more. I hope you'll be pleased." Scott opened the door and waited for her to enter.

She looked back at Brand.

Scott said, "This is company business."

Voice firm, Sahara replied, "True, but he's with me."

Scott studied Brand, as if deciding.

Brand stepped up behind Sahara, his gaze daring Scott to question it.

Instead, Scott shrugged and gestured for them both to precede him.

Once in the conference room, Scott closed the door and strode to the seat at the head of the table—a seat normally reserved for Sahara. A quick glance showed Brand that his friends weren't happy with the seating arrangement either.

Without missing a beat, Brand took Sahara's arm and drew her to the opposite end of the long table, then took the chair to her right.

In brooding silence, Justice got up, retrieved the coffee and pastry near Scott's elbow, and moved to sit at Sahara's left, offering her the food. "I got this for you."

Strangely flustered, she murmured, "Thank you," and bit into the pastry.

Miles followed suit, carrying his coffee down the table to sit next to Brand. Leese got up to take the chair beside Justice. That left three empty seats on each side of Scott.

Oddly enough, the rearranged seating appeared to satisfy her brother. He leaned back in his chair, elbows on the arms, his fingers laced together. Looking down the length of the table, he said to Sahara, "They're loyal to you."

She took a fortifying gulp of coffee. "Actually, they're loyal to the agency. They're excellent bodyguards, Scott, always in high demand, assets to Body Armor—"

Brand covered her hand. "You don't need to sell them, honey."

She abruptly stopped rambling. "No, I don't." Chin lifting, she said, "With all the new high-level business we've brought in, the results speak for themselves."

"They do," Scott said softly. "But I never doubted it, sis. You would only hire the best. I know that."

The vote of confidence cleared away her frown. "Thank you."

He segued right into business. "Now, as you know, proving that Chelsea Tuttle plotted to have me killed would be impossible."

Shooting halfway out of her seat, Sahara flattened her hands on the table. "You can't give up! I won't let her get away with this. One way or another, I'm going to see that woman—"

"Down, killer." Scott laughed. "You're always so ferocious."

"It's not funny," she snapped, some of her natural vitality returning.

"No, I suppose it's not, but relax, okay? It's working out, I promise."

"Oh." She glanced at everyone with a tinge of embarrassment, then sank back into her chair with a renewed frown. "You better tell me that she's going to prison for a very long time, because I won't be satisfied with anything else."

"All right." Scott looked only at his sister. "Ross Moran once worked for me. You know that much. I'm not sure if he explained all of it, though."

"Only that you still owed him money," Sahara said.

"Very true. Attempted murder has a way of making you forget your debts, at least for a time."

"And that the two of you had grown close?"

"I trusted Ross," he confirmed.

Leese stared at Scott. "Enough to give him the pass-code to your security system?"

Wincing, Scott explained, "He's actually a security specialist, and yes, after I had a suspicion that I was being followed, he did know the code because he helped beef up the system."

Justice snorted. "I made it better." His jaw locked. "And unlike the goon you hired, I would never break in and attack Sahara."

A flush rose up Scott's neck and his shoulders tightened. "That was unforgivable. He claims to be taken with her—"

"And that justifies attempted rape?" Miles asked.

"If I thought he would have taken it that far," Scott stated, "I'd kill him myself."

In a lethally calm tone, Brand said, "I'll handle that for you."

Scott glanced at Brand, did a double take over the seriousness of his expression, and frowned. "I already explained things to him." At that, Scott rubbed his knuckles. "When I found out he'd been in the house, and that he'd gotten out by the tree, I had it trimmed."

Sahara's eyes flared. "That was you?"

Disgusted, Scott said, "I'd snuck in to get more money by pretending to be part of a landscaping team."

"Team?" Justice asked.

"The others with me really were from a landscaping firm."

"*More* money?" Brand asked.

Scott gestured dismissively. "I kept gold and silver in a secret vault in the basement. That's how I funded myself, since I couldn't access any of my accounts."

"You snuck in?" Sahara asked, wounded by the possibility. "You were there and never told me?"

"Until I figured out who'd tried to kill me, no one could know I was alive. By not telling you, I protected you."

"By not telling her," Brand stated softly, "you left her vulnerable to the likes of Ross Moran and his gang."

"That was definitely an error in judgment, but how was I to know Ross would get enamored with her?"

Brand narrowed his eyes. "How could you think any man wouldn't?"

Scott flattened his mouth. "Believe me, he'll be very careful around her from now on."

So that there would be no mistakes, Brand sat forward and stated, "He won't be around her ever again. Period."

"As to that…" Scott shoved back his chair and began to pace.

Brand didn't like it, but he knew Sahara well enough to let her handle things—as long as she handled them in a way that satisfied his protective instincts.

"You were wiser than me, Sahara." Scott glanced at her. "You knew all along that Chelsea Tuttle was trouble."

"More than trouble," Sahara muttered. "She's sick and dangerous and—"

"You remember when she hired guards from the agency?"

"Yes." Disgust narrowed her eyes. "They reported back that she'd tried to use them in perverted sexual favors."

Since they hadn't heard the story yet, Leese, Miles and Justice stared in fascination.

"It seemed so far-fetched at the time," Scott murmured, "I wasn't sure what to believe. Overall she seemed spoiled, brazen, but mostly harmless. After she admitted to drinking too much and flirting—which she said they'd misconstrued—I tried to give her the benefit of the doubt."

"Big mistake," Sahara said.

"Clearly." He paused. "Maybe I'm better at judging men than women."

Brand snorted. Far as he could tell, her brother sucked at that, too.

Ignoring him, Scott said to Sahara, "Chelsea later told me that you'd threatened her."

"Did she?" Sahara smiled with chilling amusement. "Well, it's true. And I have plenty of evidence to ruin her socially, even if it doesn't get her locked up."

"You told her to quit her games?"

"And to stay away from you." Anger brought her brows together. "Apparently I didn't go far enough to impress my intentions on her if she contacted you again after that."

"Oh, you did. She believed you would ruin her—or worse. She made me swear I wouldn't tell you about her visit to the agency because she said she feared for her life."

"Then she's not as dumb as I assumed."

"Not dumb, no, but very cunning." Scott looked at each of the men. "I trust what I say will stay confidential?"

Leese shrugged. "As you already pointed out, we're loyal to Sahara."

"We wouldn't say or do anything to hurt her," Justice added.

"You all work for Body Armor and that gives you certain credibility." He turned thoughtfully toward Brand. "You, however, are an outsider."

Brand smiled at the absurdity of that.

Before he could say anything, Miles spoke up. "He's not officially a bodyguard, but you'd be an idiot not to see how protective he is of her."

"It's because I'm not an idiot that I'm being cautious."

Sahara cast a worried glance at first Miles and then Brand. "You can speak freely, Scott. I plan to. I have complete trust in everyone here."

Scott's skeptical gaze lingered on Brand a moment longer. "We'll talk about your role soon."

With soft menace, Brand said, "I'll look forward to it."

Throwing up her hands, Sahara said, "That's enough from both of you. We have bigger issues than macho pride." She glared at her brother. "Spit it out already."

Scott finally drew his gaze from Brand's. After running a hand through his hair, he said, "Chelsea wanted Body Armor to provide security during a special event she had planned. Of course, she wasn't exactly forthcoming on the type of event. She just wanted assurance that no one interrupted by hiring bodyguards to protect the perimeter of the property."

"Ross told me part of this," Sahara said, "but at the time I didn't realize he was talking about Chelsea."

"He knew not to mention it, not even to you. *Especially* to you. I told him I wanted you kept out of it completely."

She stiffened. "You excluded me."

"I was trying to protect you."

Leese said, "So while you were keeping her in the dark, she was taking matters into her own hands."

"Yes." Scott gave a rueful laugh. "Knowing my sister, I should have realized what she would do."

"Yeah," Miles said. "You should have."

"I could have told you," Justice added with a snort.

Sahara rolled her eyes. "You shouldn't have kept things from me, period. I would have known how to deal with her. I'm not inept."

"No, you're not," Scott assured her. "In fact, it was your reaction to Chelsea that first tipped me off and made me suspicious. I knew I had to figure out what was going on." He took his seat again. "She was already familiar with all our bodyguards, so if they got caught surveilling her, it'd come back to the agency. Since I didn't want that, I had to hire other men."

"Ross Moran," Sahara said with dawning awareness. "You hired him and his crew, didn't you?"

Justice made a sound of disgust.

"Couldn't have found someone ethical?" Miles asked.

Brand kept quiet, focused solely on Sahara and her reactions. Little by little, she was more herself, back in fighting form, and that pleased him. He just hoped her brother didn't deliver a final blow.

"Someone ethical to snoop on the niece of a prominent public figure? A woman known for her sexual deviation? A woman who operated with immunity, who apparently bought off anyone who otherwise would have complained? Yeah, where would I find a guy like that?"

Miles, Leese and Justice each raised a hand.

"None of you were here at the time."

"Because Sahara hadn't yet taken over the hiring," Leese pointed out.

Impatient, Sahara shushed Leese with a lift of her hand, then said to her brother, "Ross told me that your instincts were uncanny, so I'm guessing he discovered something?"

Scott picked up his coffee to take a sip. He spoke quietly, not looking at anyone. "Chelsea was throwing big parties where young, desperate prostitutes—women with nowhere to turn—were corralled together for the sport of all in attendance. She called it her gladiator games."

Sahara clenched her hands into fists on the tabletop. "She's gotten worse since I gathered my own recordings of her."

Brand's stomach twisted… *Since I gathered my own recordings…* Dear God. Chelsea was sicker than he'd ever imagined—and Sahara hadn't just hired someone to track the psycho, as she'd implied earlier. No, she'd done that herself.

The risks she took left him in a futile rage.

"Jesus," Leese muttered, staring at her.

"That's how you planned to ruin her?" Justice asked with horror. "You snuck around behind a twisted chick who's into pain, and you *recorded* her?"

"Yes."

Miles sat forward, his expression fierce. "I know you, Sahara. You wouldn't have stood by and let it happen just to get evidence."

"No, I didn't. But at the time I had promised Chelsea that if she quit her games and stayed away from my brother, all the details would remain private." She turned to Brand. "She broke the deal, so now I'm not held to it either."

"Agreed," he said softly, still reeling from the danger she'd chased.

Sahara drew a deep breath, released it slowly, then admitted, "While they were all busy enjoying someone else's pain, I snuck around the property and set off her fire alarms."

Scott lifted a brow. "That's genius."

Brand wanted to slug her brother for encouraging her.

Shrugging, Sahara said, "It worked. In minutes, police and firemen were arriving, but I already had at least a minute or two of very incriminating evidence. I made sure Chelsea knew that I had several copies." She looked at her brother squarely. "If you can't prove anything against her, I certainly can."

Laughing, Scott rubbed his eyes, "You're terrifying, you know that, right?"

"I know how to take care of business."

This business, Brand wanted to say—just in case her brother had missed that significant fact.

"That's obvious." Scott sat back. "To stall, I agreed to provide services for Chelsea's party. Of course, I had no intention of involving Body Armor, but I needed a strategy. While Ross was working his angle, I decided to distance myself by going out on the yacht with a girlfriend."

"And that's when Chelsea struck?" Sahara whispered.

"Men came aboard. You already know that they never recovered my date's body." Scott turned away, his gaze on the windows overlooking the city. "She and I weren't close, but I should have protected her."

"How many men were there?" Justice asked.

"Four, maybe five. They came aboard without my hearing them. We were sitting on the deck, enjoying the night, listening to music, and then suddenly they were there."

Sahara huffed. "I should have taken care of her long ago."

For some women, that would be an empty boast. Not for Sahara.

To soothe her, Brand brushed his thumb over her knuckles. "I'd rather you not kill anyone."

"And I'd rather she wasn't involved at all," Scott said.

Shifting with annoyance, Sahara said, "You're both doomed to disappointment, because it's clear that we have to do something."

"Can you ID the men who attacked you?" Leese asked.

Scott shook his head. "It was dark and it all happened so fast. I might recognize their voices, but I just don't know."

Justice said. "So we still need proof."

Scott actually smiled. "I believe Ross has it. For two weeks prior to the event, he and his men gathered intel for me, not only on Chelsea, but also on those people included on her guest list."

"Douglas Grant?" Sahara asked.

"Oddly, no. Maybe because he really does feel related to her even though they don't share blood, and maybe deep down he possesses a few vague ethics, but he's never been involved with any of her sexual escapades."

Brand had a hard time wrapping his brain around the implications. "You're saying Sahara's kidnapper has info, so he might get a free pass?"

Scott looked at Sahara. "Ross managed to record quite a bit of Chelsea's activity. He found correspondence talking about the event, what they do, how many women to expect as playthings. Even where and how they got the women." With a note of admiration, Scott added, "He's really pretty good at what he does."

Sahara gave it quick thought. "If he can bury Chelsea—"

Leese, Justice and Miles all issued protests at the same time.

Sahara turned to Brand, saying softly, "He really didn't hurt me, you know."

"It's not happening."

Anxious now, she insisted, "Taking down Chelsea is far more important than seeing Ross pay."

"Hell, no."

Scott cleared his throat. "There's more to consider. As it happens, Douglas Grant also hired Ross to kill a man. Giving Ross immunity, or at least a plea deal of some sort, means we get a two-for-one."

"We can destroy both Chelsea and Douglas?" Sahara asked with excitement.

"I think so."

"Then it's a done deal," she said with finality.

"Excuse us." Utilizing every ounce of control he had, Brand stood, gently took Sahara's arm and headed toward the door of the conference room.

Sahara didn't resist him, but on their way, she said over her shoulder, "We'll be right back. Don't talk about anything important without me!"

SAHARA UNDERSTOOD THAT Brand was upset, and she decided it wouldn't hurt to calm him before they proceeded. By seeking privacy from the others, he'd given her the perfect opportunity to see to it.

Enoch looked up as they emerged from the conference room, his smile freezing in place when he got a look at Brand's face.

"Ahem." Enoch stood. "I think I'll see if we need

more coffee." As he passed Sahara, he murmured, "Think long-term, please."

Sahara smiled at him. "That's my plan." As soon as Enoch disappeared into the room, she gave her attention to Brand.

Fury shone from his dark eyes, but she knew it wasn't directed at her. No, he was just that worried about her safety, and his concern warmed her.

Putting a hand to his jaw, she asked softly, "Are you ever going to shave?"

The question surprised him. "Maybe every couple of weeks."

She couldn't help but smile. "So you'll be semibearded, then clean-shaven, only to become semibearded again?"

He covered her hand on his jaw. "I'm not into a lot of grooming."

"Since you look sexy all scruffy, I guess that's okay."

"I'll never be a fancy dresser either."

"Fancy dressing isn't required." She leaned in and kissed him, then whispered against his firm mouth, "Ross won't hurt me."

Closing his hands over her upper arms, he stepped her back so she couldn't miss his heated glare. "You can't know that."

"If I was relying on Ross's honor, I'd agree. But I know Scott, and I know *you*." She searched his gaze. "Neither of you would let him near me."

"Damn right—although I can't speak for your brother since he's the one wanting to let the bastard skate."

His grumbling tone worried her. "Scott has deliberately tried to annoy you." She lowered her voice to a serious whisper. "That's how he chased off other boy-friends."

Brand tipped up her chin. "I'll deal with your brother, don't worry about that. The rest of this, though—"

"It's important to me, Brand." She moved closer, staring up at him, willing him to see it from her perspective. "I want Chelsea to pay. She's an awful person, a cruel, manipulative sadist. As if that wasn't enough already, she tried to take my brother from me." Sahara brushed her mouth over his. "And to see Douglas lose his authority… God, I'd love that so much."

Stubbornly, Brand insisted, "There has to be another way."

"If there was, don't you think I'd have found it by now? Powerful people don't go down easy. It takes a lot." She wound her arms around his neck. "This might be the only chance we have."

In ill humor, Brand grumbled, "Damn it, Sahara."

"You know I'm right," she insisted. "You know this is important." Imploring him, she added, "Especially to me."

He groaned.

Knowing he gave in, her heart lifted. Softly, she whispered, "Thank you for understanding."

The office entry door opened and Ross Moran started in. When he saw Sahara and Brand, he drew up short.

"Sahara." He actually started to smile.

She hastily stepped in front of Brand. "You have new bruises," she pointed out. "Did Scott do that?"

Ross touched his cheek. "Some of it." His gaze went over her head to Brand. "I already had most of them."

"And yet," Brand said, "here you are."

He looked at Sahara. "I wasn't aware my men were acting without me. You have to believe that."

"I do," she said. "Unfortunately, it doesn't make much difference to me."

"We should talk—"

"Seriously?" Brand laughed without humor. "Apparently you're a slow learner...but I can help you with that."

Warily, Ross eyed Brand. "Scott is expecting me."

Finding a new direction for his anger, Brand set Sahara aside. "That's Scott's problem."

Sahara grabbed Brand when he started forward. "Brand, no."

"Afraid so."

Panicked, she saw the resignation on Ross's face, Brand's determined stride and she knew she couldn't stop this. "Damn you two, don't you dare damage my building!"

Ross opened the door for Brand with a grand gesture. Without slowing his stride, Brand grabbed him and shoved him out first, then followed and quietly closed the door behind him.

Frozen in place, Sahara stared at the closed door. A second later, she heard a loud thump, one more followed by a groan, then the wall shook as if a body had hit it.

The sounds of combat unglued her feet. She turned and ran into the conference room, her gaze sweeping over everyone. "Ross is here and Brand just took him out to the hall!"

Scott looked up, startled.

Enoch grinned.

Leese took Sahara's arm. "Have a seat, okay? Brand won't be long."

Damn it! "What if Ross is armed?"

Miles said, "It won't help him any."

"Might just make Brand madder," Justice said with relish.

"Oh my God, you're all insane." She started to stand, but the guys surrounded her.

Justice even patted her shoulder. "Give them five minutes, okay? You can be patient that long."

She looked across the table and locked eyes with her brother. He'd lifted his eyebrows high in disbelief. And why not? Not only were these men unlike any they'd encountered before, but they were employees who cosseted her like a helpless female.

Grim, she shoved to her feet and said to the walls of muscle surrounding her, *"Move."*

Reluctantly, they each stepped aside.

Enoch rushed forward to fill the void. "Now, Sahara—"

"I won't wait here like the proverbial little woman while Brand destroys a key witness that we need to get this all settled."

"He won't kill him," Leese said. "That's not what this is about."

"He's only going to point out the error of his ways," Miles said.

Justice added, "He needs to make it clear that you're off-limits, that's all."

Being off-limits would mean that she and Brand had a commitment, and so far, they didn't. What they had was an agreement.

In any case, Brand didn't need to clear up anything with Ross because she had zero interest in any other man, but most especially a man who had kidnapped her and threatened her. Damn it, he should have trusted her to have enough sense to—

The conference door opened and Brand strolled back in, interrupting her silent rant. His shoulders were bunched, the muscles in his arms bulging, but he looked calm, calmer than he had all day.

He was even smiling.

CHAPTER SEVENTEEN

SAHARA STARED AT HIM, loving him so much that her heart wanted to burst and her stomach churned with an unfamiliar anxiety only partly due to the situation with Chelsea and Douglas.

To Enoch, Brand said, "You have a mess in the hall."

"Oh dear Lord," Enoch muttered and rushed out.

Sahara couldn't think of a thing to say. She saw no marks on Brand, but then, after having witnessed his fighting skills, she hadn't expected to.

Laughing, Leese said, "We'll lend Enoch a hand," and he started out, too, followed by Miles and Justice.

"Thanks." Brand walked up to her, his dark eyes looking deep into hers.

Sahara managed to gather her wits. "What did you do?"

"We had a discussion." He smoothed back her hair, brushed his thumb over her cheek, and said, "As long as he stays the hell away from you, I've decided he can live."

That outrageous statement said a lot, some of it serious despite the absurdity of his wording. Relief washed over her. Realizing that Brand did understand gave her an enormous smile. "Thank you."

Blustering, Scott stormed up to them. "You're *thanking* him?"

Still calm personified, Brand glanced at Scott. "You're next."

Sahara's heart had just started to settle into a normal rhythm, and now it leaped into overtime again. "No, Brand."

Antagonistic, Scott said, "Fine by me."

Facing her brother, Sahara growled, "I just got you back, you have a bullet wound on your arm and a knock on your head."

Scott's jaw flexed. "I can handle myself."

"That's what Ross said, and now he's a mess out in the hallway!"

Trying to provoke Brand, he shrugged. "Ross probably held back for fear of losing his immunity deal. I won't be hampered the same way."

Brand grinned in anticipation.

She'd never realized how foolish her brother could be. She'd always idolized him, thought him the most brilliant man alive, but now she had to reevaluate.

If he thought he could go toe-to-toe with Brand, he was worse than foolish.

Hoping to placate him, she said, "Usually, I'm sure you're more than capable, but not this time. This time," she emphasized, "you're up against a professional MMA fighter."

His eyes narrowed—and he withdrew a gun. "Then maybe I should even the odds."

"Scott!"

"I won't let any man take advantage of you, hon."

She gasped in outrage. "Who says he is?"

Growing more pugnacious, Scott rationalized his assumptions, saying, "He knows you're wealthy and influential—"

Scoffing, Brand said, "I know, but it doesn't matter to me."

"It matters to *every* man."

"You're a fool. Sahara could be dead broke and it wouldn't change how I feel."

Scott lifted the gun higher. "I'm not convinced."

"And I don't give a shit what you think." Still with Sahara in front of him, Brand kicked out—and the gun went flying. It landed on the polished surface of the table, skittered along the length of it and fell to the floor with a thud.

He'd moved so fast, it took Sahara a second to realize what had happened.

Cursing, Scott shook his hand, then clutched his fingers, his face a grimace of pain.

He cursed again when Sahara punched him in the stomach. "Ow, damn! What was that for?"

Incredulous that he would do such a thing, she hissed, "A *gun*, Scott? You would have shot him? *Have you lost your mind*?"

Scott studied her. "For you, there's nothing I wouldn't do." Then curiously, he asked, "Would you mind so much?"

"Of course I would mind!" Her shrill voice embarrassed her so she struggled to regain some control. Tone lower now, bordering on demonic, she said, "I would never forgive you if you dared to shoot him."

"He couldn't," Brand said with confidence.

She jerked around to face him. "That's enough from you."

Brand only smiled.

Scott scowled at Brand, then at Sahara. "You sound like a woman in love."

Maybe if the past twenty-four hours hadn't been so insanely chaotic, she would have thought before speaking, but never in her life had she been so frazzled, and she snapped, "Of course I love him." She waved a hand at Brand. "You've met him. You see how incredible he is. How could I *not* love him?"

After an arrested moment of silence, Brand and Scott both laughed.

ALL IN ALL, Brand thought, he felt pretty good.

Now that they had a way to lock up the threats, Sahara was finally safe.

He'd made his point with Ross. The man had finally held up both hands, saying, "Enough! No woman is worth all this."

"There's where you're wrong," Brand had told him, then he'd hit him again. He'd left Ross nearly unconscious, swearing off all women—Sahara included.

Good thing, because Sahara was his.

She loved him.

She'd shouted as much at her brother.

Brand wanted to hear it again once they were alone. They had a lot to discuss, a future to plan, but he could be patient while she and her brother settled their own conflicts.

After Sahara glared Scott into silence, he cleared his throat. "Seriously, though. He's not right for you, hon."

Knowing how she felt about her brother's opinion, Brand stiffened. Now that he knew Sahara loved him, he wouldn't let Scott or anyone else get in his way.

He took a step toward her brother. "You don't want to go there."

Scott ignored him. "I'm right, though, aren't I? He knew you were wealthy before he ever pursued you."

"Actually," she said, "I pursued him. And I don't mind admitting that he wasn't easy to catch."

Brand felt compelled to say, "That's not true. I just didn't want to work for you."

"Why work for her, when you have an easier path to get what you want?"

God, her brother was as misguided as a man could be. It was almost funny.

"You heard him," Sahara said. "My bank account doesn't matter to him."

Gently, Scott said, "I wish I could believe that."

"I love you, Scott. You've been more than a brother to me. You've been…everything. I'm so glad you're home where you belong." Sahara folded her arms. "I'd take on the devil himself to keep you here, but what I won't do is let you run my life. I'm smart and capable and I have my own inheritance. That's enough."

Damn, she was amazing, Brand thought as he gave her a slow grin. "I love you, too, Sahara."

She pivoted fast to face him, her startled expression shifting to one of utter joy. "I thought you did, but I wasn't sure."

"Why the hell hasn't he already told you?" Scott demanded.

"He's been busy rescuing me," Sahara snapped. "And that's in part because *you* kept me in the dark about things."

Scott had the sense to flush.

The way her shifting moods took her from one extreme to the other was almost humorous.

Ignoring her rigid annoyance with her brother, Brand

pulled her close, his hands rubbing her shoulders. She was as feminine as a woman could be, with a unique strength and deep conviction. He loved her more than he knew was possible. "Before we get ahead of ourselves, we need to come to an understanding."

"Here it comes," Scott predicted.

Brand's smile never slipped. He knew what her brother expected, but once a man had met her, how could he care more about money than Sahara?

Maybe because Scott saw her only as a younger sister, he didn't realize how incredible she was. Brand would never make that mistake.

He framed her face in his hands. "I love you."

After shooting a look of triumph at her brother, she smiled up at Brand and asked, "Will you marry me?"

Emotion swelled, bringing happiness and peace, even humor. He grinned. "That's a first."

She rushed on, not giving him a chance to answer. "We love each other, so it only makes sense, right? After all this time together, I wouldn't want to sleep alone, and I don't think you would either. We make a good team, too. Now that my brother is back, I won't harangue you anymore about working as a bodyguard. Going forward, hiring will be up to Scott." She managed a quick breath. "Your friends are now my friends, and your family likes me, even Becky. Before you say it, I know, I shouldn't have overstepped there. I can try to—"

Overwhelmed by her rapid-fire reasoning, Brand pressed a finger to her lips, silencing her. He waited, and when she remained quiet, he said calmly, "I want a life with you, but we need to agree on a few things."

Her brows rose in inquiry. Unlike her brother, there was no suspicion in her gaze.

"First, your inheritance is yours. I won't ever touch it. Not a single dime of it. If you're with me, we'll live in a house I buy."

Scott snorted. "I've seen what you provide your parents."

Brand paused. "My parents?" Irritation gathered, but he was determined to get through the rest of this without another explosion. "You've checked into my background?"

"As soon as I realized my sister was involved with you."

"Too bad you weren't that diligent with Ross Moran." He let that barb hit, then replied, "I'll be generous and assume you're trying to look out for Sahara—even though she doesn't need you to—but you're off base with my folks. They would never take money from me, regardless of how I've tried. They provide for themselves, and they're happy where they are."

"I love their property," Sahara stated with feeling. "It's beautiful and private, the perfect place for a family to raise a son."

It had been perfect, Brand realized. One of the few things Becky had ever done right was to give him to Ann and John to raise. He doubted he'd have so many great memories if she hadn't.

He recalled how easily Sahara had fit into the setting with his parents. No matter what Scott thought, she could be happy anywhere because her life had more meaning than luxury and wealth. He believed that, but he didn't want her getting the wrong impression. "So that we're clear, I'm not poor. I've made a good living fighting and I'm smart with my money. I've socked away a healthy savings, and the rest is earning for me."

"You're still not in her league," Scott said.

"On that we agree. I'm not sure any man could be good enough for her, but no one will ever love her more than I do."

Sahara smiled happily. "You see? He loves me. That's all that matters."

"I'll drive my own car," Brand added. "If you want something fancier, that's up to you. You won't spend anything on me, though."

The smile faded under a frown. "But—"

"I apologize for not appreciating your efforts with Becky."

Sahara blinked at the topic switch. "You apologize?"

"Are you really that surprised?" Had he been that surly about it? "You were right, you know. Life will be easier if I let that old animosity go."

Sahara rested a hand on his chest. "You have a right to your animosity. But if Becky is happy, she'll be an easier burden to bear."

Amazing that she'd understood when he hadn't. "True. It just took me a little time to see it." Already his heart felt lighter. "Don't ever feel obligated, but do feel free to do what you want with her, okay?"

She drew in a breath. "Okay."

"You should also know that I'm going to fight again. Not in Japan, but sometime after that."

Her eyes widened, but she said, "If that's what makes you happy, then—"

"After that fight, I'm retiring."

"Oh." Sahara bit her lip. "To do what?"

"I was thinking I'd be a bodyguard."

Her eyes flared again. "Here?"

"I want to be close to you."

Color flushed her cheeks as she struggled to repress a grin. "Anything else?"

He didn't bother to look at Scott when he said, "If your brother can be polite, I'll be polite. If not, he and I are going to have problems, because I'm done letting him insult you."

Objecting to that, Scott said, "I wouldn't!"

"You do," Brand insisted. "Every time you act like a man would only be interested in her money, you do her a disservice. Every time you assume she's not smart enough to make her own decisions, you underestimate her. Sahara is not only beautiful and business savvy, she's also scary smart, clever, independent, resourceful—"

Scott laughed, saying in an aside to Sahara, "I'm starting to like him."

Sahara grinned.

"You might've intimidated other guys," Brand continued, "but that's not me. She loves me, so that means I'm around for the long haul."

Sahara said to her brother. "Can't you see that he's perfect for me?"

"Because he thinks you're perfect?"

She actually blushed. "No, because he loves me as I am."

Scott smiled at her. "Then that's good enough for me. You don't need my blessing, but you have it."

Brand rolled his eyes, but since it obviously pleased Sahara, it also pleased him. "Then yes," Brand said, smiling, "I'll marry you."

Before she could get too excited, Scott said, "There's one more thing to discuss."

Sahara quickly turned on her brother. "No, Scott, there isn't. I already told you—"

"I don't want Body Armor. You need to keep it."

Brand stifled a laugh over her arrested expression. Maybe her brother was a smart guy, after all.

Floundering, Sahara whispered, "You...*what*?"

Scott took her hands. "You've done an amazing job here, sis. No one can deny that. I see you everywhere, in the new designs, in all the changes you've made. Before that, I might have run the place, but I was never a part of it, not the way you are. Does that makes sense?"

"It does," Brand said.

Scott thanked him with a small nod, then continued to Sahara, "It's yours now in a way that it was never mine. Taking it back wouldn't feel right—to me, or to the people who work for you."

"I don't know what to say."

He bent his knees to look into his sister's eyes. "It's not like you to be coy. I don't want it, but I know you do. Admit it."

"It does feel a part of me." She huffed out a breath. "But what will you do?"

"I've given it a lot of thought and decided that I'd enjoy doing some charity work for a while. I met a lot of different people while I was hiding out, people in dire situations but without my means. I'm thinking I could help, maybe make a difference."

And just like that, Brand's animus toward Scott changed to respect.

"The suite, along with everything else at Body Armor, is yours, but I'm not sure I'll keep the house. If you want it—"

She said quickly, "I don't. I stayed there only because it made me feel closer to you."

Since she'd been attacked there, Brand wondered if

the house now held negative feelings for her. He should have punched Ross a few more times.

"Where will you go?" Sahara asked with concern.

"You know the lake property Mom and Dad left us? If you don't object, I was thinking of making that my home base."

"I think that sounds wonderful."

"You'll still visit there sometimes?"

She glanced at Brand, and when he nodded, she said, "We'd love to."

Scott slowly smiled. "I guess everything has worked out."

"I guess it has." Sahara launched herself into her brother's arms, but only for a second.

After giving Scott a tight squeeze, she pressed away and landed against Brand—and there she stayed.

He helped with that, keeping his arms tight around her.

THEY VISITED HIS parents together to give them the news. After a second of shocked silence, his mom screamed, danced around the kitchen, kissed John enthusiastically, then hugged Sahara until she squeaked.

Brand couldn't stop grinning. It was a great feeling, seeing the people he loved most all together.

When Ann asked if they'd have a big wedding, Brand explained that with the arrests and her brother coming back from the dead, they had their hands full.

"You don't live a dull life," John remarked.

Brand knew it would never be dull with Sahara, but he looked forward to putting the danger behind them.

"We'll have a small ceremony," Sahara said, "as soon

as I can get it arranged. Then later, maybe a year from now, we'll have a wedding party."

"A small ceremony?" Ann asked politely, trying to keep her expression contained.

"My brother and my friend Enoch, and of course, Brand's friends and their wives."

"They're our friends, Sahara."

Smiling over that, Sahara said to Ann, "I hope you'll both join us."

With exuberant relief, Ann hugged her again. "You couldn't keep us away." Cautiously, she glanced at Brand. "What about Becky?"

"I invited her." He moved to sit by Ann. "You're my mother in all the ways that matter, so I hope you don't mind."

Ann put her palm to his face. "Oh, honey, I think we're so blessed that we should only spread happiness, not bitterness."

Damn, when it came to the women in his life, he'd struck gold. Brand smiled. "I figured you'd feel that way."

"Becky gave John and me a very special gift when she handed you over."

"She did," John agreed. "We're grateful to her."

Since he felt the same, Brand nodded. "So am I."

Understanding, supportive, always there for him... Ann's voice broke when she said, "Becky might never realize what she missed, but having you for a son has been one of the greatest joys of my life."

"Mom." Brand brushed the tears off her cheek. "I love you." He looked at his dad. "Both of you."

Suddenly he heard Sahara sniff.

Surprised, Brand turned his head and saw the tears

tracking down her cheeks. His heart softened and he reached for her.

Sahara quickly stood, saying in a brusque tone, "Show me that new gun you mentioned, John. Let's do some shooting."

His dad jumped up so quickly, it was like he'd had a spring on his butt.

Ann started to rise, too, but as Sahara swiped at her cheeks, she said, "No, you two stay and finish your chat. We won't be long."

"It's a new Smith & Wesson 9 mm," John enthused as he latched an arm through Sahara's and led her away. "Got a good deal on it, including a rebate and some accessories."

Brand grinned as he and his mom stood. "She's bossy."

Ann stared after her husband and Sahara. "In the most remarkable, loving way."

He laughed. "Exactly." Everything about Sahara was remarkable, and she was all his.

He'd been lucky as a boy, and now he was lucky as a man. That left no room in his life for resentment... only love.

EPILOGUE

THEY SAT AROUND a bonfire near the pond by the farm. Maxi and Miles had done an amazing job with the place since their wedding. The parklike setting made a perfect location for everyone to get together—and they routinely did.

Brand watched Justice and Fallon, newly married now, amused that Justice couldn't keep his hands off her. He had Fallon in his lap, and he kept nuzzling her ear. Not that Fallon appeared to mind. In fact, given the way she encouraged him, no one would ever again call her shy or reserved.

Sitting cross-legged on the ground in front of Leese, leaning back against his legs, Catalina sketched the landscape highlighted by the crimson glow of a setting sun. She was two months pregnant, and it was almost like they were all becoming dads, everyone was so excited. Leese kept a perpetual smile on his face—and he was even more protective than usual.

Next to Brand, Sahara stroked a large cat while talking about the house they'd bought together.

A house that would become a real home.

"I've almost finished remodeling it," she said. "Once we move out of the Body Armor suite, we'll have a party so everyone can visit."

"I want to see the bedroom," Justice said with a grin.

"Brand says you designed the whole thing to go around that one piece of art."

Miles stepped back into the circle with Maxi, both of them carrying trays of sandwiches and drinks they'd just gotten from the house.

Maxi said, "I thought Catalina did a painting for you."

"She did." Sahara smiled. "It's a stunning piece that now hangs in the dining room."

Miles said to his wife, "The artwork in the bedroom is something unique."

Catalina looked up. "Well, now I'm curious."

Leese lifted his beer in a toast. "What do you get the woman who has everything?"

Sahara looked around at all their friends. "It was the most romantic gesture ever." She sighed. "Brand had my shiv placed in a fancy open frame so that it fits with the expensive decor, but is accessible if I ever need to grab it."

Now that he was a bodyguard, too, Sahara's own personal bodyguard, she wouldn't need her makeshift weapon—but he knew she liked it. The gesture might have come off as a joke, at least to everyone else. After all, the men were all grinning and the women laughed.

But Sahara knew the true meaning of his gift—a symbol that she'd impressed him, that he respected her ingenuity and capability and most of all that he loved her, everything about her, including her take-charge persona.

That's why, even as she petted the cat one-handed, she leaned on his shoulder. "I do have everything," she whispered in his ear, "now that I have you."

Life didn't get much better than this.

* * * * *

Look for COOPER'S CHARM,
the lush new novel
from Lori Foster and HQN Books.
Read on for a sneak peek...

CHAPTER ONE

THE SUN SHONE brightly on that early mid-May morning. The crisp, cool air smelled of damp leaves, an earthy scent that wasn't unappealing. A mist from the nearby lake blanketed the ground, swirling around her sneaker-covered feet.

Phoenix Rose stood at the high entrance to the resort and looked down at the neat rows of RVs in various sizes, as well as the numerous log cabins and the rustic tent grounds. All was quiet, as if no one had yet awakened.

She could have parked in the lower lot, closer to her destination, but she wanted the time to take in the view. Besides, after driving for a few hours, she'd enjoy stretching her legs.

Breathing deeply, she filled her lungs with fresh air while also filling her heart with hope.

It was such a beautiful morning that her clip-on sunglasses, worn over her regular glasses, only cut back the worst of the glare; she had to shade her eyes with a hand as she took in the many unique aspects of the Cooper's Charm RV Park and Resort.

Before submitting her resume to the online wanted ad, she'd scoured all the info she could find. She'd also studied the map to familiarize herself with the design.

The website hadn't done it justice.

It was more beautiful than she'd expected.

Dense woods bordered the property on one side and at the entrance, giving it a private, isolated feel. To the other side, a line of evergreens separated the park from an old-fashioned drive-in that offered nightly movies not only to the resort guests, but also to the residents in the surrounding small town of Woodbine, Ohio.

At the very back of the resort, a large lake—created from a quarry—wound in and around the land before fading into the sun-kissed mist, making it impossible to see the full size. Currently, large inflated slides and trampolines floated in and out of the mist, randomly catching the sunshine as they bobbed in the mostly placid water. Phoenix couldn't imagine anyone getting into the frigid water, but the online brochure claimed the lake was already open, as was the heated inground pool.

She was to meet the owner near the lake, but she'd deliberately arrived fifteen minutes early, which gave her a chance to look around.

After she'd spent six months in hotel rooms, and a month familiarizing herself with the park, Cooper's Charm already felt like home. She could be at peace here and that meant a lot, because for too long now, peace of mind had remained an elusive thing.

Knowing her sister was waiting, Phoenix pulled out her phone and took a pic of the beautiful scenery, then texted it to Ridley, typing in, Arrived.

Despite the early hour, Ridley immediately replied, Are you sure about this?

Positive, Phoenix responded. She hadn't been this certain in ages. I just hope the interview goes well.

Loyal to the end, her sister sent back, He'll take one look at you and fall in love.

Phoenix grinned as her heart swelled. Through thick

and thin, Ridley was her backup, her support system, and the person she trusted most in the whole world. It didn't matter that Ridley lived a very different lifestyle, or that their goals in life were miles apart.

Phoenix loved working with her hands, staying busy and took satisfaction from a job well done.

Ridley enjoyed seeing the world in nearly nonstop travel to posh destinations, had an exquisite flair for the latest fashions and detested being messy in any way.

Different, but still sisters through and through.

She knew Ridley was still worried, and that bothered her. Much as she appreciated her sister's dedication, she wanted to portray an air of confidence and independence… just as she once had.

She didn't like being weak, and she didn't like allowing others to impact her life, yet both had happened. This was her chance to get back to being a strong, capable woman.

If all went well, today would be the start of reaching that goal.

Taking her time, Phoenix strode through the grounds, familiarizing herself on her way to the lake. She really wanted to explore the woods, and the small, quaint cabins where she would live.

More than that, though, she wanted to be at the lake when Cooper Cochran arrived. She wouldn't be late, wouldn't be nervous and wouldn't screw up her fresh start.

Unfortunately, just as she rounded a play area filled with swings and slides, she saw the lone figure standing along the sandy shore, a fishing rod in hand.

Was that Cochran?

Good Lord, he was big, and impressively built, too,

with wide, hard shoulders and muscular thighs. She hated to admit it, but that could be a problem for her.

After all, she'd learned on a basic level that big men were powerful men.

Pausing to stare, she pressed a hand to her stomach to quell the nervous butterflies taking flight at the sight of him.

The sunrise gilded his messy sandy-brown hair. As he reeled in his line, then cast it out again, muscles flexed beneath a dark pullover with the sleeves pushed up to his elbows, showing taut forearms and thick wrists dusted with hair. Worn denim hugged his long legs.

He seemed to stand nearly a half-foot taller than her five foot four. God, how she'd prayed he'd be a smaller, less…imposing man.

Finding information on the resort had been easy. Finding information on Cooper Cochran…not so much.

She stood frozen to the spot, trying to convince her feet to move, doing her best to conquer her irrational reservations, but she was suddenly, painfully aware that they were all alone on the shore. Logically, she knew it wasn't a problem. Plenty of people were around, in their RVs or cabins, so there was no reason to be afraid.

Not here, not now.

Lately, though, fear had been a fickle thing, often re-emerging out of nowhere.

As if he'd known she was there all along, he glanced over his shoulder at her. Reflective sunglasses hid his eyes, and yet she felt his scrutiny and a touch of surprise. She knew his gaze was burning over her and it caused her to shift in nervous awareness.

She guessed him to be in his midthirties, maybe nine or ten years older than her. No one would call him a classically handsome man. His features were as bold as his body, including a strong jaw, masculine nose and harshly carved cheekbones.

Not classic good looks, but he certainly wouldn't be ignored.

She could see that he hadn't yet shaved this morning, and she wasn't sure if he'd combed his hair. The breeze and fog off the lake might have played with it, leaving it a little wavier than usual.

She couldn't look away, couldn't even blink.

His scrutiny kept her pinned in place with a strange stirring of her senses.

Turning back to the lake, he said, "Ms. Rose?"

The words seemed to carry on the quiet, cool air.

Phoenix swallowed. "Yes." She watched as he cast out yet again. It almost seemed that he gave her time to get herself together. Of course, he couldn't know why she was so reserved. Still, his patience, his apparent lack of interest, finally helped her to move forward.

She watched the way his large hands deftly, slowly, reeled in the line.

Her feet sank in the soft, damp sand. "Mr. Cochran?"

"You can call me Coop."

He had a deep, mellow voice that should have put her at ease but instead sharpened her awareness of him.

"I like to fish in the morning before everyone else crowds the lake. Are you an early bird, Ms. Rose?"

"Actually, yes." A white gull swooped down, skimmed the water and took flight again. Ripples fanned out across the surface. By the minute, the mist evaporated, giving way to the warmth of the sun. "You know I had my own landscaping business." She'd told him that much in their email correspondence concerning her ap-

plication. "In the summer especially, it was more comfortable to start as early as possible. I've gotten in the
habit of being up and about by six."

"You won't need to be that early here."

"Okay." She wasn't sure what else to say. "The lake
is beautiful."

"And peaceful." This time when he reeled in the line,
he had a small bass attached. "Do you fish?"

He hadn't faced her again and that made it easier to
converse. "When I was younger, my sister and I would
visit our grandparents for the weekend and we'd fish in
their pond. That was years ago, though." This was the
strangest interview she'd ever had. It was also less stress-
ful than she'd anticipated.

Had Cooper Cochran planned it that way—or did he
just love to fish?

"You don't fish with them anymore?"

"They passed away several years ago. Granddad first,
and my Grandma not long after."

"I'm sorry to hear that. Sounds like you made good
memories with them, though."

"Yes." Fascinated, she watched as he worked the hook
easily from the fish's mouth, then he bent and placed it
gently back in the water before rinsing his hands. "Too
small to keep?"

"I rarely keep what I catch." He gestured toward a
picnic table. "Let's talk."

Until then, she hadn't noticed the tackle box and towel
on the summer-bleached wooden table.

She followed Cochran, then out of habit waited until
he'd chosen a spot so she could take the side opposite
him—a habit she'd gotten into with men. These days
she preferred as much distance as she could manage.

He stepped over the bench, dropped the towel, pushed up his sunglasses and seated himself.

Golden-brown eyes took her by surprise. They were a stark contrast to his heavy brows and the blunt angles of his face.

She realized she was staring, that he merely stared back with one brow lifted, and she quickly looked away. Thankfully, she still wore the clip-on sunglasses over her regular glasses, giving her a hint of concealment.

She retreated behind idle chitchat. "I studied the map online and feel like I know my way around. The lake is more impressive than I'd realized. The photos don't do it justice."

"I've been meaning to update the website," he said. "It's been busy, though. We lost our groundskeeper and housekeeper at the same time."

"Someone had both positions?"

He smiled with some private amusement. "No. Either position is a full-time job. But without any of us noticing, the two of them fell in love, married and then headed to Florida to retire."

"Oh." She expected to find many things at the resort, but love wasn't on the list. Love wasn't even in her universe.

Not anymore.

"You said you checked out the map online?"

"Actually, I researched everything I could about the place, including the surrounding grounds, and I'm sure I'd be a good fit for the job."

When he looked past her, she quickly turned her head to find a woman approaching with a metal coffeepot in one hand, the handles of two mugs hooked through the fingers of the other.

Cooper stood. "Perfect timing, Maris."

The woman's smile was easy and friendly. "I was watching." Long dark blond hair, caught in a high ponytail, swung behind her with every step. Soft brown eyes glanced at Phoenix. "Good morning."

"Morning."

"Coffee?" She set one mug in front of Cooper and filled it.

Phoenix nodded. "Yes, please."

Maris filled the second mug, then dug creamer cups and sugar packets from a sturdy apron pocket, along with a plastic wrapped spoon. "Coop drinks his black, but I wasn't sure about you."

Anyone who presented her with coffee on a cool morning instantly earned her admiration. "I can take it any way I get it, but I prefer a little cream and sugar, so thank you."

Cooper reseated himself. "Maris Kennedy, meet Phoenix Rose. Maris runs the camp store. Phoenix is here about the position for groundskeeper."

Slim brows went up. "Really? I was assuming housekeeper."

Cooper's smile did amazing things to his rugged face, and disastrous things to her concentration.

He explained to Phoenix, "We've never had a woman tend the grounds." Then to Maris, he said, "Ms. Rose used to run her own landscaping company. She's more than qualified and we'd be lucky to get her."

Phoenix perked up. Did that mean he'd already made up his mind to hire her?

"Especially now." Maris leaned a hip against the end of the table. "I don't know if Coop told you, but we're starting this season short-handed. We were all taking turns with the grounds and the housekeeping, so everyone will be thrilled to take one thing off their list."

Still unsure if she had the job or not, Phoenix said, "It'd be my pleasure to make things easier. If I'm hired I can start right away." She glanced at Cooper and added, "Today even."

Maris straightened. "Seriously?"

Already feeling a sense of purpose that had been missing for too long from her life, Phoenix nodded. "I'm anxious to get started."

Cooper put his elbows on the table and leaned forward. "Then consider yourself hired."

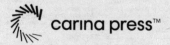

Get 2 Free Books,
Plus 2 Free Gifts -
just for trying the Reader Service!

YES! Please send me 2 FREE novels from the Essential Romance or Essential Suspense Collection and my 2 FREE gifts (gifts are worth about $10 retail). After receiving them, if I don't wish to receive any more books, I can return the shipping statement marked "cancel." If I don't cancel, I will receive 4 brand-new novels every month and be billed just $6.74 each in the U.S. or $7.24 each in Canada. That's a savings of at least 16% off the cover price. It's quite a bargain! Shipping and handling is just 50¢ per book in the U.S. and 75¢ per book in Canada*. I understand that accepting the 2 free books and gifts places me under no obligation to buy anything. I can always return a shipment and cancel at any time. The free books and gifts are mine to keep no matter what I decide.

Please check one: ☐ Essential Romance ☐ Essential Suspense
194/394 MDN GMWR   191/391 MDN GMWR

Name _____ (PLEASE PRINT)

Address _____ Apt. #

City _____ State/Prov. _____ Zip/Postal Code

Signature (if under 18, a parent or guardian must sign)

Mail to the **Reader Service:**
IN U.S.A.: P.O. Box 1341, Buffalo, NY 14240-8531
IN CANADA: P.O. Box 603, Fort Erie, Ontario L2A 5X3

Want to try two free books from another line?
Call 1-800-873-8635 or visit www.ReaderService.com.

*Terms and prices subject to change without notice. Prices do not include applicable taxes. Sales tax applicable in NY. Canadian residents will be charged applicable taxes. Offer not valid in Quebec. This offer is limited to one order per household. Books received may not be as shown. Not valid for current subscribers to the Essential Romance or Essential Suspense Collection. All orders subject to approval. Credit or debit balances in a customer's account(s) may be offset by any other outstanding balance owed by or to the customer. Please allow 4 to 6 weeks for delivery. Offer available while quantities last.

Your Privacy—The Reader Service is committed to protecting your privacy. Our Privacy Policy is available online at www.ReaderService.com or upon request from the Reader Service.

We make a portion of our mailing list available to reputable third parties that offer products we believe may interest you. If you prefer that we not exchange your name with third parties, or if you wish to clarify or modify your communication preferences, please visit us at www.ReaderService.com/consumerschoice or write to us at Reader Service Preference Service, P.O. Box 9062, Buffalo, NY 14240-9062. Include your complete name and address.

STRS17R2

Get 2 Free Books,
Plus 2 Free Gifts—
just for trying the Reader Service!